RAVES FOR THE NOVELS OF JO BEVERLEY

"A beguiling love story."
—*Booklist*

"A fabulous, intelligent tale." —Genre Go Round Reviews

"One of the most masterful writers of Regency romance."
—*Romantic Times* (top pick)

"With wit and humor, Jo Beverley provides a wonderful eighteenth-century romance." —The Best Reviews

"A delightful, intricately plotted, and sexy romp."
—*Library Journal*

"A well-crafted story and an ultimately very satisfying romance." —The Romance Reader

"[Beverley] has truly brought to life a fascinating, glittering, and sometimes dangerous world." —Mary Jo Putney

"Wickedly delicious. Jo Beverley weaves a spell of sensual delight with her usual grace and flair."
—Teresa Medeiros

"Beverley's brilliantly drawn protagonists shine in a story that puts equal emphasis on intrigue and love."
—*Publishers Weekly*

P9-CMK-530

Merely a Marriage

Jo Beverley

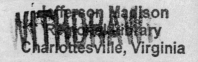
JOVE
New York

A JOVE BOOK
Published by Berkley
An imprint of Penguin Random House LLC
375 Hudson Street, New York, New York 10014

Copyright © 2017 by Jo Beverley
Excerpt from *The Viscount Needs a Wife* copyright © 2016 by Jo Beverley
Penguin Random House supports copyright. Copyright fuels creativity, encourages
diverse voices, promotes free speech, and creates a vibrant culture. Thank you for buying
an authorized edition of this book and for complying with copyright laws by not
reproducing, scanning, or distributing any part of it in any form without permission.
You are supporting writers and allowing Penguin Random House to continue to
publish books for every reader.

A JOVE BOOK and BERKLEY are registered trademarks and the B colophon
is a trademark of Penguin Random House LLC.

ISBN: 9780399583537

First Edition: June 2017

Printed in the United States of America
1 3 5 7 9 10 8 6 4 2

Cover art by Gregg Gulbronson

With many thanks to Charlie,
who has been my inscrutable muse for the last thirty-two
years; and to the WordWenches and RomEx
for all their invaluable support and camaraderie;
and finally,
to all of you who offered me love and support
on my journey here and beyond.

Chapter 1

The family parlor at Boxstall Priory was an intimate space amid grandeur, furnished for comfort rather than fashion, and easily warmed by one crackling fire. The room held many happy memories for the Boxstall family, but on this rainy November day it was a scene of discord.

A young man and woman had surged to their feet and now stood nose to nose.

"If you're so sure that making a marriage is nothing," the Earl of Langton snarled, "then you do it."

"That's outrageous!" Lady Ariana Boxstall took a step back from her brother.

"No more outrageous than you ordering me to marry."

"I didn't *order* you, Norris. I explained why it was necessary."

"Ha! Talking about it as if it were no greater matter than choosing a new pair of boots."

Both were tall, with curling amber-colored hair. Their mother formed an audience of one, observing with concern from a chair near the fire. The world openly wondered how such a tiny lady had produced two such strapping children, but so it was.

Norris, Lord Langton, was a Corinthian—a gentleman dedicated to the sporting life—and, at six foot two, built for it. He was famous for his daredevil ways.

Lady Ariana Boxstall was made along more feminine lines, for which she was grateful, but she almost matched him in height. She was sometimes described as an Amazon, or even called Hippolyta, which she deeply disliked. Her name was a variant of Eirene, the Greek goddess of peace, and she was beginning to think she should have taken a more peaceful approach.

It might have been a mistake to put the matter to her brother as soon as he arrived to celebrate their mother's birthday. Anxiety had been building in her for two weeks, however, ever since the shocking death of Princess Charlotte in childbirth had plunged the nation into mourning. Ariana and her mother wore black, and Norris sported a black cravat and armband. The Windsor funeral had occurred on the previous Wednesday and the bells of Saint Ethelburga's had tolled across the valley at the same hour.

Ariana had wept for the young mother and all who loved her. Everyone worried about the succession to the throne, for the princess had been the Regent's only child. It had been a more direct succession that had given Ariana sleepless nights. Norris's death without a son would trigger disaster, so he must marry, and soon.

"Here's an idea," he said, his sudden mildness a warning. "You prove to me that it's an easy business and I'll do it."

"You'll marry?" Ariana asked warily.

"That's what I said."

"But how can I prove it?"

"You go first. If you marry before the end of the year, I'll wed before the end of January. There's no shortage of women eager to wear a countess's coronet."

Suddenly breathless, Ariana turned to their mother. "Mama?"

"You did say it was a simple matter to choose a marriage partner, dear."

"For him! As he's just admitted, he could pick a plum off the tree whenever he wanted."

"But I don't fancy any of the plums, Mama," Norris said, "and I'm only twenty-three. The likelihood of my dying soon is small as a shrimp."

"I certainly hope so, dear."

Ariana faced her brother, who clearly hadn't grasped the key point. "Princess Charlotte was *two years younger than you*."

"I'm not about to endure childbirth!"

"But you engage in any number of risky activities."

"And have hardly ever suffered a scratch."

"Yet! Remember the Merryhews."

His brow wrinkled. "What about them? Lady Carsheld died of a carriage accident, but she was gone fifty. The old marquess was, well, old. Roger Merryhew died young, but he was in the war."

"You've forgotten *Jermyn* Merryhew!" Ariana reminded him. "He would have been marquess when his father died instead of that distant relative who crept in to take everything."

"There wasn't much to take."

"Stop harping on irrelevancies! The point is, Jermyn dillydallied about marrying, assuming he'd live to a good age, and then popped off from eating bad shell-fish."

"I don't like shellfish."

"As a result," Ariana persisted, "my friend Hermione lost her home. If Jermyn had done as he ought and married and had a son, all would have been well."

"If, if, if! If I had younger brothers, you wouldn't be raking me over the coals." Then he looked uncomfortably at his mother.

"Don't be crestfallen, dear. I would have welcomed more children, but God did not provide. In this case we must trust in his benevolence."

"We should be able to trust in Norris's good sense."

"Then we should be able to trust your willingness to sacrifice in the cause."

Her brother's triumphant smirk made Ariana want to hit him, which wasn't unusual. Only eighteen months lay between them, but she was the older and he the male and heir. There'd been rivalry between them all their lives. Typical of Norris to extend it into a matter of life and death.

Mother and brother were now both looking at her.

"It's not up to me," she protested. "Only you can produce the necessary heir, Norris. Can you truly bear the thought of Uncle Paul succeeding you? Can you? He'd evict Mama from her home, and then loot Boxstall of everything of value to throw away at the gaming tables. He might even find a way to break the entail and sell it entire."

"That might be the best outcome," Lady Langton said sadly. "I could abide our home belonging to another, but I would very much dislike to see it pillaged."

Ariana hurried to sit beside her and take her into

her arms. "Neither will happen, Mama. I promise. We only need Norris to marry."

"Which now lies in your hands," her brother said, arms folded.

Ariana knew the signs. He was generally of an amiable disposition, but he could be intolerably stubborn. Tears wouldn't move him, and she'd hate to try them. He heeded their mother, however, so Ariana decided to leave the field to her. She rose, saying, "I will leave you to come to your senses," and made as dignified an exit as she could when tears of fear and frustration threatened.

She paused in the corridor to blow her nose. How could her brother be so *blind*? Boxstall was so beautiful and full of treasures, but above all, it was their home. This part of the upstairs corridor was open to the hall below, with its gleaming wooden floor and walls loaded with paintings purchased by her ancestors, every picture an old friend.

Many were of little significance or value, but there were a Poussin, a Rembrandt, and a Rubens. She and her father had sometimes talked of turning one or two rooms into galleries in order to show off the best pieces.

Thought of her father turned her steps toward the library, their favorite haunt. Neither Norris nor her mother was bookish, so that had been their special place. Once she'd closed the door behind her, she was surrounded by the comforting scent and presence of books, but also by the ambience of sadness that had haunted the room for her since her father's death two years ago.

From her earliest years she'd spent time here with him exploring the wonderful world of books. He'd purchased some specifically for the illustrations that would please a child, but as she'd grown, she'd become his true companion on the literary explorations he'd so loved.

Papa had never had the slightest desire to travel and had even resented his times in London attending Parliament. However, when he'd visited London, he'd always returned with a carriage full of books on foreign lands and he and she had plunged into new journeys.

His particular treasures were always works about foreign parts in the past—Greece, Persia, India, and recently Egypt. He especially liked books that contained illustrations that reconstructed ruins in their glory days.

"See," he would say to her as they explored new acquisitions. "If we traveled to Greece, we could only see crumbling ruins, but here we can visit Athens in all its grandeur."

If he couldn't find a drawn reconstruction, he'd commission one. Some he'd had hung in frames around the house, but he'd displayed others here in a specially made glass-topped case.

Ariana went to it now to change the picture—a daily ritual she'd taken over when her father died. She looked through the folio, chose a print of the temple of Apollo in Corinth, and exchanged it for the one in the case.

Had that temple ever looked like that? Had the priests and worshippers been exactly as shown? It didn't matter. Her father had found all ruins sad and distressing. He'd spoken of rebuilding medieval Boxstall Priory from the mossy remnants of stone walls, but it had always been too challenging a project. Instead he'd planted trees to screen it from view.

She sadly turned the large globe on which they'd traced their travels, and stroked a hand along the map table, where they'd spread charts to mark a particular journey. She'd not had the heart to do that since he'd been gone. In truth, she'd abandoned most of their shared explorations and concentrated on the Egyptian ones, for they were the ones that had most captured her imagination.

They had all the volumes to date of the *Description de l'Égypte*, written by French scholars who'd accompanied Napoleon on his Egyptian campaigns. Her father had commissioned a monumental pedestal stand able to hold one of the twelve volumes open, and the rest closed beneath. Each book was a yard tall and three-quarters of a yard wide, but packed with wonderful illustrations and descriptions.

There were more volumes to come, but each was expensive and she wasn't sure Norris would purchase them. If not, she would. Her portion was ample. Suddenly it hit her that if her brother died without a son, she'd lose not only her home but access to this library. In fact, the library would cease to be.

Until this moment the imagined loss had been of the earldom's houses and estates. She'd accepted that the contents would also go, but not the books. This wonderful collection would be shipped off to an auction house and scattered to the wind. The *Description de l'Égypte* would be the first to go, because it would command a high price. Each volume had been printed in a limited edition of one thousand copies.

She clutched the open volume on the pedestal as if to hold it down. Could she claim these books as her own? If she said the *Description de l'Égypte* had been a gift to her, could anyone deny it? Her mother would support her.

She could seek legal advice. . . .

No, she must do more than that. She had to protect everything—the house, the estate, the art, and the contents of this library—and not just for herself. Everything must *survive* for future generations. That meant Norris must marry and fill a nursery with boys.

She hadn't expected such fierce resistance, but that couldn't weaken her resolve. She left the library to go up to her room and plan.

"What's the matter now?" asked her lady's maid, Ethel Burgis, putting aside the stocking she'd been mending by the fire.

"Norris," Ariana said.

"Ah."

Ethel was more of a companion than a maid and dressed accordingly. Her black gown was made of fine cloth and she wore no apron, nor a cap on her wiry black hair. She played the servant well enough when she and Ariana were in company, but they'd been together since girlhood, and in private they were equals and friends.

Twenty-four years ago, Ethel had been christened in the local church, Saint Ethelburga's, and, uniquely in the parish, been given the saint's name. Nellie Burgis had chosen sensible names for her other seven children—all sons, six of whom were still alive—but when finally bearing a daughter in her forty-third year, she'd credited the saint with the miracle and named the baby accordingly.

Ethelburga Burgis had immediately become Ethel, thank heavens, but even the full name didn't seem to distress Ethel. Little distressed Ethel. All the Burgises were tall, and when Ethel, the twelve-year-old kitchen maid, had shown signs of following the family pattern, she'd been trained to be Ariana's maid. Now she was an inch taller than Ariana, which served the purpose of making Ariana's height less striking, and she was of larger build as well.

Ethel wasn't fat, but she had much the same build as

her sturdy brothers and could probably have done the same hard quarry work if she'd had to. As it was, she'd learned the skills of a lady's maid and the manners to go with them, and she and Ariana were close companions. Ethel had little interest in books, but she was a well of placid common sense, too often expressed in proverbs and sayings. "All storms must pass," she said now.

"This one won't, because I can't let it. He has to marry to save the earldom."

"You addressed that subject with him."

"Of course I did!"

"As soon as he arrived?"

Ariana grimaced. "An error, I admit."

"More haste, less speed."

"And then he had the gall to throw it back at me!"

"How did he do that, then?"

Ariana hesitated, reluctant to put the absurd suggestion into words, but she never kept secrets from Ethel. "He said that if I marry by the end of the year, he'll marry by the end of January."

Ethel's brows rose. "I didn't think he had the wits for that."

"He's not stupid."

"No, but you can't expect an old head on young shoulders. He is young to be marrying."

"At twenty-five, I'm considered past hope."

"Young for a *man*," Ethel said.

"He's not just a man—he's an *earl*. He has a duty to start his nursery. His suggestion was all hollow. My marriage won't help."

"True enough."

Why couldn't Ethel share her outrage? It would never happen. Ethel was the personification of calm.

"He'll come to his senses," Ariana said.

"A leopard can't change its spots."

"Are you saying he has no sense? Mama will convince him."

"Maybe."

Ariana understood the hesitation. Lady Langton was kind and sweet-natured, but she should have been named after the goddess of peace. She disliked all forms of hostility.

"You need a ride," Ethel said.

Ariana almost argued, but Ethel was right. Fresh air and exercise would blow away her desperation and put her in a better state for deft persuasion. It even helped to put on her dark blue riding habit, for it was a relief from black. The princess's death had plunged everyone into mourning, but seeing black all around only tightened the screw of her anxiety.

Ariana went down the back stairs, hoping to avoid her brother. She was not yet in a state for sweet persuasion. An hour later she returned, much calmer but even more resolved. A ride around the estate had reminded her of how far the misery could spread. Uncle Paul wouldn't take care of anything. He'd raise rents and cut down trees for ready money. He'd neglect all repairs of drains, fences, and coppices, and especially the cottages where the farm laborers lived. There'd be no support for the church, the sick, or the almshouses.

Ariana returned to the house with stronger purpose, but plotting a more subtle course. Though she'd love to see her brother at the altar tomorrow, she could give him time to come around to the idea. True, Norris could kill himself at any moment in some sporting wildness, but it was very unlikely. Her task now was to turn his mind toward finding a bride.

As Ariana dressed in black silk for dinner, she explained her new reasoning.

Ethel said, "Bear in mind that the world's in mourning for a wife who died trying to give birth to an heir. Could turn some men off."

"Off women entirely?" Ariana asked skeptically.

"It has to make a man think."

"I can't not push him a little."

"No, but as you say, give him time. This gloomy mood will pass and everyone will forget." She finished fastening the back of the gown. "What ornaments?"

Ariana thought it sad that Princess Charlotte's tragic death might fade into the mists, but it probably would be best all in all. For now, it would serve her purpose to look a little less funereal. "My amber beads and bracelet."

Ethel fastened the triple row of beads, which sat neatly at the base of Ariana's throat, just above the high neck of the gown. Ariana added the matching bracelet at her right wrist, and pulled on short black net gloves.

She liked to wear amber because it matched the color of her hair, which was undoubtedly one of her finer features. It was even easy to manage since it was naturally curly. Not frizzy, but with a pleasant, obliging curl, which was much easier to manage now she'd had it cropped to shoulder length and shorter around her face. Curls on the forehead were all the fashion, and she had them without resort to curling irons, thank heavens.

Unasked, Ethel had brought just the right shawl—a long Norwich one, woven in a design of black and gold.

"Thank you. Any last advice?"

"More flies are caught with honey than vinegar."

"That's true."

"And it is your mother's birthday."

"Which I'd forgotten! Very well. Honeyed sweetness all evening. I must at least tempt my fly."

The meal progressed well enough, for Ariana was intent on being amiable and Norris gave a firsthand account of the events around the princess's death. Ariana and her mother had received letters, but they valued his description of how London had reacted.

"I understand the princess's doctors are being blamed," Ariana said as the second course was laid out.

"And the queen," Norris said, eyeing the new dishes with approval. He had a mighty appetite. "She wasn't there, you know."

"She isn't well, poor lady," their mother said, "and seventy-three years old. Her granddaughter's death and all the traveling and ceremonies will have taxed her."

"You fear there could soon be another funeral?" Ariana said. "We'll all be in mourning forever."

"Hope not," Norris said, helping himself to venison. "Town died on the same day. The theaters closed, and most of the shops as well. The shops opened within days, of course, and the theaters later. But no one's putting off mourning or throwing grand entertainments."

"People are truly sad," Ariana said.

"It's thrown up a few oddities," he said, adding potatoes. "Last week a foreign ambassador's wife turned up to a reception in white."

"No!" Ariana exclaimed.

"Why?" asked their mother.

"I'm told white's a mourning color in some countries. That'd make our spring assemblies pretty sad affairs, wouldn't it, with all the hopeful misses in their pale silks and muslins?"

Ariana almost said something about hopeful misses,

but managed to repress it. She did say, "I doubt you've been inside Almack's in years."

"Gads, no. Dull stuff there. Cribb's Parlour's more my style."

"Pugilism?" his mother exclaimed.

"All the thing, Mama. Keeps a fellow in trim. A man'll hear it from Cribb's if he's bellows to mend."

"Don't sink to cant, dear."

"Apologies, Mama."

"And I don't like to think of you under attack."

"It's all in good fun." Norris flashed a look at Ariana. "No danger at all."

How could he take the matter so lightly? Ariana reminded herself to keep the peace. "What do you find to do with yourself in Town amid all the gloom?"

"There are still private parties to enjoy, and other amusements. I took part in a splendid steeplechase near Chiswick. The Great All-Black."

"'All-Black'?"

"In keeping with mourning. Men to be dressed in black and riding completely black horses. The price of an all-black horse rocketed the week before, but of course I had Torrent."

Lady Langton smiled at him. "Then of course you won, darling."

Norris was a brilliant rider and could afford the finest horses. Torrent was his best.

"Neck and neck with Arden on Viking and Templemore on Beelzebub. Then Torrent put a foot in a rabbit hole and down we went. Damned shame."

"Is Torrent much injured?" Ariana asked.

"Dead," Norris said, lips wobbling. "Broken leg."

"How very sad," his mother said, "but thank heavens you were unscathed."

"Pretty well. Knocked out by a damnably placed rock. I came round to find I'd nothing but a headache and bruises, but Torrent was a goner. He was a fine beast." He pulled out a handkerchief and dabbed his eyes. "A fine beast."

"He was," Ariana said. "But . . ." She cut another piece of meat, though she wondered if she could swallow it.

Norris had almost *died*.

The idiot made light of it, but a slightly harder blow could have killed him. Or he could have broken his neck or been mortally injured in some other way. Not long ago young Lord Scorton had broken his back in a similar accident. He'd lingered a day or so, but died. At least he'd had a son.

Ariana struggled through the meal, making general remarks to conceal her inner turmoil, but the scene kept running through her head. A grim messenger bringing the terrible news, soon followed by grinning Uncle Paul, eager to throw them out and begin converting as much of the earldom as possible into funds for the gaming table.

Norris *must* marry. She knew her brother, however. Now he'd dug in his heels, nothing would move him. There was only one thing for it.

She waited until they were in the parlor and the servant who'd brought the coffee had left. Once they all had their cups, she gathered her resolution and made her announcement. "Very well, Norris. I accept your challenge."

He sipped. "What challenge?"

"If you will marry after I do, I will marry by the turn of the year."

"No, you won't. You're a confirmed spinster."

"I've had offers!"

"First I've heard of it, and clearly you've accepted none of them."

"Now I will." Despite the sick churning inside, she took satisfaction in his alarm.

"You'll accept a man you've rejected simply to force me to the altar? I don't believe it."

"To force you to start filling the nursery, I will."

He surged to his feet. "You damnable woman!"

"Norris!" his mother exclaimed.

He froze. "I'm sorry, Mama, but it's more than a man can bear to be bullied so by a sister."

"An older sister," Ariana said, also on her feet. "Older and wiser."

"A foolish woman, like all women."

"Now you're insulting our mother."

He clutched his curls. "No, I'm not! She's not supporting this mad plan. Are you, Mama?"

"Whether I support it or not, Norris, you did propose this arrangement. I don't see how you can back out now."

For their mother, it was a remarkably resolute statement, and Norris stared at her.

"It's a petticoat conspiracy, is it? Very well. I'm a man of my word. But I feel safe in the certainty that Ariana will never take herself to the altar. She'd rather marry a book!"

With that, he slammed out of the room.

Ariana found she was actually shaking. "I'm sorry, Mama. I've ruined your birthday."

Her mother patted her hand. "That's all right, dear. It's time you married, and I'll be happy to have grandchildren. But please be sure to marry as agreeable a gentleman as you can find."

* * *

"So you've gone and done it," Ethel said, helping Ariana off with her gown. She didn't seem surprised.

"I had no choice."

"Everyone has a choice." Ethel went into the dressing room to put the gown away.

Ariana called after her, "You had no choice about coming to work here at ten!"

"Every adult, then," Ethel said, returning and setting to work on the corset laces.

"Not even that, and you know it. Especially women. But this should be a simple enough matter. I only have to choose between one of my disappointed suitors."

"There's many a slip . . . ," Ethel said.

"I have three cups to bring to my lip: Lord Wilbury, Sir Charles Overden, and Reverend Aston."

"What about that Viscount Moule, who was sniffing about you?"

"The one with all the ailments and potions? Never. But the other three have asked for my hand in the past year, Overden and Aston more than once. I simply have to choose, and I can be wed in weeks."

The thought of standing at the altar with any of them seemed unreal, but once she'd committed herself, she would become accustomed.

"You had reasons to reject them," Ethel reminded her.

"And now I have reason to accept one. My mother can advise. Enough quibbling. It must be done."

However, when Ariana sat down with her mother the next morning to discuss the matter, she found it wasn't so simple.

As her mother poured them both coffee, she said, "Lord Wilbury married last month, dear. You should pay more attention to local gossip."

"It's always so trivial. But that's annoying. He was a tolerable sort."

"And Sir Charles is now betrothed to Jane Howes." Lady Langton passed over a cup to Ariana. "I wouldn't like you to disrupt their arrangement."

"I wouldn't consider it," Ariana said, but the news was a blow.

That left only Reverend Aston, the handsome vicar of a nearby parish, with a private income in addition to his stipend. Excellent, one might think, but he was thirty-two and unpleasantly full of his own importance as the cousin of a duke. In addition, he was ambitious. Ariana struggled to see herself as a parson's wife, but was definitely not made to be the wife of a bishop.

She reconsidered Viscount Moule. He was a Sussex man who'd been a guest of Aston's during the summer. She'd had no hesitation about rejecting his offer, for his conversation had been almost entirely about his ailments and the numerous odd treatments he'd taken in an attempt to cure them. He'd even been experimenting with electricity.

She tried to imagine being his wife, but it was impossible.

"Who else is there?" she asked.

"You're familiar with all the local gentlemen, and they with you. I don't think there are any particularly eligible ones, certainly not close to your height."

"My pestilential height."

"Do you dislike it very much, dear? I don't think there was anything I could have done about it, though I remember your grandmother suggesting that we feed you less."

"Thank you for not taking that advice. I might prefer to be less distinctive, but there's no purpose to that.

I do want a husband of similar height, even though Ethel says that makes no sense, given that tall men marry short women."

"Ethel is sensible, but often in a nonsensible way. The world looks oddly at a couple where the lady is much taller than the gentleman."

Ariana considered again the gentlemen of the area. She was acquainted with all the best local families. Her mother was correct. There were no other suitable tall gentlemen. She considered those slightly shorter than herself and still didn't find any who appealed.

"I must be oddly particular," she said.

"It would be odd not to be particular about the person with whom you'll share your life."

"So I was wrong to push Norris?"

"Not wrong, dear, but perhaps engaged in a somewhat quixotic endeavor. As it happens, you might have found the way to hurry him along."

"But if I marry and thus he must, he might pick unwisely."

"That is a risk, but he could do that anyway." Her mother sighed. "He's young and should be left to take his time, but disaster does hover in the wings. You'll have to look further afield."

"Visit some of our relatives?" Ariana asked, not welcoming the suggestion. After a disastrous season when she was seventeen, she'd preferred to stay in Hampshire among those accustomed to her height. Strangers did tend to stare.

"Go where there's the greatest concentration of gentlemen, dear." When Ariana frowned a question, her mother added, "Go to Town."

"To *Town*?"

"It's not darkest Africa," her mother said, with an

unusually tart edge. "November's not the most fashionable time in London, and there's the pall of mourning, but there will be a greater selection of tall, eligible men from which to choose."

"But . . ."

But Ariana remembered being stared at, and being the butt of remarks and even jokes, when all she'd wanted was to be overlooked. Given her height, hardly anyone ever overlooked her. It was no wonder that she'd failed to "take," as they said. There'd certainly been no offer of marriage.

"Don't let your previous experience color the present, dear. You were too young. I should never have agreed, but it was another piece of advice from your grandmother, and your father generally paid heed to her. She advised us to get you wed before you grew any taller."

That had been the most miserable period of her life, and some parts of it she'd never forget. The overheard comments, and the sudden silence when she'd entered a ladies' convenience room.

The awkwardness of dancing with men shorter than herself.

The cartoon displayed in shopwindows, which played upon the family name, Boxstall, showing an overdressed young lady crammed into a tall box, surrounded by people small enough to be midgets.

Then there'd been the cruelty of a man she'd begun to spin fantasies around—the handsome young Earl of Kynaston, the godlike darling of the beau monde. His looks and easy charm had been fodder for impossible dreams, but when he'd played on a lute, singing an Elizabethan love song, he'd stolen her heart.

And then he'd crushed it, sending her fleeing back to Hampshire.

Lady Langton sighed. "Perhaps Bath, then."

Ariana dragged herself out of the painful past. "Bath is full of ancients."

"Brighton?"

"In November? With the Regent in residence in his Pavilion, drowning in grief?"

Death and grief reminded Ariana of why she must marry, and soon. She wasn't seventeen anymore. She was twenty-five and had come to terms with her height. She joined in the society of this area and had many friends. She had received offers.

Despite quivering nerves, she said, "You're correct. There's nothing for it but London."

At least mourning would mean there'd be no dancing. Being partnered with a short man was so very awkward, and it was almost impossible to refuse an offer to dance.

Her mother smiled. "Wonderful! I'm sure you'll attract many gentlemen from whom to choose."

Ariana drained her coffee to fight a dry mouth. "One reasonable specimen will suffice. If we must do this, we can leave tomorrow."

"Tomorrow?"

"There's no time to waste."

"There's enough time to make proper preparations. We'll leave in three days and no sooner."

When Lady Langton made a clear statement, she was to be obeyed.

They were settling some details of the preparations when Norris came in, glowing from a morning ride. Perhaps he'd been planning a campaign of his own. He tried a smile as he said, "Let's forget about our silly challenge, Ariana. It's not fair on you. It's plain that you don't wish to marry."

"Is it?"

"As you said, you've had offers and turned the men down."

"I'm now ready to be less particular. Of course, if you remove the condition and marry soon . . ."

His smile slid into a glare. "Tell you what: your resolution is unwomanly. I doubt any man would take you, even if you weren't a giantess."

"Norris!" Lady Langton objected. "Apologize."

"No," Ariana said. "It's true that I'm too tall for a lady, and finding a husband will be a challenge. But *I* know my duty and don't intend to be too particular."

Norris growled, actually growled. "I'm leaving for Town. Now."

He stormed on his way, slamming the door, leaving Ariana shaking again. They'd not had such fights for ages, and it had been different when they were children and there'd been nursemaids to pull them apart.

"He can never hold a bad mood for long," her mother said.

Ariana wondered about that. Clearly Norris felt as strongly about his freedom as she did about Boxstall's security, which meant he'd fight for his freedom as fiercely as she must fight to take it away. He'd given his word, however, so she need only do her part.

She had only to catch a husband in the next few weeks, which for an earl's daughter with a large dowry was no challenge at all!

Chapter 2

Ariana and her mother left three days later in the family traveling chariot, followed by a simpler coach, which was carrying the servants and piled high with additional luggage. It wasn't until they were well on their way that Lady Langton made her announcement.

"We won't be going directly to the Boxstall town house, dear. I've arranged for us to stay for a few days with our cousin the Dowager Countess of Cawle."

"No!" Ariana protested.

"Whyever not?"

Ariana wanted to say, "I don't like her," but she knew she'd sound like a timorous child. Unfortunately, she felt like one. It had been eight years since she'd met the woman, and then only briefly. It had been another disaster.

"The arrangements are all made, dear," her mother said.

"But why?"

"You'll be able to stay out of sight there. Once we're

known to be in our own house, people will call and invitations will arrive, but you don't want to appear in society until your wardrobe has been refurbished."

"I'm not dressed in rags."

"First impressions are crucial, and you're sadly out-of-date. I don't think you've ordered a new gown in ages except for your riding habit."

"As everyone is in mourning, what I have will do. It's all only two years old." Purchased after her father's death.

"An age in fashion!"

"Then why do we have trunks packed with dowdy black and violet?"

"Are we to walk around in our shifts? We must wear something while new is made, and some of your clothes can possibly be brought up to style. Lady Cawle will know. She's a very fashionable and influential lady, well thought of by all."

"Well thought of? I remember being warned that a bad word from her could ruin my chances. As for fashionable, I presume she still dresses in that odd way? À l'ancien régime, waist at the waist and huge skirts. She should be a figure of fun."

"But isn't," her mother said.

"But isn't," Ariana had to admit. In a way, the eccentric Dowager Countess of Cawle ruled society.

That had been drummed into her at the time of her come-out in preparation for the visit to Albemarle Street. Lady Cawle could surround her with a halo of approval or cast her into the darkest hinterland. The lady had done neither, but she'd surveyed Ariana through a lorgnette and declared her too young and overdressed. Ariana had been so crushed that she'd turned clumsy and knocked a china figurine off a table to smash on the floor. Lady Cawle must remember that gawkish, clumsy girl.

Ariana could tell herself that she was older and more confident, but she was no shorter. She was even less able to flutter and sigh and do all the things appropriate to a husband-hunting maiden. The closer they came to London, the more nervous she felt, but she reminded herself again and again of the crucial purpose. She must marry, and could not afford to fail or flee.

Even so, when they drew up in front of the Albemarle Street house, her heart began to pound. She took a deep breath and descended from the coach, but sight of the large town house brought back such vivid recollections that a shiver went through her.

"The air's quite cold," she said as explanation, though it wasn't. They'd been having a mild November.

Liveried servants ushered them into the spacious entrance hall, but it became clear that a number of people were in the house. Music could be heard above, along with a hum of conversation and occasional laughter.

Two gentlemen who were descending the wide staircase glanced at the arrivals with curiosity, then stared. No wonder, with her so tall standing next to her petite mother. Ethel, standing discreetly a few steps behind along with her mother's maid, could not balance that.

The gentlemen continued on their way and a stately servant in black hurried forward. "My ladies, the countess is engaged in one of her musical afternoons. She is sure you would wish to progress to your bedrooms without unnecessary encounters."

Keep the country bumpkins out of sight?

All the same, it was a huge relief not to have to face Town fashionables immediately, and it had nothing to do with how she was dressed. The mere ambience of a ton party and the stares of the two gentlemen had brought back all the memories and thrown her close to panic.

You're a grown lady of high rank, long lineage, and handsome dowry. You have no reason to quail.

And she merely had to marry.

Then Boxstall would be safe and she need never come to Town again.

They were taken down a passage and up a set of secondary stairs to emerge into a luxuriously quiet corridor. Soon they were installed in pleasant side-by-side rooms. They provided everything a guest could wish for, including small dressing rooms attached to each with narrow beds for their maids.

"Most convenient," Lady Langton said. "I shall take tea in my room. Do you want some?"

"Yes, but I'll order it in here."

Her mother left in one direction with her maid, Lucy, and Ethel went into the dressing room to manage the arrival of the trunks and hatboxes. There were ingenious back stairs from the dressing rooms to the basement so that laboring servants wouldn't disturb the carpeted corridors. This place was certainly larger and grander than her family's own town house, but Ariana would rather be elsewhere.

She removed her bonnet, then rang for a servant. When a maid came, she ordered tea with two cups, for Ethel would want some. It soon arrived, with the welcome addition of small sandwiches and cakes.

Ethel came, but took her tea and some food back into the dressing room. "Maids are doing the unpacking, but they need watching."

Ariana enjoyed the refreshments and a bit of peace to collect herself. She even found some gratitude. She and her mother had been absent from Town for eight years and had no close acquaintance here. Ariana had written to her friend Hermione Merryhew, who was now Lady Faringay, hoping she might be here, but alas, no. Lady Cawle's influence and patronage would be very useful.

She was pouring her second cup when Lucy came in. "This note was received from Lady Cawle, milady."

She left and Ariana unfolded it. Their hostess apologized that her gathering was not yet over. They were to command anything they wished and she hoped they would dine with her at six o'clock.

Two hours from now.

Ariana finished her tea and rose to wander the room. The carpet was pleasantly soft beneath her feet and the brown-and-gold hangings were handsome. The fire burned generously and a scuttle of coal sat nearby in case it needed replenishing. She didn't like the smell of a coal fire, for wood was much more pleasant, but she wouldn't quibble at that.

She was provided with a handsome bed, a walnut washstand, a small table with two chairs, and two upholstered chairs on either side of the fireplace, along with fire screens to protect the complexion from direct heat. A rotating bookcase sat beside one of the chairs, holding a number of books. There was even a small desk, and when Ariana checked, she found it contained writing paper, pens, ink, wax, and anything she might need.

An excellent room for a guest, but one that rather suggested the guest spend most of her time in it, whereas Ariana needed to use her legs. She'd been sitting in a coach for five hours and would have enjoyed a brisk walk, even around the house.

Lady Cawle's guests made that impossible.

She thought of slipping outside, but the light was fading. At Boxstall that wouldn't have bothered her, but dusk made the city more dangerous, despite the gaslights, which she could see out the window were now being lit, one by one. She watched the process, muttering, "Imprisoned."

She remembered that about Town. *Don't do this. Don't go there. Scandalous to even think of going there and doing that!*

With a sigh she went into the dressing room to decide what to wear for dinner. The unpacking was almost complete, so Ethel sent the two young maids away.

Before Ariana even asked, Ethel said, "The violet silk." It was already spread on the narrow bed, and Ariana had to admit it was the only choice. Like all her winter gowns, it was long-sleeved and very plain, with only a slight trimming of purple and black beads. It wasn't fine enough for a ton event, but it would do for a private dinner.

"I might as well dress, then."

She was ready too early, with jet and amethyst jewelry, including two pins in her hair. With time to spare, she sat to continue reading a book she'd brought from home about the warrior gods of Greece and Rome. She couldn't concentrate. She felt as if she should have been preparing for the coming encounter with the Dowager Countess of Cawle as for a war. What did men do to prepare for battle? Sharpen weapons? Check guns? She shuddered at the thought.

She'd always hated war and was deeply grateful Napoleon had finally been defeated and peace reigned. Some people hadn't seemed to mind the casualty lists from a conflict so far away—as long as no one near or dear was involved, of course. But she'd always hated those lists, even if she'd recognized no name. She hadn't been able to block awareness of the grief each death must be causing to a wife, a mother, sisters, and friends. After her father's death, her sympathy had become sharper, for his was the first truly painful loss in her life. He'd died during the October after Waterloo, however, so most casualty lists had ceased.

She welcomed the interruption of a knock on the door. She opened it herself to receive another note from Lady Cawle, this time still sealed. So, it had been brought directly to her.

Intrigued, she broke the seal and unfolded the heavy paper.

> *To aid your enterprise, Ariana, here is a list of suitable gentlemen currently in Town. Their suitability consists of their rank, fortune, availability for marriage, and height.*
>
> *Viscount Churston*
> *The Earl of Sellerden*
> *Lord Blacknorton*
> *Sir Arraby Arranbury*
> *Lord Wentforth*
> *The Earl of Kynaston*

Ariana stared at the last name, then hurried to the desk. Clumsy in her urgency, she raised the lid, opened the inkpot, took up a pen, and, without checking or trimming it, dipped it and scratched thick lines through the last name on the list.

Ethel came in and saw what she was doing. The name

was still visible. "Oh," she said. Ethel had been with her during that disastrous season.

The madness had passed, leaving Ariana feeling foolish.

"What of the rest?" she asked with as casual a manner as she could as she put away the writing things. "Do you recognize any names?"

"No. Do you think the order means anything?"

"With him the least suitable of all? They're certainly not ranked by precedence."

"Height?"

"I doubt it. I should have crossed off Sir Arraby while I was about it."

"He's been unkind?"

"I've never met him as best I know, but I'd be Lady Ariana Arranbury. Impossible!"

"Beggars can't be choosers."

"I'm not a beggar yet."

The name Kynaston was still readable. Ariana tossed the list onto the fire and it felt like exorcising a curse. But then Ethel said, "Lady Cawle will expect you to have shown that list to your mother."

Blaming wretched Kynaston for all her problems, Ariana rewrote the list from memory.

But she left off one name.

At last it was time to dine. Ariana felt as if she were finally going into battle after being kept waiting for an age. Did men waiting for battle orders become impatient, or did they welcome all delays?

She and her mother were escorted to a small drawing room that was elegantly decorated with a Persian carpet on the floor and a few portraits in gilded frames on the dark red walls. It formed a perfect setting for Lady Cawle, who awaited them, magnificent in black silk. The fitted waist and wide skirts supported by cane hoops should have made her ridiculous, but with new insight, Ariana thought it made the high-waisted style dull by comparison. It certainly flattered a still-magnificently curved figure.

The lorgnette came out. "I'm pleased to see you much improved, gel." Ariana remembered that Lady Cawle even spoke in the drawl and cant of the past. "And you, Clarinda. You've been absent from Town too long."

"I don't care for it," Ariana's mother said calmly. "If I want a city, I prefer Winchester or Bath."

A twitch of Lady Cawle's brows dismissed that as folly, but she didn't argue. Dark hair and brows might have artificial help, but if so, it was skillfully done. Her complexion was largely unwrinkled. She was a very handsome woman.

"I have arranged for three mantua-makers to attend here tomorrow. They will assess your wardrobe, Ariana, and amend what can be usefully amended. They will do the same for you, Clarinda, if you wish. They will also provide some new garments within days."

"Hence the three," Ariana said.

"Glad to see you've your wits, gel. As I gather you wish to find a husband as quickly as possible, three new gowns and furbelows may be sufficient. If not, more can be provided."

"Such a pity they must all be in mourning shades," Lady Langton said. "Not that I don't regret Princess Charlotte's death, of course, but it creates a dismal atmosphere."

"In this case, that and the season are to our advantage."

"Because bright and light wouldn't look so well on

me," Ariana said, determined not to be left out of the conversation.

Again an approving look. "Precisely. Especially with the way fashion goes at the moment, with excessive trimming wherever it can be tacked on. Simpler by far to ignore the changes and carry on as one wishes."

"I should continue in the current style for the rest of my life?" Ariana asked. "But what if a new fashion comes along that I prefer? Pantaloons for ladies, for example."

The lorgnette was raised again. "Are you a revolutionary?"

"Would it be revolutionary for women to sometimes be free of skirts? When working in the fields, for example?"

"As I don't suppose you intend to trudge the fields in the next few weeks, that hardly matters. Dress as you wish for the rest of your life, Ariana, but you'll dress suitably for your current purpose."

Ariana said, "Yes, ma'am," with only spurious contrition.

"Something of a minx, are you? Remember that our purpose is to see you married, as suitably and comfortably as possible, by the end of the year, thus compelling your brother to produce legal progeny. Conceal any eccentricities until the vows are said."

"I can hardly conceal my height."

"That is not an eccentricity. It is fate."

Clearly Lady Cawle saw six feet as exactly the barrier it was, but Ariana could hardly fault her for accepting reality. As Lady Cawle and her mother discussed social details, Ariana took a closer look at the pictures on the wall.

She suspected a man in a gray wig was the deceased Lord Cawle, and a fresh-faced young man the current one. She knew that Lady Cawle had held on to the family

town house when widowed, forcing her son and his growing family to live elsewhere.

And why not? Why should a widow lose everything?
Why couldn't her mother have Boxstall Priory for life,
which would at least keep it safe from Uncle Paul?

Another portrait froze her wandering thoughts. Classically handsome features, deep blue eyes, and a close
cap of dark, curly hair. Surely it was the Earl of Kynaston, just as she remembered him!

"Lord Kynaston," Lady Cawle said, having noticed
her attention. "Handsome fellow. Perhaps you met him
eight years ago."

Ariana wanted to deny it, but would Lady Cawle
remember that they'd danced?

"I'm not sure," she lied. "Did he play the lute?"

"An oddity like that makes a person memorable.
He's my nephew. Not around at the moment."

Thank heavens for that! Even a painted portrait had
unsettled her, and not just with uncomfortable memories. It seemed as if he were looking at her, assessing her
even, which tempted her to sink into the nearest chair
before her legs gave out and ply her ornamental fan.

Lady Cawle's nephew!

"Not around at the moment" could imply that he
frequently visited. Thank heavens even more that
they'd be in this house for only a few days.

"Next to him's my daughter, Clara. Pigeon-brained,
but I steered her into marriage with another dimwit
and they seem happy enough. Bear that in mind, gel.
Choose a mental match. Now, let's dine."

The meal was more enjoyable than Ariana had expected.
The food was excellent and Lady Cawle an adept con-

versationalist. Some of her anecdotes were slightly scandalous, but to Ariana's surprise, her mother made no objection. In fact, she seemed to be enjoying herself.

When they retired to the drawing room, brandy was served as well as coffee. Ariana and her mother declined, but Lady Cawle sipped from her glass as talk turned to the matter in hand.

"I sent you a list of tall gentlemen, Ariana, but consider temperament as well as height. Looks fade, but temperament is for life, and often intensifies with age. The charmingly impetuous young man can become an erratic disaster. The romantically protective can become a tyrant."

"Surely some men improve with age," Ariana said.

"From callow youth, yes. But not from thirty onward."

"Then I shall marry under thirty," Ariana said, "and improve my husband as necessary."

Lady Cawle considered her. "Quite possibly you could."

Ariana wished she weren't blushing. "I was funning, ma'am. I don't have the knack of managing men."

"You may surprise yourself. All the men on the list are under thirty. A husband has enough excuses to be domineering without adding significant age. I'd suggest that you marry a man younger than yourself, but I doubt you'd agree."

"I've never considered the matter. I suppose he might be easier to bully."

"A threatened man is a dangerous one."

"Like a wild beast?"

Ariana was enjoying the bout with Lady Cawle, but her mother wasn't. "Don't be silly," she said, and it seemed to be addressed to both of them. "A man's

nature is not dictated by his age. My son could never
be a wild beast, but I wouldn't like him to marry a
bully. And I wouldn't like my daughter to be one."

"Again, that was only in fun, Mama. I don't care
about the age of my husband, within reasonable limits,
as long as he's sensible."

"Now she sets an impossible standard!" Lady Cawle
exclaimed, but with that gleam of amusement. "What a
pity that men no longer wear high heels," Lady Cawle
added. "Given the fashion for flat shoes for ladies"—
hers were heeled in the style to suit her gown—"it would
make some additional men of a height with you."

"Did gentlemen truly teeter around on high-heeled
shoes?" Ariana asked.

"Oh, yes." Lady Cawle smiled. "I remember when
the most virile and dangerous gentlemen did so, and
with such style. A heeled shoe shows off a man's calf
extraordinarily well."

To Ariana's astonishment, her mother joined in. "It
does. And now it's nearly always boots, or pantaloons.
I do like to see gentlemen dressed for the evening in
breeches and stockings."

The two older women continued to discuss men's fash-
ions and the way clothing revealed or concealed manly
attributes until Lady Cawle noticed Ariana's silence.
"Have you never admired a gentleman's physique?"

Hot-cheeked, Ariana said, "I don't think . . ." She'd
intended to say that she didn't think it proper, but how
could she criticize her mother? "I think a man's behavior and moral reputation more important, ma'am."

"Sounds like a recipe for a demmed bore," Lady
Cawle drawled, draining her glass. "But if you want to
marry a milk pudding, I give you leave."

"Thank you."

"Starched up, are you? I have no power to dictate to you. Nor does your mother or your brother, for you're of age. But use your freedom wisely."

"You sound as if you doubt that I will."

"Is anyone ever wise about matters of the heart?"

"Then it's fortunate that the heart has nothing to do with my quest."

"Ariana!" her mother protested. "You mustn't give up hope of love."

Ariana wished her words unsaid, for her mother persisted in believing there could be romance in this business. "I don't give up hope, Mama. But I can't insist on it. We're often told that love can grow after marriage."

"Or wither," Lady Cawle said. "Choose with a cool head, Ariana, if you're capable of it. Sweet words and flowers have snared many a poor soul to hell. You used to play the harpsichord. Do you still?"

It took Ariana a moment to catch up, but she admitted that she did.

"You played very well. There's one in the music room next door. I've had the fire lit in there and I'd be obliged if you'd play for us."

Despite the wording, it was a command, and Ariana saw no decent way to refuse. She didn't even want to. The harpsichord was an unusual instrument in these days of the pianoforte, but she enjoyed it.

She went through to the next room to find the promised music room holding a variety of large instruments and some smaller ones on display. In keeping with Lady Cawle's eighteenth-century style, there was no piano, but the harpsichord was a magnificent specimen, painted all over in rich pastoral themes.

When Ariana sat and tried out a few keys, she found it perfectly tuned. She settled to playing a familiar piece, soothed by the orderly, crisp plucks on the strings. The pianoforte was an instrument well suited to the passions, but the harpsichord was much more to her liking.

Chapter 3

The next morning the mantua-makers arrived in sequence, an hour apart. Each inspected Ariana's wardrobe and had her in and out of gowns so they could try new trimmings and overlays of gauze or net. Each departed with two gowns to refurbish and a commission to create a new one, with all speed.

Lady Cawle observed and advised. Ariana's mother had excused herself to visit an old friend. Ariana wished she'd been able to do the same, though she had no friends in Town as best she knew.

As Ethel fastened her back into a plain gray walking dress, Ariana grumbled, "I don't see why a lady shouldn't have a substitute of the same size to go through the tedium of fittings."

"Nor do I," Ethel said. "Shall we seek one?"

Ariana laughed. "You take the air out of my complaining sails. If there was to be much more of it, I would. As it is, I need a good long walk."

"Aren't you supposed to stay out of sight until you're in style?"

Ariana collapsed into a chair with a sigh. "I shall go mad." She instantly sat up again. "A newspaper! At least I can read about the wider world. Lady Cawle must take one."

"Do you want me to find out?"

"No," Ariana said, standing up. "I'll go in hunt."

"Why?"

"I need exercise! A walk around the house will be better than nothing, and this provides an excuse."

Ariana wrapped a warm knitted shawl around her shoulders and ventured out. The most likely place for newspapers was in the library, and she'd been shown the door to it last night. It was on the ground floor, but first she indulged in a brisk walk up and down this corridor.

Then she went down a floor and detoured to revisit the music room. She hadn't felt able to poke around last night, but she'd noticed that it seemed to contain quite a selection of instruments. She'd been correct, and as expected, they were all from the previous century. As well as the harpsichord, there was a magnificent harp and a variety of wind instruments. On a chest was a set of kettledrums.

She carefully opened the smoothly operating drawers of the chest to find more recorders and flutes plus a clarinet and a mandolin. Lady Cawle must frequently host musical events where the guests were invited to play. Did she try to provide every possible instrument? A cupboard revealed a cello, and a number of violins hung on the back wall. In more drawers she found viols of all sizes, and finally a lute.

Ariana firmly closed that drawer and all memories it summoned.

The harpsichord tempted, but she would be heard, so she left the room to continue downstairs to the entrance hall and, finally, the library.

It was a small room, but fully lined with bookcases except for one window and the fireplace, where a lively fire kept the room pleasantly warm. She saw two newspapers on the central mahogany table—the *Times* and the *Morning Chronicle*. Delighting in the sight and smell of books, Ariana decided she'd sit to read the *Times* in one of the large high-backed chairs placed to face the fire. She closed the door and went forward to pick up the paper, but a movement startled her.

A man was rising from one of those chairs. He stood, but then clutched onto the back of the chair to keep his balance, muttering something that might even have been a curse.

Was he drunk? At eleven in the morning!

The wretch was dressed in what seemed to be a gentlemanly jacket and breeches, but his cast-off boots sprawled on the wooden floor. Had he *slept* here? He wore no neckcloth, his shirt stood open the full six inches, and his buff waistcoat gaped unbuttoned.

Some drunken miscreant had somehow invaded Lady Cawle's house in the night?

Ariana edged back toward the door, keeping her eyes on the danger.

The slovenly mess was topped by an unshaven chin and an unruly abundance of dark curling hair that looked as if it hadn't been combed in days or barbered in a six-month. He got his balance and stared at her, and between stubble and dark brows, she saw deep blue eyes.

She might not have made the connection except for the portrait in Lady Cawle's small drawing room, but could this disreputable mess be the damnable Earl of Kynaston? Once she considered, she was sure. But why was Lady Cawle's nephew languishing here rather than in a bedroom?

Eight years ago he'd worn his hair cropped short and the tight, dark curls had made an enticing frame for his beautiful features, but it was clear that he'd taken the ruinous path she'd feared for him. His complexion was sallow, his stance unsteady, and those memorable eyes were surely bloodshot—though it was hard to tell when they were half-hidden by drooping lids. From perfection he'd become a perfect picture of slovenly debauch.

She'd intended to summon servants to throw the intruder out, but he was no intruder. She couldn't imagine how he had come to be in the library in such a state, but he was frowning at her in the same puzzlement. That was a gift from heaven. He hadn't recognized her.

She still wanted a newspaper. He seemed fixed in place. In fact, he looked as if only his clutch on the back of the chair kept him upright, but drunks were unpredictable. Still watching him as she might watch a snarling dog, Ariana edged toward the table. "I beg pardon for disturbing you, sir. I came to find a newspaper."

He gestured permission with a hand that retained much of its old elegance. She remembered that, and his signet ring—a carved red stone set in heavy gold. What a thing to recall about a man she'd spoken to only twice, and that so long ago. But she'd observed him back then— oh, yes—closely and frequently.

Keeping the table between them, she edged toward the *Times*.

He suddenly cocked his head in curiosity. "Who're you?" he asked, voice husky and slurred.

"A guest," she said, progressing another few inches. "So'm I."

Ariana realized that she should pretend not to know who he was, or that he had a right to be here. She spoke slowly and clearly. "This is the house of the Dowager Countess of Cawle."

He nodded.

"In that case, perhaps you should leave."

He blinked at her. "Why?"

She'd heard of men who ruined their bodies by endless drinking. Could it ruin the mind? In one not yet thirty? "If you're found here, there could be trouble."

"True enough. Fussing 'n' botheration." He swayed and then, giving up the effort of standing, turned and collapsed back down onto the chair and out of sight.

Perhaps he'd hidden there in the hope his aunt wouldn't discover how drunk he was.

Ariana seized the copy of the *Times* and edged back toward the door, still watching him in the mirror. He seemed only half-conscious, but then he said, "Don't go."

She realized that if she could see him, he could see her. "I mean to instruct the servants to take you home, sir."

"Don't have a home. Not in London at leasht."

"To your inn or hotel, then."

"Don't have one of 'em, either. Live here."

"This is the house of the Dowager Countess of Cawle," she repeated. He *lived* here?

"I know that," he said, frowning at her. "She'sh my aunt."

Ariana was pleased to have arrived at honesty. "Yet she doesn't know you're here?"

"Been away. 'Rived back late. The queshtion is, who are you, my gold-topped Amazon?"

Tone and faint gleam in bloodshot eyes were warning

enough. "Another guest," Ariana said, and backed again toward the door.

"Lady Ariana Boxstall," he said, making it to his feet again, brow furrowed, as if trying to remember more.

She prayed he didn't. But she couldn't resist a mischievous lie. "I apologize, sir, but I do not remember you." It was hard not to grin at the way it took him aback. Had any women ever before forgotten him?

He managed a slight bow without falling over. "The Earl of Kynashton, at your service, Lady Ariana. We danced once. At m'aunt's ball in . . . '09, yes? Musht have been '09."

Ariana hoped her smile looked merely polite, for her innards were behaving erratically. He remembered their one dance? "You have a remarkable recall, my lord. You must have danced with a great many ladies then and since."

"But none so tall. And your name does act as an aide-mémoire. Tall," he added, as if she might miss the point, "and Boxstall."

If the newspaper in her hand had been something heavy, she might have thrown it at him. As it was, her only weapon was indifference. "So it does, my lord. If you will excuse me?"

"You've improved."

Some buried part of her still stirred in foolish hope, and that broke her restraint. "As you have not, my lord! You are as arrogant as ever, and a drunkard as well. I recommend you find your bed, wherever it is."

"So you do remember me." He came toward her then, weaving only slightly, his words becoming clearer, perhaps along with his wits? "Will you steer me to my bed, Lady Ariana?"

"You're drunk, my lord, and don't know what you're saying."

"Not true, not true. I do want you to take me to my bed. To my great sorrow."

"Come any closer and I'll hit you."

Humor gleamed in those heavy-lidded eyes. "With a newspaper?"

"With my fist." Ariana switched the paper to her left hand and raised her right, clenched and ready.

He stepped forward and enclosed it with his larger hand. And then he brought their locked hands to his lips, still looking at her, challenging her. "Can't let you damage your hand, sweetheart," he murmured, his lips soft and warm against her knuckles. "Too lovely a bloom to be blemished . . ."

Lovely.

Ariana did the only thing she could and whacked his head with the newspaper. She put full force into it, but it was a feeble blow, especially left-handed. It shocked him enough to release her. He staggered back out of reach, and might have fallen if he'd not collided with the table heavily enough to move it a few inches.

"My apologies," he said, regaining his balance and perhaps sobered. He stood straight and aimed those beautiful eyes at her, full of sorrow. "Forgive me my sins?"

Her heart did something odd, something only seventeen-year-old hearts should do. Ariana turned and fled the library before the madness became complete. She ran up to her room and sank into a chair with a moan.

Ethel hurried in. "What's the matter?"

"He's here! In the library!" Ariana couldn't stop exclaiming. She felt as if her hair should be standing on end.

"Who's here?"

"Kynaston!"

Ethel sat down nearby. "Why? Has he come to court you?"

Ariana sat up straight. "Never! Do you think . . . ? No! He's Lady Cawle's nephew."

"So she's invited him, as one of your suitors."

"No!" Ariana tried to make sense. "He's disgustingly drunk. At this hour in the morning. And it doesn't appear to be an unusual state. His cravat was hanging loose, his waistcoat was undone, and his hair hasn't been tended to in months."

"You're sounding sorry for him."

"I am not! It's only that it seems a shame that someone with everything in life should sink so low."

"No one has everything in life," Ethel pointed out, "but that's the way it goes with some overindulged gentlemen. Slave to drink, rotted with the pox."

"Don't . . ."

"You still sweet on him?"

"I was *never* sweet on him," Ariana protested, and it was true. Sweet had had nothing to do with it.

He had been magnificent back then. A god. A handsome, wealthy young earl, popular, gifted, and carelessly charming. How could she not have fallen under his spell?

She'd known he was dangerous and far beyond her touch, but . . .

But, if Lord Kynaston had shown any interest, she'd have melted into his arms. If her parents had tried to stop her, she'd have eloped with him and let the consequences go hang.

"What do the servants say about him?" Ariana asked.

"I don't pay much heed to their chatter, but I'll go and find out."

Ethel left and Ariana slumped back in the chair, new horrors arising in her mind. Was it possible that she'd meet Kynaston morning, noon, and night? Thank heavens she'd be leaving in a few days, but that would be a few days too long.

Why was he here? An earl must have a town house of his own. Yet he'd said he didn't. Perhaps it was too far away for him to stagger to in his drunken state, so he'd come to his aunt's house instead? That didn't make sense. If friends hadn't seen him home, a hackney would have done the job. Whatever the reason, it was an impossible situation.

What to do?

What to do?

She rose to pace. Leaving immediately was impossible without explanation. If Lady Cawle let him stay, Ariana had no say in that. She could only continue as she'd begun. With indifference.

Trying to hit him hadn't exactly been indifferent. He'd been behaving atrociously, but a properly behaved lady wouldn't have tried to hit him with her fist.

She probably should have screamed. That would have served him right, and perhaps his aunt would have tossed him out on his ear. An opportunity missed and now she'd have to keep her door locked at night or not feel safe in her bed.

She'd go to Lady Cawle, tell her tale, and get him evicted.

But then Ethel returned.

"As you say, he's Lady Cawle's nephew on her husband's side, and she's softhearted with him—that's their words—as she wasn't with her husband and isn't with her own son. Their words again."

"What else?"

"I didn't like to ask too many questions, but Lady Cawle's maid was warning the younger maids about him. She said he's the rascal he is because his father died when he was young, so he's been the earl from a lad, cosseted by all."

"And of course he was gifted with a devil's charm." At Ethel's look, Ariana exclaimed, "It's not praise! A devil charms people down to hell."

"But some probably enjoy the journey. He has a room here, but that's recent. He's been abroad for years and only returned a few weeks ago."

"Thank God we'll soon be gone. As he clearly lives a life of dark-hours debauchery, our paths may never cross again." Ariana saw the somewhat mangled newspaper and picked it up. "Having won a copy of the *Times* at such pains, I intend to enjoy it." She sat down again and opened the paper, but her mind wouldn't stick to the words on the page.

He'd remembered dancing with her.

But only because she was tall.

"Forgive me my sins." There'd been such sorrow in that, as if he felt true repentance. Surely he couldn't remember everything about that night.

After the memorable set danced with Lord Kynaston— at the hostess's insistence, of course—she'd resumed her regular station as a wallflower. She'd felt conspicuous, as always, even when sitting down, especially when she'd just made a spectacle of herself with the object of her dreams.

Even though it was obvious his aunt had been compelling him, he'd been gracious as he'd asked her to dance. Unlike one gentleman she'd heard whispering, "Gads, no, ma'am, please. A veritable maypole!"

Alas, she'd paid him badly for his courtesy. She'd been a well-taught dancer, but being so close to her idol had made her clumsy, which had made her even clumsier, as had awareness that every eye was upon them— because he was a god and she was freakishly tall.

When the set was over, he'd returned her to her mother's side, but she'd felt every eye was upon her. She'd used the excuse of needing the ladies' retiring room to escape. She'd spent as much time there as possible and then lingered on her way back, taking a circuitous route. She'd found herself in a corridor, able to hear men's voices from a room ahead. The door had been ajar and so she'd hesitated, wondering if she could walk past without being seen. Then she'd realized they were indulging in a cruel review of the young ladies present.

One miss was a giggling pink rabbit, and another a pudding bag with her bulk tied into a white dress. Then some wit had turned to ornithology. Miss Penty was a big-breasted buzzard, because of her hawklike nose and large bosom. Miss Sallicome, who had pimples and sadly crooked teeth, was a lesser-spotted crossbill.

Each sally had brought louder guffaws, and she'd stood there, fists clenched, desperate for the courage to storm in and call them a gaggle of lesser-brained vultures. But then she'd heard Kynaston's voice.

"And let's not forget the big-footed Boxstall longshanks!"

How they'd hooted and choked. She'd fled back the way she'd come, aware as never before of her feet, of the slap they made as she ran and how they must look in white satin slippers trimmed with pink rosettes to match her gown.

At the memory, the agony of embarrassment washed over her again, as if she were seventeen again, and her hands crushed the edges of the unread paper.

A knock brought her out of the past, but Ariana was instantly alarmed that it would be him. She didn't want to see him, not even if he'd come to apologize. When Ethel opened the door, however, it was to a maid bearing a folded paper.

From him?

Apologizing?

It was a letter, however.

"From Hermione Faringay," she said with relief. The letter had been addressed to the town house and sent on. "Perhaps she's coming to Town after all."

Ariana broke the seal with anticipation, but her friend's first words were that she and her husband were fixed at Faringay.

But she continued:

I'm so pleased you're in London again. You've been much too inclined to stay in the country, and I'm sure you'll enjoy all London has to offer. Never mind the trivial social whirl. You must visit the British Museum and any number of other intelligent diversions. I mention the British Museum because they have Egyptian artifacts there, including the Rosetta stone, and I know that's an interest of yours.

You may also want to visit my great-uncle, Mr. Peake. He has recently acquired a town house where he can display the items he brought back from the East. He's also amusing himself by hosting gatherings of a society called the Curious Creatures. They are people who share an interest in anything odd or obscure, and in new ideas and developments.

His last letter said that he'd acquired some Egyptian pieces. They are mostly small items, but there's a reproduction of a wall painting that he seems pleased with and hopes to mount in his drawing room. I've sent him a letter to alert him to your being in Town and I'm sure he'll invite you to look at his acquisitions. If you wish to write to him yourself, his address is 29, Burlington Street.

Ariana refolded the letter, cheered by the prospect.

Ethel read her mind. "You're supposed to stay out of sight until you're fashionable."

"The devil. I might as well be locked in the Tower. But I might be able to go on this one expedition."

"How?"

"This Peake is a merchant. I'm only hiding from fashionable people. I won't meet any of them at his house."

"Fools rush in where angels fear to tread."

"Fortune favors the brave," Ariana shot back, and sat to write the letter.

She received a reply only a few hours later, suggesting that she come on the afternoon of the next day.

"There," she told Ethel. "All settled. And there's the added benefit of removing me from this house for a while." Where a black-mopped, red-eyed Kynaston lurked.

"He'll likely dine here," Ethel pointed out.

"Are you determined to ruin my mood? But in that case, I will dress with dignity."

All Ariana's finer gowns were in the hands of the seamstresses, but it suited her to go to dinner in an almost drab, plain black gown. She could have enlivened it with a rich shawl, but she wrapped herself in knitted brown and an air of perfect indifference.

He wasn't there.

For which she was grateful, she assured herself, aware of Lady Cawle's silent disapproval of her appearance. That was all Kynaston's fault, and he was doubtless out in some low tavern getting soused again. That was no concern of hers.

After the meal, in the small drawing room, Lady Cawle again asked Ariana to play, adding, "As you are in practice, I suggest you play as often as possible. It shows you well, as before."

"It does," Ariana's mother agreed warmly. "I remember how much your playing was admired, dear."

Ariana sat to play, unsettled by a view of her time in London that she'd forgotten. Now she was prompted, she remembered that she'd played on a few occasions and not disgraced herself. Admired, though? That was coming it too strong.

Perhaps there would be occasions when she could perform, however, and it was something she could do sitting down.

Ariana was comfortable in the certainty that she'd meet none of the fashionable set at Mr. Peake's house, but she decided not to request permission.

"Discretion is the better part of valor," Ethel said.

"I don't need permission to go anywhere," Ariana stated, and she put on her dark gray pelisse and a black velvet beret and went downstairs, Ethel a step behind.

However, Lady Cawle must have had some means of knowing everything, for Ariana was halted in the upper corridor by a request that she visit her hostess. She told

Ethel to continue down into the hall and was taken to Lady Cawle's white-and-gold boudoir.

"You are going out?" Lady Cawle asked.

"As you see, ma'am."

"Where?"

"Is that not for my mother to ask?"

"Have you asked her consent, gel?"

"No," Ariana said, irritated to be made to feel like a naughty schoolgirl. "I'm on my way to visit the elderly relative of a friend. He has Egyptian artifacts, but he's a merchant. I will not be revealing my shabbiness to the ton."

"Egypt is fashionable these days, but very well. You may go, but with an escort. Ah, there you are."

Ariana turned, to find Kynaston coming in.

His eyes were still bloodshot and the general slackness remained, but he was shaved, his hair was cropped short, and his jacket, breeches, and boots were in perfect order. Ariana was an honest woman, and had to admit that despite everything he was once more distressingly godlike.

"You required something, Aunt?" His tone suggested resentment or even something more arrogant, but that didn't deter Lady Cawle.

"Make yourself useful and escort Lady Ariana to some eccentric relative of a friend. Don't let her go to any fashionable spot."

Kynaston's dark brows rose. "How far am I allowed to go in restraining her?"

"Don't be tiresome. It's a simple task, and shouldn't be beyond even you."

Clearly he'd been taxing his indulgent aunt's patience, which wasn't surprising.

Ariana thought he might refuse, but Lady Cawle's power seemed to hold. "Do we use the town carriage?" he drawled.

"It could draw attention. A hackney will suffice."

He bowed to his aunt and opened the door for Ariana. She sought a way to avoid this situation, but short of changing her mind and remaining at home, she saw none. She wanted to see the Egyptian artifacts and wouldn't let a dictatorial woman and a disreputable wretch steal the opportunity. Ethel would be with her. Together they could handle him if he proved troublesome.

She went through the door and along the corridor in the direction of the stairs down to the hall.

Titus Delacorte, Earl of Kynaston, had no desire to visit an eccentric collector.

He had no desire to go anywhere that required him to dress and behave as a gentleman should.

He particularly had no desire to be escorting Lady Ariana Boxstall, not when she stirred feelings he'd renounced. Despite the drunken haze yesterday, he'd responded to her bright eyes and vibrancy, but he'd hoped he'd felt only an irritation that would fade. But today had been the same. She'd plagued him with a direct gaze that had spoken of her low opinion of him. Hardly surprising after their last encounter, but he didn't want anything to do with the woman. She was too disturbing to his mind and his purpose. She had looked directly at him, not up at him. Excessively tall women usually had the grace to hunch in an effort to reduce their height, but she'd stood tall and bold.

Damnable Amazon.

Damnable aunt!

Aunt Claudia had been good to him, however, even at times when he'd not been appreciative—especially then—and she asked little in return. Of course she was match-making, which was strange when she'd been glad to see the back of her own husband, but she seemed moved by Lady Ariana's quest. He could appreciate a desire to save an estate from a wastrel, but was surprised that such an Amazon would make a martyr of herself.

She'd taken the lead down the corridor, straight-backed, poised, and confident. She hadn't been so confident all those years ago, but she'd been young then, and on her first season.

He'd also been young.

So very young.

Clearly her life had been less troubled than his.

Unfortunate that their first encounter in years had gone so poorly. He couldn't claim that being badly foxed was unusual, but to have passed out in the library and still been there at nearly noon had been uncouth. Memory of her raised fist stirred a smile. She'd meant business, as she'd shown by whacking him with the newspaper. Not a painful blow, but rather like a slap with a glove.

A challenge.

Had she meant it that way?

Any husband she chose would have a challenge. Perhaps an exciting one. But that man wouldn't be him. Aunt Claudia had to know that—or did she think she could change anything by the force of her will? Probably.

At the top of the stairs Lady Ariana halted and turned to face him, eye to eye. "There's no need for you to inconvenience yourself, my lord." Such bright eyes. Such healthy, glowing skin . . .

"If I don't obey, my aunt will be displeased. It's never wise to displease the Dowager Countess of Cawle."

"It's a blessing that you heed somebody, sir!"

"What a low opinion you have of me."

"Hardly surprising after our previous encounter."

He really should have apologized, but better by far if she despised him. "I promise not to assault you in the cab," he said.

"You'd be most unwise to attempt it."

Without waiting for a response, she set off down the stairs. He followed, damnably tempted, despite everything. But then he saw the woman waiting for them, plain clothing and demeanor declaring her to be some sort of lady's maid or companion.

She was as tall as her mistress, but more broadly built, and not in a feminine way but with mannish jaw and shoulders. Black gloves covered very solid hands. He appreciated Lady Ariana's warning. This creature could be a female pugilist if she wished.

"Lord Kynaston is to escort us, Ethel. My lord, this is my companion, Miss Burgis."

Miss Burgis dipped a very slight curtsy, not trying to hide guarded hostility.

Good.

Do your job.

He inclined his head, then summoned the hovering footman and sent him for a hackney. By then his valet stood ready to assist him into his greatcoat. He pulled on black gloves and set his beaver hat on his head, aware of the difference short hair made. The hat fit better, but it felt strange. He should have summoned a barber sooner, but he'd felt that losing his locks would be some sort of Rubicon, with only disaster on the other side.

Shades of Samson?

Was Lady Ariana Boxstall his Delilah? If so, what destruction would follow?

He caught her frowning at him. She instantly looked away, but he was bruised by her concern. What was he to her, or she to him? She'd be gone from this house in a few days—off on her husband hunt. May she soon be safely shackled.

The carriage arrived and they all left the house. Miss Burgis climbed in unaided. He handed Lady Ariana in, asking, "The address?"

"Twenty-nine, Burlington Street."

He gripped the edge of the door to keep his balance.

"Is that not a street?" she asked, concerned. "I'm sure that's what—"

"It's a street," he said.

It was no great matter. Just one more trial in a sequence of them, and all must be endured. He repeated the direction to the driver, then entered the carriage.

Miss Burgis had taken the backward-facing seat, as a servant should, but that meant he must settle down beside Lady Ariana. It shouldn't disturb him, but as the carriage moved off, he accepted that it did. She was an alluring woman and, despite her height, beguiling in a very feminine way. Her lips were full and soft, demanding to be kissed. She was shrouded in dull outer clothing now, but he could remember from the day before that she had a magnificent bosom.

He still wasn't immune to such things.

Alas.

The silence was becoming uncomfortable, so he asked, "You are to visit Mr. Peake?"

She turned her head to look at him. "You know him?"

"I know of him."

"Is he a famous eccentric, then? He's the great-uncle of a friend, and she tells me he has many curiosities from the East, as well as the Egyptian artifacts."

An eccentric. Perhaps the house would be completely changed. That would be a blessing.

"He's a nabob of sorts," she continued, "and spent most of his life in the East, returning rich."

"A fortunate man."

She frowned at him, and no wonder. He was doing his best to behave as normal, but her warm closeness made it a strain. A glance at the other woman showed dark eyes steadily on him, alert for a threat. Perhaps she'd protect him from himself.

"I assume the house isn't in a fashionable area," Lady Ariana said, "Mr. Peake having been a merchant."

"Not particularly fashionable now, though it was more so a century ago." He escaped into detail. "Fashionable London is a shifting sand, always drifting, and always westward."

"Because the only space is to the west. London has always grown along the river, and the east already has the City, the docks, and many activities to do with shipping."

"You study such matters, Lady Ariana?"

"It's common knowledge, my lord."

It was. He was in danger of appearing an idiot. "And now we no longer depend upon the river for transportation, we are breaking free to the north. Hence the Regent's plan for his grand road and park, ripping through anything in his way."

When he'd returned to England, to London, he'd been affronted by the drastic plans, but he'd have welcomed them if they'd flattened Burlington Street.

Silence settled again and he embraced it, but then she spoke. "Where is your town house, my lord?"

"I don't have one," he said, and looked outside. That should put an end to that.

Ariana met Ethel's interested eyes. Yesterday Kynaston had said he had no nearby home and now he'd confirmed it. That was hardly believable of an earl. Unless . . .

Was he all rolled up, as the saying went? Had his rakish ways ruined not only his body and mind, but his fortune? In that case, Lady Cawle could be trying to capture Ariana's very large dowry for her wastrel, bankrupt nephew. He'd been on the list, and perhaps she'd summoned him from wherever he'd been to make the most of his chances. Had he arrived drunk out of resentment?

Forewarned is forearmed, as Ethel would doubtless have said. Ariana resolved to avoid all future attempts to throw them together.

The carriage stopped on a street of terraced brick houses. Kynaston climbed down and paid the driver, then handed down Ariana. He escorted her to the glossy black door. She'd expected somewhere eccentric, but Mr. Peake's house was one of a conventional brick terrace probably built a century or more ago. As Kynaston had said, this had once been a fashionable area.

The door knocker was more promising, being a gargoyle with long tongue protruding. Kynaston used the tongue as it was intended, to rap the knocker, and the door was opened almost instantly.

Instead of a footman or maid, however, the door opener was a fashionably dressed lady of middle years wearing black and a dashing dark blue velvet turban ornamented with a black plume. She smiled and said, "Welcome," but then walked off into a nearby room, where a number of people seemed to be engaged in lively conversation.

Surprise fixed Ariana in place until Kynaston pushed her forward with a hand on her back. Even through gown and pelisse she felt the shock of his touch, and she hurried forward, hearing Ethel close the door behind them. There were no servants in the narrow hall to assist them.

A brown-haired gentleman, probably in his forties, was coming downstairs and he smiled at their confusion. "At a meeting of the Curious Creatures, Peake has the servants stay out of the way, so whoever is closest to the door attends to it. Your outer clothing can be left in that reception room over there."

He continued on toward the back of the house.

"Curious Creatures indeed," Ariana said, unsure about removing anything. The modest hall was comfortably warmed by a fire, but did she want to stay in this madhouse? She turned to Kynaston, but he was looking around blankly, and no wonder. They were surrounded by a jumble of the conventional and the extraordinary.

An elaborately woven cane chair sat next to a stern seventeenth-century oak one. A deeply carved chest of rosewood set with mother-of-pearl and semiprecious stones was flanked by a conventional longcase clock and a tall pot holding spears. More weapons hung on the walls and up the staircase, many of them richly ornamented and of a style never used in Britain. They were interspaced with grotesque masks, one of which seemed to be covered by small squares of gold.

Many of these items must be precious, but there was a distinct smell of rot.

Kynaston twitched as if coming out of a reverie. "I'm inclined to leave."

That firmed Ariana's spine. "I wish to stay."

"You, too, are a curious creature?"

"It would seem so."

He didn't like that, but he said, "Then onward to the improvised cloakroom."

They went into the room, but it clearly was not improvised. The walls were lined with hooks, and there were a number of stands to take more cloaks, pelisses, greatcoats, hats, and anything else a guest might wish to shed.

Ethel hung up Ariana's pelisse and then took off her own cloak to put on a nearby hook. Kynaston shed his greatcoat and hung it up. His gloves and hat went on a side table and then he adjusted his sleeves and the cuffs of his shirt. He stepped in front of a wall mirror to check his black cravat before turning away.

Such instinctive attention to his appearance, and yet yesterday in the library he'd been a mess. Neat when sober, scruffy when drunk?

"Shall we explore?" he invited.

But now Ariana hesitated. "I'm not supposed to appear before the ton yet. The lady who opened the door looked rather fine."

"Could you not have developed cold feet before we undressed?"

The word "feet" did it. Ariana marched out to face the fashionable foe.

As they entered the hall, someone knocked on the door. No one hurried to open it. Ariana waited for Kynaston to do so. When he didn't, she opened it herself. She couldn't remember ever opening a front door for others in her life. A plainly dressed couple nodded their thanks, entered, and went to the cloakroom in the manner of those well accustomed.

Ariana laughed. "I didn't mind opening the door, but rather resent being left to close it after them. What a wealth of new experiences from a simple visit."

"With more to come, I'm sure."

"Clearly you disapprove, my lord. Having escorted us here, you may leave if you wish."

"I'm entrusted with your care, Lady Ariana, and I confess to some curiosity of my own. Shall we go up?"

Ariana could hear conversation upstairs, so she agreed, telling Ethel to come with them.

Ethel's status was always a little delicate, sitting as it did between lady companion and lady's maid. In this relaxed household there seemed no reason to separate, and Ethel might find aspects of the place enjoyable. Her sturdy appearance could make people think her stolid, but she had a lively, curious mind. If Kynaston objected, he kept it to himself.

In fact he seemed withdrawn. Perhaps he had a drunkard's head.

The simple doglegged stairs opened directly into a large room, which seemed to take up most of this floor. It was full of chairs and sofas, many occupied by people engaged in animated conversation. Everyone wore sober colors, but the style ranged from Puritanical to high fashion. Ariana could still smell something noxious, almost as if a rotting animal lay in some corner, but no one else seemed disturbed.

She looked for somewhere to sit, but an elderly man rose and came over, using a cane, but lightly. He was gray-haired and somewhat rawboned, but dressed in the latest style.

"Welcome, welcome! I hazard a guess that I have the pleasure of addressing Lady Ariana Boxstall, friend of my dear great-niece."

Ariana dipped a curtsy. "Then I suspect I have the pleasure of meeting Mr. Edgar Peake."

"You do, you do." He looked behind her and Ariana made the introductions to Ethel and Kynaston.

"Lord Kynaston, is it?" Mr. Peake said with sharp interest. "What do you think of the place, eh?"

"Novel," Kynaston said in a drawl that was almost insulting.

Certainly Mr. Peake was something of a rough diamond and showing no discernible deference, but if Kynaston disliked low company, he should have left when invited to do so.

"I've already seen so many intriguing items," Ariana said with a smile. "And I'm curious about the Curious Creatures."

Mr. Peake gestured around. "An admirable group— a club of sorts, which meets occasionally in Town to investigate oddities. It used to gather in a tavern, but now I have this house, I make it available. One benefit is that more ladies attend. We'll have a presentation shortly on the possibility of life on the moon."

"You plan to live on the moon?" Kynaston asked, in the same insulting manner.

Mr. Peake wasn't at all deterred. "All things are possible in our marvelous modern age, my lord. Perhaps we'll find a way to use coal gas to fire a rocket there with a man on board."

"That sounds terribly dangerous," Ariana said.

"And impossible," Kynaston murmured.

"Nothing is impossible," Peake said. "To think so is to be blind to opportunity. Gas will revolutionize the world—you mark my words, my lord—but we haven't perfected it yet. Hence the faint aroma of experimentation."

"So there isn't a corpse lurking here," Ariana said.

Peake chuckled. "Unless you count the one in the basement. Come, come! I gather you will be particularly interested in my Egyptian acquisitions and they are still down there." He urged them toward the stairs.

Despite mention of a corpse, Ariana was keen, but she would happily shed Kynaston's disdainful company. "Do you wish to remain here, my lord?"

"You might escape into fashionable dissipation, Lady Ariana. So, no."

She shrugged and went with their host, noting that the Earl of Kynaston had not improved with keeping, as the saying went. He'd lost all his smiling charm and become arrogantly rude. At least that was wearing away at any lingering enchantment.

As they returned to the hall, the knocker sounded again. Mr. Peake went to answer it and was soon greeting new guests—a couple with two sons in their teens.

They chattered away, and then Peake remembered them. "My dear Lady Ariana, Lord Kynaston, my apologies! My lord, would you be so kind as to take Lady Ariana and her companion down to the cellars? I'm sure you know the way. I must take these fine young fellows up to meet Inkman." With that, he returned to his new guests.

Ariana looked an apology to Kynaston, for Peake's request had been beyond anything. No wonder he looked at the edge of his patience. "There's no need," she said.

"You wish to see his Egyptian artifacts. Come." He didn't wait, but walked away toward the back of the house.

"Why would he know the way?" Ethel muttered as they followed.

"He must have visited here in the past."

"Visited the cellars?"

Ariana shrugged and hurried to catch up.

She'd never considered a man's back before, but remembering the way her mother and Lady Cawle had assessed the gentlemen, she indulged herself. Though awake to all Kynaston's faults, she couldn't help but be aware that his back view was fine. Broad shoulders, slim hips, strong legs that moved him forward in a very smooth, athletic way. No matter what debauchery he'd sunk into over eight years, he was still in good physical shape.

He halted and opened a plain door to reveal a narrow staircase. "Take care on these stairs. They were built for people with small feet."

Ariana froze.

The monster!

From behind her, Ethel whispered, "He's having trouble, too."

He was. Ahead of them, Kynaston was having to put his booted feet sideways on the narrow treads. Ariana still might have retreated if Ethel hadn't given her a shove. She went down, big feet sideways on the inadequate stairs, hating him, her feet, and the cruelty of being a tall lady. He had to duck at one point to go under a dip in the ceiling, which at least warned her to do the same.

Then she arrived in a basement area lit by two small windows high in the walls, and wonder wiped all grievance from her mind.

A part of one long wall was covered by Egyptian

figures, portrayed in that distinctive style, with the faces shown in profile but shoulders square to the viewer. Brown skin, black straight-cut hair, and mostly white clothing that left the men's legs bare. Hieroglyphic writing presumably described the scene, but no one knew exactly what those images and shapes meant. It looked as if a harvest was being gathered and presented to a pharaoh or a god. She knew that at times the pharaohs themselves had been considered gods.

Ariana wanted to move closer, but the floor was almost entirely covered by wooden crates, bundles, and shrouded objects. There were only a few narrow passages, none going toward the mural.

The light suddenly increased and she turned to see Kynaston replacing the glass on a hanging oil lamp. A tinderbox sat nearby.

"Thank you, my lord." Ariana turned back to the wall painting, which had become brighter and more alive. "Isn't it magnificent?"

"Impressive," he agreed, moving closer. Given the lack of space, that meant very close.

"It's not real," she said, heart suddenly beating faster. "I mean . . . it's a reproduction."

"You can detect that?"

I can detect your smell. Subtle and clean, but something else. Something I didn't know I remembered from a hot, perfumed dance.

"My friend told me," she said quickly. "Lady Faringay, Mr. Peake's great-niece. She wrote to me about it."

"Stand aside," he said, which was barely possible. He squeezed past her, their bodies pressing together for a shocking moment. "My lord!" she protested, but by then he was in front of her, blocking her view.

The oaf!

But he tested one crate and then lifted another to place on top of it. He pulled the cloth off an object to reveal a very odd wooden statue. He picked that up, looked around, and found a safe spot for it on top of some soft-looking bundles.

Then he turned and gestured. "My lady?"

He'd made a space for her in front of the mural.

Against her will, Ariana was charmed—by his thoughtfulness and by a hint of true warmth on his face. This was more like the man she remembered, and her body was still humming from that outrageous moment of close contact.

But the picture summoned, and she went forward into the space he'd created. He didn't retreat, so he was still close, but not as close as before.

Which might be a shame.

Focus on the mural, Ariana.

"It's as if it is a wall," she said.

"Probably painted on plaster laid on wood."

"So quite easy to do. Anyone could have such a thing created."

"You would?" he asked.

"I might. My father would have."

"It would be an odd addition to a lordly seat."

"But an interesting one." She glanced at him. Which was a mistake when they were so close. The light hung behind them, casting his face in shadow. That concealed all his shortcomings but hid none of his perfections.

"It would certainly excite conversation," he said, their eyes only inches apart.

There was a kind of intimacy, as if of nighttime and privacy, and . . .

Ariana stepped as far from him as she could, until the backs of her legs pressed against a box. She excused her movement by turning to inspect the mural more closely. Carefully, she touched it, finding a stonelike surface.

"You're correct, I think. Plaster, or perhaps stucco, on wood. I wonder how it was brought down here, and how it will be taken out."

"There's a door to the outside."

A dip in awareness told her that he'd turned away to look for that door. She'd known his old magic lingered in her mind, but after his disgusting behavior yesterday, she'd never imagined it might still have power over her.

Or perhaps she had.

Even yesterday, in a wretched state, he'd captured her attention in every way.

She composed herself and then turned to look around the room for herself. "So many mysterious shapes and intriguing containers."

She peered into a tall, ornately painted urn and caught a ghost of stale spices that was almost as disturbing as the smell of rot in the house above. How old was it, and what had it contained? She was ready to face Kynaston again and did so. But he was standing stock-still, staring into a corner—at a mummy case.

The dead body in the basement!

It stood upright, tilted back slightly against a wall, and half in shadow.

As always, it was shaped like a bundled person—narrow at the feet, wide at the shoulders, and then head-shaped above. The case was elegantly decorated in black, brown, and ocher with touches of gold, but the most striking aspect was the portrait set into the head where the face might be. It wasn't the stylized picture she would expect, but a vivid, lifelike portrayal the equal of modern artists such as Lawrence and Phillips.

Ariana edged sideways to take hold of the base of the hanging lamp and move it to throw more light. A young woman's dark eyes seemed to come to life, looking directly at her, holding a slight, questioning smile, as if she were wondering, *Who are you?*

Her brows were as dark as her eyes, but lighter brown hair clustered in curls around her face in a style that would pass as fashionable now. Her lips were pink and full, and despite a complexion somewhat too dark for English fashion, she was lovely.

"It's as if she's alive," Ariana whispered. "I assume that's a picture of the . . ." She'd been about to say "the corpse," but it seemed cruel under that lively gaze. "She looks so young. Perhaps less than twenty . . ."

She heard a sound and turned to see Kynaston going back upstairs. He stumbled on one step, then hurried on.

Chapter 4

"Upset him, that did," Ethel said.

She'd stayed by the stairs and Ariana had completely forgotten she was there. Had Ethel sensed anything of Ariana's reactions to Kynaston, or had everything appeared normal? And why on earth had Kynaston fled, discourteously abandoning his escort duty? From fear of an ancient coffin?

Ariana let the oil lamp return to vertical, returning the mummy to the shadows. "It upsets me," she said. "Doesn't it bother you?"

"Why should it," Ethel said, coming forward, "any more than any other tomb or memorial? I wonder why we've never thought of painting portraits on the outsides of coffins."

Ariana shouldn't have been surprised that Ethel was discussing the matter in a prosaic way, but she was tempted to tell her to be quiet. That would have been irrational. The vibrant image was of a person long dead, and as Ethel said, it was no more eerie than the stone effigies in Boxstall church.

"It's a clever portrayal," Ethel added, "but no one would see it once the coffin was buried. Did the Egyptians not bury their dead?"

"There were different practices at different times," Ariana said, trying to be as calm. "But I don't think mummy cases were buried."

"Then did the bereaved visit them as we visit graves?"

"Possibly." Ariana wasn't sure that seeing such a picture of her father on his tomb would comfort her.

Ethel might have had the same thought. "Do you think they painted them as they were in death, or in their prime?"

"What a question!"

"But if you die at eighty, would you want to be remembered like that or as you were as a young woman?"

"I'd like to be remembered at my best. Who wouldn't?" Ariana said. "So this lady might have died of old age after a long and blessed life."

Ariana liked that idea, but when Ethel said, "I doubt it," she wasn't surprised.

This wasn't a portrait of a woman in the prime of life, but of a girl on the brink. She could have been as young as sixteen, and no more than twenty. A tragedy lay behind the mummy and Ariana couldn't bring herself to poke among the other contents of the room. All the same, it seemed cruel to leave—to abandon the girl once more to her dusty corner.

Ethel picked up her disquiet. "She's been dead two thousand years or more. She can't care."

Ariana extinguished the lamp and picked her way carefully back up the awkward stairs, knowing that was true, but feeling like a traitor all the same.

Then there was that moment with Kynaston at her side to disturb her. It clearly hadn't meant anything to him, unless that was why he'd fled the cellars.

As she emerged into the hall, she saw Mr. Peake approaching. "I was just coming to find you, Lady Ariana. The talk is about to begin. You won't want to miss it."

Ariana might, for it sounded like nonsense, but she wanted more information about the lady in the mummy case.

"The Egyptian mural is lovely," she said as they went toward the stairs. "And it seems you have many other treasures below."

"I do. I do. Soon I'll find places for them around the house."

Even the mummy? That felt wrong.

"Lord Kynaston is still below?" Peake asked.

"He came up first. I wonder where he is."

Mr. Peake shrugged. "The nobility have their ways," he said, ignoring the fact that Ariana was also noble. She rather liked that. "Come along."

As they started up the stairs, he said, "That Egyptian stuff isn't mine. I mean, I didn't collect it. Never been to Egypt. Belonged to Lord Ombrow, but he's rolled up from too much collecting and too much card playing. Sold up and gone abroad. Seemed a shame to see the collection broken up, so I bought it."

They were about to enter the drawing room, where people were seated, ready for the talk, so Ariana quickly asked, "The young woman?"

"Remarkable, isn't she? Painted in hot wax, which is why it has that depth."

"Oh, I've read of such things. There are very few examples."

"So I gather. It wasn't Ombrow's. Came across that two weeks ago and snatched at it. Some people grind up mummies, you know, believing the powder is a potent cure for everything that ails them. Atrocious if that happened to such a rare thing."

"Yes, indeed," Ariana said, almost sick at the thought, but what her mind conjured was that happening to a young woman, not a mere antiquity. "Is anything known about her?"

"There's no writing. I'll have some experts in to have a look."

"Have them treat her with respect. She seems so real. Alive even." Ariana shut up before she sounded entirely mad.

She found she needed to name the young woman. Cleo. That sweet, curious person could never have been a resolute queen, but the name pleased. She was Cleo, and she must be treated with respect. That meant she couldn't remain in the corner of a basement forever, but where should she be?

Peake said, "I see two chairs over there. Come along."

Ariana followed him, looking around for Kynaston. He wasn't there. Was he so squeamish about an ancient corpse that he'd fled the house? Ah well, she was capable of making her way back to Albemarle Street.

She thought the lecture about the possibility of living on the moon more fancy than fact, but it was entertaining. A quite serious discussion followed, including speculation on the various means of getting there. Someone even suggested a ladder, citing Jacob's ladder of angels. Ethel said nothing, but Ariana could read her expression.

Eventually a door was opened to reveal a room set with refreshments, but Ariana realized time was flying by. She found her host and thanked him. "I must leave now, Mr. Peake. I've enjoyed this very much."

"You must come again when I have fewer guests, my dear."

"I'd like that, but I fear I'll be engaged in social fripperies."

"Break free of them."

She considered him. "You seem very sure I can."

"I've lived a long life, Lady Ariana, and rarely done what I was supposed to."

"You're a man."

"A definite advantage, yes, but I've known women who made their own way. If you can't return sooner, the Curious Creatures now meet every two weeks on a Tuesday. The meeting after next falls on Christmas Day, so we'll be a small gathering, but we'll have a feast and a discussion of the Christmas star."

"I'll be at Boxstall then."

But at that moment Ariana realized that if her plan worked, she wouldn't be. She could be spending Christmas at the home of her new husband. Why had she never thought ahead to that point?

"Then perhaps when next you return to Town," Peake said.

Such confidence of life rolling on, year to year with few changes.

"If I can," Ariana said, and added, "Lord Kynaston seems to have left, so I'll need someone to summon a hackney."

"There's a bell in the hall that'll summon a servant, but the earl might be lurking somewhere, avoiding fancies about the moon."

"I doubt Lord Kynaston ever lurks."

"All wise men do when advisable, Lady Ariana,

and he'll know the quiet spots. This was his house, you know."

"*His* house?"

"Bought the lease off him. Through his agents, that is. He was abroad until recently. I hope the changes didn't upset him."

Some of Kynaston's behavior now made sense. "I think perhaps they did."

"Odd the way people sell a place, then expect the new owners to keep it as it was. I must return to my guests, Lady Ariana. Ring the bell by the hall fireplace and a servant will come up."

He hurried off and Ariana and Ethel went downstairs.

"That must be why Lord Kynaston's living at Lady Cawle's," Ethel said.

"But why sell? This place had probably been in his family since it was built."

Ethel had no answer to that. They went into the cloakroom, where Ethel took down Ariana's pelisse and helped her into it.

Ariana answered her own question. "He's probably squandered his all, like the owner of the Egyptian artifacts. That would explain him living abroad as well. Any number of people are doing so for cheaper living, even one of the Regent's brothers."

"Idiot wastrels."

"The end of the war has created unanticipated problems, even for the more careful," Ariana said, pulling on her gloves, then realized she was inventing excuses for Kynaston. "Nothing excuses bad manners, however. The wretch has abandoned us."

"Some people are very afraid of death."

"An ancient mummy is no more threat than a grave-yard."

"Some don't like to pass near a grave," Ethel said, but then added, "His greatcoat's still here."

Ariana saw that was true. "Lurking after all?"

She was tempted to leave without him, but supposed she should make a minimal effort. She went into the hall and checked the nearby rooms. A half-open door led into the reception room, which had been abuzz with talk earlier. It was unoccupied now.

She opened a closed door to find a conventional dining room. The next door opened into a library. The shelves were half-empty, but a number of unopened boxes on the floor could hold books. She immediately wondered what treasures they contained, but she'd found the lurking wretch.

He was lounging in a chair to her left, looking completely at home, legs stretched out toward the fire. Clearly he'd not hesitated to order service as if he still owned the place. He had a glass in his right hand and a decanter stood on a table close by. If it had been brought to him full of wine, he'd made inroads.

At her entry he looked around; then he put down the glass and stood with a lazy grace that denied inebriation. "You're ready to leave, Lady Ariana?"

"If it's not too inconvenient, my lord." Ariana allowed herself sarcasm, but resisted an urge to criticize his drinking.

It must have been upsetting to see one's family home in the hands of another and so drastically changed. The threat to Boxstall had driven her here to London in search of a husband. Her success would lose Boxstall to her forever, but her home would be preserved.

He accompanied her out of the room and went to the cloakroom for his outerwear.

In a turmoil of emotions, Ariana tugged the bellpull hard and heard the jangle below. Perhaps she'd sounded impatient, for the young man who hurried up was still shrugging into his jacket. Given the order, he dashed out. Kynaston joined Ariana and Ethel in the hall, but he made no attempt at conversation, so neither did she.

The servant returned. "Coach's here, milord!"

Kynaston gave him a coin and they went out. He instructed the driver to take Ariana and Ethel to Albemarle Street, handed them in, and joined them, and the coach set off.

The silence continued. Ethel never chattered when Ariana was with other members of the nobility, and Kynaston looked fixedly out at the passing streets. He might as well have shouted that he didn't want to talk about anything.

Ariana let him be. He was probably contemplating the road to ruin that had led to the loss of his house and who-knew-what-else.

His primary country estate would be entailed and thus safe, but he could have sold off any contents that were legally free. Secondary estates would have gone. She could only hope they'd been purchased by better landlords who'd take care of the tenants and laborers as he doubtless had not.

Did he have family who'd been dragged down with him? A mother, brothers and sisters? She should have been furious at him, but instead she felt the ache of threatening tears. She'd known, even at a raw seventeen, that he might be heading for disaster. That such a glitter could not last. Or was that simply the wishful thinking of the outsider?

The rich must be miserable.

Luck must run out.

Beauty will fade.

In fact, the poor were more often miserable than the rich; some people lived blessed lives even without doing anything to deserve them; and though the bloom of youth passed, some people were beautiful all their lives, through good bones and graceful movement.

Kynaston was an example. As he was turned away, she felt able to study him. Despite his ruined life, his features were still classically fine, and the years had added strength. He could model for a marble bust of a god. Apollo, she thought, remembering a bust of the god at Boxstall. A noble head set perfectly on a strong neck, curls on the brow.

"A perfect Apollo" meant the epitome of manly beauty. The nobility of his high brow, the straightness of his nose, the fullness of his perfectly formed lips . . .

Kissable.

Ariana twitched away from that thought, looking away and praying Ethel wasn't watching her and guessing her mind.

He was a ruined wretch! He'd been blessed with everything and thrown it away, probably to the ruin of his family, servants, tenants, and all. No wonder he feared death. He'd go straight to hell.

Perhaps that mummy had reminded him of some particularly vile betrayal of a charming young woman. If so, she hoped it had seared his soul and would haunt him all his days.

Chapter 5

When they arrived back at Albemarle Street, Kynaston separated from Ariana with only an inclination of his head, presumably to go in search of brandy to try to blank out his sins. She wished him joy of it.

She went to her room, took off her outer clothing, and washed her hands. Ethel was unusually silent and Ariana didn't probe that. Instead, she went to join her mother and Lady Cawle in the small drawing room. She gave an account of her visit, but left out any mention of Kynaston's distress or drinking. She'd not carry tales back to his aunt, and in any case, Lady Cawle must have been aware of all his faults. She was having to house him and hadn't hesitated to be tart with him.

"I might like to meet this Mr. Peake," Lady Cawle said.

"He's somewhat eccentric," Ariana warned.

"So am I. I would like to see the mummy you mentioned. I will ask him to bring it here."

Ariana had already been thinking that Lady Cawle

and her skirts would never get down into the basement, but this startled her.

"Do you think that appropriate?" she dared to ask.

"Whyever not?"

Clearly commanding others to fetch and carry was normal, so Ariana said, "It is a person, in a manner of speaking."

"Then it, or she, should not be in a basement."

Ariana had no argument to counter that. "I was told that Mr. Peake's house was once Kynaston's."

She'd succeeded in surprising Lady Cawle. "This Peake has bought the Burlington Street house?"

"So it would seem."

Ariana's mother said, "How odd that he sell."

"It's on the fringes of the current fashion," Lady Cawle said, "and he's spent years traveling abroad, during which it's often been rented out. We are to go to the theater tonight, Ariana."

That was a clumsy change of subject. Lady Cawle didn't want Ariana to know Kynaston was ruined.

"I thought I was to lie low until I have my fashionable wardrobe."

"An early foray will be useful preparation and the theater won't involve extensive mingling. You have one adequate gown."

"I do?"

"Madame d'Estreville delivered your dark blue refurbished with black trimmings, as agreed."

Ariana wished to object simply because she hadn't been consulted, but she'd enjoy a trip to a London theater. Nothing outside London quite compared.

When she went to her room, Ethel already had the gown spread on the bed, and it did look well. The addition of black Vandyke lace on the bodice and at the hem made the deep blue gown more sober, yet grander at the same time. Black gloves and slippers and all would be complete.

When she dressed that evening, Ariana added jet jewelry. She wanted nothing odd to attract attention.

Once she was ready, she considered herself in the mirror. Anyone who might remember her last visit to Town would find her much improved. Back then she'd been dressed in conventional pale shades, with too many frills and flowers. She winced at the memory of rosettes that had drawn attention to her big feet, but then buried that memory deep. Now she at least had dignity.

"Will Lord Kynaston be accompanying his aunt to the theater?" Ethel asked.

"I dearly hope not."

"He's nice and tall."

"Even so."

The less she saw of the man, the better. But of course his aunt would have demanded his escort as part of her plan to match them up. Ariana went downstairs braced for another encounter, and there he was, looking particularly magnificent in dark evening clothes. The only color about him was his red ring and the large ruby on the pin that held his black neckcloth in place. Ariana couldn't deny that spending more time with him would be . . . interesting. But then Lady Cawle introduced her, with particular emphasis, to the gentleman standing at Kynaston's side.

Lord Churston. Another of her listed suitors.

He was of a height with her and pleasant in appearance, though his dark brown hair was a little thin, and arranged to disguise that. It was unfortunate that he be standing by Kynaston, but Churston had the edge in having the healthy air of someone who never overindulged in anything. Here was an excellent possibility, so Ariana smiled warmly at him, ignoring Kynaston's rather cynical expression.

The third gentleman, Sir Norman Ffoulks, was some twenty years older than the others and both shorter and leaner. He had a worldly air and soon proved to be a sophisticated flirt. Ariana wasn't surprised to find him the main focus of Lady Cawle's attention. Sir Norman could easily be imagined in the satin and lace of a bygone era, heels high and small sword on hip.

That left Ariana and her mother with Kynaston and Churston. Lady Langton immediately drew Kynaston's attention with questions about the location of his estates—which turned out to be Wiltshire—and then launched into gossip about other people she knew in that county.

Of course, Churston was on The List, and as far as her mother knew, Kynaston was not, but the effort should not be wasted. Over dinner, Ariana directed as much of her attention as possible at Lord Churston, trying to draw out his finest qualities.

It wasn't easy, for the seating of such a small company meant that of necessity Kynaston was on her other side, talking easily to her mother. The scraps she overheard were intriguing.

Italy? He'd spent some time there?

Churston was her target, she reminded herself, and asked him if he had traveled abroad.

"Only briefly, Lady Ariana. I find Britain has everything I could want."

"What is your native county, my lord?"

"Shropshire."

That was in the north, far from Hampshire, but Ariana knew that was probably her fate. Wiltshire, however, adjoined Hampshire. Delacorte couldn't be close or she'd have known that. It probably lay on the far side, many miles away. But closer than Shropshire.

She focused on Churston again. "Is your principal estate close to Wales, then, my lord?"

"It lies to the east of the county, ma'am. Not far from Bridgnorth."

Ariana would look that up on a map later. If it lay close to a good road, the distance might not matter.

Kynaston mentioned a Phyllis.

Who was she?

Churston wasn't an easy conversationalist and Ariana was struggling for a new topic when Lady Cawle addressed the table as a whole, mentioning the visit to Peake's house, and inviting her to give an account. Ariana was pleased to do so, but she tried to avoid anything that might make Mr. Peake or his friends seem ridiculous.

Even so, Churston said, "Sounds like an odd fellow. Merchant, you say?"

"Something of a nabob, I gather. And related to Lady Faringay."

"Ah." Clearly the connection made Mr. Peake slightly more acceptable, but Churston's attitude made him less so to Ariana. He showed every sign of being a snob.

"Collecting's quite the thing," Sir Norman said. "Has been forever, of course. There was Sloane gathering stuff from all over back in the last century, and then getting the government to set up the British Museum to house it all."

"I hope to visit the museum," Ariana said, directing the words and a smile at Churston.

She was inviting him to invite her, but he said, "I fear you'd find it dull stuff, Lady Ariana."

Her mother intervened then. "Ariana is quite interested in antiquities."

Churston's polite smile was skeptical.

"Sloane reminds me of Soane," said Sir Norman. "An architect, but also a collector. I've been told he has all kinds of antiquities in his house in Lincoln's Inn Fields and admits select people to view them."

"Including ladies?" Ariana asked.

"I've not heard that he refuses them," Sir Norman replied. "Or you could visit the Egyptian Hall, Lady Ariana. The place was built in the Egyptian style, but I can't say it's accurate."

"Napoleon's carriage is housed there, is it not?" Churston said. "More your thing, I'm sure, Lady Ariana."

Ariana was saved from making a caustic comment when her mother exclaimed, "Oh yes! I heard that when it was first displayed, the place was packed with tonnish gawkers."

"Mayhem," Lady Cawle agreed. "As when Napoleon was on board ship in Plymouth harbor. People traveled down from London to try to catch a glimpse."

"He had been our direst enemy for so long," Ariana said.

"The most appropriate treatment for a villain is to ignore him," stated Lady Cawle. "Some people seek notoriety."

Sir Norman was bold enough to challenge this view of Napoleon, and a lively discussion swirled about the ex-emperor's aims, abilities, and ambitions. It was an unusual dinner conversation, but Ariana enjoyed it. She noticed, however, that Lord Churston played little part. Did he disapprove, or was he simply dull-witted?

Whichever, she was beginning to fear that he would not do.

They didn't linger after the meal, but left for the theater, scurrying under umbrellas to the two carriages. Lady Cawle and Sir Norman used her town carriage and the rest had a hired one. It was from a livery, however, and almost as fine.

As they rattled over cobblestones, Ariana became nervous again. The trip to Peake's house had exposed her to some fashionable people, but they'd all seemed more interested in life on the moon than in her. This would be a different sort of affair—one where many of the theatergoers would be there to see and be seen.

As soon as she entered the Theatre Royal, Covent Garden, she felt her peculiarity. Even with tall Lord Churston at her side and Kynaston nearby, she was the focus of stares. All she could do was ignore them as she and the others went up to the boxes.

Thus far, Churston's height was all she'd discovered in his favor. After suggesting that the museum might overstretch her mind, he'd had nothing interesting to say at dinner.

She'd ceased trying to draw out conversation, but as they went slowly up the stairs, he remarked, "Bit of a crush." A little later he added, "Not as much as usual. Mourning, you know."

It was only polite to do her part. "Do you prefer plays or opera, my lord?" Ariana asked.

"Plays, as long as they make some sense. There's a great deal of nonsense on the stage."

"Isn't nonsense sometimes the point, my lord? Consider *A Midsummer Night's Dream*."

"Ah well, but that's Shakespeare, Lady Ariana. I was thinking more of the modern nonsense such as ladies running off with highwaymen and gentlemen marrying dairymaids."

"Perhaps it's hard to write a play about ordinary people doing ordinary things."

He surprised her by agreeing, but then added, "Not much point to theater at all, really, is there? But people will go, even the lower orders. Not good for them. Gives them ideas."

He was not only dull but pompous, and thought his every opinion correct. Intolerable.

When they reached the Cawle box, Ariana sat with relief, for when she was seated, her height was less obvious. Churston took a seat beside her, but she couldn't expect perfection. Lady Cawle had taken a seat at the front, with Sir Norman and Ariana's mother. Kynaston was somewhere behind her, which made Ariana distinctly nervous.

To cover it, she raised the subject of the gas-lighting in the theater, and to her relief, Churston talked sensibly enough about it and the increased safety of gaslit streets. She moved on to the current social unrest, and he pointed out the poor harvests of 1816, which had made it worse, and how they had arisen from the eruption of Mount Tambora.

Ariana was beginning to think he'd do after all until he said, "But I mustn't bore you with such matters, Lady Ariana."

"I'm not at all bored."

"Now, now, you don't have to humor me." He actually patted her hand. "I know you'll be more concerned about the style of hats and the latest dances."

Fortunately the performance began then, but as Ariana focused on the stage, she accepted that he was a hopeless case. Thank heavens the play was excellent and made the evening worthwhile.

At the first intermission the ladies remained in the box and a stream of people came to pay their respects to Lady Cawle and her guests. Kynaston remained at the back, a darkly silent presence. Was he pining for drink?

Then Ariana had to pay attention to a new arrival. Lord Blacknorton was another of Lady Cawle's listed possibilities, but Ariana knew from the start that he'd never do. It was shallow to reject any man for his appearance, but there it was. She had to assume that Blacknorton had shaved before attending the theater, but his heavy jaw was already dark. His black brows almost met in the middle and his short hair was a spiky thatch. Even his spatulate fingers were furred with black and she feared he could be thick with hair all over.

However, with Kynaston already off the list, and Churston and Blacknorton impossible, that left only Sellerden, Wentforth, and Sir Arraby Arranbury. She was still prejudiced against a man with such an ill-suited name, but perhaps Ethel had been right.

Beggars can't be choosers.

"Is something the matter, dear?" her mother asked.

No one was close, so Ariana said quietly, "I'm developing a greater appreciation for princesses and such who are forced to make marriages without any choice."

Her mother's lips twitched. "I didn't think Churston quite to your taste."

"Nor Blacknorton. So hairy."

"I'm sure some women find that appealing."

"That's good, for I'd not like to think of him rejected all his life."

"You have a kind heart, dear, but be careful to marry

no man out of pity. And you mustn't marry simply to force Norris. If disaster falls, it will be his fault, not yours."

"Then why am I here?"

"To see if there's a man who will suit."

So, her mother had sought this way to matchmake, had she? Ariana knew that her single state worried her mother, but it wasn't such a terrible thing, especially when a lady had a comfortable income of her own. She was beginning to regret insisting so forcefully that a quick, practical marriage would be easy. It would gall her to lose her contest with her brother, but all the same, perhaps the need wasn't so urgent. . . .

As if to reinforce her resolve, the threat personified entered.

Ariana hadn't seen her uncle, Paul Boxstall, since her father's funeral, when his superficial resemblance had been particularly upsetting. It had been as if the same mold had produced one perfect specimen and one that was badly flawed. It was an offense against heaven that the badly flawed one, the dissolute one, still lived.

Uncle Paul's skin was even more deeply seamed now, his eyes more pouched, his lips slacker, but his smile was the same crooked sneer. "My dear sister, and my niece. In Town at last."

Lady Langton had to introduce him to Lady Cawle, who responded in a way that should have frozen him on the spot. Of course, he didn't care. He was probably enjoying embarrassing them.

Ariana noticed Kynaston move forward as if he'd take action and Lady Cawle gesture to him to hold fire. It was oddly comforting that he be there. Ariana didn't exactly fear her uncle, but he was capable of any sort of unpleasantness.

For a start, he was drunk, though a lifetime's practice enabled him to stay upright. He was perfumed, but nothing could disguise a slight sour smell of decay. Ariana wished she could believe he was dying, but it was probably just a lack of soap and water over too many days or weeks, and a complete lack of attention to his shabby evening clothes.

"M'nephew with you?" he asked.

"No," Ariana's mother said, trying to be as icy as Lady Cawle, though it wasn't in her nature.

"Pity. Got a business prospect he might like." He looked around as if seeking a seat to collapse into, but Kynaston moved forward, took him by the elbow, and steered him out of the box without untoward drama.

A very useful skill!

Ariana said, "I hope Norris has more sense than that."

"I'm sure he has," her mother said. "He must bump into the man here and there all the time. Such a sad case."

"From what you've said, he's been like that from the cradle."

"That can't quite be true, dear, but for most of his life, certainly. He had looks and charm of a sort once, but threw away every chance."

That unfortunately sounded too much like Kynaston's course, and Ariana hated to think of him like Uncle Paul one day. It was for his family and friends to prevent, however, not for her. She had a marriage to make and a renewed purpose. Uncle Paul must never, ever inherit Boxstall.

But she was already down to three candidates.

Perhaps there were others.

As the bell rang for the end of the intermission, she

surveyed the opposite theater boxes and even the pit in search of tall young men. She saw a few. Some might have been married, and some ineligible, but there had to be more than six possibilities in the beau monde.

At the second intermission Ariana decided to face the world standing. Lady Cawle and Sir Norman remained in the box, but the rest of the party left to stroll the box corridor. Ariana would have liked to partner Kynaston, but her mother took up her duty and linked arms with him. Ariana had no choice but to endure more of Churston's dull company.

"It was well-done of Kynaston to remove my uncle," she said.

"He would have left of his own accord in due course, Lady Ariana. There was no call for the possibility of a scene."

"But there was no scene, my lord."

"You do not fully understand these things, dear lady."

Ariana was immensely glad when two tall men in regimentals came to join them.

Churston introduced his brother, Captain Pace, and Captain Pace introduced his friend Captain Grant. They were both excellent company, but it was clear Churston disapproved of their high spirits. In Ariana's opinion, men who were willing to risk their lives for their country were entitled to as much high spirits as they wished.

The officers moved on, and a lady with two daughters came over to greet Churston and be introduced. It was clear Mrs. Motely had him in her sights for one of her chicks. She was welcome to him, but mother and daughters were all petite, making Ariana feel like a maypole.

Amazon, she reminded herself. If she had to be anything, she'd be a warrior, but she wished the Motelys would move on. Kynaston and her mother were part of a group who were enjoying some sort of joke. Heavens, Kynaston was laughing!

It quite transformed him. . . .

"Lady Ariana Boxstall!" The Motelys had gone and a couple was coming over.

Ariana recognized the lady who'd opened the door at Mr. Peake's. "Very unconventional to introduce myself, but I do think that opening a door for you allows it. I'm Lady Hatchard, and of course, my husband, Lord Hatchard." They were a genial couple of middle years and middle height, but for some reason Ariana didn't feel excessively tall in their company.

She curtsied. "It was kind of you to let me in, ma'am. Do you know Lord Churston?"

They did, and they all four conversed. Or rather, all three did, for the Hatchards wanted to talk about life on the moon. Churston showed no interest except for muttering, "Piffle," more than once.

Then Lord Hatchard said, "I understand that you were invited to investigate Peake's cellars, Lady Ariana. A rare honor."

"Is it? Most items down there are boxed or shrouded, but there are some interesting pieces. If most haven't seen them, I won't spoil the surprise."

Lady Hatchard laughed. "You have my husband exactly, Lady Ariana. He was trying to wheedle out some details."

"You could ask Lord Kynaston," Ariana said. "He was with me."

"In the *cellars*?" Churston asked.

Why did she have to blush? "Mr. Peake asked Lord Kynaston to take me down there. I understand it was his house."

"Indeed it was," Hatchard said. "Understandable that

he sell it, of course." His move to a sad tone confirmed Kynaston's ruin, and was a bracing reminder of reality.

The Hatchards moved on and Churston said, "I cannot think it wise of you to go off alone with Lord Kynaston, Lady Ariana."

Ariana was about to tell him that Ethel had been with her when she recognized an opportunity to get rid of him for good.

"Thank you, my lord," she said, layering her words with frost, "but my behavior is none of your concern."

"A lady being alone with a man like Kynaston is any gentleman's concern."

She looked him in the eye, pleased, and not for the first time, to be able to do it. "No, it is not, sir. I wish to return to the box."

In moments, Ariana could settle back into her seat, satisfied with her work. She'd not have to fend off an offer from Churston, explaining why he would not do. He'd avoid her from now on.

He had to take his seat beside her, but immediately leaned forward to speak to Lady Cawle. "Apparently Lord Kynaston was showing Egyptian artifacts to Lady Ariana in some cellars."

The blaggard! She'd told him off, so he was trying to stir trouble, and Kynaston wasn't yet here to intervene.

Ariana was about to explain, but Lady Cawle turned to say, "So I understand. I did ask my nephew to escort Lady Ariana to Mr. Peake's house." Then she added, "Are you suggesting that they are *compromised*, Churston?"

He spluttered. "I'm sure it's not so bad as that, ma'am."

"I'm sure you're correct," she said with a catlike smile.

Churston turned toward the stage, his stiff shoulder registering his affront. Ariana shared a grateful smile with Lady Cawle, but she had to wonder if her hostess had hoped Churston would say yes. Had she wanted him to make a great pother over the incident and force Ariana to the altar with her nephew? If it came to that, Ariana simply wouldn't go. Though she intended to marry, and soon, she would never allow herself to be forced in such a manner. Never.

When Kynaston returned with her mother, Ariana tried to register indifference with every part of her body. As the curtain rose, however, a new thought stirred. Had Lady Cawle peopled her list with undesirables in order to give her nephew a clear field? Ariana glared at the back of the lady's head, promising, *You'll catch cold at that, my lady.*

For the last intermission, she remained safely in the box. Churston abandoned her, which suited her perfectly, though she was left with only Lady Cawle. Would Lady Cawle attempt to plead her nephew's charms? If the lady had any such intention, she was foiled by a visitor. The man paid homage to Lady Cawle, but then turned to Ariana. "I wonder if you remember me."

He was tall, with a long, lean face and thin lips. His tight, wasp-waisted jacket and elaborate neckcloth marked him as of the dandy persuasion. She did remember him, but couldn't produce a name. Something in his smug manner made her happy to be able to say, "Alas, sir, I do not."

She remembered lying about that to Kynaston—who had left with her mother. They were probably both enjoying themselves more than she was.

"The curse of time!" the man said. "Frank Fettersby, at your service, my lady."

"Ah, Mr. Fettersby. Now I remember. You tried to steal a kiss."

"Who could not?" he protested.

"All the other gentlemen in London."

"Sluggards."

"Gentlemen," she corrected. "I was seventeen, sir, and you already well into your twenties."

"A mere twenty-five. I have never forgotten you."

"Was I the only one who hit you on the nose?"

He smiled. "The only one."

She liked his boldness, but she was remembering a great many things, including him being a fortune hunter with a very shady reputation. He'd clearly failed in his hunt for eight years, and it was insulting that he now think her easy prey.

"Your kisses haven't snared a lady of fortune yet, Mr. Fettersby?"

His faced pinched, but he tried to be gallant. "Perhaps I never forgot you."

"Doing it too brown, sir. Are you enjoying the play?"

Clearly he didn't give a damn about the play and soon left.

"Glad to hear you bloodied his nose," Lady Cawle said.

"Alas, ma'am, I didn't manage to draw blood."

"You were only seventeen. I'm sure you could do better now."

"I probably could." But Ariana was remembering raising a fist, and that fist being overwhelmed by a large, warm hand.

A *drunkard's* hand.

"Ah." Lady Cawle raised her lorgnette to look across the theater. "I didn't know he was in Town. Viscount Dauntry, standing behind the lady in the excessive silver turban. Blond, handsome, stylish. And tall."

"Dauntry? He's recently come into the title, hasn't he? My friend Lady Faringay wrote to me about it. He had no idea he was in line."

"Thus he's probably seeking a bride."

Lord Dauntry was a friend of Hermione's husband, which made him an attractive *parti* to Ariana. She missed her friend.

Trying not to be obvious about it, Ariana assessed him. Perhaps she'd misjudged Lady Cawle, for she'd pointed out an attractive possibility. Dauntry was elegant and fashionable, but his ease of manner countered any suggestion of fop. He said something that amused those around him, which suggested he wasn't a bore.

A knot of anxiety loosened. It was too soon to decide anything, but Lord Dauntry seemed to have everything to recommend him.

See.

She'd known it couldn't be so very difficult in the end.

Chapter 6

Back in Albemarle Street and undressing, she told Ethel all about the evening, including the encounter with Uncle Paul.

"A cesspit of a man," Ethel said, unfastening Ariana's gown. "Who inherits if your uncle dies?"

"A distant cousin. A better option, but almost anyone would be."

"Then perhaps you should kill your uncle."

Ariana turned to stare. "What!"

"Man like that, if he fell off a bridge and drowned in the river, no one would wonder or care."

"I couldn't dream of such a thing."

"Easier, I'd think, than marrying to force your brother."

"One's illegal and a terrible sin, and the other isn't."

"Less likely to get you hanged, true enough."

"Of a certainty."

"I meant, killing your uncle," Ethel said. "When you kill your unpleasant husband, you'll be the first suspect."

"I'm not going to kill anyone," Ariana said. "The

very idea! And I'll find a tolerable husband. There has to be at least one."

"This Viscount Dauntry?"

"I've not even met him." Ariana sat so Ethel could take the ornaments out of her hair.

"True, it's early days yet," Ethel agreed. When Ariana's hair was free, she began to brush it. "So you ran Lord Churston off."

"Thank heavens. I can't believe that he tried to scold me."

"You could have said I was with you in the cellars."

"I could, but that would have diluted the deterrent. As it is, I'm free of him, at least."

"But no additional suitors other than Dauntry."

"Whom I've not yet met," Ariana reminded her. "Frank Fettersby tried to court me."

"The fortune-hunting rake?"

"The very one. If he learned not to sneer when rebuffed, he might have more success."

"People don't change," Ethel said, putting down the brush. "I'm not going to become excitable. You're not going to become meek. The Prince Regent's not going to become frugal."

Ariana turned to look up at her. "What of all the sermons about repentance and reform?"

"I don't reckon they change people's natures, but they might change what they do with them. You're going to continue to be determined, but you're going to use that to choose the right husband."

"Yes, I am," Ariana said, standing.

And I'm going to remember that the Earl of Kynaston has always been on the road to ruin, and people don't change. So, he was pleasant this evening and behaved quite normally, but beneath that exterior, he's a wreck.

* * *

Ariana settled into bed pleasantly tired, but hours later was still awake, at least in part because of thinking about a certain wretch's potential for reform. Tinkling clocks around the house and more sonorous chimes from church bells farther afield told her it was two in the morning of what the French called a *nuit blanche*. She didn't often suffer them, but she knew how it would be. Simply lying there wouldn't bring sleep, and soon her legs would become irritated and might even cramp.

She climbed out of bed, shivering in the cold air. The fire had died long ago. She drew back the curtains to let in the moonlight, and then wrapped herself in her thick woolen robe, even pulling the hood up over her head. Her fur-lined slippers would help keep her feet warm. Even so, she needed to be vigorous if she wasn't to become chilled through.

A few circles of the room told her this wouldn't do.

At home at these times she walked the corridors. There were no long corridors here, but there was more space outside this room and staircases to go up and down. Clearly the whole house was asleep. No one would know.

She used the tinderbox to light a candle and then ventured out. The only sounds were from ticking clocks. She walked briskly up and down this corridor, her slippers making little noise. It was a short corridor, however, so she started downstairs. She'd been too inactive in recent days. That was why she couldn't sleep. At home she enjoyed a long walk or ride on most days, and sometimes both. Merely going around Boxstall involved considerable walking.

Her sleeplessness was from other causes, however, and more than damnable Kynaston. As she turned to go downstairs, she accepted that she was more worried about her situation than she'd admitted to Ethel or herself. The death of the princess had brought all her worries to the fore, but once she'd busily engaged in her plan, the hovering disaster had moved backward in her mind. The encounter with Uncle Paul had brought it back to the front. Some fatal folly by Norris, and Uncle Paul could have Boxstall and all attached to it tomorrow. If she left her brother to himself, it could be years before he took up his duty. Her mother expected him to fall in love, but not everyone did. There were far too many middle-aged bachelors. She had to force him, but she was coming to see that his complaint had some value. It was no easy matter to find a congenial spouse, and to marry someone uncongenial would be horrible.

She walked up and down the carpeted lower corridor, fighting uncertainty and guilt, past the doors to the small and large drawing rooms, and then the music room. And who knew what else? Lady Cawle had her private chambers there, but the house remained silent.

Ariana's candle flame flared with the passing air, just as her mind churned over her problem. Should she leave her brother to settle in his own good time? That would release her from her husband hunt. High rank brought responsibilities, however, and that was the end of that.

Tired of the limited space on this corridor, she looked longingly down into the hall. There was much more open space there.

It was deserted, lit only by a glass-shielded candle, which stood on a side table. Her own was burning down rapidly under the wind of her movement, so she blew it out before going downstairs. She'd be able to relight it before returning upstairs.

Once in the hall, she put her candle beside the lit

one, then took advantage of the larger space. She marched down toward the rear of the house and then returned to circle the hall, grateful that the floors were wood and not marble. The cold of marble might have penetrated through leather and fur to chill her feet. As it was, she was warm from the exercise and her troubled mind was settling.

She must stick to her course. She could afford to be particular at first, for the perfect husband might be available, but if she didn't find him soon, she'd take whichever gentleman was the most tolerable.

Even Kynaston?

Neither tolerable nor suitable!

All the same, once summoned, the wretched man would not be driven out of her mind. He'd returned to the house with them earlier, but immediately gone out again. Probably to some drunken wallow. It was positively tragic and someone should drag him back from the brink. Lady Cawle was forceful enough in other respects, but she seemed to treat him as if he were fragile.

Earlier Ariana had tried to raise the subject with her mother, but Lady Langton had only praise for Kynaston as an escort and a companion. He was all that was amiable. Ha!

Yet perhaps he was better than she'd thought. Perhaps that drunken moment had been only that—a moment. He'd clearly charmed her mother, and she'd seen him part of a cheerful group at the theater. She'd glimpsed his better side in the cellars when he'd cleared a space for her and they'd discussed the mural. Did he still play an instrument and sing? Music, said William Congreve, had charms to soothe a savage breast. Or was it beast?

Beast Kynaston. That fit, yet against her will that memory returned—the memory from eight years ago of Kynaston playing the lute and singing an old song. As best she remembered, he'd been at ease about performing and seemed to enjoy it. She'd been struck by that, because most young bucks were more awkward about being musical.

Such an excellent performance meant practice, and practice meant discipline. She remembered thinking that he couldn't be as much the Town idler as he'd seemed. Her obsession had led her to find out more about his choice of song.

"Pastime with Good Company" had been written by Henry VIII before he became king, but it had remained popular to the present because it had a good chorus. When Kynaston had performed, many of the men had joined in that chorus:

> For I delight to hunt, sing, and dance!
> My heart is set on all goodly sport
> To my comfort. Who shall stop me?

Hunt, sing, and dance. Men these days were as fond of hunting as back then, but many were less keen to sing and dance.

It wasn't long after that performance that she'd fled back to Boxstall, but some of the fascination had lingered. She'd looked up the song and found both the original lyrics and modern versions that came more easily to the tongue, including the one Kynaston had sung. She'd even practiced singing it—in private, for it was a man's song.

Ah, foolish seventeen.

The lyrics had truly fascinated her, however, especially when they'd been written by a young man destined to be king. On first reading, the song seemed a celebration of passing time in good company, but underneath was a commentary on wastrel youth.

Had Kynaston understood that, even then? She didn't know if he ever sang the last verse.

Pastime with good company I love, and shall until
    I die.
Grudge who may, but none deny, if God please,
    thus live will I.

Then the jolly chorus, well suited to stamping feet, even in the original:

For my pastance hunt, sing, and dance!
 My heart is set on all goodly sport
To my comfort. Who shall stop me?

And indeed, who would have stopped a prince? Or a young, rich earl?

But in the third verse the tone changed to advice to be wiser.

But every man has free will, the best to choose, the
    worst to refuse.
My plan will be, virtue to use, vice to refuse. That
    shall be me.

If Kynaston had sung that, he'd not taken it to heart.

Suddenly weary, Ariana picked up her candlestick, preparing to relight the candle and return to bed.

A key turned in the lock of the front door.

She stared for a second, but then realized a thief wouldn't have a key, and a servant wouldn't use the front door. She ran down the corridor toward the rear to lurk in the shadows there, then remembered to raise her hood in case her hair caught the candlelight. She heard the door shut, and a mumbled curse. Then a clatter and another curse. She guessed that he'd dropped the key.

Drunk again?

She leaned slightly to see. The one candle lit the scene like a theater stage. Kynaston, in greatcoat and tilted hat, was making his way toward the candle—with considerable difficulty. Definitely drunk, and badly so. He was weaving his course and almost tripping over his own feet.

When he arrived at his destination, he clutched onto the table with both hands. Perhaps without that support he would have crumpled to the ground. Ariana could almost feel his effort to firm his legs and straighten. He kept one palm flat on the table as he very, very carefully lifted off the glass surround to liberate the candle. It immediately began to flicker, probably in response to unsteady breathing.

"Plaguey thing," he slurred, perhaps to the glass, the candle, or some other insubstantial offender.

He grabbed the candlestick and turned toward the staircase. He reached the newel post but then, clinging to it, must have decided the mountain was too steep to climb. He loosed his grasp and staggered, still muttering and cursing, toward the library. When he shut the door, the hall was plunged into a darkness that seemed an echo of the darkness Ariana felt about his state.

She stayed where she was, furious at Lady Cawle. But then, what could the lady do? Lock him up? Punish him in some way? Maybe she did lecture him and even berate him, but housing him might have been the only kindness in her power.

Ariana felt the inevitable temptation to go to the library to see if there was anything she could do. That candle could be a danger in such unreliable hands. It would be folly, however, and whatever the Earl of Kynaston needed, it wasn't her preaching at him.

She no longer had any way to light her candle, but the moonlight coming in through the fanlight over the door was sufficient for her to make her way up the first flight of stairs. As she turned into the next flight, that light ended, so she had to feel her way back into her bedroom.

The moonlight there was startlingly bright after such darkness and she easily returned the candlestick to its place, took off her robe and slippers, and got back into bed. There was still enough warmth between the sheets to comfort her and she snuggled down.

She was ready for sleep now, and she would not let a miserable ruin of a man below prevent her.

Surprisingly, after a while, that proved true.

Ariana normally woke early, but the next day Ethel had to rouse her before the dressmakers arrived in half an hour. Ariana washed, dressed, and ate her breakfast, unable to stop reviewing last night's scene.

Was there anything she could have done?

Was there anything she could do today to help Kynaston in some way? She wasn't fool enough to take him on for life, but she would help him if she could—restore the damaged treasure. But some ruins, like those of old Boxstall Priory, were beyond human effort. She must stick to the possible—her marriage. She went off to do her duty to fashion.

Her mother came to observe and advise, and Ariana said, "You should get some new gowns, Mama."

"Oh, no. What I have is perfectly suitable, especially for a widow of advanced years."

"Advanced years? You're only just past fifty."

"Old enough not to have to fuss over my clothing, dear, for which I am very grateful. Now, if you have no need of me, I have an engagement to visit an old friend, Lady Bumford. We will probably happily forget that we're in our dotage."

Ariana smiled and gave her mother her blessing, pleased to see such light spirits. Her mother didn't have the temperament to be gloomy, but she'd never truly recovered from her husband's death. Living quietly at Boxstall these past years had perhaps not been the best thing for her, but it had been part of Ariana's cowardly hiding away. Whatever had happened, that must cease.

When the dressmakers left, Ariana decided to read another newspaper. She'd missed doing so yesterday out of sheer cowardice, avoiding any possibility of encountering Kynaston again in the library. Given what she'd witnessed last night, she might have been wise, but she wouldn't pander to him anymore. She went to the library and walked in, braced for unpleasantness.

The room was uninhabited—blessedly so, she assured herself—and in perfect order. No boots lying on the rug before the fire. No brandy, nor even the smell of it.

It felt strangely empty, but Ariana put that folly out of her mind and picked up the *Times*. The two chairs set before the fire looked much more comfortable than the one in her bedroom, so she'd read in here. She sat down in one—but not the one Kynaston had been in the first day. That forced her to accept that his presence lingered anyway.

He'd been limp with drink here two days ago, but there'd been a trace of humor in him. Last night he'd been grim. Had he been in a gaming hell? Gaming was folly at all times, but drunken gaming was a sure road to ruin. Had he lost everything that remained to be lost?

Had he shot himself?

Nonsense. A shot would have been heard and the house would be in an uproar.

Poison, then.

Cut his own throat.

"Stop it."

Her voice startled her back into sense. Kynaston was sleeping off his debauch, and she was going to read the newspaper, blessedly undisturbed.

She was engrossed in an article about South America when the door opened behind her. Quickly she rose and turned, heart pounding with expectation—to see only Ethel.

"Lady Cawle wants to see you in her boudoir."

"Why? What's happened?"

"Are you expecting some disaster?" Ethel asked, brows raised. "I'm simply passing on a message from her maid."

Ariana calmed her mind as she replaced the newspaper on the table and then set off for Lady Cawle's boudoir, but she couldn't stop the worry. Had Kynaston achieved some terrible disaster? If he'd managed to stake and lose the family seat, Lady Cawle might push for the marriage to rescue him.

Ariana entered a white-and-gold boudoir to find her mother also there, but no great air of emergency. Lady Cawle was reclining on a chaise, dressed in a loose silk robe, and some hothouse lilies released a light perfume.

Feeling foolish, Ariana sat down, determined to be sensible.

"We have been discussing your progress thus far," Lady Cawle said. "What is your state of mind now?"

"Churston is pompous and boring."

"Blacknorton?"

"Too hairy."

"What *do* you find attractive?" Lady Cawle asked.

Pinned to the spot, Ariana actually stammered. "I . . . I'm not sure. Height?"

Lady Cawle dismissed that with a wave of a plump hand. "Dark or fair?"

Dark. In reaction, Ariana said, "Fair. But that's not a fixed preference. Character and temperament are more important."

"As long as the gentleman is not hirsute."

"If that means excessively hairy, then yes."

"Lord Wentforth is blond and bookish."

"That sounds hopeful."

"Sir Arraby Arranbury is a very amiable man."

"Then I look forward to meeting him."

"Stop badgering Ariana," Lady Langton protested. "She's only attended one event."

"I understood that there was no time for shilly-shallying." Lady Cawle's gaze returned to Ariana. "What of Kynaston?"

"What of him?" Ariana asked blandly.

"If you spent time in the cellars with him, you must have formed an impression."

"What!" Ariana's mother exclaimed.

"We were looking at Egyptian artifacts, Mama. Ethel was with us and the house was full of guests."

Lady Cawle smirked. "Many undesirable things have happened in the dark corners of houses full of guests. What do you think of him?"

"Very little," Ariana said, pleased with the ambiguity.

Her mother was looking puzzled, and Ariana remembered that she'd rewritten the list with his name omitted. She plunged on. "I gather he has financial difficulties."

"Kynaston?" said Lady Cawle. "Of course not."

"He sold his house to Mr. Peake."

"A person may sell a property without being in danger of the Fleet. Unless you are ahead of me in the news, gel"—a clear impossibility—"Kynaston's fortune is intact. He is purchasing a new house in Grosvenor Square."

Ariana was speechless. Was Lady Cawle lying? Or had he deceived her? If true, what did it mean?

"Do you have anything else against him?" Lady Cawle demanded.

Ariana used the only weapon she had. "He's a drunkard. I came across him drunk in your library here on my first morning, and then found him drinking in Mr. Peake's library." She couldn't mention the third offense without admitting to eccentric nighttime wanderings.

Lady Cawle's expression revealed that she was not unaware. "He's not a sot."

"Are you going to tell me he's not a womanizer, ma'am?"

"Less of a one than you might think, but if you're seeking a gentleman of monklike chastity, gel, your task will be exceptionally hard."

Ariana was annoyed to find herself blushing at the frank discussion. She reached for the only escape. "I did like the look of Lord Dauntry."

"Who is Lord Dauntry?" her mother asked. "He wasn't on the list."

"I wasn't aware that he was in Town." Lady Cawle considered. "Lady Lieven is hosting an entertainment tonight. Dauntry might be there." Ariana probably looked lost, for Lady Cawle added, "Lady Lieven is the Russian ambassador's wife."

"I know that, ma'am."

"It was in her box that I saw Dauntry last night. I hadn't thought to have you appear at a significant affair yet, but we will attend."

Ariana wanted to ask if they had invitations, but the Dowager Countess of Cawle was probably invited everywhere and, if not, would never be refused admittance.

Things were running out of control. A mere mention of Lord Dauntry to deflect attention from Kynaston, and now her hostess had him in her sights. But that wasn't intolerable. Any target other than Kynaston was a relief, and she couldn't be dragged to the altar with any man she didn't want.

"Despite mourning," Lady Cawle said, "there will be dancing. Dancing gives an excellent opportunity to assess a man."

Dancing! Ariana had thought mourning would spare her that. "It seems rather soon after Princess Charlotte's death."

"Life goes on beneath the mourning veil. You've come to Town a-courting, gel. Have some spine."

"I have plenty of spine. If such a statement makes sense. If I have a suitable gown, I'll be delighted to attend." Ariana felt safe in the knowledge that she did not.

Lady Cawle's smile should have warned her.

At four in the afternoon Mrs. Lassiter arrived. She had been given the task of enlivening Ariana's black silk evening gown. Lady Cawle must have instructed her to make all speed, for the woman entered Ariana's bedroom in triumph, followed by an assistant bearing a white muslin bundle. It was unwrapped to reveal a transformation.

The densely black evening gown had been ordered

in the early days of mourning, modestly cut with a high neck. Now the bodice had been lowered to an alarming degree. The gown was made of crepe fabric to avoid shine, but now black satin ribbon work gleamed around bodice and hem, and the work on the bodice seemed designed to emphasize the wearer's breasts.

As a finishing touch, bodice, hem, and long sleeves were also ornamented with a dark gold braid woven through with metallic gold thread, which caught the light.

It had become rich and rather splendid, in only two days.

Mrs. Lassiter was so proud of her work that Ariana obliged with warm thanks, even though she'd wished the woman had been a slow and clumsy worker. She was going to have to attend the ball, but even worse, she was going to have to dance.

She danced with pleasure in Hampshire among people she'd known all her life, but she hadn't danced elsewhere since that dreadful time eight years ago, when she'd danced with the godlike young Earl of Kynaston.

Later, dressing her hair for the ball, Ethel said, "Stop twitching!"

"I can't help it." Ariana let the word out. "Dancing."

"You dance very well."

"But this will be among strangers. Of all sizes."

"You can hope only tall gentlemen ask you to dance."

"But if a short man asks, I must accept or declare I'm too fatigued. . . . But I can't do that for the first dances."

"Or later," Ethel said. "Or you'll be sitting out all night."

"I might prefer that. No, it would make me an odd-ity of another sort. Oh, to simply be unremarkable!"

Ethel chuckled. "I doubt you could ever be that."

"It might be pleasant as a novelty. Perhaps Lady Cawle could hold a tall ball."

"Then she wouldn't be able to attend, would she? There, that looks well enough."

Mrs. Lassister had provided a bandeau of black and gold to match the gown, and it sat well on Ariana's amber hair, hardly adding another inch.

Ariana stood, trying to be optimistic. "Dancing is a good way to meet a number of gentlemen without it being particular. I felt awkward about having Churs-ton's escort once I realized I couldn't marry him."

"He might not want to marry you."

Ariana turned to stare. "Goodness, how arrogant to think they're all waiting for my nod! And indeed, why should tall men particularly wish to marry a tall woman?" *With big feet* slithered out from the back of her mind. "Most men seem to want wives shorter than themselves."

"The better to look down on them." Ethel picked up the gown from the bed and put it deftly over Ariana's head. "But what's to say a man who's interested in you will be in a hurry? That Lord Dauntry, though. He might be. You could cut through the dither by asking him yourself."

"I couldn't possibly!"

Fastening the back, Ethel said, "Reckon you can do anything you set your mind to."

"I can't stand for Parliament, or join the army or navy, or go to a university. Or vote."

"True enough," Ethel said calmly, passing over a

black lacquered fan. "But you *could* ask a man to marry you."

"I could walk down the street in my shift," Ariana retorted. "Ability and possibility are not the same thing. I'm not made to be outrageous."

"True enough."

Ariana eyed her. "Would you ask a man to marry you?"

"I might," Ethel said, "if it seemed he wouldn't get around to it himself."

That was probably true. Ethel had no allegiance to conventional ways.

Ariana turned to survey herself in the mirror. She did look striking. Too striking?

Outside of mourning, black was rarely worn, and within strict mourning all color was avoided. The gold against the black was truly magnificent, and it seemed to pick up the color of her hair. She'd much rather be in plain, dull black, but if she had to do this, she'd do it boldly.

"I'll wear the golden parure." Gold was a little bold for mourning, but this was an odd sort of mourning.

The set of golden ornaments in an Egyptian design had been a gift from her father on her twenty-first birthday. Soon she was wearing the coiled gold necklace and matching earrings. The snake bracelet should be worn on the upper arm, but with long sleeves that was impossible.

Ariana considered herself again and realized that the colors and some aspects of the design recalled the mummy. But here, instead of that brown-eyed, quizzical face she saw her porcelain complexion and blue eyes. Eyes that looked fearful rather than inquisitive.

Who are you, Ariana Boxstall, and what do you truly want?

She turned away but was still tangled in thoughts of that poor girl, trapped in her coffin in a basement. It didn't seem right, but where could she be put with decency? Even a museum would put her on public display—but that would avoid the danger of her being ground up to make potions. No wonder Kynaston had been so upset. He might have been showing a sensitive side.

Or a guilty conscience, she reminded herself.

That was much more likely, and at least he wouldn't be escorting them tonight. Lady Cawle had already stated that. He had other commitments.

With a brandy bottle, Ariana assumed.

Ariana couldn't believe her state as they traveled to the Russian ambassador's residence on Harley Street. Her innards felt knotted, and it was all she could do not to grip her black-gloved hands tightly together. At least she didn't have a suitor to contend with. For escort, Lady Cawle had summoned Norris. At heart her brother was an amiable man, so he was doing his duty with good grace, and looked very fine in his black evening wear.

His elaborately tied gray silk cravat was pinned with silver. Ariana's mother was in black with jet jewelry. Lady Cawle was not traveling with them, but in one of her elaborate sedan chairs. "Four in a carriage is a crush," she'd declared, and it certainly would have been with her hoops. She, too, had been dressed in black, but a glossy black striped with deep blue. With it she was wearing magnificent sapphires. She'd approved of Ariana's golden touches.

As they rolled along the streets, Ariana noticed Norris

studying her, as if to assess the danger. In the end she said, "No. I haven't chosen a husband yet."

"I didn't say anything," he protested.

They completed the journey in silence. Conversation, even dispute, would have been a welcome distraction from the coming trial.

A crowd had gathered outside the ambassador's house to witness the fashionable guests going in. Their eager faces were illuminated by flambeaux, which weren't truly needed on the gaslit street, but which created drama.

Ariana would rather have slipped inside in the dark, but she would not show fear. However, she was grateful for the fact that Lady Cawle's chair opened first. The countess could have been carried into the house, but the weather was fine and perhaps she liked display. She emerged, cloak open, sapphires flashing, creating a ferment in the crowd, then swept into the house without acknowledging the attention at all.

Ariana tried to follow her example, but it wasn't in her nature to be arrogant. She was pleased by some overheard appreciation of her appearance—until one person said, "Mighty tall, though, i'nt she?" She entered the house feeling rawly exposed.

You're only imagining that every eye has turned to you!

One eye had, and was welcome. Blacknorton hurried to her. She couldn't marry him, but she could greet him warmly simply for being tall, and she was happy to promise him the first set. One hurdle overcome! In the patterns of a country dance she'd have to encounter other men, some of them shorter, but she'd mostly dance with her partner.

They shed their cloaks and went upstairs to make their bows and curtsies to the ambassador and his wife. Lady Lieven had not been in London when Ariana had last been there, and she was interested to meet such a famous lady.

Countess Lieven was only a few years older than Ariana and as pretty and charming as reported. Even in a brief encounter Ariana saw sharp intelligence. No wonder she was said to play a major part in her husband's embassy. Why, then, were most women expected to hide their talents?

The assembly room—for mourning reasons this was not to be described as a ball—was large but already well filled with the powerful and great of London. The overall color tone was somber, but some of the men wore military uniforms, which provided welcome splashes of color, as did the sashes and medals of orders.

As for the ladies, all wore gowns in dark shades, and most wore ornaments of pearl, silver, and jet. Sparkling gems were less common, as was gold. Ariana wished she'd worn jet—but only for a moment. Her height could never be disguised, so she'd be bold in all ways.

The room had been decorated in a subtle way that did not quite disregard mourning. Most of the floral displays were simply evergreens and any flowers were white. The magnificent curtains were of pale gray velvet and all the seating was shrouded in gray cloth. The music being played at the moment was stately with subtle religious tones.

Despite this, the guests smiled, chattered, and sometimes laughed. Life went on beneath the veil.

Lady Cawle sailed across the room to a gray-shrouded sofa and established herself there, wide black skirts taking up most of the width, her sapphires afire. Ariana was surprised that none of the older ladies present had already claimed the seat, but perhaps any who'd made the attempt had been quietly warned off.

Norris escorted Ariana and her mother to chairs beside the sofa and then fidgeted.

"You may go and find other amusement, dear," their mother said, and he escaped.

People were hastening to talk to Lady Cawle as if she were holding court, and she made introductions to Ariana and her mother. There were some who remembered Lady Langton from the past, but none who remembered Ariana. Or admitted to it.

She wondered if any of the gentlemen here had been in that drunken gathering all those years ago. She'd recognized Kynaston's voice, but none of the others.

Would anyone remember the yellow-tufted, big-footed Boxstall longshanks?

Her resolve to be bold began to seep away. She realized she'd tucked her feet back, as if to try to hide them, and forced them forward again. She plied her black fan and set herself to appearing normal, hoping Blacknorton would keep his promise to dance the first set with her.

When he approached, she could have beamed at him, but remembered to be merely pleasant. She mustn't raise false hopes. She took her place in the line, trying to put herself mentally in comfortable Hampshire, and then embarked on the dance.

It went better than she'd expected. Certainly there were awkward moments, such as when she had to take a turn with a particularly short gentleman, but she remembered what her father had said to her once.

"Short men are uncomfortable about their lack, my dear, so you must do your best to ignore it."

So she'd smiled kindly at the little man. He'd smiled back, clearly relieved that she wasn't offended.

Dear, darling Papa. She was in danger of new tears over losing him, but she smiled, as she knew he'd wish and ended up enjoying herself. As Blacknorton took her back to her mother, she only slowly realized that she'd smiled too warmly at him.

He clasped her hand in parting and looked into her eyes. "A pleasure, Lady Ariana. Such a pleasure."

When he walked away, she wished all her warmth undone.

To make matters worse, she was now having to stand, as her mother was bracketed by Lady Cawle's sofa on one side and an occupied chair on the other. She made sure to stand tall. She'd long overcome any temptation to hunch.

Then she heard Lady Cawle say, loud and clear, "Kynaston. I was not aware that you meant to attend."

There he was, some yards away in perfect evening wear, as elegant and polished as could be. He came over to bow to his aunt. "I'm escorting Phyllis."

Phyllis, again!

"I wasn't aware she was in Town," Lady Cawle said.

"Nor was I. She arrived today with the Weathersteds."

Ariana had overheard that name at the theater and now she regretted that she hadn't asked her mother for more information. This Phyllis was clearly a lady of significance to him, and also well-known to Lady Cawle. Even, perhaps, well liked by the lady?

Ariana was ashamed to recognize jealousy.

"Where is she?" Lady Cawle asked, raising her lorgnette to look around.

"With some young people somewhere," Kynaston said. "We old fogies are of little interest."

Ariana had to squeeze down a grin. Had anyone

ever told Lady Cawle she was an old fogy? The lady's slight smile had disappeared, but Ariana thought she saw a hint of it in her eyes. So, she liked being teased. Probably only by handsome men.

And, Ariana realized, Kynaston wouldn't speak that way about this Phyllis if she was his ladylove.

"Lady Ariana."

Ariana turned to find Churston by her side. "May I have the pleasure of the next dance?"

She was surprised by the offer, but had to agree, and another tall partner was to be welcomed. It was a shame she'd miss any further exchanges between Kynaston and Lady Cawle.

"How are you enjoying your time in London, Lady Ariana?" Churston asked as they strolled toward the dance floor.

She was about to respond with a polite platitude, but remembered that she needed to drive him off. Brightly, she said, "I enjoyed the meeting of the Curious Creatures, my lord. The one at Mr. Peake's house. It's most interesting to consider life on the moon, don't you think?"

He gave her an insufferably indulgent look. "Pure folly, dear lady."

"Are you sure? There was some serious discussion of means of traveling there."

"I'm sure the folly would easily be exposed by any man of sense."

Any *man*. The bit between her teeth, Ariana said, "Our grandparents couldn't imagine the speed at which we travel the roads now."

"The improvement of roads is a relatively simple matter."

"Then what of balloon flight? If people can rise high that way, why not further?"

"A balloon to the moon? My dear Lady Ariana—"

"We cannot know the future, my lord. I am *most* interested in such matters."

His smile lingered as they took their places on the dance floor, but she felt sure she'd delivered a killing blow. He probably thought her mad, but even at best he knew her for a woman with an active, curious mind, and one bold enough to interrupt him. He'd never marry such a woman.

One down, she thought as she curtsied. Two if she included Blacknorton. But then she remembered that reducing her suitors was not precisely her purpose.

Lord Dauntry. He was tonight's target.

As she danced, Ariana kept alert for him, but also took note of all the tall gentlemen around her. Some would be foreigners, and she'd not marry abroad. Others would be married. However, there must be any number of tall eligibles. She noted a few possibilities, but didn't see Dauntry.

She returned safely to her position near Lady Cawle and her mother. Kynaston hadn't taken part in the dance and was now with a lively group of ladies and gentlemen.

Ariana felt as if she'd slid into the past.

There he was, at ease, charming, handsome, and, of course, adored. At least two ladies had a predatory glint in their eyes and one gentleman seemed to be drinking in every word he said. Ariana deliberately summoned the memory of his recent debauchery and turned her attention elsewhere.

At last, she saw Dauntry across the room. People were supposed to be able to tell if they were being stared at, so she stared, hoping to attract his attention. However, he hadn't responded when the next dance was announced, and Lady Lieven presented a Mr. Vavasour as partner. He was just a little shorter than she and paunchy, but he'd do.

It was a line dance with two lines, and she saw Kynaston in the other. That was as well. She didn't want to meet him in the dance and perhaps have her wits softened further. He was partnered with an ordinary-looking woman whom Ariana judged to be married, which was excellent.

Which was nothing to do with her!

Mr. Vavasour was an able dancer with no interest in chatter, so she could enjoy her time with him. Even better, the very short man was in the other line, so she didn't have to manage that. All was well, but then as the set ended, the next was announced to be a waltz.

The beauty of the waltz was that she would be with the same partner throughout, so there'd be no danger of passing encounters with short men or Kynaston. On the other hand, if a man of medium height offered, she'd be stuck in a slightly awkward situation throughout.

Dauntry would be ideal. She looked at him again, trying to draw him to her side.

But then she became aware of a man approaching her purposefully—the very short one from the earlier dance! She turned away as if she'd not seen him, looking around desperately for some other partner. Any other. She was willing to grab one if necessary.

Lady Cawle spoke in a particularly clear and carrying voice. "You promised the waltz to Kynaston, did you not, Lady Ariana? Where is he?"

The words silenced all around, and he turned. Anger flashed in his eyes and for a terrible moment Ariana thought he'd refuse the summons. She wouldn't blame him. But then he came over, even smiling, with lips at least.

"My apologies, Lady Ariana."

His eyes were so cold.

Heavens above. Did he think there was some plot to snare him?

She was trying to think of a way to reassure him, when a voice behind said, "Lady Ariana! Did you not promise the waltz to me?"

She had to turn to the short man. He was quite handsome and well formed, but perhaps not even five feet tall. What possessed him?

Hating being the center of attention, she said, "I think not, sir, as I am already committed to Lord Kynaston."

"Then the next waltz."

"Alas, sir, I'm promised for that one, too," Ariana lied. What else could she do?

He understood the rejection and turned to stalk away.

"I don't even know his name," she murmured.

"Lord Inching," Kynaston said. "Yes, slightly unfortunate."

She glanced at him, hoping to see humor, but he was still cold. "Why would he wish to dance a waltz with someone so . . . tall?"

"Inching is very much attracted to taller ladies, and ladies as tall as you are uncommon."

"You mean he might persist?"

"Very possibly. If you are sufficiently desperate in your husband hunt, Lady Ariana, he would be an easy target."

The vile beast! But she reminded herself that he had some reason for his sour humor at the moment. "I apologize for Lady Cawle, my lord, and I thank you for the rescue."

"But you don't deny seeking a husband."

Ariana turned away, wafting her fan and idly surveying

the dance floor as couples moved into place. "Why should I, my lord? Nearly all the single ladies here are interested in marriage, and probably many of the gentlemen seek a wife."

"True enough. Positively barbaric, isn't it?"

"You have a jaded view of the world, my lord."

"A realistic one. Come, let us take our place."

She put her hand in his extended one, registering his strong reluctance.

He didn't want to dance with her.

Perhaps he was remembering their last dance, when the dazzle of being his partner had turned her clumsy. In a country dance such a situation would be awkward, but if they were stuck together in a waltz, it was going to be excruciating for both of them. Ariana felt that old pull toward the ladies' retiring room, but it was far too late to escape, especially after Lady Cawle's intervention—and she didn't want to. She was feeling all the tremulous excitement she had eight years ago, but this time she would dance perfectly! She put aside all other thoughts as the circle of couples began the progressive step.

In time, however, came the turn.

Many thought the turn of the waltz risqué and even scandalous as it put the couple into each other's arms for a while, face-to-face, the gentleman's hand in continuous contact with the lady's waist. Ariana had thought that a mere quibble.

Until now.

Turning, almost eye to eye with Kynaston, his hand warm through the silk of her gown, built her feverish unsteadiness to a danger point. Despite all good sense, she was still wildly attracted to him!

She tried to summon memories of the slovenly drunkard, but at this moment Lord Kynaston was any lady's dream. Close to, his face was even more handsome than from a distance, and she could sense his body beneath the dark formal wear.

He's a sottish wretch, she tried to remind herself, but was relieved to switch again to the forward step and not have to look at him at all.

According to Lady Cawle, he wasn't insolvent, but he was still a rake on the road to ruin. When they waltzed again, she made herself look over his shoulder at nothing in particular, and dance perfectly. Perhaps her performance was why a number of gentlemen offered for the next dance, giving her the choice. That, or Lady Cawle's actions had made her notoriously interesting.

Whatever the cause, she was grateful, even though Dauntry wasn't one of the suitors. She passed over two taller men to choose one slightly shorter than herself simply because he had smiling eyes. Mr. Tongford was as amiable as she'd expected and made an excellent dancing partner. Perhaps he was a possibility.

She was bracing for the challenge of the next choice when she saw Lady Cawle's eyes upon her in a commanding manner. Ariana was very tempted to give her the cold shoulder, but the woman was her hostess. She went to the sofa.

"I'm sure you need a chance to catch your breath, Ariana," Lady Cawle said.

"I'm not at all winded, ma'am."

"It is more ladylike to pretend to be so. Sit down."

There was just enough space on the sofa for Ariana to sit without crushing the hoops beneath Lady Cawle's skirt, so she obeyed, wondering if she'd added bumptious good health to her other flaws.

Lady Cawle languidly waved her fan in front of her lips and spoke quietly. "Tongford is a fortune hunter, and Irish to boot. Irishmen often have charm, but be wary. He's a better specimen than most, but without a feather to fly with and looking for a lady to give him plumage."

Ariana's irritation faded. That was a useful warning. "I might not mind, if I liked the man."

"That is for you to decide. You danced well with Kynaston."

Ariana also plied her fan. "I wish you hadn't done that, ma'am."

"No thanks for the rescue?"

"Yes, very well. Perhaps you can now command Lord Dauntry to my side."

"If he doesn't approach of his own volition, I will. Note that Inching is definitely to be avoided. His interest in tall ladies approaches an unhealthy obsession. Your brother should warn him off."

"I can't imagine Norris doing that."

"Then what use is he? Sir Arraby, Lord Sellerden, and Lord Wentforth are not in attendance, so you must please yourself when it comes to the next dance."

"If only I could."

Lady Cawle turned her head to study her. "Whom would you choose?"

"I'd choose to leave."

"I have no patience with cowards, gel. Leave if you wish to."

"How?"

"Walk."

"What of Mama?"

"She's old enough to take care of herself."

Ariana was very tempted, but her sudden disappearance could be ruinous and Lady Cawle knew it. "Why tease me so, ma'am?"

"To see how foolish you are. Very well." She surveyed the room and then raised a finger.

As Lady Cawle couldn't have magical powers, she must have been looking to see which gentleman's attention she could catch, but it still seemed extraordinary that a man came to them, not seeming annoyed. Sir Tom North was tall, handsome, and amiable, though he must have been in his thirties, at least. All the same, Ariana loosened her criteria a little, especially when he proved to be an excellent dancer. Ariana mentally added him to her list. As it was the supper dance, she went with him to eat, anticipating light conversation and delicious food, and an opportunity to learn more of him.

Small tables were set out in a number of rooms, many already occupied by ladies as their partners went to the buffet to select food. North steered toward a table where two ladies were settling, each with a gentleman standing behind.

Something about a plump lady and her companion suggested a married couple, but a handsome, dark-haired lady was being seated by Kynaston. Phyllis? No, the lady must have been in her thirties at least.

All the same, Ariana didn't want to take supper at the same table as Kynaston and looked around for an alternative. When she knew so few people, it was impossible.

Kynaston saw them approaching and his cold look implied again that Ariana was pursuing him. She desperately wanted to deny it, and even to tell him exactly what she thought of him. Being a well-mannered lady was a great impediment.

Introductions were made and Ariana discovered that

the couple was Lord and Lady Eastonholme, and the lady Mrs. Manners.

Wife or widow?

North seated her and then went with the other gentlemen to find food.

"I don't know why we can't select food for ourselves," Ariana said.

Lady Eastonholme smiled. "One of the many advantages about being married, Lady Ariana, is that my husband knows just what I like."

"Another reason to regret that I'm a widow," Mrs. Manners said, adding, "I feel the need to say that. With everyone in mourning it's not instantly clear and gentlemen keep asking me to dance."

"My condolences, ma'am," Ariana said, annoyed by a pang. She didn't want Kynaston, so why begrudge him to another woman? Mrs. Manners would be an odd choice, however. She was a good-looking, well-bred woman, but her clothes and ornaments didn't suggest a rich widow, and she might have been as much as ten years Kynaston's senior. She certainly didn't seem a likely match for a rake.

"In addition to that," Mrs. Manners said, "I'm Lady Phyllis Delacorte's companion, and not quite an equal of this company. So thoughtful of Lord Kynaston to partner me for supper."

"I'm sure he enjoys your company, ma'am," Lady Eastonholme said kindly. "May I ask, was your husband a military man?" When Mrs. Manners said that he had been, she added, "One of our sons died at Quatre Bras."

The two women began to share their experiences, seeming to find comfort from it.

How sad that such a bond be so likely. There seemed to be scarcely a family in Britain untouched by the losses of war. If peace prevailed, there could come a time when a similar coincidence would stir astonishment. May that be so.

Ariana was also digesting the fact that Lady Phyllis was probably Kynaston's *sister*. Delacorte was the family name. It was remarkable that he partner an employee and she had to give him credit for that. She truly couldn't imagine a match there, so she felt more kindly toward Mrs. Manners. Major Manners had died of wounds suffered at Waterloo, but only recently. He'd been brought home, where he'd lingered for nearly two years. Mrs. Manners seemed to treasure that time, even though there'd never been hope of recovery.

"I'm very fortunate to have my position," she said, smiling. "Lady Phyllis is a good, quiet girl and can be relied upon to be sensible. Lord Kynaston agrees and told me I need not hover over her."

A kindly brother and a considerate employer. Can it be believed?

Ariana said, "I assume you and Lady Phyllis have been living in the country?"

"At Delacorte, yes, but a problem developed with the roof that made leaving the house for a while advisable."

Ah, rack and ruin. That fits the picture better.

"It can be so hard to keep a large house in good repair," Ariana said, seeking more evidence.

Mrs. Manners didn't oblige. "We were to visit a relative in Cambridgeshire, but then some neighbors, the Weathersteds, invited us to come to Town with them."

"Much preferable, I'm sure," Lady Eastonholme said. "Especially for a young lady."

"She's only seventeen," Mrs. Manners said. "Her brother thinks her too young."

"Not if she's as sensible as you say, ma'am. A little

experience at a quiet time will be just the thing. When did you first come to Town, Lady Ariana?"

"At seventeen," Ariana admitted.

"There, see."

Lady Eastonholme and Mrs. Manners settled happily to discussing young ladies and society. Ariana gazed around, seeking Dauntry, but instead saw Lord Inching approaching. He was partnering a young lady only a few inches taller than himself, but his attention was on Ariana. There was no way to prevent him from claiming the two remaining seats, but why did one of them have to be at her side?

He was obsessively attracted to tall women, and something of that glittered in Lord Inching's eyes. She was remembering an elderly gentleman in Hampshire who'd been in constant pursuit of plumply bosomed young women. Apart from his age, there'd been nothing particularly to object to, but his attraction had become a kind of mania. When he'd progressed to lurking in wait for his targets and then rushing out to grab their breasts, his family had installed him in a home for the demented. Everyone had been most relieved. Thus far there'd been nothing to object to about Lord Inching's behavior, but it was a relief when he went to the buffet of food, leaving Miss Cushing at the table.

Kynaston, Eastonholme, and North returned, and the food North had selected was satisfactory. She'd never before thought of food selection as a means of choosing a husband, but perhaps it could be useful. She noted how easily he spoke to the other ladies, especially to Mrs. Manners, who was on his other side.

Ariana gradually became aware that he was *particularly* interested in Mrs. Manners and that the lady, while composed, was not unaware or displeased. North had only just been added to her list and now she must cross him off! Wine was served, and Ariana took a deep drink of hers. Husband hunting was a slippery affair.

However, despite Inching returning to the seat at Ariana's side, the supper went well for a while. Then she felt a touch on her ankle. She twitched, thinking, *Mouse!* but then realized it was the despicable Inching. She moved her feet away from him, but went too far and touched North's. He slid her a rather surprised look.

She didn't think her cheeks had heated as much in years, and across the table Kynaston was watching her sardonically. "Is something amiss, Lady Ariana?"

"No, of course not." She tucked her feet backward, wishing she could engage in lively conversation with North, but he'd turned back to Mrs. Manners.

"I believe this is your first Town ball in quite some time," Kynaston persisted. Was he intent on embarrassing her? Was he, for heaven's sake, recalling her last one?

"I've attended many in Hampshire," Ariana said, "and in general prefer rural entertainments."

"Rural entertainments!" exclaimed wide-eyed Miss Cushing. "In preference to an ambassador's assembly?"

"In the countryside, one knows everyone."

"How unexpectedly unadventurous," Kynaston said in a drawl, and turned to pretty, tiny Miss Cushing. "You, I see, are more eager for new experiences."

The girl blushed, clearly not immune to his magnificence. "Tonight was my very first waltz, my lord."

"Then may I hope you'll dance the second with me?"

The chit's blush deepened and she giggled, but she

agreed with enthusiasm. Ariana caught Inching looking at her in an odd way, and remembered telling him
she was engaged for the second. Which she wasn't. What
was she to do about that?

She thought he might ask again, but instead he raised
the subject of the Amazons, asking whether their military abilities were likely to be true. "They must have been
very tall women," he added. "And stalwart. Is it possible
for women to be so muscular?"

Mrs. Manners said, "Some women do hard work in
the fields, my lord, and even in mines. We are not
designed by God to be feeble."

"How true, ma'am. I have seen female pugilists and
wrestlers."

"There were many resolute women in the history
and myths of the ancient world," Kynaston said, frowning at Inching, "and not all of them warlike. Demeter,
for example, the goddess of the harvest, who cast the
world into eternal winter until the lord of the under-
world returned her daughter, Persephone."

"Or Psyche," Ariana said, to support the effort to turn
the subject. "She was mortal but succeeded at a series of
impossible tasks in order to win her beloved, Eros."

"With help from the gods," Kynaston pointed out,
"including Eros himself."

"You imply that women can never be heroes on
their own, my lord? Male heroes also generally had
friends and allies among the gods."

"She has you there, Kynaston," said Lord Eastonholme with a chuckle.

"And then there's Cleopatra," his wife said. "True
queen of Egypt. Of course, we English don't find a strong
female monarch astonishing, having had Elizabeth, but

they were rare in the past, were they not? I don't believe there were any female rulers of Rome."

"Quite right, my dear," Lord Eastonholme said, beaming at her.

How lovely it would be to grow old with an amiable companion.

"That's probably why Rome collapsed," Lady Eastonholme continued. "Insufficient power and influence for women."

Ariana supported her. "Even France is an example, for they have never had a sovereign queen."

"I doubt a female monarch of France would have prevented the Revolution," Kynaston said. "Especially as Queen Marie-Antoinette was a principal cause."

"Perhaps unfairly blamed," Ariana protested.

"We could have had a Queen Charlotte," Mrs. Manners said, "if not for her sad death." But then she looked consciously at Kynaston. "I'm sorry, my lord."

Was he such a tyrannical employer that she feared dismissal for intruding into a conversation to play peacemaker?

He was certainly not pleased, but he said, "We can hardly avoid all mention. As for Cleopatra, there is a great interest in Egypt these days. I admit, I'm not an enthusiast for it as a decorative style."

It was a clumsy diversion, but it worked because Miss Cushing came to life again with enthusiasm for crocodile-legged furniture and palm motifs. Lady Eastonholme was happy to debate such matters, so Ariana could largely observe. Kynaston did the same, except for intervening if Inching tried to turn the conversation back to his obsession.

She had to admit that she'd enjoyed their brief debate.

Clearly his intellect hadn't been entirely eroded by drink, and he'd spoken to her as if she had a brain and opinions worth considering. She noted that tonight his consumption of wine had been moderate. If he was to stop drinking alcohol completely, could he be reclaimed?

A choral performance was announced so that everyone could digest their food before exerting themselves again in the dance. Kynaston and Mrs. Manners rose together, but Ariana could tell that North and the widow would prefer each other's company.

She stepped close to Kynaston and took his arm. "Our discussion of Marie-Antoinette was disturbed, my lord."

He tensed as if he'd push her away, but then he looked beyond and must have understood the situation. "North, if you could escort Mrs. Manners to the music? Lady Ariana wishes me to prove that I'm correct."

They all turned to leave the room, along with a stream of others. Soon the other couple was well ahead.

"You don't object?" Ariana asked.

"How could I confess it?"

"Not to escorting me, my lord. To North and Mrs. Manners."

"I should tear them from one another's arms, breathing fire?"

"She is in your employ."

"How do you know that?"

"She told me. Told the whole table. She seemed to want matters clear."

"She's an admirably honest lady."

"And you won't interfere?"

"God forbid. If North's to her taste, I wish them both well."

As they turned to go up the stairs as part of a stream of couples, she considered him. "You mean that."

"Wholeheartedly."

"Then it's to your credit."

"As little else is?"

She let that pass. This wasn't the time or place to fall into an assessment of his folly. "It will leave your sister unsupported," she said.

"Indigent widows are not scarce. The sorry remnants of war."

"It is a terrible business," she agreed, and would have said more, but they'd arrived at the drawing room, which was now set out with rows of chairs, many already taken.

Ariana spotted Lord Dauntry and remembered her particular purpose. He was already seated, but with two spaces to his left. She steered firmly in that direction. Dauntry was with a pretty blond lady, but Ariana chose to assume he was squiring an absent friend's wife, or perhaps even a sister.

As they approached, she approved of his fine-drawn features and elegantly dressed blond hair. They would have angelic children together. She sat beside him, and took a bold tack.

"We've not been introduced, my lord, but I'm Lady Ariana Boxstall, friends with Hermione Faringay. She's written to me about you."

He smiled in a very pleasant way. "And to me, to ask me to remember her to you if we met in Town."

Hermione had probably expressed concern and asked him to help if he could, but Ariana would ignore that.

"A shame she isn't in Town, for it's an age since we met, but as Christmas approaches, many are settling onto their country estates."

"Will you spend Christmas at yours?" he asked.

"Of course," Ariana said, but then remembered that she could be married and elsewhere by then.

He proved perceptive. "You would rather not?"

"I will delight in it," she replied with a bright smile. "It's such an enjoyable time of year in the countryside."

"Have you ever spent it in Town?"

"No."

"That, too, has its charms. But I suspect my wife will want a country Christmas."

He was *married*? Despite the shock, Ariana maintained her smile, but how had Lady Cawle not known that? Why had Hermione not told her?

"Only *suspect*, sir?" she teased. "Should you not know?"

"We marry next week and still have much to learn about one another."

Thank heavens the music was introduced then and Ariana could turn her attention elsewhere, if not her thoughts.

A Russian male choir began singing deep and sonorous songs, which suited her mood. She was beginning to fear that her quest was cursed, and matters were not improved by Kynaston leaning close and murmuring, "So much for that prospect."

"Did you know?" she murmured back, eyes on the choir.

"The purpose of your coming here? Yes. His imminent marriage? No."

She glanced at him to assess the truth of that, and was caught for a moment by those splendid blue eyes. Yes, they still showed a trace of his debauchery, but they were magnificent at such close quarters and there was something in his expression. . . .

She turned hastily forward.

She must guard against that, for it would be folly to deny his ability to heat her body and addle her wits. She needed a sensible, reliable husband, and must work harder at that. The candidates were dwindling, and no new ones had presented. North had been a new possibility, but he was interested elsewhere. Dauntry was soon to wed.

After a while she realized that she shouldn't be surprised.

It was true that many unmarried members of the beau monde were intent on changing their state, but people weren't attracted to every member of the opposite sex they met, especially oddities such as excessively tall ladies. When she considered the matter, no man ever had captured her interest or stirred her emotions in a powerful way.

Except one.

Who sat beside her, emanating something that made her want to lean closer, or move a hand closer to accidentally touch . . .

None of that!

This was her first social foray, and she had weeks ahead of her. She settled to appreciating the deep-voiced harmonies, trying not to hear sorrow and tragedy in every note.

After the performance, everyone moved toward the ballroom. Once there, Dauntry asked Ariana to partner him. Kynaston, of course, made no objection and offered a hand to Dauntry's companion, a Mrs. Lansing. Things could have been worse, Ariana told herself. She had a tall and amiable partner and was becoming more relaxed about Town dancing all the time. For the rest of the night, she would simply enjoy herself, especially as she had a choice of partners for every dance.

She was enjoying being part of one of a number of eights, when she almost missed a step—because Norris was dancing in the nearest one. He usually avoided dancing as much as possible, but Lady Lieven must have dragged him to his duty. He seemed remarkably cheerful about it. That was probably because he was partnered with a very pretty young blonde who smiled at him as if he were a god, and danced with exceptional grace.

He even grinned at Ariana as if he was enjoying himself, too.

Heavens! Was he to be her salvation by falling in love?

When the dance ended, she returned to Lady Cawle's side, but kept an eye on her brother. He and the blonde had joined another couple—a dandified young man and a hopelessly dressed plain girl—but he still looked all aglow.

Ariana asked, "Do you know the young lady with my brother, ma'am?"

"The pretty flibbertigibbet? A Miss Weathersted, I understand."

Weathersted. Why did that name seem familiar? Then she had it. "I met a Mrs. Manners who is companion to Kynaston's sister. I believe she said that Lady Phyllis is visiting Town with some neighbors called Weathersted."

"Ah. The Weatherteds are Phyllis's godparents. That's her with them."

The plain, badly dressed girl was Kynaston's sister?

Ariana had begun to feel a little kindly toward the man, but here was yet more proof of his fecklessness. He could do little about his sister's looks, but he could ensure she was better presented.

Lady Phyllis's dark hair was scraped back from her

nondescript face without a trace of curl, and she was wearing a plain black round gown that was only barely suitable for this occasion. She must have felt particularly uncomfortable when constantly in company with a beauty like Miss Weathersted.

Ariana would like to have words with Kynaston, but then the second waltz was announced, wiping away all other thoughts. She'd told Inching she had a partner and was about to be proved a liar.

Across the room, Inching was watching her, probably ready to leap into the breach.

Then a very tall man entered her line of sight and bowed. "Count Lubinoff, my lady," he said in a heavy accent. "Do you forget you promised this honor to me?"

No matter how Lady Cawle had arranged this, presumably with the assistance of Lady Lieven, she was saved, and in spectacular fashion. Count Lubinoff's deep blue uniform was festooned with gold, and he topped her by at least six inches. Ariana would have been grateful for any suitable partner, but she gave him her warmest smile as she rose to go with him onto the dancing floor.

The count wasn't the most graceful dancer she'd ever partnered, but his height made her feel positively petite, which was a novel sensation. How odd to begin to realize that she didn't like it. She'd become used to being as tall as, or taller than, most men and didn't much care for being so overwhelmed, for having to look up, for having to stretch her arm to match his.

She was so engaged in assessing this peculiarity that she only belatedly noticed that Norris was dancing again. Astonishing, especially the waltz, which he claimed to find embarrassing. His partner this time was poor

Lady Phyllis. He'd have been obliged to offer, of course, but the girl was flushed with pleasure, and looking up into his eyes in a very particular manner.

Ariana saw Kynaston standing against a wall, observing them with a glower. Perhaps he was realizing what a sight his sister was, or more likely that she was glowing with false hope. Ariana resolved to have a word with Norris later. He probably didn't realize what a handsome, eligible prospect he was.

She had no time to observe or interfere for the rest of the ball, for gentlemen positively competed to partner her. They weren't all her height, but none were tiny. Inching didn't attempt to approach again. She thoroughly enjoyed the event and she knew her mother was relieved and pleased. She'd have been happy for the dancing to continue until dawn, as it often did in the summer, but at this time of year dawn came late, and mourning dictated an early end. The music ceased at one in the morning.

Ariana went down to the hall, intending to thank Lady Cawle for ensuring she'd had so many suitable partners, but the lady was already settling into her sedan chair. It had been brought inside and she was soon carried away by her liveried chairmen, an armed footman trotting alongside.

There was definitely something to be said for a sedan chair.

Eventually the Boxstall carriage was called and Ariana went outside with her family, finding the ground wet from recent rain, but the air fresh.

As they rolled through the dark, damp streets, her mother said, "You remember we're to move to the house tomorrow, Norris?"

"Of course I do, Mama. What do you take me for?

All is in order, and Mrs. Milner is looking forward to having a lady take charge." After a moment, he said, "I was thinking we might hold a small entertainment once you're settled."

"An excellent idea," Lady Langton said, but with some surprise, and Ariana knew why. She couldn't remember Norris ever taking an interest in hosting an entertainment. Not one that involved ladies, that was.

He flushed a little. "For Ariana."

Or for a pretty blonde.

"Aren't you afraid it might facilitate my wooing?" Ariana teased.

He seemed startled by the notion and looked away, shrugging. "You'll woo wherever you are. Thought you might like it."

Ariana resisted the urge to tease him some more and thanked him, feeling more at ease than she had in days.

Norris was smitten and surely ardent young love was impatient. She couldn't imagine Miss Weathersted making any difficulty about becoming a countess by Christmas. Thus, they could all celebrate the season at Boxstall, problem solved and life back to normal.

Of course Miss Weathersted would then be mistress of Boxstall, and Ariana agreed with Lady Cawle's assessment that she was a flibbertigibbet. However, no one could command her brother to marry a sensible woman and all that was truly needed was marriage and an heir.

After they'd dropped off Norris at the Boxstall town house, Ariana said, "I think he might be interested in young ladies at last, Mama."

"I know. Isn't it exciting? I may see both of you married by the spring."

Ariana hoped her mother wouldn't be too disappointed

to have only one wedding, and that one much sooner than spring.

Everything was suddenly bright. Her brother was falling in love, and tomorrow they would move out of Lady Cawle's house. There'd be no further risk of coming across Kynaston in his cups, and little chance of seeing him at all.

That would put an end to any temptation to be foolish.

Chapter 7

After that comforting thought, Ariana was aggrieved to arrive back at Lady Cawle's house at the same time as Kynaston. He was paying off a hackney cab as their carriage halted, and came over to hand them down. Ariana would not have believed that the contact of gloved hands could be significant.

Ariana's mother went ahead toward the open door, so Ariana was left to walk to the house with him.

"You leave tomorrow, I believe," he said.

"You will be pleased to see us gone."

"It would be most discourteous of me to agree."

This was an opportunity to clear away one matter. "I am not eyeing you as a future husband, my lord."

He raised his brows at her. "You're eyeing all the men of London that way, Lady Ariana."

Angry words rose, but they were passing through the doorway by then, with servants and family ahead, for Lady Cawle was waiting to see them safely returned.

Ariana said, "Not Lord Inching, I assure you," and

Lady Cawle put in, "That dreadful man. Keep your distance from him. Good night." With that, she went upstairs.

"Lord Inching?" Ariana's mother asked.

"The very short man. Apparently he has something of an obsession for tall ladies."

"Then definitely to be avoided. I hope your sister enjoyed the dance, Kynaston."

"She's in alt." His tone was distinctly sour, and no wonder.

"Every young lady is thrilled by her first ball," Ariana said. "Such events soon become humdrum."

"I wished to keep her out of the social whirl a while longer," Kynaston said, "but circumstances forced my hand."

A poorly maintained roof, Ariana remembered, which had led to his sister being here by charity of neighbors, but with no money for pretty gowns. Lady Cawle had denied that Kynaston was in financial straits, but he could have concealed the truth from her.

"She's seventeen, is she not?" her mother said. "Not too young for a first dabble."

"But too young for marriage, ma'am."

With those stern words, he wished them a good night and walked off toward the library. That room again. Did the servants know to have a decanter of brandy there, waiting? Ariana was tempted to run in there and smash it.

"As if she's going to marry within days of her first Town dance!" Ariana's mother remarked, heading for the stairs. "But my older brothers were the same. As bad if not worse than my father."

"Because they knew what young men get up to?"

Her mother chuckled. "I'm sure you're right, dear."

When they reached their rooms, Ariana's mother said, "Good night," and went into hers, but Ariana lingered in the chilly corridor, thinking that no young man had ever tried to get up to anything with her. In Hampshire she'd had admirers, but they'd all behaved with perfect propriety. Exactly as it should have been, but she couldn't help wishing that some fevered gallant had tried to clasp her in his arms and seize a passionate kiss.

Just once.

Especially if it were Kynaston . . .

Memory of Fettersby returned like a dose of salts. He'd tried to kiss her against her will and she'd thumped him on the nose for it. Probably every other man had sensed she'd do the same thing, since she was an Amazon of a woman.

Which had her remembering Kynaston clasping her raised fist.

Ariana hesitated, knowing she mustn't do what she was thinking of doing.

She wouldn't smash the brandy decanter, but perhaps she could talk sense to him. He'd not been drunk at the ball, or just now when returning here. He couldn't be crazed with drink yet.

Ethel would be waiting in her room, hot water ready.

But powerless to resist, Ariana went back downstairs, realizing why. There'd been something in his manner when he'd escorted her inside—something that disturbed her more than the thought of him drinking. Beneath his guarded good manners, she'd sensed a darkness. Even despair.

The servants who'd greeted them had disappeared below and the only sound in the deserted hall was the slowly ticking clock. The glass-shielded candle waited for Kynaston to stagger out of the library and weave his way up to his bedroom. It threw a pool of steady light, but created many shadows, through which Ariana must walk on her way to the library door.

There, she hesitated again.

He was none of her business except that he was suffering in some way. The cause was probably years of indulgent debauchery and the consequent financial straits, but she was plagued by an urgent need to prevent disaster.

She realized exactly why she was here.

She was imagining him preparing to shoot his brains out.

Every scrap of reason shouted that was nonsense, but the idea, the vision of it, would not be dismissed. Yet she couldn't make herself open the door.

She could enter and claim to be looking for a book to read.

At gone one in the morning?

He was simply in there drinking, good sense argued. Thus, she should turn and walk away. She should go up to her room and to bed.

She couldn't do it.

Heart thumping, she turned the knob and opened the door.

By the light of a branch of candles she saw him standing by the fireplace, looking into the sultry red glow. There was no glass in his hand.

He turned, face shifting from bleak to furious. "What the devil do you want?"

Ariana opened her mouth to say, "A book," but the lie wouldn't come out. "I was concerned for you."

His eyes closed briefly. "There's no need, I assure you."

"Then why not come upstairs to bed?"

A wry smile twisted his lips. "Is that an invitation?"

She'd already blushed at her own words. "No. You know what I mean."

"Sometimes I can't sleep. Take your own advice, Ariana. Go to bed."

Ariana. He'd used her name without the "Lady," which seemed intolerably intimate.

Like a breath of air, she found a reason for being there. "I wanted to speak to you about your sister."

"About Phyllis?" He seemed blankly surprised. "Your interfering concern extends to her?"

Despite the edge to his words, she persisted. "She needs better clothes."

"If she'd warned me she was planning to come to Town, I would have provided them."

"You will now?"

The simmering anger tightened his lips. "Damned interfering female. Perhaps you'd like to take her under your wing."

"I will if you won't."

"You'll find her an uncomfortable chick."

"Why say that?"

"She has a mind of her own."

"So do I."

"Yes." He came toward her. "What's in your mind, Ariana? Why are you here?"

The closer he came, the more her heart pounded, and not entirely with fear. "I told you. Concern."

He was in front of her then, eyes meeting hers. "You thought I'd be drowning in brandy."

"Yes."

"Only to escape. Tonight was my first ball in a long time."

"Assembly," she corrected, numbed by his being so

close. His lips so close, and the intimate smell of him weaving through her senses. "Because of mourning."

He touched her cheek, light as a feather, so that in the dimness she couldn't be sure he had touched her at all. Then he touched his lips to hers, as featherlight and ethereal, but with fiery power.

"Why?" she breathed.

"A farewell kiss. A Judas kiss."

"I see no betrayal."

"Perhaps an ambush. Be on guard."

"Against you?" *I'd give you everything, here, now, if you asked for it. . . .*

"I pray not." He stepped back. "I'll pose no danger to you, Lady Ariana."

"I fear none," she said, wishing for the courage to pursue, to capture. And yet she sensed he'd resist, to the death even. "Do you fear death?" she demanded. "Is that the problem?"

He spoke so softly that she could hardly hear him. "I'd welcome death."

"A pistol would be quicker than brandy." But she regretted the tart words as soon as they were out. "I'm sorry!"

"It would be, wouldn't it? I'll remember your advice."

"Don't! I mean . . . don't do anything. I . . ."

Humor touched his lips. "Lost for words, Lady Ariana? Unusual, I'm sure. Go to bed. You leave here in the morning."

She didn't want to go. Now or tomorrow. How could she abandon him? And yet she knew—she sensed—that he truly wanted her gone, now and tomorrow. Pride could not withstand that.

"Good night, then," she said.

"Good night."

There was nothing for it but to leave, abandoning him to his dark devices, but once out of the room, she ran upstairs as if he might pursue. She paused in the upstairs corridor to catch her breath and gather her wits. He wasn't following her, no matter how much she might wish he was.

What devil haunted him?

Was he given to fits of perilous melancholy?

She'd known one gentleman in Hampshire who'd seemed to have everything for a contented life but had slowly withdrawn from society and then one day walked out to sea, even though he was unable to swim.

Once thought of, a similar deep melancholy seemed all too likely. It would explain why Kynaston neglected his responsibilities, even why he'd been abroad for years. He could have been seeking treatment. Perhaps brandy helped. No wonder his aunt treated his shortcomings so gently, but such a mental affliction was a tragedy beyond anyone's mending.

Ariana gathered her composure and then went into her room to give Ethel a brisk account of the assembly.

"Shame about Lord Dauntry," Ethel said.

"Yes," Ariana agreed, but at the moment she had no space in her mind for such minor disappointments.

Kynaston looked at the closed doorway, drawn to the brandy decanter that would be waiting in a cupboard to his right. It did no lasting good, but it brought temporary relief. Sometimes it even made him feel normal—which was dangerous, especially with Ariana Boxstall around.

She'd be gone tomorrow, and he must be glad of it.

That first encounter, first in recent times. He'd been

so deeply sodden, he'd made lascivious comments. Damnable woman.

She was right about Phyllis, but dull clothes might save her from disaster. She wouldn't wear pretty frills anyway, and everyone was in black.

But then he remembered Lady Ariana's black gown and the way the bodice exposed the swell of her lush, creamy bosom. The pagan gold jewelry had declared that she was no conventional woman. The braid on the gown—ah, the golden braid that brought to mind that mummy case and that quizzical face.

Seraphina.

The decanter called from its concealment like a siren, but he left the room, and once he was sure Lady Ariana Boxstall wasn't hovering anywhere, he went to his room and his sleepless bed.

But he did sleep, until he was woken early by an odd sound. Then he realized it was the harpsichord. His room lay over the music room, and he'd noticed this before—that music played there carried upward, perhaps up the chimney. Generally his aunt held musical events in the afternoons and evenings, when he wasn't in bed and usually not in the house, which was a blessing.

The player was skilled and the notes precise. Lady Ariana Boxstall, giving a farewell performance?

He'd heard her play eight years ago and admired the skilled precision that seemed at odds with the ill-dressed, awkward girl. Despite her shortcomings, she'd made an impression on him, but a fleeting one. Now she was back, grown into herself. . . .

Thank God she did not sing.

Thank God Lady Ariana Boxstall would soon be gone from that house.

*   *   *

Ariana had suffered a restless night, constantly disturbed by trying to work out what exactly had happened in the library. His touch, his kiss—there'd been something insubstantial about both, as if he'd hoped they weren't happening.

Why? Because he feared her husband hunt?

Or because he knew there could be nothing lasting between them.

Thank heavens she'd soon be gone from this house.

Even after she'd settled into bed, she'd been tempted to go back down to see what state he was in.

After the clocks struck three, she'd slipped out of her room to look down into the hall. All had been dark. The waiting candle had gone, so he must have come up to bed. She had no idea where his bedroom lay, and if she did, it would be clear madness to invade there.

After that, she had fallen asleep for a while, to suffer disturbing dreams, but none she could remember. She'd woken again at seven in the morning, knowing she could sleep no more. And so she'd gone down to the music room, seeking solace. The harpsichord had no volume control, but she'd hoped no one would hear and be disturbed as she tried to banish disturbing thoughts.

It didn't entirely work. Later, as she picked at her breakfast in her room, she foolishly wished she weren't about to leave. He didn't need her. He had a sister and a loving aunt. All the same, if she were here, she might be able to help. They would certainly meet and she felt all the pain of unfulfilled, insubstantial kisses. . . .

"We'll need an extra trunk for your new gowns," Ethel said, and Ariana was grateful for the distraction.

"I'm sure Lady Cawle can lend us one. Go and ask."

When Ethel had left, Ariana climbed out of bed and forced her mind to other matters.

Boxstall and marriage.

Norris had definitely been enjoying Miss Weather-sted's company, but that might come to nothing. She must pursue her plan until she was sure. In any case, it was time for her to marry. Idiotic to draw back from that because of one impossible man.

She took out her list of eligible gentlemen and crossed off Churston and Blacknorton. That left Wentforth, Sellerden, and Sir Arraby Arranbury. She would *not* be prejudiced against the latter because of his name. He could be the perfect contender.

Ethel returned to help Ariana dress, and then scooped up the various small items to add to the last trunk. Ariana went to take farewell of Lady Cawle.

As she walked along the corridor, Kynaston came out of a room, almost close enough to collide. He slept so close? They both took a step back and he frowned at her.

"We are to leave shortly," Ariana said, almost breathlessly.

"Yes," he said, in a dull-witted way. Had he drunk the night away after all? "From where you plan to hook and wind in a husband. Any husband."

"Only a tall one," she retorted.

"Have you no sense?"

"I have plenty of sense, sir. Kindly step out of my way."

He grabbed her wrist and dragged her into the room he'd just left, shutting the door.

It was his bedroom.

Mad. Definitely!

He released her, but stood between her and the door. Ariana looked around for the bellpull. Unfortunately it was by his bed, but she inched toward it. "My lord, think what you're doing."

"What do you think I'm doing? Planning a rape?"

"As you're clearly insane, anything is possible!"

"I'm not insane. Stop acting a theatrical scene. I merely wish to talk to you."

"*Talk* to me? The drawing room would be more suitable."

"You invaded the library last night."

"Which is not a bedroom."

"Yet I have slept there, as you know."

She was close to the bellpull now, which meant she was very close to his bed, and he was watching her in a particularly perilous manner. She stepped away from the bed. "Kindly move away from the door, Kynaston."

"Not yet. I mean you no harm. Quite the opposite." He seemed calm and sincere. Parts of her wished he weren't, but she walked toward him, speaking firmly and meeting his eyes. "Step aside, my lord."

"You need my advice."

"I *need* to leave this room. We can go to the drawing room for more conversation."

Unmoved, he leaned back against the door and folded his arms. "This will do."

She bumped into something and glanced down to see the chest at the foot of his bed—and the object on it.

A lute.

The recollection rolled over her of him singing and playing.

But this lute was unstrung and neglected, along with all the rest of his sad life. She could have screamed and brought a dozen people there, but she wouldn't bring scandal down on him if she could avoid it. She folded her arms in imitation of him. "You wanted to talk to me? Do so. In brief."

She'd swear he was disappointed.

What did he *want*?

"Very well," he said. "You're not desperate enough to marry Inching, but don't marry Churston, either."

"He's a pleasant enough gentleman."

"He'd bore you to death and dislike you objecting."

Ariana feared he was right. "Thank you."

"Blacknorton would be incapable of fidelity."

"Perhaps I wouldn't mind."

"Then choose him. He's otherwise an amiable fellow."

"What possible business is this of yours?"

"I'm Lady Cawle's nephew. You're some sort of distant cousin. We share a family tree."

"Are you suggesting that you have some *right* to interfere?"

"I understand that your height has made it difficult for you to find a husband"—*her height!*—"but some choices would be worse than spinsterhood. I'm offering manly advice."

Ariana inhaled, exhaled, and then walked toward him. "Move."

"You need to—"

"Move!"

Suddenly wide-eyed, he stepped sideways away from the door.

Ariana took command of the doorknob before turning to face him.

"My marriage is my affair, my lord. Mine alone. I deny any and all family connection. Turn your scrutiny to your own deplorable state—your finances, your estates, and your family—for you are not of sound mind!"

With that, she escaped, but rushed back to her bedroom to collect herself. The arrogant, insufferable . . . madman!

She'd been crediting him with deeper, more substantial burdens, but put simply, he was an insane drunkard who was neglectful of all his duties. A gentle lady in his employ was afraid of speaking out of turn. What sort of tyrant was he to his poor sister? Perhaps she'd come to Town in desperate search of a husband so as to escape him.

And his lute lay neglected.

> *Pastime with good company.*
> *Virtue to use, vice to refuse . . .*

"Take your own words to heart, my lord," Ariana said aloud. She blew her nose, straightened her spine, and went to find Lady Cawle.

She found the countess in her boudoir, on a chaise, still in dishabille.

"It was very kind of you to have us to stay, ma'am."

"It's been interesting, gel, and even amusing. You're embarked on an unusual quest."

"I thought every unmarried lady in London was seeking a husband."

"Because our world leaves them little alternative, but few are so urgent. Don't marry into misery. Nothing is worth that."

That echoed what Kynaston had said. Ariana almost mentioned his outrageous behavior, but she wanted nothing more to do with him. Doubtless his aunt knew all.

"Ah, Clarinda," Lady Cawle said. "Take care of your daughter."

Ariana's mother had come in, but she looked between them, puzzled. "I always do."

"Then you're a ninny to let her get into this situation, but then you always were."

"I must object to that," Ariana said.

"Of course you must," Lady Cawle said, "but it's true. She's too softhearted. I'd have had your brother married by now without all this pother."

"No, you wouldn't, because I would have stopped you. Or her . . ."

"Cease before you tie yourself in knots." But Lady Cawle was smiling. "Visit me if you wish. If not, I'm sure we'll attend some of the same events."

Ariana and her mother offered their formal thanks and took their leave.

"I'm sorry she abused you so," Ariana said.

"That's all right, dear. She's right. In the past heirs were often married off before their majority gave them any say in the matter, and she did exactly that with her own son. But I don't think you and Norris would have been any happier for being raised by her, and your father would certainly have disliked being married to her."

Ariana chuckled. "You have almost as much good sense as Ethel."

Chapter 8

The town house in Brook Street was nearly as strange to Ariana as Lady Cawle's, for she'd stayed there for only a few weeks eight years ago. It was considerably smaller, but it was their own and there was no danger of running into Kynaston in any part of it.

She would not feel regret over that.

Her mother set to taking command of the management of the house and Ariana explored the library. Her father had spent short times here each year when doing his duty in Parliament, so there were some interesting books on the shelves. As she browsed, she remembered that London offered a wealth of bookshops to plunder, and this time the books would clearly be her own.

At lunch she and her mother discussed the husband-hunting plan, but Ariana said, "There are a number of places I want to visit, Mama. The British Museum—I understand one must write to make an appointment. Mr. Soane's private collection, and the Egyptian Hall."

"Didn't you say that was a rather tawdry imitation, dear, and currently housing Mr. Bullock's stuffed animals?"

Ariana chose some pickled herring. "Yes, but I'd like to see it."

She couldn't say that her father had wished to visit the place to see just how poor a job had been done. His health had declined before he'd been able to do so, so she would complete his mission.

"Then seek a gentleman's escort, dear," her mother said.

"I don't need protection."

"An hour or two in a gentleman's company will be helpful. Dancing is all very well, but simpler pursuits can be more revealing."

"At the moment, there's no gentleman I can summon whose escort I'd want. Churston and Blacknorton won't do, and I've not yet encountered Lords Wentforth and Sellerden, or Sir Arraby."

"Then ask Kynaston. Why stare? He escorted you to that Mr. Peake's house."

"Very unwillingly. I'd not impose."

"Then perhaps Norris can take you."

"Mama! He'd be bored to death and it would serve no marital purpose. I need to meet the other candidates before I can request their escort."

"I'm sure you will. We already have a number of invitations. If you're finished, we could go through them."

Ariana participated, but they had no way to tell which events Sellerden, Wentforth, and Arranbury would attend.

Considering an invitation to a talk on the Highlands of Scotland, she said, "Perhaps I'd like to travel."

"Not north," her mother said firmly. "But you might enjoy a wedding trip to those places you and your father found so fascinating. Greece, Rome, Carthage, and such. Though they all seem to be hot, dusty, and uncomfortable."

Ariana chuckled. "How unromantic you are, Mama."

"I can't see any romance in heat, flies, dirt, and dreadful roads. Let's talk of more pleasant matters—Norris's entertainment. We don't have a wide acquaintance as yet, but we can hold it in a week or two."

"Sooner," Ariana said, realizing that Norris or she needed to be well on the way to the altar two weeks from now.

She was ready to argue her point, but her mother said, "You're right, dear. Town will thin out as we get closer to Christmas."

There was another problem Ariana hadn't foreseen. Her eligibles could even now be planning their departure for rural estates.

"Next week, then," she said. "And we'll invite Lords Wentforth and Sellerden, and Sir Arraby."

Her mother nodded. "Something simple. Cards—not for money, of course—and music. You can play, which always shows a lady off well."

"Did I really perform when I was in Town before? I don't remember."

"Only two times, dear. You were a little shy, but you were warmly applauded."

How selective memory was. All that had stuck in her head were the excruciating balls.

"Some readings, perhaps," her mother continued, "and some books and prints on display in the library. I'll leave that to you."

"Perhaps Lady Cawle will attend. She'll bring half of the ton in her train."

Her mother looked up in alarm. "I do hope not. I prefer a comfortable gathering to a crush. But you're more in favor of the lady now?"

"I admire her confidence."

"Don't try to emulate her yet, dear. Wait until you're married."

"Isn't that rather deceptive, Mama? Shouldn't a gentleman see the true goods before he buys?"

"What a way to put it! I'm sure any suitor will try to show you only his best parts."

That put Kynaston out of the running. But she already knew that.

She looked through a few more invitations, but then pushed away one to a view of the *presepe*, or Christmas scene, at the Italian embassy. "Have you thought that if I win this challenge, I won't be at Boxstall for Christmas?"

"Oh dear. No, I hadn't. Oh."

Ariana squeezed her mother's hand. "I'm sorry. I've upset you."

"Silly of me. It's the way of things when a lady weds. I could hope you'd not move far, but as we've dismissed the gentlemen of the area, I fear you will."

"I'm not sure why more women don't rebel."

"Most women are pleased to leave their father's house and become mistress of their own. I certainly was."

"Perhaps you and Papa were too indulgent of me. You should have made me less comfortable."

"Raising children is a very complicated business. Even though you'll be sad to leave Boxstall, Ariana, you may well come to love your new home just as much, especially if you love your husband."

Love, love, always love. Ariana smiled for her mother

and said, "I'm sure that's true." She'd have to pretend that it was true, for her mother's sake, but she'd count herself fortunate if she could even tolerate the man.

That evening they attended a literary party held by Mrs. Montecute. Lady Phyllis was there, attended by Mrs. Manners, which meant Sir Tom North hovered nearby. The older couple seemed truly attached, so Ariana went over to speak to Lady Phyllis to give them some private moments. She might also be able to learn a bit more about Miss Weathersted.

"I'm acquainted with your brother, Lady Phyllis, and with your companion."

The plain girl smiled, and it certainly improved her appearance. Ariana couldn't help mentally choosing a better wardrobe for her as they spoke. Nothing frilly . . .

"He took Della into supper at Lady Lieven's," the girl said. "That was thoughtful of him."

Soft greens and blues to pick up her eyes. Which weren't as glorious a blue as her brother's.

"You seem surprised," Ariana said.

Lady Phyllis blushed slightly. "I didn't mean that, but I've been in the schoolroom and he's been abroad in recent years. We're only just becoming reacquainted. He's my half brother, you know."

Ariana should have suspected that. There must have been ten years between the two.

"So you've never known each other well."

"He was my only family when I was young. Our father died when I was in the cradle, and when my mother remarried, she left me at Delacorte."

It was said in a prosaic way, but Ariana felt for the small child who'd been, in effect, orphaned, and had only an older half brother to call her own.

"Of course I had servants," Lady Phyllis continued, with no hint of self-pity. "My old nurse is still at Delacorte and fusses, and in time I had an excellent governess, Miss Truscott. I wouldn't have minded her staying on, but she's a truly dedicated teacher and preferred to seek new pupils."

"I confess to having been happy to see the back of my governess," Ariana said. "But my father had always guided my education, and continued to do so." None of this was to the point. "Did you take lessons with your friend Miss Weathersted?"

That brought a smile to the girl's eyes. "Not at all. In any case, she went to a school."

Generally the choice of less wealthy families, and most schools did a poor job of educating girls. Neither mattered. Norris wouldn't be best suited to a blue-stocking, and he didn't need a bride with a large dowry.

"Are you both enjoying Town?" Ariana asked.

"Cessy is in alt over the company and the shops, but not so interested in London's history. I suppose it's unfashionable of me to want to visit the Tower and Westminster Abbey."

It was, rather, but Ariana felt in sympathy. "I'm sure visiting such places at least once is acceptable. If no other opportunity arises, perhaps we could go together."

Lady Phyllis's eyes brightened. "That would be delightful. Perhaps your brother would escort us?"

Ariana remembered too late that the girl had shown signs of admiring Norris. However, she could only say, "Or if not him, some other gentleman."

"Kynaston would oblige, I suppose," Lady Phyllis said, but without great enthusiasm.

They were in accord on that, at least.

The next reading was announced and conversation

came to an end as everyone found a seat. Ariana's mother beckoned, indicating an available seat by her side. Once she was settled, her mother introduced the blond gentleman on her left with rather the air of an angler showing off a prize trout.

Lord Wentforth!

And a very praiseworthy trout indeed! Wentforth had good looks without being showy, and a relaxed, agreeable manner. He took part in an easy flow of conversation, and didn't blanch if Ariana revealed knowledge or opinions.

They listened to a lady reading her own poem about dead babies, which Ariana thought unhelpful in the present mood of mourning. She didn't say so, and the next reading was a nice relief, being about travel to Norway.

That was followed by a scholarly lecture on the various forms of sonnets, which almost had Ariana fidgeting in her seat. However, when it was over, Wentforth took up the subject with enthusiasm. Heavens, he was a true enthusiast for poetry. How much analysis of sonnets could she bear in a lifetime? She put aside her qualms, but then a little later he rose to read a work of his own, which turned out to be on admiration of an unnamed lady. He frequently looked at Ariana as he declaimed. Perhaps it wouldn't be too distressing to have poetry composed in one's honor.

This poem couldn't have been written with her in mind, but it seemed as if he found phrases such as "splendid as the rising sun" and "ocean-deep in nobility" suited her. But then the description "dainty" occurred three times, followed by praise of the lady's tiny dancing feet. Not only wouldn't he suit her; it was obvious that she wouldn't suit him!

She returned home and crossed Wentforth off the list, beginning to feel anxious. Time was passing, and she might have to wait until their Wednesday entertainment to meet Lord Sellerden and Sir Arraby.

"Down to two," Ethel said, glancing at the list. "You need to get some new names."

"Perhaps there aren't any."

"I hear tell there are a million people living in London."

"Few of the men would be a suitable husband for me, no matter how I stretch my requirements."

"Martyrs don't count the cost."

"Then I'm no true martyr." Ariana put the list back in her desk. "Do you remember Tessa Cornwell lamenting that when a lady was well into her twenties, all the best men of her generation were already taken? Perhaps it's true, especially now with so many men lost in the war."

"You could look at younger men. Your brother's friends, perhaps."

"Heavens, no! But I will try to find more suitable possibilities. We'll be attending church tomorrow."

St. George's was full and there were many men present. When everyone stood for a hymn, Ariana assessed the tall ones. They all seemed to be with ladies, and some were clearly with families. Two were possibilities, but how could she approach them? In fact, without a connection to introduce her, she couldn't.

As they walked home afterward, her mother told Norris about the Wednesday entertainment. "I assume that will be all right, dear?"

"Anything you want, Mama. May I add a few names to your list?"

"Of course. Some younger guests would be pleasant."

"Then Stuckley and Mifflin-Pole, both excellent fellows."

Ariana resolved to seriously consider them if they had the height. A few years' difference in age wouldn't be impossible.

"Stuckley may want to bring his sister, who's a decent sort. Perhaps also Miss Weathersted and Lady Phyllis Delacorte?"

Of course he wanted Miss Weathersted to attend, and Lady Phyllis could hardly be excluded. But Kynaston might escort her.

Ariana's expression must have been revealing, for Norris said, rather huffily, "You object, Sis? They're agreeable ladies."

"I'm sure they are," she said quickly.

"They'll be most welcome," Lady Langton assured him.

"Kynaston will probably attend," Norris said, and he seemed as unhappy at the prospect as Ariana. "He's always hovering over Lady Phyllis."

"There's nothing amiss about a protective older brother," his mother said.

There wasn't, but Ariana would have preferred that he be neglectful. "Kynaston can be difficult," she said, "but that's neither here nor there."

"Difficult?" her mother asked, making Ariana regret her words.

When they arrived home and Norris took himself off, Lady Langton said, "I wasn't aware that you'd spent time with Lord Kynaston. Apart from that waltz."

"I encountered him in the house a few times," Ariana said. "He seemed somewhat morose."

"Lady Cawle is concerned, which is only natural. It's a sad case, and she's very fond of him."

A sad case. So everyone knew he was sunk in drink and melancholy and beyond hope.

Monday was taken up by the usual Town tedium of morning visits, but they were an essential part of becoming known. A number of ladies were old friends of her mother's, and many gentlemen remembered Ariana's father warmly. A Lady Knightly invited them to take a stroll around the shops, which Ariana found tedious. It was all bonnets and lace and no books.

That evening, after dining at home, Ariana, Norris, and their mother attended an assembly at the Admiralty. The invitation came from an admiral Ariana hadn't known was on the family tree, and she went in hope of uncovering a whole new batch of possibilities. Naval officers were often away at sea for long periods, and an absent husband might suit her best.

Alas, she found the company rather short. Perhaps the cramped conditions on board ships deterred tall men from the career.

On their return Ariana looked again at her list of two. "I need new candidates." She sat at her dressing table so Ethel could unpin her hair. "Tomorrow I'm going to rebel against morning calls. The company is mostly ladies and I have so many other activities in mind. I want to visit the British Museum, the Egyptian Hall, and Mr. Soane's. And return to Mr. Peake's to study his collections more closely."

"None of them are likely to produce a candidate for the altar," Ethel pointed out.

"You never know. I might quite like to marry a scholar." It was a new idea, but not an unpleasant one. "In any case, I intend to command gentlemen to escort me on most of my ventures. As my mother said, an hour

or two in a man's company could be much more revealing than a dance. Speaking of which, I must visit Lady
Cawle. She will have additional suggestions."

"*He* might still be living there," Ethel said, putting
away hairpins.

"Lord Kynaston will either be out or sunk in bran-
died gloom."

But Ariana admitted to herself that a mere two days
out of his orbit and she needed to know how he was. As
best she could tell, Lady Cawle was making no attempt
to help him, and his sister was young and living elsewhere.

She still worried that he might do away with himself.

A note to Lady Cawle brought an invitation to visit
at one in the afternoon. Ariana approached the Albemarle Street house, trying to divine if Kynaston was
inside. If he was, he didn't appear as soon as she entered,
like a lurking fox after a chicken. Ethel took herself off
downstairs, and Ariana was soon with Lady Cawle.

"How goes your project?" Lady Cawle asked.

"Poorly. I can't like Churston or Blacknorton, Dauntry is to wed soon, and I suspect Wentforth has a lady
in mind."

"Dauntry is to wed? To whom?"

"I don't know. Within the week, he said."

"How very intriguing. Why do you think Wentforth
out of reach?"

Ariana told her about the poetry evening, but she
didn't mention "dainty" or "feet."

It was not surprising, therefore, that Lady Cawle
asked, "You couldn't tolerate a poetical husband?"

"Perhaps I could," Ariana said, but moved on. "Ma'am,
do you truly think Sellerden or Sir Arraby might suit
me?"

"I put them on the list, didn't I? As you're being unreasonably particular, I can't tell."

"I was told Blacknorton's a womanizer who's unlikely to be faithful."

Lady Cawle raised her eyes to heaven. "Now the gel demands fidelity in a husband!"

"Is it so impossible?"

"It severely limits the possibilities, and in truth can never be guaranteed. I've known the most meek and comfortable gentlemen wander and some of the wildest become faithful. Take Lord Arden. Heir to the Duke of Belcraven. A rake of the first order, but he married a schoolteacher and has become a saint."

Ariana's friend Hermione Merryhew had been a guest of the Ardens in Town, and had written from there. She'd liked Lady Arden, but found the marquess arrogant.

"He married a *schoolteacher*?" Ariana asked.

"The whole world was agog, I assure you. On the other side, we have Lord Rawstall, who seemed good and pious enough for sainthood. A few years of marriage sent him off to loose women and he now has not one but two mistresses housed and waiting for him, one in Town and one near his country estate."

"His poor wife."

Lady Cawle shrugged. "It was never a love match. Impossible to know what she thinks, but four babies in five years might have made her grateful for relief. Do I embarrass you with such blunt talk?"

Ariana would have liked to deny it, but she was blushing. "A little. We are taught that fidelity in marriage is the most important thing."

"Ladies are taught that, because gentlemen like to

have some hope that their nurseries are full of their own get."

"Lady Cawle!"

"Don't expect me to be mealymouthed. I suppose you want more names. Of course there are plenty, but the fashionable world is thin in London at this time of year. There may be some merchants or professionals worth a look."

Ariana knew she should agree, but she didn't think she'd make a good wife to a merchant or a lawyer. She found she was clasping her hands. "I didn't think details would matter so much."

Lady Cawle assessed her. "Are you sure you have a completely open mind?"

"I just confessed that I have requirements."

"I wonder if you have some notion in your head of the perfect husband. That would get in your way."

A person popped into her head, which made her say, "There are some aspects I could never like, especially rakish behavior. And may I point out that two of my failures have been because the gentlemen are unavailable."

"True. I'll think on it and send you what names I can conjure." It was only when Ariana had risen to leave that Lady Cawle said, "Again, you haven't mentioned Kynaston."

"I know he wouldn't suit."

"I assure you he's not bankrupt."

"I was told his sister is in London because the roof of his country seat is falling in."

"A gross exaggeration. Some neglect, yes, but he will attend to it."

"Can you assure me he's not a drunkard?"

"He drinks." Lady Cawle stated it as a correction. "At the moment."

"I'm supposed to believe that he'll stop?"

"Why not?"

Ariana was surprised to find Lady Cawle so besotted, but it seemed unwise to argue.

"Then I hope for it, but I don't have time to wait for his reform."

"How very trenchant you are, gel. As you will. I will send any names I think of."

Ariana took her leave, and as she walked home with Ethel, she related the conversation. "I think she must have been intending to match me with Kynaston all along, and now she's angry to be thwarted."

"Let her be," Ethel said. "She can't do you any harm."

"I don't fear her." But Ariana remembered Kynaston saying that it wasn't wise to offend the Dowager Countess of Cawle. Ariana resolved to be on her guard, and to treat any further suggestions of candidates with caution.

That evening they went to a dinner, the theater, and a supper, but no new candidates appeared. Ariana tried to widen her selection to include gentlemen an inch or two shorter than herself and those not of the nobility. It did no good, and it wasn't surprising. She was realizing that deep inside she did care about whom she married. In fact, she'd rather not marry at all than marry in even a lukewarm way.

Sweet stars in heaven, she wanted love!

She'd never suspected such folly, and for Boxstall she'd have to be more sensible. There was a better course, however. Norris must wed Miss Weathersted. How could she promote the match?

He wasn't with them this evening, but he wasn't with his lady, either. He hadn't been specific, but she guessed he was attending some amusement that was packed with young aristocratic bachelors who, like him, were avoiding the more conventional events.

She looked around at the company and saw mostly older people and couples. She was hunting the wrong ground.

The next morning, when Ethel brought her breakfast, Ariana said, "I'll be going out shortly for a long walk through the parks."

"You could do with some exercise," Ethel agreed. "You're looking peaked."

"It's not that. It's a time when gentlemen like to ride. I might meet, or at least see, some new possibilities."

When Ariana was ready, she visited her mother, who was still in bed, to say where she was going.

"Take a footman, dear."

"There's no need, Mama. Anyone lurking with attack in mind will not take on two Amazons."

They were soon in Green Park. "Ah, this is better," Ariana said as she strode along a path. "Such an open space reminds me of the countryside, and a nip in the air is particularly refreshing."

"You could have brought one of your horses to Town so you could ride," Ethel said.

"It didn't seem worth it for a short visit. I didn't even bring a habit."

"You could send for one and hire a horse."

"I could. But I hope to . . . have this settled soon."

She'd almost said "be home soon," but she might never be home again.

She put that out of mind and they walked along in

companionable silence. It was enjoyable, but not suc-
cessful as a husband-hunting venture. There were few
people out at this time of day, and no riders. She'd find
them when she reached Hyde Park.

Then Ethel said, "Who's that short man over there,
staring at you?"

Ariana looked, then turned to walk on. "Lord Inching. An unpleasant creature. Ignore him."

"Not hard to do when we've turned our backs on
him. But that's not wise if he's dangerous."

"He's not dangerous in that way. He simply has a
ridiculous attraction to tall women."

"Perhaps he'll take to me, then. Think I could become
'my lady'?"

Ariana chuckled, but then eyed her maid. "Do you
want to marry? I'd not stand in your way."

"I might, but no man has taken my fancy as yet."

And you have all the time in the world to wait.

Ariana disliked feeling watched. She glanced behind,
but saw no sign of Inching. *There, see. Gone.*

As expected, the open expanse of Hyde Park contained
a number of gentlemen riders, some going at speed. Ariana watched them enviously, but also assessing.

A tall man required a tall horse, and a well-to-do
one should have a fine horse, unless he was a poor
judge of horseflesh. She saw a few riders who could
qualify on both points, but discovered no way to meet
them.

Run in their way and risk being knocked down? Hardly.
It could risk death.

Eventually Ethel said, "If you keep walking, you'll
leave London entirely."

Ariana halted and laughed. "Wouldn't that be lovely?

But yes, we have gone too far. Time to return to Brook Street."

As they walked back, she continued her survey of the riders, wondering if there was some way to attract attention. She was admiring a particularly fine bay, when it turned in her direction. She realized that the rider was Norris—and in company with Kynaston.

Norris reined up, bright with morning exercise. "What do you think, Sis? Need a replacement for Torrent, so I'm trying this one out."

Ariana stroked the horse's nose and looked it over, trying to ignore the other rider, but unavoidably aware of him all the same. "Seems excellent. Have you had a chance to try it at speed?"

"Not properly yet, but I think it'll do."

Ariana really couldn't ignore Kynaston any longer, so she looked up at him, assessing his state. Quite healthy, all in all. "Are you, too, trying out a purchase, my lord?"

"Merely borrowing. I don't have my horses in Town at the moment. Do you not ride, Lady Ariana?"

"Ride?" asked Norris. "She's a regular Nimrod!"

"You hunt?" Kynaston asked with surprise.

"There's no reason I shouldn't," Ariana said, even though it wasn't considered suitable for ladies, "but I don't care for it. My brother was being a little imprecise."

"She's a grand rider," Norris corrected impatiently, "on the flat and over fences. If she did hunt, there'd be few to beat her."

Ariana was surprised by her brother's words. When the riders continued on their way, she said, "I've never heard him praise me like that before. Do you think he does it all the time away from me?"

"Or he wants something."

"Ah, yes. But what?"

"For you to give up your plan?"

"I don't see how praising my riding skills would achieve that." A little while later Ariana said, "I wish Lord Kynaston hadn't been with him."

"Looked in good trim, though. Perhaps he was drinking because there were guests in his aunt's house."

Ethel meant it as a joke, but Ariana considered it. Could the man be mad enough to hate strangers under the same roof as well as anything that reminded him of death?

"I'm wondering *why* Kynaston was with Norris. There must be eight years or more between them."

"Happened to meet and rode together. He was looking at you in a very particular way."

"Norris?"

"Lord Kynaston."

"Nonsense!"

"How can you tell if you weren't looking at him? Which you weren't, most of the time."

"He was probably wary of some attack."

"Been attacking him, have you?" Ethel asked.

"Only when he's attacked me." Ariana instantly regretted her words and marched on. "We've received a satisfying number of acceptances for tonight's entertainment, including from Lord Sellerden and Sir Arraby Arranbury."

"So you'll meet them at last."

"Yes." Perhaps by tonight the matter would be settled and she could be at peace again. "And the Weathersteds will attend." So Norris's wooing could progress.

"With Lady Phyllis?"

"Yes."

"Her brother'll probably come, too," Ethel warned.

"True, though I wish he weren't going to be there."

"If wishes were horses, beggars would ride."

"Don't continually refer to me as a beggar!"

Ethel raised her brows. "Those who don't have all they need are indeed those in want. But those content with what fate brings are as rich as princes and kings."

"Fate hasn't yet brought me a husband to be content with," Ariana replied, and set a brisk pace home, where she spent the day helping her mother with the details of their entertainment.

One extra footman and two extra maids had been hired and some of the food was being brought in from Fortnum and Mason, but there was still much to do.

In December there were few flowers available, but the persistent mourning tone made the lack of them acceptable. Instead, they used extra candles amid greenery and white ribbons, wherever possible in front of mirrors.

"Very clever, Mama," Ariana said as they made a last survey before their guests arrived. "No one can mute the brilliance of flame, so it's completely acceptable."

The library was set up with card tables—hired—and the drawing room with extra chairs from around the house, for that was where the poetry and music would be performed. It contained a piano, a harp, and a harpsichord, and some other instruments lay to hand in case they were needed. She saw a violin, a flute, and a recorder. Not so grand a selection as in Lady Cawle's house, but reasonable.

But there was no lute.

It was an unusual instrument, which made her wonder why Kynaston had taken it up. More evidence of madness, and from a young age? It couldn't truly be seen as mad, however. There were clubs for the performance of early music. It simply wasn't a normal choice for a young gentleman of the beau monde.

The dining room was ready for refreshments to be set out, but as the event wouldn't run late, there'd be no supper, so no extra tables were needed. Thank heavens, for there was no room for them.

It would soon be time to dress, but something teased at Ariana's mind and would not be ignored. It was a foolish thought, and even a dangerous one, but it wouldn't go away. The servants were all busy, so she sent Ethel off to the music shop. Soon a hired lute lay alongside the other instruments in the drawing room.

Ariana hoped it would be used. She truly wished to hear Kynaston play and sing again.

Ethel would quote, "Music has charms to soothe," and perhaps that was part of the plan. If he played, would it heal him? After a meaningless contemplation of the glossy instrument, she went to prepare.

She'd chosen to wear one of her new gowns. It was in mourning hue, but closer to deep lilac than to violet. The cut of the bodice was daringly low and wide, dipping between her breasts and exposing her shoulders. An almost transparent veil of pearly gauze was a nod to sobriety, but concealed nothing.

"Wicked, that is," Ethel said, but in approval.

Ariana felt a slight tug toward changing into something else, but she wouldn't be a coward. She was husband hunting, and for that, the gown was perfect. At least two possibilities would be here tonight. In addition to the daring bodice, the cut of the silken skirt seemed designed to cling, with the deep froth of gray-and-lilac lace at the hem enhancing that.

She considered that trimming with concern. The lace might draw attention to her feet. She could do nothing about that. Her dark gray silk slippers were as discreet as possible. She was as she was.

She wore her pearls, with the long string wound around the base of her neck so as to not interfere with the view below. More pearls at her ears, and a brooch between her breasts. She wore nothing on her arms and hands other than long gray silk gloves.

Many-headed hairpins gave the effect of tiny seed pearl flowers scattered throughout her curls, and there she allowed some sparkle. Each had a diamond chip at the heart.

Perhaps it was all a little light and bright for mourning, but she felt ready for the fray.

To avoid overstretching the servants, they were dining before the gathering alone. As the dining room was unavailable, they were to eat a simple meal at a table set up in the library. When Ariana joined her brother and mother there, Norris goggled in a very satisfactory way.

"I say, Ariana . . ."

"You disapprove?"

"A fellow's not used to seeing his sister—"

"Decked out for husband hunting? Are you worried that in this garb I'll win?"

"No, no!" he said, but then babbled, "Mean to say . . . Look splendid. That's what I meant."

"Dear Norris," their mother said, "have you only just realized that Ariana is a very handsome woman?"

Ariana smiled thanks at her mother, but was it foolish to wish that just once someone would substitute "beautiful" for "handsome"?

She worried that reminding Norris of the plan and

his fate would cast him into a bad mood, but he was behaving well. In fact, he was in high spirits.

As they ate a pear tart, Ariana said, "It's almost as if you're looking forward to this evening."

"I am," he said. "Good to see the house used for proper entertainment."

"The contrast being 'improper'?" she teased.

He even took that in good part, chuckling. "Aye, I've hosted a few gentlemanly parties here, Sis. But nothing beyond the line," he assured his mother.

"I'm sure not," their mother said. "You are looking as fine as Ariana, dear. That neckcloth is cunningly arranged."

Ariana hid a smile. She and her mother had often been amused by the fuss men made over the way they tied a strip of cloth, giving different knots particular names. Doubtless the twists and turns of Norris's gray silk had taken him and his valet a great deal of time.

He was blushing with pleasure. "It's a Braydon. Very tricky. But I think we pulled it off."

They left the library so the evidence of their meal could be removed, and made a final check of the arrangements. The lute in the drawing room now seemed like evidence of stupidity and her mother spotted it.

"I didn't know we'd provided a lute."

Ariana found no response other than the truth. "Kynaston plays, or did. I heard him once. If he can be tempted, it will provide variation."

"It certainly will. What an excellent idea."

Ariana distrusted her mother's bland tone, but she wasn't about to poke into that pile of trouble.

The hired musicians began their soft music from a corridor on the first floor and so the family gathered in the hall to prepare to greet their guests.

Soon the house began to fill in a most satisfactory
way. Ariana did her duty, but she was alert for her targets. There were no formal announcements of guests,
so she hovered near the door to hear people give their
name and invitation to the footman as they came in.

Kynaston arrived with the Weathersted party. Ariana noted that her words had not had effect. Poor Lady
Phyllis was as ill dressed as before.

Norris hurried forward to greet the Weathersteds.
Perhaps her problem was solved, but she wouldn't count
her chickens.

At last she heard a man say, "Sir Arraby Arranbury."
What a mouthful. But she saw a tall, rather gingerish
man—she would not be prejudiced against ginger—with
a square chin and a pleasant expression.

She moved forward. "Sir Arraby, welcome. I'm Lady
Ariana Boxstall."

He smiled and bowed. "Honored, ma'am. From Hampshire, I believe."

"Yes." A maid came by with a tray of wine. Ariana
took a glass from it and presented it to him.

"Thank you, ma'am, but I don't drink."

She almost said, "Not even water?" but was mainly
dismayed by the implications. She managed a smile.
"Very wise, I'm sure. Do you forbid all inebriating beverages in your house, Sir Arraby?"

"I permit small beer for the servants. Abovestairs
we drink tea."

"Tea is an excellent beverage," she agreed.

His smile became approving, but Ariana knew another
candidate had tumbled off her list. She wasn't addicted to
alcoholic drinks, but she enjoyed wine with her meals, an
occasional glass of port, and even a small brandy now and

then. She didn't want to live in a house where only small beer and tea were allowed. What was more, she wondered what other restrictions on pleasure ruled there.

She took him over to her mother. "Mama, I present Sir Arraby Arranbury. He is as fond of tea as you are."

With that, she escaped.

"Arranbury not to your taste?"

She turned to find Kynaston by her side, with a glint of amusement in his eye.

"I assume you know his ways."

"You could tipple in your boudoir."

"He'd know."

"And read you a lengthy lecture on the subject."

"At which I'd throw the chamber pot at him."

Ariana realized with a start that she was chatting to Kynaston in much the same joking way she might talk to Norris. Perhaps it was because he was looking normal again, and humor warmed his eyes. She squashed down any lusty reactions. She wanted information, and he might be the man to provide it. She moved into the corridor toward the back of the house, where they wouldn't be observed. He followed.

"Very well, my lord. What do you know of Lord Sellerden?"

"Nothing to his detriment."

"But you know of my mission and whom your aunt recommended. Every one of them is problematic."

His dark brows rose. "I believe I was on the list."

"A case in point."

He actually seemed puzzled.

"You drink," she said.

"You just rejected Arranbury for not drinking."

"You, sir, drink to excess. You also molested me."

"You assaulted me."

"After you laid hands on me."

"After you threatened to hit me."

"Then you manhandled me into your room!" Ariana remembered where they were. They were both keeping their voices low, but someone might come by. "Whatever the rights and wrongs," she said, turning away, "we would not suit."

"On that point, at least, we agree. If you think Lady Cawle put together a list of impossibles, you're wrong. Sellerden may be acceptable."

His agreement that they wouldn't suit was almost painful, and him thinking unmet Sellerden might suit her irritated her. Or perhaps her underlying distress came from his presence, here in shadowy privacy, so close. . . .

She waved her fan to cool her blood. "Tell me more about Sellerden," she said, turning back to face him.

"He's a bit dull, but that's from my perspective. He's a decent, good-humored, responsible gentleman with large estates."

"Positively ideal. Where's his seat?"

"Cheshire."

"A long way from Hampshire."

"Don't let such a detail deter you."

He truly was urging the case of another man. But that was good. He was correct in saying that they would not suit. "I look forward to meeting him," she said with an enthusiastic smile.

He captured her fan and plied it for her. She had no idea why she allowed him to do it, or why she was looking into his eyes.

"Are you truly going to marry in order to force your brother to the altar?"

"If Lady Cawle has told you all, you know the answer is yes, and why."

"Give him time. He'll fall in love and manage the business on his own."

You haven't. Thank heavens those words didn't escape. "Not all men do, and not so young."

"There are so many bachelor pleasures." His purring tone was positively wicked.

She made sure her tone was brisk when she said, "Yet most men with estates to consider pay attention to their duty."

"As your brother will. Give up your plan."

Ariana narrowed her eyes. "Has he set you to this?"

"Of course not."

"Then I can't see it's any business of yours."

"You didn't hesitate to poke into my concerns."

"So you play tit for tat?" She snatched back her fan. "Look to yourself, Kynaston, for you have many more problems than I do."

She returned to the hall, and heard, like a rescuing bugle, the name Lord Sellerden. She went over to brightly welcome her last hope.

He was exactly as Kynaston had implied—a pleasant, healthy man with brown curls, excellent manners, and a couple of inches on her.

He'd do, she decided, squashing down all temptation to be more particular. She could sense some dullness, but it wasn't extreme.

She chatted to him, introduced him to her mother, and then, most of the guests having arrived, took him up to the drawing room for the first entertainment. This was a reading by a new author whose novel was a humorous take on society's foibles. As it was gently done, everyone chuckled along and applauded warmly at the end.

That was followed by a piano performance, and Ariana could exchange a few quiet words with Sellerden. How to set her hook?

"It's many years since I visited Town, my lord. What new attractions should I sample?"

"What sort of attraction would interest you, Lady Ariana?"

Another point in his favor that he asked rather than prescribed. She decided to be honest. If he couldn't tolerate her true nature, she'd have to extend her search.

"I confess to an interest in ancient history, my lord. Greece, Rome, Egypt, and such."

He didn't seem dismayed. "Then have you visited the British Museum?"

"No, and I do want to."

She expected him to offer to escort her there, but he missed his cue. "There's also the Egyptian Hall," he said. "Only a few years old, mind you, but generally admired."

"Oh yes!" Ariana said, layering on the enthusiasm. "I gather it isn't particularly authentic in its portrayal of Egypt, but I *definitely* wish to visit it."

This time it worked. "Be delighted to escort you there, Lady Ariana, if you wish. At your convenience."

She beamed on him. "How *very* kind of you, my lord. I'm free tomorrow morning, if venturing out before noon is not too unfashionable."

He looked taken aback by the haste, but agreed. "Shall we say eleven?"

Rather later than Ariana had in mind, but she agreed. She paid attention to the music for a while, and then excused herself with the need to check on other guests.

She left the room feeling satisfaction and even virtue.

She was keeping to her dutiful course, and there was every chance she could get Lord Sellerden to the altar before the New Year. Whatever his virtues and vices, he seemed easily led.

It would be preferable, however, for Norris to be at the altar instead. Where was he?

She looked into the library, where eight people were playing whist with two others watching. A young couple was going through some prints she'd put out on display. From their manner, they were using the activity as an excuse to court. Indeed, the very angle of their bodies spoke of it, and of a sweet, innocent yearning she'd never experienced.

She shrugged off regret. People were different, and she'd never attempted to fit a conventional mode.

In the dining room, some were already enjoying the dishes laid out, and the servants there seemed to have everything under control. Norris had insisted on a smoking room being set up toward the back of the house. She couldn't intrude there, and could only hope few men would lurk there for the whole evening—especially him.

She went down to the kitchens to be sure there were no hidden disasters, and then took the servants' stairs back up to the drawing room floor. She could hear that the pianist was still playing, so she decided to go up one more flight to check her appearance in her bedroom before returning to the company. The kitchen had been rather hot and steamy.

The mirror assured her that she'd not stained her gown or acquired a smudge on her face. She adjusted some pins to catch stray wisps of hair and reapplied a slight touch of rouge to her lips, wondering if Kynaston would find that attractive or too bold.

She couldn't imagine him finding anything too bold for a certain sort of woman—the sort he doubtless preferred.

Did her lips look scandalously pink?

She tried to scrub off the rouge with her handkerchief, but it mostly remained, and now her lips were redder from the scrubbing.

She shook her head and turned her mind to her brother.

She must find Norris and, if he wasn't with Miss Weathersted, make it so. As for Sellerden, she had her arrangement for tomorrow and didn't want to seem in hot pursuit. Any wealthy, titled bachelor in Town had to know he was a tasty quarry, and he might take flight.

Norris, however, might need a little help.

A glance in the mirror showed her lips still too pink, but she couldn't hide away forever. She emerged from her room and startled to find Kynaston in the corridor frowning at her. "Are you hiding, Lady Ariana?"

"Of course not. What are you doing up here?"

"I was concerned for you."

Was that a deliberate echo of what she'd said to him in Albemarle Street?

"Why?" she asked. "And why up here?"

Then she wondered if he remembered more about her London season than she'd thought, and knew that she'd often hidden away when she could. That intolerable thought brought heat to her cheeks and anger to her aid. "As usual, you are being impertinent, sir, but nothing is amiss."

He'd placed himself between her and the main stairs. She could turn and go down the servants' stairs, but be damned to that. She pushed past him.

He stopped her with a hand on her arm. It was a mere touch, nothing forceful, but she did stop.

"My lord?"

"Your situation troubles me, Lady Ariana."

"As I've tried to make clear, my lord, my situation is no concern of yours."

"I'm not claiming a right," he said slowly. "More of a need." He raised a hand and touched her cheek. "I wouldn't want to see you unhappy."

Ariana tried to ignore that butterfly touch. "I'm not unhappy. . . ."

"In the future."

"I won't be unhappy in the future. Please, my lord . . ."

He took a step closer, cradled her head in his hands, and kissed her. Shock dissolved in an instant under a wash of pure pleasure. And satisfaction. She'd wanted this.

She'd been kissed before, but not like this. Though his lips were gentle, her whole body responded with warmth and then with weakness, so she had to clutch the sleeves of his coat.

And then he deepened the kiss. He tilted his head and his tongue teased at her lips, coaxing her to open. The intimate heat shocked—she'd never been kissed like this before!—but instantly excited, and then delighted. She leaned into him, wanting to be closer, ever closer. . . .

Her breasts suddenly tingled and the heat everywhere intensified into hungry need.

She must have pushed forward, for he moved back against a wall. A strange growl came from her own throat. Or perhaps from his. Or both. They were crushed together by desperate arms, but trying to get closer, ever closer.

But then he pushed her away, his eyes dark and wild.

"My lord. I apologize!"

"What the devil for? I started that."

"I should have rebuffed you from the first." She stepped out of his hold and fussed with her gown. "We will forget this, if you please."

"Can you?"

She had to meet his eyes to give her word force. "Certainly."

"Liar."

Did he know she was still feverishly hot, and aching, in extraordinary places? She turned away. "I must return to the guests."

Again, he stopped her, with a hand, this time tight on her wrist. Sensation rippled up from his hold and she looked at him, fearing . . . she knew not what.

"Take a moment to look less hectic," he said.

"Let me go."

"Ariana, I kissed you to try to show you what marriage is about."

Wickedly unfair to use the weapon of her name. "I understand what marriage is about, my lord."

"Then don't go to the altar lukewarm."

"Many a hot-blooded marriage has ended in disaster."

It was as if she'd hit him. His grip loosened and she twisted her wrist free.

"My marriage is no concern of yours," she said again, as if repetition would give it force.

"I can't feel that way."

Then what do you want? she wailed inside. The old magic was back. He need only say the word, especially after that kiss. How could she live without such kisses when one had stirred a passion she'd never known lived in her?

"But I'll interfere no more," he said.

He meant it. Pride demanded a cool response. "Thank you, my lord. I expect you to keep your word."

He captured her hand again, and raised it for a kiss. "I will."

"Thank you," she said, but unsteadily.

How could a light kiss on her silk-clad knuckles be as powerful as one on her bare lips? As if he knew, he turned her hand and placed a kiss deep in her palm, murmuring, "Farewell."

And then he released her and strode away, leaving her shaken almost to collapse.

What had that been?
What had it meant?

She realized she was leaning back against the wall for support and forced herself upright. She wanted no such wild dramas in her life, and Sellerden would be her tranquil refuge. After a few moments she was able to return downstairs. She found a poet was reading in the drawing room, and noted with surprise that her brother was in the audience, seated between plain Lady Phyllis and pretty Miss Weathersted. The power of love. Norris didn't care for poetry.

Thus she felt free to go in search of Sellerden. She found him in her mother's boudoir, which had been adjusted into a conversation parlor, but he was part of an amiable group with no spare seats. Observing him, she acknowledged that her future husband was completely suitable. Duty called for her to do her best to secure him, and it might be easy.

She felt nothing but sour emptiness inside.

This cool selection of a suitable partner was what she'd demanded of Norris, and now it appalled her, but the need was still crucial. However, if Norris was truly in love with Miss Weathersted, she could escape the worst. His listening to poetry was an excellent sign, and yet something bothered her.

She returned to the drawing room and saw that on Miss Weathersted's other side sat one of Norris's friends. Mr. Mifflin-Pole was a fresh-faced young man with hair arranged wildly in a windswept manner and a very high shirt collar. He was slouched in a way that suggested that only the company of a pretty girl had brought him into a poetry reading and he was wondering if it was worth it.

Ariana sat on a chair at the back, understanding her concern. Norris needed help. He was seated between Miss Weathersted and Lady Phyllis, but on Lady Phyllis's other side sat an elderly couple. For some reason, Norris had ended up paired with Lady Phyllis and let his friend partner the lady he desired.

She'd wait here and correct that situation when the reading ended.

It took quite some time.

The poet was reciting his long poem about the Battle of the Plains of Abraham. Ariana found any warlike topic unpleasant and this was made worse by a dramatic deliverance. Had the plump poet ever raised a weapon with intent in his life?

Finally the reading ended with a celebration of General Wolfe, who'd won the battle, but died in the fighting. After applause people rose to move about and perhaps go in search of refreshments. Ariana moved in on her brother's party.

"Somewhat bloodthirsty," she said.

"Stirs the blood!" declared Mifflin-Pole, causing Miss Weathersted to look at him adoringly. She was probably just the sort to unthinkingly urge her lover or even her husband off to the fray. Ariana truly did not want her for a sister-in-law, but if she was Norris's choice, so be it.

Lady Phyllis said, "Though I respect our gallant soldiers who saved us from Napoleon, I don't think it quite right to celebrate battle and death in such a way."

"I say," Mifflin-Pole objected. "What of Waterloo? Worthy of celebration, eh?"

"I think Lord Byron's reflections on Waterloo much more deeply considered." She spoke as quietly as she looked, but with clarity and purpose.

"Byron! That blaggard was a supporter of Napoleon!"

Norris intervened, annoyed, and with reason. "No need for that tone, old fellow. Especially with a lady."

Mifflin-Pole flushed and apologized. "Carried away. Forgot myself."

Lady Phyllis didn't seem upset, but Ariana wanted to give her some support, especially as she agreed with her.

"Battle is battle," she said, "no matter who has the right or wrong, or who is victorious. It is a bloody business and inherently tragic."

To her surprise, Norris chimed in again to support her. "Didn't Wellington say something about there being nothing worse than a battle won than a battle lost? Or something like that?"

He'd mangled it, but caught the gist.

"He did," Ariana said, "and he would know."

Miss Weathersted, clearly bored, said, "Weren't we going to the refreshments?" She addressed that to Norris, so she knew what she wanted.

Ariana moved between her brother and Lady Phyllis, which put Lady Phyllis in the natural position to partner Mifflin-Pole. But Mifflin-Pole sidestepped to offer his arm to Miss Weathersted, and Norris did nothing to prevent it! Then Norris had no choice but to politely partner Lady Phyllis.

Ariana watched the two couples leave the room. Of all his many faults, she'd never suspected her brother of such spinelessness. Miss Weathersted was his for the taking, but he wasn't taking command. Kynaston would never allow such . . .

No, she would not think of him.

A young lady sat at the harp. Ariana was in no mood for twanging strings, so she left. She was in no mood for company, either, and when she found her mother's boudoir empty, she sat there to collect her thoughts.

Norris would be regretting his spinelessness by now and that should impel him to be more forceful later. Mifflin-Pole was supposed to be a friend. A word to him should sort it out, because Ariana had seen no sign that Mifflin-Pole was in love with anyone. He probably simply hadn't wanted to partner Lady Phyllis because of her serious mind and lamentable appearance.

Lady Phyllis's gown tonight was a particularly ugly shade of gray and excessively full and shapeless in the skirt so as to conceal any hint of her curves. It was equally nunlike in the bodice, which ended tightly around her neck with only a slender white frill for ornament.

How painful it must have been to have an Adonis for a brother and none of his looks or charm. She didn't even have his curls. Ariana had always been grateful not to have to use a curling iron, but if she had such straight hair, she would. Everyone wore curls around the face these days. Everyone. Why wasn't someone advising the girl about these things? Where was Mrs. Manners? Probably somewhere with North, neglecting her duties. Even Lady Cawle had failed to take the girl in hand.

Ariana realized her fretfulness rose from the lingering hurt of her first experience of London. Nothing could have altered her height, but she could have been more attractively dressed. Lady Phyllis would never be a beauty, but she could show much better than she did.

She remembered what the girl had said of her family. Her mother had been the earl's second wife, and Kynaston's father had died when Kynaston was quite young. About ten, she thought. Then Phyllis's mother had remarried and, it seemed, abandoned her daughter at Delacorte.

It must have been a sad situation, but Phyllis had said her half brother kept an eye on her. That had been kind, but as he'd reached adulthood, he'd abandoned her, in particular by traveling abroad and neglecting all his responsibilities. Poor girl. But Kynaston was back in England now, and no matter how short of funds he was, he should spend on his sister, especially when he himself was dressing finely.

As if summoned, he entered the room. "More trouble?"

She regarded him wearily rather than with anger. "You said you'd cease your interference."

"On the matter of your marriage. From your dismal pose I thought something was amiss with the entertainment."

"Then be assured that all is well." Ariana knew it would be wiser to send him away, but this was an opportunity. "I was thinking about your sister again."

"Why?"

"She's appallingly dressed."

"She's young as yet."

"Even so, she's here. It can't be pleasant to know oneself poorly turned out."

"She's expressed no discontent to me."

"She probably doesn't want to cause you extra expense."

"That would be foolish, and she's not. May I point out that this is no business of yours."

"Tit for tat?" Ariana rose, and felt better to be even with him. "It must be the business of any woman with a kind heart. When she planned to come to Town, someone should have provided her with a new wardrobe."

"I didn't know she was coming until she arrived. If I had, I'd have taken action."

"Then clearly you're not well enough informed about her movements."

"I grant you that. I'll keep a closer eye on her in future."

As he was said to be opposed to his sister's early marriage, that might not suit, but Ariana didn't see how to object.

"She seems a sensible, well-informed young lady," she said.

"Bluestocking tendencies, but they should keep her safe."

"Safe from what?"

"Folly."

"You fear she'll follow in your footsteps?"

"Perhaps I do."

"Then set a good example and cease ruining yourself through drink!"

"I haven't had a drink in days," he snapped.

"Which has put you in a foul mood."

"But addiction to alcohol could be easier to recover from than a bad marriage. Give up your plan."

"Not that again! What do you *want*?" she asked, suddenly at her limit. "Why can't you leave me alone?"

It was as if she'd hit him. He even stepped back. "I apologize. I did promise not to interfere." He bowed. "My sincere apologies, Lady Ariana."

With that, he turned and walked away.

Ariana collapsed back into the chair and rested her throbbing head on her hand. Why did she become so ridiculously dramatic whenever she was in his company? She couldn't seem to control herself. Of course, put like that . . .

Oh no.

What did such irritation have to do with the sweet sentiments of love poetry? With sighs and blossoms and gentle adoration? Her situation felt more in tune with Sappho's poem about the ruinous love of Helen of Troy. Her father had introduced her to that as part of their exploration of the story of Troy. Ariana had never learned Greek, so he'd made a prose translation for her, and she could remember the gist.

Consumed by insane desire for Paris, son of the king of Troy, the beautiful Helen had left her good husband without a thought for him, her child, her parents, or any consequences.

Helen's action had puzzled people through the ages. Some tried to make it a story of rape and abduction, but the ancient texts put the blame on female weakness and the power of lust. Ariana and her father had leaned toward some sort of derangement of the mind. Now she saw that what she and her father had failed to recognize was that love itself could be madness, especially an unrequited or a forbidden love.

Perhaps her father and mother and others like them, people who'd met in comfortable normality and progressed to marriage with universal approval, felt only the slightest flickers of love's mad flame. Perhaps love needed the fuel of problems to create an inferno, as with Romeo and Juliet, Abelard and Héloïse, and Helen and Paris.

All tragedies, she noted.

Ariana shook her head, eyes closed, weighed down by the disastrous truth. She loved—no, she was possessed by a demented obsession with—the Earl of Kynaston. The awareness, the sensitivity to him, had always been there, but it had taken that corridor kiss to reveal the blazing truth.

Was this why every other man had been unpalatable to her?

Had she been infected for eight long years?

There'd been reasons to reject Churston and Blacknorton, though in Blacknorton's case perhaps not reason enough. Dauntry was unavailable, and perhaps Wentforth as well—though she'd given up on Wentforth easily. She'd felt nothing for Arranbury and was hiding here because she didn't truly want anything to do with acceptable Sellerden.

She wanted Kynaston.

Kynaston, who was addicted to brandy, no matter what he said, and who she was certain had wasted his inheritance. Kynaston, with his damnable beauty and charm, which he employed to trap and use women.

No, not charm. That was too sweet a word. It was a kind of magnetism, and all women were iron to it. She was astonished no woman had snared such a prize. Certainly he would have resisted having his freedom constrained, but there had to have been determined campaigns.

Were all women more sensible than she? Did they see how disastrous it would be?

She made herself stand, and it did help. She was

overwrought, but she wasn't mad and she wouldn't be consumed by this. She needed an antidote. She left the room to seek normal company. But as she walked along the corridor, she heard the unmistakable sound of a lute. Slowly she turned her steps toward the drawing room. When she entered, she found a large audience silently attentive as Kynaston plucked strings to produce a calm and stately melody.

He was seated much as he had been eight years ago, but she thought perhaps not quite so much at ease. His attention was all on his instrument and his hands, perhaps because he was out of practice. All the same, the music had a pure clarity that seemed in conflict with all she knew about him now.

Was that why he'd been drawn to the lute? Because it lent itself better to coolness than more modern instruments like the violin and piano? A counterbalance to his nature?

Then, with a brief look up at his audience, he began to sing. His voice wasn't as pure as it had been, but it had gained depth and a mellow timbre from time and perhaps hard living.

He sang in Italian, which surprised her. She didn't know the language, but she knew Latin and could make out much of it. It was a love song of sorts, but lamenting his failings. She remembered his reaction to Cleo and knew she'd been right—the mummy had reminded him of some wrong he'd done to a young woman.

Causing her death?

Too melodramatic by far, but the song had power, and not just over her. The room was spellbound. She recognized the approaching end and that she was standing. She quickly sat down. Though he'd performed for a roomful of people, she felt as if she'd illicitly observed a private lament.

He finished, stood, bowed, and returned the lute to its place. There was a heartbeat gap before the applause, but then it came warmly, followed by appreciative comments. Ariana could hear surprise. Was he no longer in the habit of performing? Of course, he'd been traveling in recent years.

He was leaving the room, which brought him close to where she sat. He saw her and paused as if to speak, but then moved on.

Ariana was glad of it. He'd said he'd trouble her no more and she must cling to that, for the music had been the final straw. If he'd taken her hand then and led her from the room, out of the house, and to her destruction, she would have gone, just as Helen had left Menelaus. She would have been powerless to resist. It would not have led to war and devastation, but it would have wrecked her and her world and grievously wounded others around them.

Thank God he'd not tempted her. At that inopportune moment her mother smilingly called for her to perform. There was nothing she wanted less, but she had no choice other than to try to appear in calm good humor and sit at the harpsichord.

She chose a piece by Handel that she knew by heart, realizing only too late that it was in a minor key and had a dark, dramatic tone. Or was that merely her imagination? She cut it short after a few minutes and rose to curtsy thanks for the applause.

There were many eager to show their skills and a lady rose to perform in her place.

She was free—to do what? There was only one thing

on her mind and so she went in search. She wouldn't force her company on him, but she needed to see him, even from across a room.

A tour of the public rooms failed to find him. Secreted somewhere again with brandy? But when she asked the footman stationed in the hall, he told her that the Earl of Kynaston had left.

The house suddenly felt colder and emptier and she was in danger of revealing tears.

She must conquer this! If not, she'd end up like Lady Caroline Lamb, a scandal—and, worse, a figure of fun—for her shameless pursuit of Lord Byron. Reading of the scandal, Ariana had found it as inexplicable as Helen's elopement with Paris, but now she understood.

Love was a form of madness and, if thwarted, fuel for tragedy and destruction.

"Lady Ariana?"

Ariana pulled herself out of melodrama and turned to find Lady Phyllis at her side.

"Do you need something, Lady Phyllis? I gather your brother has left." Now, why had she added that unnecessary sentence?

"I merely wished to compliment you on your playing."

"Thank you."

"I might attempt the harpsichord myself. I was taught the piano, but it and I never seemed to go along well."

"I felt the same," Ariana said, but she was regaining her wits and recognized what was going on. Lady Phyllis had fallen in love with Norris, and was trying to please his sister. Perhaps the sister could gently persuade her that they'd never suit?

"Shall we take some refreshment?" she suggested.

Soon they were seated at a small table with glasses

of wine punch and small delicacies that they both ignored. Around them others chattered, but it was private enough.

"Are you very fond of music?" Ariana asked, preparing to point out that Norris was not.

"In truth, more to listen to than play. I have no patience with the practice."

"Yet I wouldn't suspect you were idle."

"Unless reading is considered idleness, which it is by some. I understand you are quite a scholar yourself, Lady Ariana. Of ancient Egypt?"

"Is it general knowledge?" Ariana asked with surprise.

"I don't know. Lord Langton told me." Ah, the revealing blush. "He said that was why you'd not visited Town for many years."

"He often misunderstands things," Ariana said, sliding in a warning, but surprised that Norris and this girl had fallen into personal conversation. "I simply prefer rural life, but we do have an excellent library at Boxstall."

"Your father was also a scholar."

Lady Phyllis was beginning to irritate Ariana. Her direct gaze and lack of any girlish mannerisms seemed unnatural, and she seemed intent on dissecting the Boxstall family.

"Neither of us were scholars," Ariana corrected. "Mere amateur enthusiasts, but that can be enough. What do you like to read, Lady Phyllis?"

"Poetry, philosophy, history, but I confess to an interest in mathematics and natural philosophy as well."

Certainly an oddity, but Ariana liked her honesty.

"I know a gentleman in Town called Mr. Peake," Ariana said, "who shares your interest in natural philosophy.

He hosts a gathering once a fortnight for a group of people who call themselves the Curious Creatures. You might enjoy that, if not this year, in future."

"I might well," Lady Phyllis said, and then dug beneath the ample skirts of her gown to produce a leather-bound notebook with attached silver pencil, in which she made a note.

Ariana could only hope no one noticed. No one had pockets beneath evening gowns anymore, and if a lady carried a small tablet of paper, it would be prettily bound with ivory or silk.

Truly, Kynaston should . . .

But she would not use this as an excuse to seek a meeting.

She remembered her purpose—to warn Phyllis off Norris. It was even more imperative now. Without seeking a way to lead into her subject, she brightly said, "I do worry about the Boxstall library now my brother is the earl. He has no interest in such things."

Lady Phyllis stowed her notebook and said, "I'm sure he wouldn't deprive you of it, Lady Ariana."

"I'd hope not, but once I marry and live elsewhere, he might see no point to the more rare and valuable volumes. I can't remember when he last entered the room."

"Then perhaps he'll give you your favorite books when you leave."

Ariana could never accuse her brother of a lack of generosity, so she had to say, "He might. If he thinks of it."

"I'm sure he will."

"You seem sure of a great many things," Ariana snapped before she could help herself.

Lady Phyllis blushed, and for once looked her age. "I'm sorry. I've presumed too much. It's only—Lord

Langton seems a kind man, and from a few things he's said, he's fond of you."

"Yes, he is, and I of him. I apologize. Steering an event like this can be wearing on the nerves."

"It's delightfully arranged, but I shouldn't claim any more of your time." Lady Phyllis rose, and Ariana knew she should protest that she'd enjoyed every moment, that it had been a pleasant relief. But she let the girl leave, words unsaid. She drank from her punch. She should have done more to convince Lady Phyllis that she and Norris would be a bad match, but where was the purpose? Norris was drawn to pretty Miss Weathersted. Moreover, logic had no part in love, or she wouldn't be overwhelmed by her feelings for Kynaston.

He'd left the house. She wouldn't meet him again tonight, and if she could possibly arrange it, she'd never meet him again. Ever.

She stood to take up her duties again.

She did her best to act normally as the party progressed toward its end. Pretense helped restore normality, so as the last guest left, she could almost laugh at her drama. She was still powerfully attracted to Kynaston, but not madly enough to ruin herself over him.

She certainly couldn't marry him. That would be a union of passion and strife and quite probably a disaster of epic proportions, because she didn't believe he would change. He'd never cease his drinking, and he'd squander her money as quickly as he'd run through his own. As Lady Kynaston, she could end up counting pennies in a house with a leaking roof, with tiny mouths to feed and her husband off carousing with low friends and vile harlots.

But now she couldn't marry any other.

She tried to fight that truth, but failed. Such a marriage would inflict misery on an innocent man.

Thus, Norris must marry Miss Weathersted.

Her brother was standing across the hall, so Ariana
joined him to say, "That went well and you did your
duties excellently."

"Don't know why you're so surprised."

"I'm sorry if I doubted you. Did you enjoy it?"

"In parts. Not too keen on poetry."

She went directly to the point. "Miss Weathersted is
very pretty."

"She is, but prettiness isn't everything." His tone surprised her, as did the sentiment.

"I'm glad to hear you say so. Is she kindhearted as
well?"

"She's kind to Phyllis, I suppose," he said, with the
beginning of a doting smile.

"*Only* to Phyllis?" Ariana teased. "Not to you?"

"Of course she's kind to me. I'm an earl."

She was amused by how firmly his feet were on the
ground, but she wanted him to be in love. Madly in
love. In part that was because she wanted some crazed
lovers in the world to find happiness. But she had a
more practical reason. If he was madly in love, he'd
permit no delay in getting to the altar.

"I'm surprised that Lady Phyllis and Miss Weathersted are friends," she said. "They're not very alike."

"Wouldn't say they're friends exactly. Neighbors,
and the Weatherstdeds are Phyllis's godparents."

"So they stepped in when Kynaston's roof started to
leak on her."

"Exactly. Bit of a rum do, that. A man ought to take
care of his place."

"He certainly should."

"Truth is," he confided, "Phyllis finds Cessy Weath-ersted a bit of a trial and always has."

An unpleasant worm of an idea slithered into Ari-ana's mind. He kept referring to Kynaston's sister as Phyllis. No "Lady" attached.

Plain, ill-dressed, studious Lady Phyllis?

She tossed out a test. "Lady Phyllis seems a very serious-minded young lady."

"Yes, isn't she?" And he blushed as if describing per-fections.

Ariana was so astonished as to be speechless, but she quickly seized on one thing—if Norris was attracted to Phyllis, it wasn't any shallow, facile emotion. He must truly be in love, perhaps even in the sort of wildfire way she needed.

"She's young," Ariana said.

"But mature. More mature than me really."

He could recognize that. What a change in a man.

"Do you think you'll suit?" Ariana asked.

He blushed and seemed startled, as if he believed he'd been keeping his feelings secret. Ariana prayed she was a better actor than he.

"Perhaps," he mumbled.

Ariana smiled. "Then I wish you well. She'll be an interesting sister."

He smiled back in a moonling way. "She is marvel-ous, isn't she? So kind and wise. Mother will love her."

"I'm sure she will." Ariana had all kinds of doubts, but his besotted love solved her problems. He'd rush to the altar and they'd all be together at Boxstall for Christ-mas. "So now our challenge is moot," she said.

It was as if he snapped out of a dream. "What? Oh, no. You're not getting off so easily. You'll have to admit you're beaten."

It went against Ariana's instincts, but she was still sane enough to agree. "Of course I will. I'll give up my quest and admit defeat as long as you promise to marry before the end of the year."

"End of January was the arrangement."

"Very well, before the end of January."

She thought the deal was done, but he pulled a face. "There's nothing I want more, but I don't even know how Phyllis feels."

"I'm sure she won't refuse you."

"But she's a serious-minded girl and I'm more of a lightweight. I can't always keep up with her, but," he added, his voice softening back into besotted tones, "she speaks so well on so many topics, and has a lovely voice. Doesn't she have a lovely voice?"

In Ariana's opinion it was average, but she agreed.

"I'm sure I'll learn to be a better man."

"So am I. But have you thought, now such a gem is in society, many other men will see what a treasure she is? You'll want to win her hand before someone else steals her away."

"By Jupiter, you're right! But that means talking to her brother. Difficult man, Kynaston."

"Even so, he can have no objection."

"Can. Didn't want Phyllis to come to Town at all. Said she's too young. Doesn't want her to marry for years. She complains he'll want to keep her locked up until she's gray."

Clearly Norris and Phyllis had spent more time together than she'd known, but his words were dismaying. Phyllis was young and only just taking her first steps in society, so even a sane and sensible brother might insist on a long betrothal. An unbalanced one might indeed want her to wait for years.

In four years Phyllis would come of age and be able to marry as she wished, but that was far too long.

"You must try," Ariana said. "Make an appointment to speak to Kynaston tomorrow and put it to him. At least you'll know where you stand."

"He'll probably banish her back to Delacorte."

"The roof leaks."

"Then to some other distant, rural stronghold."

Ariana had to chuckle. "You're sounding like a Gothic novel, but in that case I'm sure you can gather a force of trusty knights and lay siege to rescue your lady."

He grinned. "This love business does make a fellow a bit silly. I don't think Phyllis would think much of an armed assault."

"You never know. Even the most serious-minded lady might be charmed by being treated as a damsel in distress just once."

He nodded, standing straighter. "I'll beard Kynaston tomorrow. Thanks, Sis."

Ariana smiled tenderly as she watched him go to his room. This marriage could be the making of him. Her smile faltered, however, when she recognized a new problem. If the plan worked, she'd have Kynaston as a brother-in-law! How could she survive that and remain sane?

At best, Phyllis would be constantly mentioning him, speaking of his actions and breaking Ariana's heart with worry over his road to ruin. At worst he would frequently visit Boxstall and torment her in the flesh.

Very much in the flesh.

This marriage business had all seemed such a simple matter once.

Had the gods laughed over her confidence that day at Boxstall?

*   *   *

Ariana knew she should go to her room, but she didn't want to face Ethel yet. Ethel had a way of guessing what was going on, or at least that something was going on. Ethel also had access to servants' gossip, and heaven knew what had been seen and heard.

Below in the hall, servants were tidying up with busy footsteps and the occasional clink or clatter, but saying little. They must all have been tired and keen for their beds. There was a smell of wine, from the amount that had been drunk as well as some inevitable spillage, and even a whiff of pipe smoke.

She went quietly downstairs and to the back room that had been set apart for the gentlemen who enjoyed a pipe. It hadn't been cleaned yet, so used pipes lay on the hearth and some tobacco had been spilled onto the table by the box. She picked up a little and smelled it.

Her father had enjoyed a pipe, but only in his study, never in the library, where the smoke could infiltrate the books. A wave of sadness made her blink against tears, and she wished desperately that he were here to advise her. What would he say about Norris and Phyllis, and about her own terrible impulse toward self--destruction?

He'd advise against marrying Kynaston, but he'd advise against marrying Sellerden as well, not for fear of hurting him, but to avoid anything lukewarm. He'd said as much once. They'd been reading Sappho, and some of the woman's more passionate verses had embarrassed her. Stuff about a trembling heart, deep aches, and a flush of heat along the skin. Ah, yes, she understood that better now.

"That's the truth, Ariana," he'd said. "We dress it

up in ribbons and lace, and some poets prate on about sweet smiles and tender hands, but you'll find real poets address the power and fury of it. If there's no fire and never the slightest touch of pain, it's weak tea."

That conversation had been years after her season, years after Kynaston's cruel words, and she hadn't recognized the fire and pain of that incident. Now she saw that it had hurt so badly because she'd cared so deeply, even back then. She'd had no hope or expectation of winning him, but she'd yearned with all her young, defenseless heart and soul, and probably unwittingly, he'd trampled on both.

Only a fool would let him do that again.

She brushed tobacco off her gloved hands and went back to the hall to go upstairs. Her mother came out of the dining room. "Not in bed yet?" she asked.

"On my way there. It went well, didn't it?"

"Very well. I enjoyed arranging a Town party again." Despite the late hour, her mother did look bright, and even younger.

"Did you ever do it before?" Ariana asked.

"Of course! In the early years I came to Town when your father did and entertained for him. Once you came along and then Norris, I generally stayed at home. I didn't mind, especially as your father never stayed in London longer than he had to."

Thoughts of fiery passions invaded, but Ariana pushed them aside. Despite her father's words, she couldn't think of her parents that way.

As they turned at the top of the stairs, her mother said, "You probably don't remember the times we brought you and Norris here when you were young."

"No."

"Your father wanted to show you the wonders that London has to offer."

"Now I do remember some things. A visit to Westminster Abbey?"

"Yes, and other places. You were six when Norris became ill in Town with some fever and nearly died. After that, we didn't bring either of you to London again."

"Oh, I do remember that. It was frightening and I was taken away by someone. Uncle Willoughby?"

"That's right. We wanted you far away in case it was infectious. Fortunately no one else caught it and Norris recovered, but we were all very alarmed."

"We think we know about our family and our world, but much is forgotten, or not spoken of."

"Perhaps we should all be diarists for our children and posterity, but I never had the patience for that."

"Nor did Father." They'd reached her mother's bedchamber. "May I come in for a moment?"

Her mother agreed, but said, "Is something amiss, dear?"

"Not at all. Or not really." Ariana didn't want to speak of her insanity. "I think Norris might be seriously interested in Lady Phyllis Delacorte."

"The plain one?" her mother asked, and Ariana wondered how much it hurt to be constantly referred to that way. Like "the tall one."

"Say rather that her looks are quiet," Ariana said.

"I suppose so. She'd be greatly improved by colors."

"Then we'll hope the mourning ends soon. He plans to ask Kynaston tomorrow, but he thinks Kynaston will want them to wait."

"No harm in that." Her mother smiled happily. "I told you he'd fall in love."

"Yes, but he might not marry for years."

"If they love, I doubt they'll wait quite that long."

"Mama, have you forgotten the purpose behind all this?"

"No, but I refuse to even consider the prospect of Norris dying in my lifetime."

"I can't ignore it."

"Ariana, surely you're not thinking of continuing with your challenge now. How could you? If you manage to marry by the end of the year, Norris would be honor-bound to follow you to the altar."

"Isn't that the point?"

Her mother was looking at her as if she'd run mad. "But if Kynaston won't allow Phyllis to marry for a while—and that seems completely as it should be— Norris would have to marry someone else."

Ariana put a hand to her head. "Oh, Lord. I'm an idiot! This all seemed so simple once."

"You were wrong about that, but I knew there was no point in saying so."

"Am I so unreasonable?"

"No, dear, but headstrong. Once you get an idea, it can take time to purge it, even if it must be purged. Being purposeful is an excellent quality, especially if you now pay attention to finding yourself a husband you can love."

Love, love, love.

Ariana couldn't keep the words in. "What do you think of Kynaston?"

"Goodness. Are you considering him after all? Not the easiest of husbands, I'd think."

Ariana backstepped hurriedly. "I meant as a brother-in-law! And son-in-law." She was hot-cheeked, but her mother didn't seem to notice.

"I don't suppose he'd visit Boxstall very often."

"No."

"He is a handsome, virile man."

"Mama!"

"Am I not supposed to notice such things?" She looked directly at Ariana. "Tell the truth, dear. Are you considering him as a husband?"

Ariana looked away. "His behavior is unstable. He drinks too much and can behave tempestuously."

"Tempestuously?"

"Never mind."

"Ariana, what did happen in that cellar?"

Ariana looked back. "Nothing! Ethel was with me."

"Ethel is perfectly capable of turning a blind eye if she wants."

"She didn't. Nothing untoward happened except Kynaston becoming upset by a mummy and leaving without us."

After a silent consideration, Ariana's mother said, "Very well. I trust your good sense, dear. I know you'll do the right thing."

Ariana escaped to her room, wishing she had such faith. She didn't say a thing to Ethel about Kynaston, and did her best not to let a hint slip. If her mother had picked up her interest, Ethel easily would. It was the first time she'd kept anything of importance from Ethel, and that made her think. Once she was settled in bed, candle extinguished, she made herself review the situation.

Truly, she'd had a fit of madness. She remembered with mortification that it had been Kynaston, not she, who'd broken that kiss. If he'd persisted, she'd have continued, even to her ruin. And he must have known it. He'd stopped—because he hadn't wanted to go that far.

He'd only been doing as he'd said, and teaching her a lesson.

She wanted to shrivel into a ball and roll into a hole

in the ground. She wanted to flee Town at first light tomorrow and never return. Certainly never see Kynaston again.

Who was probably going to become her brother-in-law.

He'd hate that as much as she would. Would he refuse Norris on those grounds? That would be horribly unfair, but he was capable of it. Very well, she'd reassure him. She'd avoid him, but when they met, she would be cool, calm, and composed, so he'd have no need to fear that she'd tear off his clothes. That thought didn't help her cool, calm composure, but she forced her mind to practical matters.

Tomorrow she was to visit the Egyptian Hall with Sellerden. She couldn't easily cry off the engagement, but she mustn't encourage him in any way. Now she couldn't marry soon. It would cause a disaster.

Instead she would turn all her efforts to smoothing Norris's way to the altar with Lady Phyllis Delacorte.

Chapter 9

The next morning Ariana awoke to rain. That didn't augur well for a pleasure trip, but suited her for the outing with Sellerden. Perhaps the weather would literally dampen his enthusiasms. She could only hope it would extinguish any lingering idiocy she had about Kynaston. She'd been plagued by dreams. Such dreams . . . !

For Sellerden's benefit, she chose an outfit that was quietly fashionable but as unalluring as possible. Her black-striped walking dress covered by her gray fur-lined redingote should do that. On her head she wore a low black velvet hat that she knew was close to ugly.

"Why that one?" Ethel asked.

"It has to be worn sometimes." Ethel clearly wasn't satisfied by that. "Very well, I've decided Sellerden won't suit, but I've committed myself to this."

"What's wrong with *him*, then?"

"He's boring."

"There are worse fates."

"I couldn't endure it. In fact, I'm giving up my husband

hunt. My brother is falling in love with Lady Phyllis Delacorte, and I intend to push them to the altar with all possible speed."

"Oh," Ethel said. "You going to remain a spinster all your days, then?"

"Very likely. You disapprove?"

"It doesn't seem natural."

"You're a spinster," Ariana pointed out.

"That doesn't mean I'll always be one."

Ariana remembered Ethel suggesting that she'd like to wed. "You'd like to be married?"

"If the man was right."

"Who would be right?"

"I don't know. I haven't met a right 'un yet."

That made Ariana laugh, which was a good start to the day. "Off we go, to politely repel Lord Sellerden."

She was at her bedroom door when a maid burst in, gasping, "Lady Langton wishes to see you in her boudoir, my lady! Now!"

No point asking a maid what was amiss. Ariana hurried there, mind jangling with possible disasters—Norris?—to find Lady Cawle installed and glaring at her.

"You," Lady Cawle declared, "are a scandal!"

"I? What? *Why?*" Ariana looked to her mother, who seemed close to tears. "What's happened?"

"In the papers!" her mother gasped, pointing to one that lay sheet-scattered on the carpet.

Ariana bent to start reassembling it, but then realized how pointless that was. She straightened to face Lady Cawle. "Tell me. I've done nothing."

"It's what people think you've done that matters, gel. And you've entangled my nephew."

"Kynaston? What is he claiming?"

"Innocence, of course, but who'll believe him? According to the *London Intelligencer*—a scandal rag of the lowest sort—you and he were fornicating in the cellar of that Peake's house."

Ariana was grateful for a nearby chair to collapse into. "It's not true."

"But who will believe that?" Lady Cawle demanded.

"You said it was a scandal rag. Who on earth reads that thing?"

"Not me," said Lady Cawle, as if she'd been accused. "Someone sent me a copy with a weasely note about my needing to know."

"Because of Kynaston. If anyone believes the lies, it will be because of him, not me."

"How does that matter? You'd best leave Town."

"*What?* Why can't he leave Town?"

"I've told him to do so. His estates need attention. But you cannot stay."

Ariana looked toward her mother. "If I run, everyone will believe it's true."

"They'll believe it if you stay, Ariana. It will be horrible."

"Ethel was with me. We can make that clear."

"Maids have connived at sin before now," Lady Cawle said. "There's nothing to be done but let it die down. Meanwhile, I and others can spread the word that it's malicious nonsense, but it will take time to extinguish the last ember. The best thing would be for you to quietly marry in Hampshire."

"If I could have married in Hampshire, do you think I'd be here?"

"Lower your standards."

"To the cowboy?" Ariana snapped. "No, I won't. I'm innocent. Can't I sue?"

"*Sue?*" Lady Cawle asked, outraged.

"I've read of such cases. Slander or libel. I can sue the newspaper, and then the truth will come out."

"That you *weren't* in the cellar with Kynaston?"

"That Ethel was with us!"

"We've dealt with that."

"We weren't there long enough."

"It doesn't take very long."

Ariana wasn't sure what that meant, but she tried not to show it. "What does Kynaston say about this?" she asked. "Will he simply let it die down?"

"He has gone to speak to the editor of the foul rag."

Ariana relaxed. "Then there'll be a retraction in tomorrow's paper."

"You have great faith in him," Lady Cawle said, narrow-eyed.

"He's an earl. If he pushes hard enough, they'll print that the moon is made of cheese."

"The press is not so cowed by the nobility as it once was, but you could be correct. However, mud sticks."

A tap at the door brought the footman with a note for Ariana. She took it eagerly, expecting it to be from Kynaston. It was from Sellerden, apologizing for having to disappoint her, but he'd been called to the country by a family emergency.

She folded it, chilled by the first breath of disaster.

"What was that?" her mother asked anxiously.

"I was to go to the Egyptian Hall with Lord Sellerden, but he's been called out of Town."

Lady Cawle expressed her opinion with a grunt. Ariana's mother sagged back. "We'll not be received anywhere. Truly, Ariana, we should go home."

Ariana feared it would come to that, but it would seal her fate. "I'll wait until I hear from Kynaston."

* * *

Kynaston was entering the shabby backstreet premises of the *London Intelligencer*.

"Mr. Yarby?" he demanded of the sour-faced, shirt-sleeved man who was sorting through sheets of paper on a counter.

"Who wants to see him?"

"The Earl of Kynaston."

The man's prominent Adam's apple bobbed. "I'll see if he's in, milord."

He went toward a door, but Kynaston stepped forward and pushed him out of the way. He opened the door himself to see a man at a desk in a musty, ramshackle room that teetered with books and papers. The editor of the *Intelligencer* was a spare man with hollow cheeks and a blotchy complexion.

"What do you want?" he demanded, unawed by an obvious gentleman.

"An apology, a retraction, and a name. I am Kynaston."

Again a swallow, but then the man smirked. "If you can prove that anything I've printed is untrue, my lord, I will certainly apologize and retract."

"My word should suffice."

"Not for my readers, my lord."

Kynaston slammed his furled umbrella down onto the mess on the desk, stirring a cloud of dust and something that scurried away.

Yarby shot to his feet. "None of that, my lord! The days are gone where the likes of you can threaten the press."

"If you believe that, you're a fool. If you don't print a groveling retraction, you'll next see me in court, and I'll sue you for every penny you have and more. You'll end up in the Fleet, and I'll see this place torn down. Now, the name. What's the source of your lie?"

"Don't know. Truly, my lord! Anonymous letter."

"Show me."

Yarby scrabbled among the papers on his desk, discarding most onto the floor, and then snatched one. "Here it is, my lord. If it's a lie, you can't blame me."

Kynaston didn't bother to respond to that. He took the letter and read the words. Yarby had printed them almost exactly. Of course there was no signature, but when he turned the letter to see the address, he saw the man had signed it there to pay for delivery, and he shook his head.

Idiotic Lord Inching had franked the letter.

He folded it and put it in his pocket, then left without another word.

The newspaper office was located some distance from Mayfair, but he chose to walk back, even in the rain, in part to work off some of his simmering fury, but also in order to think.

He'd not led a virtuous life, nor one free of notoriety, but he'd never before been involved in this sort of scandal. The wrong reaction could fan the flames, and the one to suffer most would be Lady Ariana.

He searched his conscience. Had he done anything to precipitate disaster? In fact, yes, if anyone had known of that hot corridor kiss, but not in Peake's cellar.

It was as if the universe were intent on making him suffer. He deserved that, but not at another woman's expense.

He should put an announcement in the papers. *Warning to all women! Keep your distance from the Earl of Kynaston or be caught with him in the wrath of heaven!*

Lady Ariana should have been warned. She was magnificent, but part of her magnificence was her caring heart and a streak of powerful determination. She cared about the fate of her home, and was set on a trip to the altar to save it. He'd berated his aunt for some of her selections, but she'd argued reasonably enough that she hadn't known that Churston disliked clever women—or, indeed, that Ariana was a bluestocking— or that Arranbury was opposed to drink. Now Ariana was left only with Sellerden, but he should suit her well enough—as long as Kynaston hadn't ruined everything with that kiss.

That kiss.

Had he truly wanted to teach her something, or merely to kiss her? He'd needed to kiss her from that time in the library, but he'd thought it drink-insanity then. The impulse had never left him, however. Perhaps it never would.

He dragged his mind from impossibilities to the service he could do her now. This mess must be sorted out and leave her blameless.

He wanted to thrash Inching, but it would be more suitable to call him out. That itself would be a new scandal, however, especially with their differing heights. The cartoonists would make hay of that, and though his reputation wouldn't be dented by notoriety, Ariana could be ruined.

That brought to mind that cruel cartoon from years ago, of Ariana, enormous in her box, surrounded by midgets. He hoped she'd not seen it, but probably she had. A popular cartoon could be printed off in thousands and displayed in shopwindows all around London. Even if she'd avoided seeing it that way, people shared such things with the targets—all in sympathy, of course, and because they "needed to know."

Sometimes—frequently—the world disgusted him.

Perhaps it was time to grasp the nettle and visit his

estates. Phyllis had not spared him in her description of the problems at Delacorte and his steward's shortcomings, but his spirit still shrank from it. He'd already rid himself of the town house, but he could hardly shed Delacorte, even if the entail allowed. The house had been his family's home for centuries.

If only he'd not returned to England.

With a sublime piece of misprognostication, his aunt had commanded him to return in time for the celebrations of the birth of the next in line to the throne. As an earl, she'd written, he must be present to represent the house of Delacorte. That, added to Phyllis's pleas, had brought him back—to be assaulted by tragedy and embroiled in this protracted mourning.

Since then, he'd not attended to much except the brandy glass.

Until recently, when Lady Ariana Boxstall had entered his life.

Reentered, to be precise, though he could scarce remember her from years ago except for her height. She presented a great deal better in dark colors than pastels, but perhaps the improvement also came from maturity. She'd grown into herself, as some did, men and women. Others outgrew a youthful glow to become more ordinary as they aged.

He'd been heading toward Albemarle Street, but changed direction. He must visit Ariana.

Ariana felt in danger of one of her sick headaches. She'd not suffered one for months, but then despite her anxiety over Boxstall, her life had been orderly. Until now.

Her decision to wait until Kynaston arrived had not silenced anyone, and soon Lady Cawle and her mother had been joined in a chorus of disaster by a Mrs. Scott and a Lady Jerome, who were apparently bosom bows of her mother's.

Ariana hadn't paid close attention to her mother's comings and goings in Town, but it seemed almost a betrayal that she now had old friends who felt entitled—obliged, even—to come to support her in her time of trial. Especially when both ladies clearly believed every word of the scandal. Tired of protesting her innocence, Ariana retreated to her room to take off her outdoor clothing and tell Ethel what was going on.

As Ethel removed the hat, she said, "So someone can print lies in a newspaper and everyone believes it?"

"So it would seem." Ariana rubbed her aching head.

"Oh, dear," Ethel said, and took over, massaging the base of Ariana's skull.

"That's wonderful, thank you."

"It's a long time since you've had one of your headaches."

"This situation is enough to make a Stoic ill."

"And it'll make no difference if I tell the world I was there the whole time? Crazed, it is. You two didn't even touch!"

"You can tell them, and some will believe it, but you know that horrible saying—there's no smoke without fire. It's Kynaston's damnable reputation that's to blame. If I'd been there with Churston or Sellerden, no one would believe it for a moment."

"You say he's gone to speak to the newspaper. He'll sort it out."

"I hope so. He might make it worse, though."

"How?"

"Murder the editor."

"He's not insane."

Is he not? Ariana managed not to voice the query,

but Kynaston was unpredictable and could act wildly, and even now could be making everything worse. She wished he would come to report his actions.

At last a maid came to say that Lord Kynaston had arrived.

Ariana rose to go, but then said, "Come with me, Ethel."

"To the drawing room?"

"Why not? You're a witness."

"Lady Cawle's probably still there."

"I need you, Ethel."

"Very well, then."

When they entered the room, Ariana's first look was at Kynaston. He looked grim but not wild, and her feet took her to him, whether she willed it or not.

He took her hand. "How are you?"

"Shocked." *Especially at the magic of your touch.*

She hoped she concealed that, but perhaps not, for he said, "Sit down," and led her to a sofa. Ariana liked his caring attentions all too much.

Ethel would have stood behind, but Ariana patted the seat beside her and asked her to sit there. She needed her friend and stalwart support, but also she didn't want Kynaston sitting beside her. She'd give herself away and she couldn't bear that, but more to the point, it would toss fuel on the fire. People might think that indeed they'd been up to no good in that cellar.

He returned to standing beside the fire and said, "I visited the newspaper. There will be a retraction."

"But the harm is done," Lady Jerome pointed out.

Lady Langton protested. "We must be more positive, Julia."

"We must face facts," Lady Jerome countered. "You always did live with your head in the clouds, Clarinda."

"Ladies." Kynaston's voice cut through. "If you will assure all you encounter that there's nothing to the tale, it will blow over."

"Madness," snapped Lady Cawle. "At such a dull time of year, fresh blood will stir the hunt, and I gather you can't deny being in that demmed cellar."

"With my maid," Ariana pointed out.

Her mother shook her head. "We must leave Town."

"I won't run."

"Then you'd best marry him," said Lady Cawle.

Ariana's heart leapt, but she was still sane enough to be furious. "That's what you've been wanting all along, isn't it? Did *you* send that information to the papers?"

The visitors gasped and Ariana's mother went pale, but Lady Cawle merely curled her lip. "I would be amused if not for your low opinion of me, gel. If I had wanted to spread a scandalous story, it would be in a finer publication."

"You do want me to marry your nephew, though, don't you?"

"In a mild way. Other men would have suited you."

Kynaston broke in again. "There is no question of marriage here. It would only imply that the story was true."

"Exactly," Ariana said. "As would fleeing Town. We must carry on as usual."

"Are you sure that's wise?" asked Mrs. Scott, looking distinctly uneasy.

But Lady Jerome raised her chin. "I shall support you, Lady Ariana."

Lady Cawle smiled at her. "Then you, ma'am, will be my guest in my theater box tonight. Mrs. Scott, I'm sure Clarinda can depend upon you scotching the story on every occasion?"

Lady Jerome flushed with gratification, Mrs. Scott with awareness of the snub. As Kynaston had said, it wasn't wise to displease Lady Cawle.

Lady Cawle turned her guns on her nephew. "You will be with us at the theater, looking, if you please, bored rather than like a vengeful god. Bring Phyllis."

"No," Ariana protested. "Don't embroil her in this."

"Her presence will be a declaration of innocence. Well?" Lady Cawle asked Kynaston.

His vengeful-god demeanor made it hard to tell how he felt, but he said, "If she's willing to attend, she may. For now, I'm going to visit my lawyer in order to crush that rag altogether. And I have someone else to deal with."

With a curt nod to the company, he strode out, leaving a singe of violence like the acrid smell that hung after a fireworks display.

Ariana shivered slightly and the other ladies were silent, but then the spell broke and she rose to pursue him. She ran downstairs and caught him as he was taking his umbrella from the impassive footman.

She tried to sound casual as she said, "A word with you before you leave, my lord."

He almost refused, but then followed her into the dining room. Once inside, she left the door open, but moved as far from it as possible.

"Whom else are you going to deal with?" she asked.

"You needn't concern yourself."

"How could I be less concerned could I be? Are you planning a duel?"

"No."

"I have your word on it?"

"You doubt my word?"

"I must. My reputation hangs on a thread here."

"Which is why we shouldn't be alone together in this room, even with the door open. Ariana, this is all my fault—"

"No!"

"It's my reputation that makes people think the worst."

"Or your nature." Ariana was aware of wild energies, ones grown from his kiss last night and her weak reactions to his dangerous appeal.

Her mother came in. "I think perhaps you should have a chaperone."

Ariana exhaled and smiled. "You're right, of course. I merely wish to know what Kynaston knows and what he's going to do."

"Perhaps it's best to leave it in his hands, dear."

That would be the conventional thing, but Ariana turned back to her target.

"Unwomanly," he said, and it stung, because it was true and clearly he saw it as a mighty flaw. She didn't relent, however. With a sigh, he said, "The newspaper editor gave me the letter that brought him the information." He took it out of a pocket and passed it over.

Ariana unfolded it and read, grimacing at the vile words. "You're going to find out who sent this. How?"

"Turn it over."

She did and saw the signature. "The idiot! Mama, Lord Inching franked his anonymous letter!"

Her mother hadn't come to look at the letter, but she did now. "What a silly man."

"Silly? He's done his best to ruin me, and only because I refused him a waltz." She gave the letter back to Kynaston, glad to have the disgusting thing out of her hand. "What are you going to do?"

Some of the fury left him. "There's the question.

His small stature makes him almost untouchable by a man like me. Perhaps I should hire a tiny firebrand—"

Then Norris burst in, his banyan open over an open-necked shirt and breeches, hair on end. "What's this I hear? You've created a scandal with my sister?"

"Norris!" Ariana protested. "It wasn't his fault. It was Lord Inching."

"Inching! That worm."

"Whom you can touch no more than I can," Kynaston said.

"I can step on him."

Ariana quickly related the whole story, and then Norris had to read the letter for himself. "I have to do something."

Ariana rescued the paper from his throttling hands.

"Violence will only put fuel on the fire," his mother said.

"Then private violence," Norris snarled. He could actually have been grinding his teeth. "Thrash the man. Drive him out of Town. Out of England!"

"Keep your head, man," Kynaston said. Norris's wild response seemed to be calming him, and Lady Langton set to soothing Norris.

Ariana went to Kynaston. "I'm trying to think how Inching knew of the events at Peake's house. I don't believe he was there."

"From what I know of him, he has no curiosity beyond what will win at the races and what lies beneath a tall woman's skirts. . . . I apologize for that."

"There's no need. It's clearly true. Hardly anyone knew we were in that cellar. Mr. Peake?"

"He might speak of it, but with Inching?"

"I can't stand these uncertainties! Tell me the truth. Can we brazen this out?"

"If your nerve holds. Which it will."

She saw admiration in his eyes. True admiration, and that warmed her, top to toe. Perhaps that kiss, that passion, had not been false. Perhaps . . .

But Norris came over then, wanting a council of war with Kynaston.

Ariana remembered then that her brother had planned to speak to Kynaston today about Lady Phyllis. Now this mess would get in his way. There was nothing she could do about that at the moment, so she went to her mother to discuss what to do next.

But her mother said, "We should leave the gentlemen to deal with this." Ariana didn't agree, but when her mother added, "I must talk to you about all this, Ariana," she saw no choice.

They left the dining room, closing the door. They said nothing in front of the footman, but as they walked toward the stairs, someone rapped at the door. They both turned back, sure another blow would fall.

The footman opened the door—to Mr. Peake.

Ariana went to him. "Come in, sir. I suspect I know why you're here."

"Aye. A nasty business."

"All lies and fabrications," Ariana said, grateful for the opportunity to say that before the servants.

"Of course it is. You and your maid weren't in my cellars for longer than ten minutes, and among a dusty clutter of urns, statues, and other stuff."

Ariana smiled at the clever old man. The servants would carry that downstairs, and from there it would spread around Town. She took him up to the drawing room, feeling that matters were already improving.

Outside the door she paused to say, "Forgive me for

asking, sir, but did you speak of Lord Kynaston and me being down in your cellars? We're wondering how the news got out."

"Not that I can recollect, Lady Ariana. There were more interesting things going on. And of course, my servants were belowstairs unless summoned."

"That's what I thought," Ariana said, and continued on into the room. There she found that the guests had left, and Lady Cawle was on her own.

She didn't seem enraged at having been abandoned. Indeed, she said, "Good to see Kynaston exercised about something useful again."

"I'm concerned he'll make matters worse by committing murder."

"Of a *newspaper* editor?" Perhaps Lady Cawle wouldn't consider such a death murder at all. Ariana decided not to tell her about Inching. The lady focused her lorgnette on Mr. Peake. "Whom have we here?"

Ariana made the introductions. Mr. Peake made his bow to the dowager, being as pleasant and unawed as he was with everyone.

"What is your opinion of this debacle, sir?" Lady Cawle asked.

"That it's nonsense, my lady. As I said below, Lady Ariana and Lord Kynaston, along with Lady Ariana's maid, weren't down in my cellars for more than ten minutes. I'd say it'd take that long to find a spot for sin among the clutter."

Lady Cawle actually chuckled. Perhaps she'd been more unsure than she'd implied. "Sit beside me, Mr. Peake, and tell me of your adventures."

He sat down, but asked, "All of them, my lady?"

"Especially the scandalous ones."

He grinned at that.

Ariana's mother ordered fresh tea and stayed to serve it. Ariana stayed because Peake's stories offered escape from more pressing matters and were keeping her headache at bay.

Except that anguished thoughts wouldn't be controlled. What were Kynaston and Norris planning? She didn't entirely trust the good sense of either, but was glad Kynaston was involved. He was older and would surely restrain her brother from rash violence and even murder. Odd to think of Kynaston as a rock of stability.

"Ariana will take me to visit your house, sir."

Her name startled Ariana into paying attention.

Lady Cawle continued, "I will see your cellars for myself."

But Peake said, "That'll never do, ma'am. Your skirts'll never fit unless you trim your sails."

"Impudent man!" Lady Cawle snapped.

Ariana wondered if she'd demand structural alterations, but she rose and took her leave. Mr. Peake offered Lady Cawle a polite good-bye, and left with Ariana.

"An odd lady," Peake said as soon as they were out in the corridor.

"A very powerful one," Ariana told him.

"She won't knock any chips off me, Lady Ariana, but I'm sorry if I've made your situation more difficult."

"I don't think so. She's not petty. Again, I apologize for your involvement."

"I, too, must be on my way, but be sure I'll do all I can to scotch this. It's a few lines in a gutter rag, lass. It'll be forgotten by tomorrow."

As he left, Ariana hoped he was an infallible prophet.

"Your appearance at the opera will clear this away,"

Lady Langton said as she appeared at Ariana's side. "I've decided we should not leave Town. We should brave this out after all."

"You needed to speak to me, Mama?" Ariana's head was aching more and more.

Her mother knew the symptoms. "Oh, my poor dear. Not at all. I'd only go over and over it all to no purpose. Go and lie down."

Ariana gratefully obeyed. In her room she lay on a chaise while Ethel massaged her temples, using a lavender-and-rosemary cream that generally helped. Ariana had been prone to these headaches all her life in times of stress. She'd not suffered from one for years until Princess Charlotte's death, and then seeing a course of action had driven them away. Now this. She hadn't felt so helpless since that season so many years ago.

The aroma and gentle touch soothed and she drifted off to sleep. When she awoke, tucked under the coverlet, the headache was gone, though as always she felt somewhat fragile.

Ethel was sitting nearby, reading. "Better?" she asked.

"Much. Thank you."

"Hungry? It's nearly one o'clock."

Ariana gingerly sat up. She couldn't face solid food.

"Soup," Ethel said. "I'll get it for you."

Once Ethel had left, Ariana carefully stood and washed her face with the cold water in the bowl. Feeling better, she went to look out at the day. The rain had stopped, but passersby were well wrapped up, so it must have been cold. It would be brisk and fresh, however, and she might like a walk after she'd eaten. But then, could she face the world?

Ethel returned with a tray holding soup for both of

them, bread and butter, and all the necessities for tea. It was a large and heavy tray, but she made nothing of it. Soon they were sitting at the small table, enjoying chicken soup.

"So," Ethel said, sipping her second cup of tea, "what happened when you went after Lord Kynaston? Them belowstairs say your brother was breathing fire."

"Norris was in a state, but I think Kynaston will have talked sense into him. The oddest thing. He—I mean Kynaston—discovered that it was Lord Inching who sent the information to the newspaper!"

"That little man? The one who chases after tall ladies?"

"The very one. Fortunately that means Kynaston doesn't feel able to challenge him, and I assume Norris will be persuaded of the same."

Ethel took another piece of bread and buttered it. "Doesn't seem fair that big men can't beat up little ones. My brothers wouldn't hesitate if some inchworm spread scandal about me, even if it was true."

"Inchworm," Ariana repeated with a smile. "So appropriate. Gentlemen's code, I suppose."

"But that's letting the worm get away with it."

"Perhaps he depends on that."

Ethel shook her head, but made no further comment on the odd ways of the highborn.

Ariana poured herself more tea, added sugar, and sipped at it. "I asked Kynaston how Inching knew we'd been in the cellar, and I still wonder. He wasn't at Peake's house."

"There'd have been gossip."

"By whom? Only the three of us and Mr. Peake knew we'd been down there, and he said he hadn't mentioned it."

"Servants."

"Remember, at a meeting of the Curious Creatures the servants stay belowstairs unless summoned."

"A proper puzzle, then."

"Mr. Peake must have mentioned it to someone, and that someone must have related it to Inching. Let's ignore the dismal subject. Kynaston and I are to appear at the theater tonight to show the world we're not at all disturbed by the silly lies. What shall I wear?"

"The unaltered black?" Ethel suggested. "It's still high in the neck, and you don't want to look bold."

"I don't want to look penitential, either."

"You won't with the amber beads. I could weave your fine gold chain around them. That'd glitter a bit in the lights."

"That might work."

"It will." Ethel rang for a maid to clear away the lunch, then turned from the bellpull to say, "May I have an hour, Ariana? I have an errand to run."

Ariana was surprised, but she said, "Of course. I shall sit quietly with a book."

She did that, but she didn't take in much of the text. Her mind kept fretting around scandal and malice and Kynaston and desire with eccentric diversions to marriage and happiness and . . .

. . . *leaking roofs,* she reminded herself.

And *drink.*

All the same, she longed for Kynaston to be there now, perhaps even to be in his arms, where she'd feel safe and protected, if only for a moment. It was a blessing when Ethel returned, putting an end to all such folly. Ethel went into her tiny room to take off her pelisse and bonnet and returned to sit down. "Lord Inching got his information from Lord Churston. Lord Kynaston could call Churston out."

"Churston! But I don't want anyone calling anyone out. How did you find out?"

"I asked Lord Inching."

"You went to speak to him?"

"Seemed the easiest way. I thought that with his interest in tall women I'd probably get in."

Ariana was slack-jawed. "You simply went to his door?"

"And asked to see him. I suspect his footman—a very short footman—has orders to admit any tall woman."

"They probably thought you a whore."

"More than likely."

"I can't believe . . . What *happened*?"

Ethel smirked. She truly smirked. "He answered my questions."

"Dear heaven. What did you have to do?"

"Nothing much. He was like a cat in catmint. Perhaps he likes women who are big as well as tall. His eyes were almost crossing, especially when I let him have a glimpse of leg. He answered every question I asked and I'm not even sure he's aware of it."

Ariana collapsed into laughter, which was a wonderful release. "I wish I'd been there!" When she'd sobered, she reviewed what Ethel had said. "How did Churston know?"

"Mr. Peake said something and it spread from there."

"I suppose so." But then Ariana remembered. "Oh, Lord, at the theater! That woman—Lady Hatchard. She mentioned us meeting at Mr. Peake's and my having been allowed into the cellars. Peake must have spoken to her or her husband about it. Then her husband wanted to know what was down there, and I said Kynaston was with me. This is all my fault!"

"There, there," Ethel said. "You couldn't have known."

"That's no excuse. I should tell Kynaston."

"What? Confess your sins?"

"Tell him who's truly to blame."

"So he can call him out? Churston's tall enough."

"Oh no, you're right. Best that Kynaston never finds out. But if he confronts Inching, the worm will spill all."

"No fear of that," Ethel said smugly. "Apparently Lord Kynaston had been to Inching's house earlier, but the man had denied being in. He'd no notion of his guilt being known. He simply doesn't welcome tall gentlemen. When I told him Kynaston knew all, it threw him into a panic, so I suggested he leave Town immediately. He's off to visit his estates, which are nicely distant in Cumberland."

"What a worm, but thank you, thank you! Even though I hate to think of him getting away with his malice."

"Perhaps he'll never dare come south again."

"I can hope for that. Churston must be punished as well. He tried to ruin me simply because I didn't favor him."

"And because you're unnatural," Ethel said. "There's one with a low opinion of any woman with a thought in her head."

"That's not so rare, alas."

"We could go to his house and give him a thrashing. He'd be too embarrassed to mention it."

Ariana seriously considered it. It would be so very satisfying. Perhaps she'd beat him about the head with an encyclopedia. She sighed. "Regretfully, no. I need this storm to blow over, which means the visit to the theater. There, I will give a perfect performance of innocent, even empty-headed, purity."

*   *   *

Later, Ariana assessed her appearance in black and amber and decided it was as good as could be. Ethel's idea of the fine gold chain around the beads worked to add some very unpenitential glitter.

She, her mother, and Norris traveled together to Lady Cawle's house, where they were received by Kynaston and Lady Phyllis. Norris went immediately to Lady Phyllis's side, even though she was as poorly dressed as always.

Was Lady Phyllis's poor appearance not carelessness, but a deliberate attempt by Kynaston to keep her unmarried? He was frowning at the couple as if he'd like to split them up. Or he might simply have been puzzled. Ariana still found it hard to believe that a serious girl like Phyllis could tolerate her brother, and there was no air of happy lovers about the two at the moment. She should go to Kynaston, for he was to be her partner for the evening, but she felt odd about it. Shy.

Shy?

She put on a bright smile and walked over to him.

He raised his brows at her. "You look in surprising good spirits."

"Are we not all acting tonight? Perhaps you shouldn't look so grim." Merely being close to him sent a tingle along her skin.

"We're not at the theater yet, but I shall remain grim. It is my appointed role to be vengeful."

"I'm not allowed to be angry?"

"Please, scowl along at my side."

That brought a laugh. "So tempting, but then people will think us together under duress and come to all sorts of conclusions." He was showing no particular sensitivity to her presence, so pride kept Ariana cool. "Instead

I shall be bored by the whole thing, which in part is true. Have you discovered anything from Inching?"

"He's turned tail and run. I was tempted to pursue him up the Great North Road, but I'm needed here. For now."

Sir Norman Ffoulks arrived along with Reverend Corby, a dean of Westminster Abbey. Big guns indeed! Corby was to partner Ariana's mother, while Lady Cawle enjoyed the company of her favorite attendant.

Lady Cawle joined them and they all went to dine. Conversation flowed, but no observer would have imagined them at ease. It was a relief to leave for the theater and get the ordeal over with. Ariana reminded herself of the many times she'd seen lovers try to conceal their feelings, but give themselves away with every look and word. She'd not make that mistake, but that added an extra layer of performance to the evening.

Tonight they were to visit the Drury Lane theater. When Ariana stepped into Lady Cawle's box and went to a seat at the front, a sea of faces turned toward her. If this was how it felt to be onstage, she'd never be an actor. She maintained a calm smile, and turned at the last moment to make a casual comment to Kynaston. He responded, but kept his grim face on.

She prayed Churston wasn't here or she might let her feelings show. If Kynaston noticed—disaster! She realized she was probably looking grim now and put on a slight, relaxed smile. Acting was a great deal more difficult than she'd thought.

Once the curtain rose, she focused on the play. It was a comic opera called *The Haunted Tower*, with exactly the sort of twisted plot that was diverting. The play was set in France, where the Baron of Oakland, an

Englishman, was a false usurper and the true baron
was in disguise as a French peasant, but in love with a
grand French lady who was pledged to marry the Baron
of Oakland, but in love with the true one without knowing who he was. To escape, she was impersonating her
maid, who was in love with a plowman. . . .

When the curtain fell for the first intermission,
Ariana could naturally turn to Kynaston to say, "My
head is aching with the attempt to follow that."

"I suggest you don't try. It doesn't bear close inspec-
tion."

"But it's relaxed you," she said, "and it's very well
performed. I particularly enjoy the maid, Cicely."

"A lovely singing voice and spirited charm."

Was he attracted to her?

Oh, no. Not that fatal trap for the besotted—irrational
jealousy.

Fortunately Dean Corby joined in the conversation
then. "The play's translated from the French, Lady Ariana, and was originally set before the Revolution there.
That gives the conflict between the peasants and the
baron a different reading."

"It would, Dean. Did he end up under the guillotine
in that version?"

"I believe so. And of course the English were all
villains and the French the heroes."

"Whereas in this one, that's reversed."

Despite the scandal, Lady Cawle's power held, and
the usual number of people came to visit her box. The
visitors must also talk to her guests, including Ariana
and Kynaston. If eyes were sometimes sharply curious,
no one mentioned the scandal. Until one lady—a Mrs.
Overstall—said archly to Ariana, "It would seem we can
expect an interesting announcement, Lady Ariana."

"Can we?" Ariana asked, sincerely confused. But then she wondered with alarm if the woman thought she was with child.

"You and Kynaston," the lady said with a chuckle. Ariana was grateful that Kynaston had left her side to speak to a one-armed gentleman, a Major Beaumont.

"Such a fine couple you make," Mrs. Overstall said. "And after all that's happened . . ."

"Happened?" Ariana queried. "I hardly know Kynaston, ma'am. Oh, you refer to that ridiculous bit of gossip! Lady Cawle suggested that we appear together tonight to put it to rest."

"Oh, I see. Probably wise, but such a shame."

The lady left, but Ariana felt the power of her words. It was a shame that she and Kynaston couldn't make a match of it.

"Has Lizzie Overstall upset you?"

Ariana turned to Major Beaumont. On introduction, she'd noted by instinct that he was tall and seemed intelligent and decent. His war injury wouldn't deter her at all. What a terrible husband hunter she'd become.

"She seemed to think Kynaston and I were obliged to marry. And that it would be a desirable outcome."

"Many women think any marriage better than none."

"Then they're wrong."

"I agree. Are you enjoying the play?"

It was a conventional conversational gambit, but Ariana was grateful for it. She must continue to act carefree. "I'm having a little difficulty keeping the characters straight, especially the hero, who changes costumes and even sex quite frequently."

He chuckled. "It is a demanding part."

"I'm enjoying the maid. The way the actress expresses her feelings and her saucy meanings with her body, and her lovely singing voice. Her white hair is a some-what strange device, however, for a fairly young woman."

"Mrs. Hardcastle went white at an early age, and has made it her special feature, rather than disguising it with dyes or wigs."

"I admire her for that," Ariana said, but couldn't help thinking that nothing could disguise her height. The warning bell sounded and Major Beaumont left the box.

Lady Cawle seemed able to follow all the conversations around, for as everyone began to settle for the next act, she said to Ariana, "Beaumont's my godson. He's married to Mrs. Hardcastle. Quite enchanting, isn't she?"

"Extremely," Ariana said, reviewing the conversation for fear she'd said something less than glowing. Apart from the comment on the actress's white hair, she hadn't.

"She makes a quite magical Titania," Lady Cawle said.

"I'm sure she must."

As the curtain rose and Cicely began a new song, Ariana considered the Dowager Countess of Cawle's acceptance of her godson's lowly bride. His marriage to an actress would have been a scandal, and Ariana doubted the highest sticklers in society accepted the major's wife, yet Lady Cawle didn't seem to mind.

What was the world coming to? Perhaps she should read more gossip and understand it all better.

When they went to supper later, she found the answer to her question about society's acceptance. Beaumont and his wife joined them without any apparent awkwardness. Mrs. Beaumont—as she was offstage—was as lovely and charming as she'd seemed, and completely at ease, even among the highest of society.

And they were among the highest of society. Lady

Cawle did nothing by halves. The Lievens were present, and the Hungarian ambassador, Count Esterhazy, and his wife. The Duke and Duchess of Leeds and the Earl and Countess of Warwick sat at the table, and even the prime minister, Lord Liverpool, had accepted the invitation, along with his wife. He was seated at Lady Cawle's right hand. Everyone seemed at ease with the actress and they all politely ignored the scandal.

Until Lady Cawle raised the subject. "Liverpool, don't you think the government should ban scandal sheets?"

He looked resigned. "I might, dear lady, if anyone could distinguish between them and the valid purveyors of information."

"In days past, no one would dare to print lies about members of the nobility."

Kynaston said, "But we live in more enlightened times, Aunt."

"That is a matter of opinion. You want to give everyone the vote, even the penniless."

Ariana glanced at him in surprise. He was for reform? She didn't need more virtues to put against his vices.

"A vote for everyone of modest property," he amended.

"Even women?" asked Mrs. Beaumont from across the table, eyes twinkling.

Kynaston laughed. "In due course."

Ariana hadn't seen him laugh for eight years and she found it magical—but it was at the teasing of a charming lady of normal size.

Lady Cawle gave a very disapproving humph, but Kynaston turned to her. "You don't think your opinion of value, Aunt, when it comes to who governs our country?"

Ariana had an impression that everyone held their breath, but did some of the other women feel the same as she did, that he was making an excellent point?

"Women over fifty, then," Lady Cawle said. "Not young flibbertigibbets."

Ariana couldn't resist. "Are there no young *male* flibbertigibbets, ma'am?"

"Enough of this," Lady Cawle said, moving off losing ground. "The fact is that the credulous masses believe every bit of nonsense they see in print, so something should be done."

She left it at that, moving on to the nonsense of some theater plays, but her comment might shift some wondering minds. No one here would want to be seen as part of the credulous masses.

Talk soon moved to education for the poor, with some supporting the idea and others suspicious of it. Kynaston was in favor and Ariana noted that his drinking was moderate. It was something that he was able to behave correctly in public, but a marriage would involve a great deal of privacy. She must remember that, especially when she was fighting a powerful physical attraction that made him the focus of her attention. She hastily looked away and said something to Lady Lieven.

The discussion was unusually meaty for a supper party, but this was a gathering of intelligent people who took a keen interest in public affairs, and Lady Cawle was managing it to suit her purpose. As the supper drew toward its end, she raised the subject of Mr. Peake's collection.

"Lady Ariana and Kynaston gave such an interesting report of Peake's curiosities that I thought of visiting his house myself, and especially his cellars, but I was informed that the steps down are steep and narrow."

Eyes sharpened. Everyone knew another act of the play had begun.

Ariana took up her part. "That's true, and it's a shame,

for he has intriguing items stored down there. There's a replica Egyptian mural and I glimpsed a statue of Anubis. Unfortunately I couldn't get close enough to inspect it. I might have begun moving chests and bundles except that there was a talk about to begin in the drawing room and Kynaston had already gone ahead upstairs."

He gave a slightly indulgent smile in return. "Finding eventually that I hadn't been followed. I didn't realize how difficult it would be to drag Lady Ariana away from anything Egyptian."

People chuckled.

"Egypt is so fascinating," said the Duchess of Leeds. "I, too, would like to see these items. Are there any mummies?"

Ariana knew she should say yes, but Cleo should not be crudely exposed to curiosity. Yet she didn't wish to outright lie.

"Mr. Peake has a great many non-Egyptian items," she said, "having traveled extensively in the East. There are some quite terrifying masks. All these are in the main part of the house, of course, but I saw many unpacked boxes as well."

"A treasure trove!" said Ffoulks.

"It is," Ariana agreed. "I'm sure Mr. Peake will welcome appreciative visitors once he has his house in order. He's not been there long."

"He purchased the lease on my house a bit over a month ago," Kynaston said. "That was why Peake asked me to take Lady Ariana down to see his Egyptian treasures. I knew the way."

Another useful drip of information.

"Surprised you were there at all," Leeds said, and Ariana wondered why he gave it such weight.

"Curiosity," Kynaston replied lightly, but others around

the table were treating the matter as significant. Why? Then she realized. No matter what Lady Cawle claimed, everyone knew the lease had been sold to pay crushing debts.

Lady Liverpool turned the conversation. "Have you visited the British Museum, Lady Ariana?"

Ariana replied that she hadn't, but intended to, and talk moved on to other interesting London locations. Ariana settled to confirming her interest in ancient civilizations. It would be useful in the scandal to be seen as a bluestocking with no interest beyond the academic, and it could be paving the path to the future. She was even more sure that if she couldn't marry Kynaston, she could marry no one. She might as well be an eccentric bluestocking.

Later, when she returned home, she gave Ethel a cheerful account. "I believe we've seen the last of the nasty business."

The next day proved her wrong.

Chapter 10

Ariana was enjoying her morning chocolate when her mother came into her bedroom with such an expression that Ariana asked, "What's wrong? Not . . . not Norris!"

Had he plunged into a duel? With Churston? Been *killed*?

"No, no, but, oh dear, Ariana . . ."

Ariana scrambled out of bed. "What is it? What's happened?"

Her mother had a crumpled piece of paper in her hand and she thrust it forward. "I should burn it. But you have to see."

It was cheap, rough paper with a printed picture on it. Ariana smoothed it out, her heart already pounding with trepidation. When she could make out the picture, she gasped. "How? *Why?*"

Her mother sat, a hand to her chest. "The how is easy enough. A bit of skill with pen and ink and the

ability to etch it. Why, I can't imagine. Why would anyone be so cruel?"

The cartoon was not the best drawn Ariana had
seen—not nearly as fine as the one of her in a box—but
it was clear enough, with the meaning made absolutely
clear in bubbles of speech.

The scene was a crowded space containing sketched-
in statues, urns, and boxes. A woman sprawled on a sarcophagus, her skirts revealing her legs, and she wasn't
wearing drawers. *Lady A B* was crying a wild invitation
to the finely dressed gentleman, whose flap was already
down. *The Earl of K* was saying, "Don't worry, my
Amazon. I'll satisfy your bold desires."

The whole thing was titled "The Peake of Pleasure."

Ariana sat on the chest at the foot of her bed, her
legs actually failing her. "I don't believe it. This isn't
possible."

But it was, and this was far worse than the small
item in a cheap newspaper.

This was a *print*. That meant it would have been run
off in hundreds, even thousands, and sent around to
every print shop for display and sale. It was certainly
being hawked on the streets for a penny. If it became
popular, it would be sent around the country and even
abroad, enclosed in letters that gleefully explained the
scandalous situation in full.

The letter slipped from her nerveless hand.

Ethel hurried in. "What's amiss?" She grabbed the
paper and looked at it. Her silence was eloquent.

"Perhaps you should marry Kynaston after all," Lady
Langton said.

But Ariana straightened at that. "No! That would
only confirm the lie. Oh, heavens. He'll make things

worse." She struggled to her feet. "I have to speak to him."

"I don't see how things could be worse, Ariana."

"He could *kill* someone. Ethel. Clothes. Now."

Her mother wrung her hands. "Oh dear, oh dear. But who could he kill for this?"

It was a good question. Had Inching or Churston been behind this? Would either go so far?

Ethel had put the cartoon on the bed and hurried off to gather clothing. Ariana picked it up. Without looking at the picture, she searched the edges for the name of the artist or printer. The printer's name, at least, was usually at the bottom. There was nothing there. Whoever had done this did not mean to be caught, but Kynaston would already be on the hunt, murder in mind, and this time sanity might not hold him back.

And Norris. What would her brother do? "Does Norris know?"

"I haven't told him." Clearly her mother saw the same disaster there.

Kynaston, then. A letter.

She opened her writing desk and the first thing she saw was the list. She'd crossed out his name on the first day and then burned the paper. This was the one she'd written, with all the names crossed out except Sellerden's, and yesterday he'd crossed himself off. The whole idea of the challenge to her brother had been rash, but it had paved the way for this disaster. She'd offended Inching and misled Churston, leading to that item in the paper, which had somehow led to this. *All* her fault, and thus hers to deal with.

She took out a clean sheet of paper, dipped her pen, and began to write.

"What are you doing?" her mother asked.

"Writing to Kynaston."

"You can't dictate to a man in a situation like this. He's going to want blood."

"And he can have it," she said, "but I can't allow him to make matters worse."

She soon received a response, but it was from Lady Cawle to say Kynaston was investigating the cartoon and attempting to have all the copies destroyed. He would come to her as soon as possible.

"She adds again that I should marry him," Ariana told her mother and Ethel.

They were in the library by then, supposedly drinking tea, but the cups stood cooling, almost full. They would have sat in the drawing room, but that faced the street, where a crowd had gathered in hope of a glimpse of the scandalous Lady AB.

Norris, raging as expected, had wanted to send for the magistrates and the military to drive them away. He'd even threatened to shoot some of them. Ariana had persuaded him to leave to join forces with Kynaston in the hope there was some sanity there.

"A marriage does paper over a lot of cracks," her mother said. She was dry-eyed now, but mangling a damp handkerchief.

"I hate how this is distressing you, Mama. I wish I could waft it all away."

"But you can't. We can't even leave the house!"

"It will blow over," Ariana said, but she didn't believe it. This was a true disaster.

The crowd outside their door would have to dissipate in time, especially as it was threatening rain, but could she ever appear in Town again? Even if people didn't exactly believe the picture, it would be in their minds whenever Lady AB entered a room.

"Perhaps Kynaston will discover the culprit," her mother said.

"But will that help?" Ariana asked. "Probably some lowly printer saw that item in the paper and decided to exploit it for profit." But then she frowned. "If he's anonymous, how is he earning his filthy money?"

"There's a good question," Ethel said. "Paid up front?"

"If so, by whom?"

"Not Inching."

"You seem sure of that."

"Lord Inching would never sink so low," Ariana's mother said, clearly thinking no nobleman would.

Ariana wasn't so sure, and Churston was also in the mix. She realized she'd told no one what Ethel had discovered.

"We will leave for Boxstall," her mother declared.

This time Ariana had to agree, but she said, "Not until we have some idea of how this came about." There was nothing more to be said, but the silence became intolerable. Ariana surged to her feet to pace the room. "Where the devil is Kynaston?"

"Ariana!" her mother chided.

"This is not the time to fuss about language! I wish I knew some more heinous language. This is all so unfair!"

Her mother broke into tears again. Ariana rushed to her and rocked her, longing for someone to comfort her. To be a child again with faith in hugs and the power of others to make things right. Despite what might happen in the next few days, this scandal would hang around her neck for the rest of her life.

In decades to come, people who heard her name would ask if tall Lady Ariana wasn't the Amazon who'd been caught in a cellar *in flagrante delicto* with wicked Lord Kynaston. Even worse, such stories grew over time. Eventually she would have been discovered by dozens, naked in the act, and would have borne bastard triplets, each marked with a mysterious pagan hieroglyph. And then, decades hence, people would marvel that such a dried-up old spinster could ever have been racy, and she would have wasted away her life, hiding in libraries because books were her only friends.

Her brother returned.

"Norris!" Ariana exclaimed. "What's happening?"

"Devilish little," Norris complained, "but Kynaston told me to come to give an interim report."

"Then do so."

"Don't take that tone!" he snapped, making Ariana wonder if this hellish situation wasn't driving them all mad. "We've been making enquiries, with the assistance of the magistrates and some Bow Street Runners."

"That sounds excellent," she said, trying to be calm. "Has anything been discovered?"

"Would you like tea, dear?" her mother asked, making Ariana want to scream at her.

"Ale," her brother said.

Ethel went out to arrange for it and at last Norris sat down to make his report.

"The editor of the *London Intelligencer* has fled London and possibly the country, so it's suspected that he was behind it. His press might have been used, but there are no plates or other incriminating evidence there."

Ariana sat down opposite. "Why would he do that at his own expense? He had no reason to hurt me."

"He might not see it that way. Kynaston laid down

the law to him about the piece in his paper and was taking action to shut him down. Apparently he's a resentful sort given to using his paper to attack anyone he sees as an enemy. But it's all supposition as yet."

So Kynaston might have triggered this new disaster, but she'd caused the root of it.

"We were wondering how the printer would make a profit from this, but if it was his own vile plan, that wouldn't bother him." She realized something else. "If you don't have the plates, they can't be destroyed, can they?"

Norris grimaced. "I fear not."

"Which means there's nothing we can do. I find that intolerable."

"As do I."

Ethel returned, followed by a maid with a tankard of ale and some slices of cold game pie. Sensible Ethel knew that food would calm Norris. He set to with appetite, but Ariana wondered if she'd ever be able to eat again.

"How can this happen?" she demanded of the room and the world in general. "I'm not ripe for scandal. I've lived a quiet, respectable life. Why is this even believed?" No one had an answer, but she did. "Because of my height. I'm a freak, and therefore anything is possible, even this."

"Oh, no, dear," her mother said, but her heart wasn't in it.

On instinct Ariana fought back tears, but she was tempted to surrender to them. Perhaps then someone would cradle her and make every problem go away. Perhaps Norris. But no. He was taking the manly part, but he was still her younger brother. He and her mother began to go over everything, worrying at it like dogs with a shredding ball, creating nothing but mess. Ariana went to a front room and peered around the edge of the curtain. The crowd was growing.

She moved away before anyone saw her. She'd have liked to go to her room, but that seemed like a cowardly retreat, so she returned to the library. She didn't sit, however, but browsed the shelves, as if she could be considering sitting to read a book.

Then the door opened and their footman said, "Lord Kynaston."

He took in the mood of the room. "What new trouble?"

"None," Ariana said, wanting to rush to him with relief. Instead she resumed her seat at the table. "Only acceptance of disaster. Do you have hope to offer?"

He seemed more weary than angry, however, and not at all hopeful. "Only that this will pass. It's clearly nonsense."

"I'm not sure people care. They relish stories of pig-faced men and women giving birth to rabbits. Is anything being attempted?"

He sat in the chair next to her, turning to face her. "A magistrate is interrogating Yarby's print man, but he's a tough nut to crack. It's as if Yarby sees this as a holy crusade against the sinful rich."

"But it's a *lie*."

"All in a good cause."

"You're sure this Yarby is behind it?"

"It's the most likely explanation."

Ariana considered her next words, but Kynaston sought purposeful action and so did she. "I do wonder," she said. "Yarby must have been raged at by victims many a time, so why take such action now? Could he have been urged to it, and even paid to do it?"

"By whom? Inching?"

It was time to tell everyone what Ethel had discovered. "Inching got wind of the story from Lord Churston. Might he have urged Yarby to this extra step?"

Everyone stared; then Norris exploded, "*Churston!* I'll have his gizzard! But why?"

"Because I found his assumption of superiority intolerable and made it plain, and he doesn't approve of women with firm opinions."

"But how did he find out about events at Peake's?" Kynaston asked.

She turned to him. "That's my fault. At Covent Garden, a Lord and Lady Hatchard mentioned my being in Peake's cellars, trying to tease out information about what is down there. I was with Churston at the time. They added that you'd been there with me, and Churston was shocked. I should have said that Ethel was with us, but I wanted to be rid of him, so I let him think what he chose. I'm sorry."

"You couldn't have known he'd turn to spite. How did you find this out?"

"Ethel did. She went to Inching and he confessed all."

Everyone looked at Ethel.

"Very enterprising," Kynaston said, but in an odd tone.

Ariana wanted to protest that Ethel had done nothing but show some leg. But even that seemed too much and Ethel was smirking. She wasn't at all ashamed.

Ariana turned back to Kynaston. "You are not to call out Churston."

"I'll do as I think best, but I'm more likely to take him to court if Inching will stand evidence."

"You can't depend on that, and if Inching and Yarby keep their mouths shut, you'll have no case."

"Damnation," he muttered, and no one complained.

"We have to do something," Norris said. "Let it stand and Ariana is ruined."

All the fighting spirit drained out of her. "I dislike fleeing the field of battle, but Mama and I must leave Town for a while. I'm sorry if this touches your sister in any way, Kynaston."

"If it does, it's not your fault."

And what will become of Norris's hopes? Ariana wanted her brother married for the sake of Boxstall, but above all, now she knew love, she understood the painful necessity. She must do her best for him. She stood and said, "I must prepare to leave Town, but I would like to speak to you alone for a few moments, Kynaston, before we leave."

He'd risen but clearly didn't relish the idea. Her wild emotions were not reciprocated. She wouldn't let that deter her. Ethel, Norris, and her mother decided they had work elsewhere, leaving them alone together. As if in accord, they both moved closer to the fire, but farther apart.

"Your maid should have stayed," Kynaston said.

"Are you afraid to be alone with me?"

She meant it as a tease, to lighten the moment, but he astonished her by replying, "Yes."

"You think I'll do you *harm*? I've only ever tried to help you, Kynaston."

"Good intentions don't always absolve you of guilt."

"True. I wanted to apologize fully for embroiling you and your sister in this disaster. It is all my fault."

"The last thing I expected from you is an oversensitive conscience."

"It's a fact, as I explained, though why not wanting to dance with a short man and being a bluestocking should be offenses enough for this I have no idea."

"They aren't. And it's possible that Churston only intended a small piece in a minor newspaper, and that my anger at Yarby caused the cartoon."

"Perhaps, but I believe we're responsible for the consequences of our actions, even the unintended ones."

"That's harsh."

"I don't mean it so, but people will say that they never meant any harm as if it should absolve them! Often a little thought would have prevented all."

"Come, come. You think you should have realized that refusing to waltz with Inching would lead him to such malice?"

"Perhaps not. But I might have realized that being so abrasive with Churston would anger him."

"Stop this. It's his sin, not yours."

"But you've become embroiled through no fault of your own when you already have more than enough problems on your plate. I ask that you not make it worse by dramatic action."

She expected agreement, and was shocked when he said, "I'll not be shackled by you."

"Not even when my life will be affected more than yours? I'm likely to be *ruined* by this, Kynaston, but you will simply continue to be a rake."

"If I don't deal with this, I'll be the man who allowed a lady to be unfairly ruined."

"But you *can't* deal with this! Don't you *see*?" Damnation. Tears were threatening again, at the worst possible moment.

He closed the distance between them and pulled her into his arms. "Don't," he said huskily. "Don't cry. I'll find a way to make all right."

"How?" she wailed, but she was encompassed in strong arms, her head resting on his broad shoulder, his body

warm along her whole length. She'd never been held like this since she'd been a girl, comforted by her father. Her mother's hugs had always been awkward unless they were seated. Those gentlemen she'd flirted with and kissed had never been so familiar.

She could stay like this forever. She realized he might appreciate a little comfort from her, and tightened her arms. A moment later he gently separated them, but he looked into her eyes as if assessing her condition.

She smiled for him. "Don't worry. I don't have the nature for tragedy. I will survive, even this."

"I hope for better for you." He gave her his hand-kerchief and she wiped her eyes. "Please put aside any guilt over this, Ariana." His use of her name and the way he said it caught her breath. "We can't go through life striving to never offend anyone, especially those who deserve it."

"I think the sermonizers would say we should."

"Then I'll go to hell. But it will be a little less hellish if the same sin sends you there, too."

He left then and Ariana stared after him in a daze.

That had almost been a way of expressing eternal togetherness, but it could also have been a proclamation of . . . *love*? She clutched the white handkerchief as if it were precious.

But then she saw that those odd words could as much be a warning as a promise. Hadn't she thought for herself that marriage to Kynaston would be a kind of hell? A drowning person would climb into any boat, but sometimes it might be wiser to drown.

It was time to prepare for their departure, but she put the handkerchief in her pocket.

She and Ethel began to pack trunks, but then she received a letter from Peake.

My dear Lady Ariana,

I cannot express my shock at the scurrilous image that has been created from an innocent incident.

I must confess that I might have been the source of gossip. When we spoke, I said I hadn't mentioned your being in the cellars with Lord Kynaston, for I couldn't imagine doing so, but I have since recollected that Lord Hatchard remarked on seeing you emerge and demanded, in a humorous way, why you were so privileged and he was not. I can't imagine Hatchard using the information in any malicious way, but talk can spread.

For that reason, and as the incident occurred in my house, I intend to do my utmost to correct the situation.

I am recruiting the Curious Creatures and various others to point out how impossibly absurd the cartoon is, and this evening I will allow any of them who wish to inspect the cellars. They will have to brave the mob that has gathered here, but I have informed the magistrates, who have offered troops to keep the peace if the gathering turns unpleasant. I don't wish to disperse them, because I hope that seeing the bon ton arrive will erode their belief that this is a house of sin.

Be assured, dear lady, that I will do everything in my power to correct this great injustice.

> *Your servant,*
> *Edgar Peake*

"Poor man," Ariana said. "It will do no good, but at least he can do something, whereas I can only run."

She looked at the half-filled trunk and rebelled. "Stop. I won't run away." But then she sat with a sigh. "But what can I do?"

"Fortune favors the brave," Ethel said, which might have been true but was of no practical use.

"Of course! I must attend Peake's event. That will make the point more strongly." In her excitement she rose with some energy.

"Maybe, but how are you to get there? That lot outside will tear you apart."

"They can't be angry with *me*."

"A day out in the cold with nothing to show for it? Then there's the hawkers selling them mulled ale."

Not just a mob, but a drunken one? "You told me to be brave."

"But he who fights and runs away lives to fight another day."

"Stop it!" Ariana sat to think. "Norris went to Lady Cawle's to speak to Kynaston. I could join forces with them there."

"How?"

"Dress as a servant?"

"You're too tall."

"You're tall," Ariana pointed out, but she took the point. "It's a shame this house doesn't have a back entrance."

"You could dress as a man," Ethel said.

Ariana stared, but then thought about it. "I'd never get away with it."

"It'd only be for a moment if a carriage stood ready. You could wear some of your brother's clothes."

"What of you?"

"I doubt Lord Langton would want me wearing his clothing."

"He won't want me to, either, and I need your company. Bring his valet to me."

The passing minutes gave Ariana ample time to see all the risks and dangers of the plan. If she was detected in men's clothing, the mob would attack her with even more vigor. But put simply, she had to do *something*, or she'd go mad. She went to the mirror and gathered her hair, imagining it under a hat. How could that work? Wasn't her face too feminine?

Robert, Norris's valet, came in, looking alarmed. Clearly Ethel had told him of the plan. He was not the sort to refuse an order, but he could make objections.

"You don't have his lordship's shoulders, my lady, if you'll excuse me saying so. Or his sturdiness elsewhere. His clothes will hang off you."

"They won't hang off me so much," Ethel said, "and couldn't Lady Ariana wear a greatcoat?"

The valet didn't like that suggestion, but he couldn't deny it. "Perhaps," he said, and tried again. "But his boots . . ."

"Are you saying my feet are too small?" Ariana asked, rather amused. "If I wear pantaloons, I could wear my own half boots and it might not be noticed. People see what they expect to see. I hope. I must at least try the effect, Robert. Take us to my brother's wardrobe."

With drooping shoulders, the valet led the way.

Ariana first tried on Norris's traveling greatcoat, with its layers of capes. It was oppressively heavy, but it certainly concealed her lack of sturdiness. She next tried one of his tall beaver hats, but her hair gave her away.

"We'll pin it up tightly," Ethel said, "and with the high collar you could pass." She quickly gathered all they needed and carried it back to Ariana's room.

Ariana took off her gown and put on the pantaloons. Her bunched-up shift helped fill them, but even
the draw-laces at the back couldn't tighten them at her
waist. Ethel produced pins.

"Even so," Ariana said, "I look ridiculous."

"The greatcoat will cover all. But you need a shirt
and jacket on top."

Ariana put on a shirt, but refused the large jacket.
She put on the greatcoat again, and truly, from the neck
down she could pass. For once in her life her height
was to her advantage.

"There's still the problem of my hair."

"We could cut it short."

"I'd rather face the mob!"

"Then we'll pin it up."

Ethel brushed Ariana's hair up to the crown of her
head, pinning and pinning it until it stayed put. As a
hairstyle it was horrendous, but when the hat went on
top, it merely looked a little odd. Wisps of curl were
escaping all around. Ethel applied skin cream to the
wisps, darkening them and making them look lank.

Ariana considered herself again in the mirror. She
still looked much like herself, but none of the mob
knew her. They'd be waiting for a scandalous woman,
not a poorly presented gentleman.

"Here, put on the gloves." The leather gloves were also
too large, but they did give the impression of large hands.

Ethel was getting into a full set of Norris's clothing,
this time with breeches. His boots were large on her,
but not too large, and her shoulders almost filled the
jacket.

"You're much more convincing," Ariana said.

Ethel admired herself in the mirror. "I am, aren't I?
I might like to dress like this at times and swagger

around." She plaited her wiry dark hair into a pigtail and tied it with a ribbon, creating an old-fashioned style, but one some men still wore. With a hat on top it looked easily believable. She went to the fireplace and poked her finger into the soot, then dabbed a bit above her lips and around her chin.

"You really could fool anyone," Ariana said. "Should I try the soot?"

"Maybe a tiny bit. Your skin's too pale and delicate. You're obviously a young sprig. I'll thicken your eyebrows just a bit."

The effect made Ariana laugh, but it wasn't ridiculous. It merely made her look an even-less-prepossessing specimen. She put on her black leather half boots and then practiced a bold, manly walk, the cane tucked under her arm.

Ethel looked out through the window. It faced the back, so it told them nothing about the mob, but she said, "Fortune does favor the brave. It's begun to rain."

Ariana went to confirm it. "It will disperse the mob?"

"Not heavy enough for that, but it'll excuse an umbrella."

While Ethel went to get one, Ariana wrote a note to her mother. She'd leave it with a servant, however, for her mother would be sure to forbid this enterprise.

Ethel returned with a man's black umbrella. "Nothing ventured, nothing gained!"

Ariana was heartily tired of proverbs, but as she left the room and went downstairs, she appreciated the sentiment.

The footman had been sent to summon a hackney, and a wide-eyed maid kept a lookout for it. "It's here, milady!"

Ariana gave the note to the maid, doing her best to

ignore a panicking heart. She couldn't faint. When Ethel opened the door, she strode out, immediately opening the umbrella as she headed for the hackney door, which was held open by George.

"Where's the lady?" someone called.

"Aye, where's the Amazon?"

"Shameless hussy!"

For a moment Ariana thought she'd been caught, but it was an insult to the absent. She thrust the umbrella into George's hand and entered the coach, immediately pulling down the grubby blind closest to her. Ethel snarled, "Be off with you, you lowly scum," in an admirably deep voice, before joining her. George slammed the door and they rattled away.

"My, but I enjoyed that," Ethel said.

Ariana had a hand to her unsteady chest, but she said, "I think I did, too, now it's done. Never again, though. Never again."

They were soon in Albemarle Street, where they saw no gawkers. Either a sinful man was too commonplace or Kynaston had dealt with them—he or Lady Cawle, who could probably summon the army to her assistance if she wished. Ethel went to rap the knocker, and as soon as the door opened, Ariana hurried inside, leaving one of Lady Cawle's servants to pay the hackney.

Kynaston came out of the library, seeming puzzled for a moment. Then he recognized her. "The devil! Come in here."

Ariana and Ethel went into the room and he closed the door.

"I needed to escape," Ariana said, suddenly feeling foolish. "And this was the only way."

"Very enterprising." He smiled at Ethel. "You, ma'am, are most convincing."

"Sturdy stock, my lord. Here, my lady, let me take off that greatcoat. You must be sweltering."

Ariana surrendered it gratefully, but then realized she was exposed in her ridiculous baggy pantaloons and her brother's large shirt, which she hadn't bothered to fasten at the neck. It hung down, exposing her corset. She quickly gathered it together, but she'd seen a reaction from Kynaston.

A most interesting reaction.

Chapter 11

"I'd best go and make arrangements," Ethel said, and left.

Ariana stared after her, but Kynaston said, "Someone mentioned obliging maids?"

"I don't know what's come over her." But Ariana did, and she was hopeful, especially after the way Kynaston had looked at her.

"She's matchmaking," he said. "A pity it's to no purpose."

It was like a blow to the heart. She should have been grateful for honest bluntness, but she felt like crumpling to the floor in despair. Pride rescued her. "Indeed. A ridiculous notion. I came here, Kynaston, for a purpose."

"I should hope so," he said, but he turned away to put more coal on the fire, which was already burning brightly. A sensitive man, to give her a moment to pull herself together, but she hated that he might guess her feelings.

Why couldn't she have a grand, tragic, impossible

romance? Instead, she was a victim of unrequited love. Was there anything more pathetic?

When he turned back, she told him about Edgar Peake's letter. "I want to attend, and I think you should, too. But not together. Not as a couple, I mean." She was tangling herself. "Would Lady Cawle attend?"

"I doubt she could resist."

"She won't make it into the cellars with her hoops."

"She will reign from on high."

"So you could come with her, and I with my brother and mother."

"Except that you are now separated from your wardrobe."

His eyes flickered down and she realized she'd let go of her shirt. She fumbled behind for one of the pins holding the pantaloon waist together, but he came toward her, pulling out his cravat pin. He offered it, and she used it to hold the shirt together.

"Why did you come here?" he asked.

She had no answer, or none she wanted to give. In the end she repeated, "I wanted to escape." It was, in part, true.

"Perfectly understandable. Why hasn't your brother dispersed the mob?"

"I persuaded him not to. There were only a few at first. Then he left. I thought he'd come to speak to you."

"He did, but then stormed off to find some friends and rampage around the print shops gathering copies. I thought it was the least harmful outlet for his passion."

"He's young."

"I might have done the same if I'd thought it would do any good. As it is, Peake's plan with your elaboration might serve a better purpose. I have also come up with another notion. We could have a different cartoon drawn."

"A *different* one? For what purpose?"

"Nothing so interestingly scandalous, but an accurate illustration of Peake's cellar with a few fashionable notables poking around in it."

"Would that interest people?"

"Not as much as sin, but it will be a curiosity for a few days."

"It might help. Is there a glimmer of hope?" she asked.

"I said I wouldn't let this ruin you."

"But you aren't God."

"I'm an earl," he said lightly, "which is close enough for the purpose."

She could point out that Norris was one, too, but let it pass. Kynaston had a power and maturity her brother might never have. But where did that fit with the drunken wretch she'd come across in this room not much over a week ago? She glanced around and saw no sign of spirits.

She looked back at him. "Why were you drinking?"

His face shuttered and she thought he wouldn't reply at all, but then he said, "I had space and time enough."

She knew she should let the subject drop, but she needed to understand. "When your life calms, you'll return to brandy again?"

"Oh, for a calm life! I believe we discussed your unseemly interest in my affairs."

"I'd be concerned over anyone who was wasting their talents as you seem to be."

"Any talents I have are being used in your service at the moment, Lady Ariana. There, your interest should stop."

It should have, but a madness had taken grip of her. "Why is it to no purpose?" she demanded. "We might not suit, but you rejected the idea of a match so absolutely. Am I so repulsive a person?"

"God, no! If you must have it, I will marry no one. It is nothing to do with you."

His words hurt, but for the most part Ariana was puzzled. "You don't feel a duty to your line?"

"Can you never let anything go?"

"Not when it's important. Why?"

"It's obvious, you harridan. I won't kill another woman!"

Ariana stepped back, in part in shock but also in fledgling horror. He'd murdered someone? A wife? It made no sense.

He was staring at her. "You don't know, do you?"

She shook her head.

"How, I can't imagine. My wife died in childbed, three years ago."

Ariana abruptly sat in one of the upright chairs by the library table. "I didn't know you'd married."

"Have you lived in a hermitage?"

"No, but I've never been interested in gossip. It's late to offer commiserations, but I do."

"I doubt you can truly share my misery. There would be no purpose to my marrying other than to fill a nursery, as they put it—as you command your brother to do—and I will not do that."

Things began to fall into place. "That's why you sold your house. It happened there." She didn't wait for a response. "That's why you don't want your sister to marry."

"She probably will in time, but I won't encourage her to it."

"You'd forbid all childbearing if you could?" He didn't answer, probably because he had no answer, but yes, he probably would if he could. It was all too tangled for Ariana to cope with at the moment, but she remembered Norris.

"My brother has fallen in love with your sister."

"Then he'll have to wait."

Ariana wanted to argue the urgency, but now that seemed a minor matter.

"I've finally silenced you," he said with wry humor. "Truly, I didn't know that you didn't know. That might have made me rough with you at times."

But Ariana was thinking about those times. "That first night, in this room, you made an approach to me."

"One of the perils of drink. I never said my willpower was perfect."

"The more reason not to drink."

"Which I remember, most of the time. We should consider plans—"

"*And* you kissed me."

"To make a point."

Ariana met his eyes.

"Very well," he said. "I am attracted to you. Nothing will come of it."

Ariana couldn't help a smile, and a rather pathetic "Truly?" escaped. "Attracted to me?"

"Zeus, surely you know you're beautiful!"

"I'm too tall to be beautiful."

"Have you been locked away in a tower for the past eight years?"

"As good as, perhaps. But here in Town men haven't been falling at my feet. Except for Inching, I suppose."

"Have they not? You have been so focused on your list that you've ignored the rest. Shorter than you on the whole, but not intolerably so. You're the toast of the clubs."

"I can't be. You're confecting this to try to soothe my hurt feelings."

"I wouldn't insult you that way. Churston was probably driven to extremes because he found your unsuitability intolerable. He wanted to capture the latest prize. Wentforth has written a poem about you. He does tritely make you Hippolyta, queen of the Amazons, but it's a paean of praise. I had Count Lubinoff here today, trying to call me out for dragging your name through the mud."

"Oh, I'm sorry!" Ariana said, but she was fighting delight. "I never imagined."

"Where did you get the idea that you were an antidote?"

She could have told him, but she knew it would hurt. It had been a bit of youthful thoughtlessness and he'd not imagine any of the ladies would have heard of it.

"I wasn't a great success when I last came to Town," she said.

"What were you, sixteen?"

"Seventeen."

"Some girls are enchanting at that age, but few boys are. I remember being gangly with big feet."

Still she twitched at that, but he was speaking honestly.

"At that age I tried at times to dress like a beau," he continued, "but I was advised to wait, and to enjoy being a youth. He was right. Have I offended you by comparing you to a boy, Ariana? It's perhaps a matter of growing into one's height."

"I'm not offended, no," she said. In fact she was drawing in this quiet, intimate conversation like a precious feast, to be savored in later days. "My grandmother pushed my parents into bringing me to Town early for fear I'd grow even taller."

"The perils of good intentions."

"I've never thought of her as having good intentions. Heavens above, perhaps I'm like her! She always pushed for action. She wanted my mother to starve me in the hope it would stunt my growth."

"Let that be a lesson to you, then."

She met his eyes. "I'm not to try to bully you into sense?"

"It would be painful for both of us."

"It will be hard." She could say that she'd marry no other, but that would be to put a burden on him. She probably should marry someone else to ease him, but she wasn't sure she was capable of that.

"Time heals," she said briskly, standing up. "And it also flies. How do we arrange for the new cartoon? And how do I get back into my house for my clothes?"

In the end, Kynaston left to find Norris and remove the mob from the Brook Street house so Ariana's mother could emerge later without harassment. Ethel went back to the house to collect everything Ariana would need, and returned in her female form. Ariana was left with nothing to do but wait and go over her time with the man she loved.

How could she not have known of his marriage and his wife's death? Because she'd never been interested in gossip unless it was millennia old. In a sense she had indeed locked herself away in a tower, safe from hurt.

The death of Princess Charlotte had afflicted everyone. She herself had been spurred to drive Norris toward the altar, but she'd never thought that "filling his nursery" would involve putting her brother's wife at risk. It was the way of things, and most women survived. If not, the death of the princess wouldn't have hit so hard. Everyone had taken a healthy birth for granted. Babies died too often, as did young children, but mothers much more rarely. The queen had given birth to many children.

Then Lady Cawle came in. "I have only just been informed that you're here, gel, and I can see why. If you had to dress in men's clothing, could you not have done it with more panache?"

Ariana laughed. "I don't see how. The greatcoat did cover the worst of it."

"Come to my boudoir."

Walking across the hall and up the stairs, Ariana did feel exposed and ridiculous, but she was soon in the elegant room. Lady Cawle settled onto a sofa and said, "Tell me your side of the story."

It didn't take long.

"Mr. Peake's idea is good," Lady Cawle said, "and I will attend. The idea of a new print is also good. More than one. A pity the Regent has returned to Brighton."

"I thought he was fixed there in mourning."

"He was in Town yesterday and gathered his Privy Council today, but has already left."

"He wouldn't wish to attend any social event."

"Probably not," Lady Cawle said, but it was clear she would have made the attempt. "It must be a glittering affair surrounded by complete propriety."

Ariana had to ask. "Kynaston said I'm generally admired."

"Why are you surprised?"

"Because I'm accustomed to thinking of myself as a freak."

"Folly. You are distinctive, but that is no bad thing,

as you see." Lady Cawle was referring to herself. "You are a handsome woman, Ariana, with grace and poise."

"He said beautiful," Ariana said.

She was still cradling that to her heart, despite her sadness. Not handsome—beautiful. And perhaps he loved her—and even desired her despite his vow. Heavens, she had her tragic love!

She'd much rather not.

"Did he?" Lady Cawle said. "He's right, of course."

Ariana had to recollect the conversation. "He also told me about his wife."

"You didn't know?"

"I've never been interested in gossip."

"It was rather more than gossip, gel. He and Seraphina were a celebrated couple, celebrated for their looks, charm, and wealth. They were viewed as favored by the gods, which made such an end a particularly shocking tragedy."

"Like Princess Charlotte."

"Quite. If I'd had any expectation, I would have never urged him to return, but it seemed a reasonable excuse. His estates were being neglected, as was Phyllis. She was reaching an age where she needed her brother's attention."

"Seraphina? That sounds like a foreign name."

"Italian. She was the daughter of a musician. Not a suitable match, though in fact the family is of the Umbrian nobility. Very lovely, but also a truly kind and charming young lady. They shared a love of music. They would perform together. Their voices were perfectly matched."

Ariana suddenly had a thought. "Was she a little dark of complexion, with brown eyes?"

"Yes. Not unusual for Italy, though her hair was a

golden brown. I have a small portrait of her." Lady
Cawle rose and went to a drawer to take out a painting.
"I have others. After Seraphina's death, Kynaston took
her body to her family in Italy. I thought that on his
return he might destroy all remembrances of her, so I
gathered them to keep them safe. He didn't return at
all until I pressured him to."

She gave the painting to Ariana, and it was shock-
ingly similar to Cleo. Seraphina had worn her hair in a
more modern style, but soft brown curls clustered around
her forehead, and her large brown eyes were full of anticipation for the joys of life.

No wonder he'd been shocked to his core.

No wonder he'd resorted to brandy.

Ariana stood up and gave the portrait back to Lady
Cawle. "Your pardon, ma'am, but I must write a note
to Mr. Peake."

"Use my desk."

Ariana sat to do so. Cleo must be hidden away. She
must be preserved from the idly curious, but above all,
Kynaston must not confront that mummy case again.

Within half an hour she had a reply to say that the
mummy was now in a bedroom, which would of course
not be open to the public. That didn't solve the problem of what to do with Cleo in the long term. Perhaps
she'd buy the mummy and secrete it at Boxstall, where
it seemed she was destined to spend her days, unwed.

There was only one man she could marry, and even
if she could in some way force him to it, it could be a
cruel act.

As Ariana prepared for the visit to Peake's house, she
said to Ethel, "My Town career has hardly ever been

pleasant, has it? Terror of dancing, impossible suitors, performances for cruel stares. Why can't it be normal?"

"All things must pass," Ethel said, which wasn't one of her better efforts.

"Are you all right?" Ariana asked. "Has anyone been unpleasant to you over this?"

"They'd never dare," Ethel said, so dismissively that Ariana envied her. "I'm just thinking about a lot of things."

"Would it help to talk about your concerns? I've been wrapped up in my own affairs."

"With reason. Are you not going to marry Lord Kynaston, then?"

Ariana merely said, "It seems unlikely." She hadn't told Ethel about Kynaston's tragedy, and it seemed too intimate to share, even though to anyone accustomed to social news and gossip it was no secret at all. Lady Overstall's comment in the theater now made sense. She'd hoped he was recovering from his grief and resuming a normal life. The understanding over him selling the lease of his house had been because of the memories that lingered there, of Seraphina both at her happiest and at her death.

"Why not?" Ethel demanded. "I've asked around, and no one thinks he's bankrupt."

"Don't meddle. He doesn't want to marry me."

"I've seen the way he looks at you."

"Ethel, stop! It won't do and that's an end of it."

Seen in the mirror, Ethel's expression was mutinous.

"You're not to try to throw us together," Ariana said. "I simply want to survive tonight, and then we'll probably return to Boxstall."

She was wearing the dusky blue again, but with the gold jewelry for boldness. The evening was cold enough to warrant a fur-lined cloak that would cover everything. Just in case, and for those inside the house, she was wearing a black gauze fichu to fill in, or at least veil, most of the low neckline. Ethel was to attend her, in part because she'd been present at the crucial time, but also for support. She was wearing a gown made of red silk shot with black to excellent effect.

"That's handsome," Ariana said. "I haven't seen it before."

Ethel admired herself in the long mirror. "I had it made here, in case I needed anything grand."

Ariana felt slightly unsettled, as if Ethel was changing, but any unease was only part of her trepidation about tonight. "And now you do," she said cheerfully, "so you were very wise."

"A problem foreseen is half-avoided. Let's be off, then."

When Ariana emerged from the house with her mother, her brother, and Ethel, the coach was waiting. Some people still lurked, but Norris had hired guards to keep them at a distance and there was no shouting. Ariana did her best to look composed and confident, but was glad to be inside the coach and rolling on their way. She didn't lower the blinds. Let people see.

As the coach passed by avid eyes, she tensed in fear of thrown dirt, or even a stone. Earlier in the year someone had thrown a stone at the Regent's coach and broken a window. It seemed no one felt so angry at her, for they left the street unscathed.

Norris was scowling, however, so Ariana said, "Please try to stay calm. Yes, this is infuriating, but any anger will only make it worse."

"As long as that blackguard Churston doesn't turn up."

"Heavens, might he?"

"Only if he's a fool. Kynaston's let him know his part is exposed."

"What was his reaction?"

"To deny everything. Unless Inching will confront him with the accusation, there's nothing anyone can do. Short of a duel."

"No!" Lady Langton said.

"No," he agreed. "Don't see how a man could come up with a pretext for it without dragging Ariana's name down again. Kynaston's dead set against that."

"For which I'm grateful," Ariana said. "I'd celebrate to see Churston in the dust, but most of all, I want all this over."

He patted her hand. "After tonight, it will be, Sis."

Ariana didn't have such faith. What if the beau monde didn't take up Peake's invitation? He was a merchant and little known, and people might have already made up their minds.

Chapter 12

When the carriage turned into Burlington Street, it had to join a queue that was letting people out at Mr. Peake's door. A crowd had gathered, but they seemed mostly to be enjoying the spectacle rather than expressing any outrage. Then Ariana saw a small army of men holding them back.

Norris left the coach first and then handed down Ethel. Ariana heard a stir and a murmur but nothing extraordinary. Her mother left the coach next. Then it was her turn. The prime attraction. She was tempted to hunch, but she held her head high and kept a slight smile in place, grateful for Ethel at her side.

As they walked toward the door, she heard someone ask another, "Which one is it?"

"Blond, wasn't it?"

"Aye. But look at that. Two Amazons!"

"Was he dallying with both of 'em, do you think?"

The absurdity made Ariana smile more widely, which was probably as good a way as any to enter the house, especially as the modest entry hall was packed with people, and ahead the simple staircase held streams going up and down. Clearly the event was being seen as a rout, and some, having seen what they'd come to see, were already preparing to leave.

A Mrs. Pelman paused by Ariana and her mother to say, "I knew there was nothing in it, of course. But a very interesting collection of curiosities, even if some are a little risqué."

Ariana smiled and thanked her, but she wondered what Peake had dug out to put on display.

He worked his way through the crowd to greet Ariana. "The whole world seems to be here. I've scattered curiosities around the house to keep them amused."

"And even titillated?" she asked.

He winked. "Distraction."

Then Kynaston was at her side. "All well?"

Now that you're nearby. But Ariana agreed that it was, keeping her smile. He still looked ready to murder someone. She shed her cloak into Ethel's hands and decided to tease. "Someone outside speculated that you were frolicking in the cellar with Ethel as well as me. They didn't seem outraged."

"The tide's turning among the common people. Now they're simply enjoying the play. It's the sticklers in the ton we have to convince."

"Are they here?" Ariana couldn't see any of the fashionable lions.

"A few. They won't be in the first surge. As it is, there's a queue to go down into the cellars. Peake's unshrouded many items there, but it's otherwise much as it was."

He didn't mention the absence of Cleo.

"No sarcophagus?" she asked.

"Definitely not, and hardly space to move."

"Is your sister here?" Ariana asked.

"She wouldn't be kept away, but the Weathersteds didn't care for it, so I brought her. Ah, over there."

Being tall gave Ariana easy sight of Lady Phyllis with two other young ladies, now with Norris in attendance. Ariana glanced at Kynaston, but couldn't see if there was an additional layer of grimness. Soon she was going to have to push the matter of Norris and Phyllis. Someone should have a happy ending.

"We should probably move through the house," he said, reminding her of the matter in hand.

"But not looking like an amorous couple," she said.

"Definitely not. Mere acquaintances."

It hurt, but she smiled. Ariana turned to her mother, but saw her chatting cheerfully to a small group, so she moved on with Kynaston, Ethel rather awkwardly behind. They must make an impressively tall trio and impossible to miss. People continuously came to assure Ariana that they'd always known the cartoon to be a scurrilous lie, and she could comment that her companion, Miss Burgis, had been with her all the time.

Perhaps Ethel, with her stalwart build in fashionable dark red silk, was even more of a curiosity than Ariana. A few men even set up a conversation with her, to which she responded with composure. Ariana remembered Ethel indicating that she wouldn't mind marrying. May she have her chance.

Then Ariana remembered that this had once been Kynaston's home. His happy home with his lovely wife. She paused to ask, "Do you mind being here again?"

He looked around at the Oriental furniture and weapons, and the grotesque masks on the wall. "It's so different that any ghosts have fled."

"I'm glad." Perhaps in time the portraits of Seraphina that Lady Cawle had preserved would be valued.

They didn't go down into the cellars, but they stood for a while in the corridor nearby so that those emerging could give their shocked assurances.

"Not that there aren't some pieces down there which might incite others to unfortunate behavior," said Lord Liverpool.

"There are?" Ariana said, raising a brow at Kynaston.

"I thought it best not to mention them, Lady Ariana. They weren't uncovered when we went down there last week."

"For which you should be grateful," Liverpool said.

"Should I?" Ariana murmured, when the prime minister had moved on. "They sound educational."

"'Inciting' was the word. Behave."

"I'm giddy with relief. It's going to be all right, isn't it?"

"Probably. That couple over there—the Duke and Duchess of Belcraven. Quite a coup, and now they're joined by the Yeovils, and all apparently on good terms with Peake. I wonder how he managed that. They're going down to the cellars. With new images out tomorrow of such fashionable elites in the cellars—without the more scandalous pieces, we hope—the drawing of us will be seen to be a lie. Where next?"

"The library," Ariana said.

It held memories of him nursing his shock at seeing the mummy portrait, and any place reminiscent of him would always have importance to her, but she found it changed. The packing cases were gone and many of the shelves now held books. Ariana would have liked to explore, but instead must be seen and be assured again and again that no one had ever truly believed that picture.

A number of people were clustered around a table, so she led the way there. Some Oriental prints were on display beneath glass. They were almost a rebuke to the artist who'd produced that clumsy image of her and Kynaston. There was nothing lewd about them, for the men and women were in rooms and gardens and fully clothed in rich, brightly colored clothing. Yet something about the curves of their bodies, the angle of their heads, and the gestures of their pale hands spoke of desire. What they talked of and planned was probably crude, but at the moment they were simply beautiful.

"I would love to own such pictures," she murmured.

"I suspect they are high art and quite rare."

"Even so. Why do people choose crudeness over this?"

"Low tastes? We should move on, perhaps up to the drawing room?"

Ariana left the table reluctantly. She would return to look her fill, and she'd ask Peake where she might find something similar, but would that be wise? Already she was imagining being with Kynaston in a similar way, perhaps walking in a garden together, heads close, hands touching a sleeve or a shoulder.

How delicious . . .

The drawing room was almost as packed as the hall and the windows stood open to cool the air, but so many people, some not the cleanest, created a smell to rival the one she'd noticed on her first visit. How long ago that seemed, but it had been only a week.

She was plotting a course toward a window when she saw someone waving—a brown-haired lady with shining eyes at the side of a handsome dark-haired man.

Ariana sped in that direction. "Hermione! How do you come to be here?"

Lady Faringay seized her hands. "Uncle Edgar wrote

to me about the item in the paper—he's a great gossip—
and I convinced Faringay we must come to give you
support. We'd no idea it would become worse. Oh,
this is my husband. Faringay, my friend Lady Ariana
Boxstall. And you, I suspect, are the wicked Earl of
Kynaston."

She teased so charmingly that Kynaston smiled back.
"Only by reputation."

"Then you should have more care to your reputation, sir!" Hermione shot back.

"Especially given this unpleasant entanglement," Lord
Faringay said. He spoke pleasantly enough, but Ariana
caught an edge. Not another man feeling he should kill
someone for this, perhaps with Kynaston in mind.

"And all my fault," Ariana said with emphasis. "I was
so curious to see Mr. Peake's Egyptian treasures."

"But I alerted you to them," Hermione pointed out.

"Then I used the incident to deter a suitor, deliberately not mentioning that my companion was with us.
Oh," she said, looking around, "where is Ethel?"

"I think she stayed in the library," Kynaston said.
"I'm sure she can fend for herself."

Ariana supposed that was true, but she hoped Ethel
wasn't prey for unscrupulous men. It was odd to think
of her as vulnerable, but Ethel wasn't accustomed to
venturing into tonnish ways on her own.

"Where are you staying?" Ariana asked her friend.

"Here," Hermione said. "We could escape the heat
by going to our room."

"Alas," said Kynaston, "if Ariana and I disappear,
some will think the worst."

"Do you want to retire, my dear?" Faringay asked,
with concern.

"Don't fuss." Hermione rolled her eyes at Ariana.

"I'm increasing and he's hovering. Oh, don't you, too, start thinking about poor Princess Charlotte! That doesn't predict the fate of all women."

Lord Faringay obviously didn't share that opinion and Ariana hated to think how Kynaston was reacting.

"Should you be traveling?" she asked her friend.

"No," said Hermione's husband.

"Why not?" Hermione argued, and it clearly wasn't a new subject. "As our local midwife said, if a carriage ride could shift a babe in the early weeks, there'd be a lot fewer bastards in the world."

"Hermione!" Faringay protested.

"Isn't it true?" Hermione demanded, sending her husband a saucy glance. His lips twitched and it was easy to see the love and trust between them. That, of course, would make any loss all the harder to bear. Ariana turned to Kynaston to see how he was reacting to the topic. He was surveying the room as if he wished he were far away.

Ariana turned back to the Faringays. "Wise or not, I'm grateful to you for coming. Tomorrow Lady Cawle will be at home for morning visits to give yet more curious the chance to ogle me and decide if I'm wanton. If you're fit in the morning, perhaps I could visit you then."

"I haven't been sick at all as yet," Hermione said cheerfully, "so of course. We have much to catch up on. My family, your family. Your adventures."

She flashed a look at Kynaston, clearly implying he was an adventure destined to the altar. Ariana gave a little grimace to head that off. Hermione was capable of saying something direct and to the point.

"We should circulate a little more," she said. She linked arms with Kynaston and steered him away. "I'm sorry about that," she said quietly, "but one can't avoid all mention of childbearing."

"I know that."

"Perhaps in time . . ."

He halted them to look at her directly. "I've had three years, during which a host of women have given birth without disaster. However, none of them were put in danger by me, and none will be."

"Smile," Ariana said, following her own advice. "Or people will think we're in discord, and heaven knows what they'll make of that." Smiling, they approached the Esterhazys, who were happy to discuss the impossibility of enjoyable sin in Mr. Peake's cellars. They continued to move through the house, generally being greeted with assurances that the whole story was clearly a fabrication and wishes that the culprits could all be flogged.

An account of the popular event was already on its way to the principal newspapers, accompanied by an illustration of prominent people in the cellars. The newspapers wouldn't be able to use the illustration, but it would enforce the story. By the morning various prints would be posted in shopwindows, their appeal enhanced by the presence of notables, including ambassadors and dukes. Ariana couldn't imagine how Mr. Peake had enticed such big guns to his impromptu event, but then a very grand cannon arrived—Prince Frederick, the royal Duke of York.

He arrived with a modest entourage, but apparently he'd agreed ahead of time that he could be shown in an illustration, taking an interest in Peake's stores of exotic items—that was, the unlikely scene of the crime. He dutifully visited the cellars, and then went through the house, being amiable to all and showing what seemed to be a genuine interest in Peake's collection.

He paused by Ariana and Kynaston to commiserate with them at being the target of baseless malice. "In the royal family, one has to become accustomed, but it's beyond anything that ordinary people be a target for such malice." Ariana supposed an earl and an earl's daughter were very ordinary to a prince.

Peake drew them aside to his small private office, to give them the first proofs of tomorrow's prints to look over. He went away, leaving them alone.

"We'll stop them using that one," Kynaston said, pointing to one that showed him and Ariana against a display of spears. It definitely gave the impression that an announcement was to be expected.

"It's to show us fully dressed and decent," she said. "Anything in the cause."

His lips tightened, but he didn't protest further.

"The prince in the cellars will be popular," she said, "and the reproduction of the Egyptian mural. That should set the right scholarly tone."

"You're being relentlessly cheerful."

"What else am I to do?" she asked, even though her heart was aching. This evening had been the longest time they'd spent together, and now they were alone, but a shield stood between them, created by his will. He'd made himself absolutely clear. He would never put another woman in danger of childbirth, and thus he wouldn't marry.

She might argue for a celibate marriage, but she knew it wouldn't be possible. Even when they were in public and acting a decorous part, the fires had stirred. Now she hungered to insist upon a kiss. A kiss like the one they'd shared, but more so.

Leading to more.

Walks in gardens would never be enough. . . .

Perhaps he sensed her thoughts, or even felt the same temptation. "We should go," he said, and steered her out of the room. His touch on her arm sent shivers through her.

This was intolerable and so unfair! How could she change his mind? Perhaps Hermione would have some wisdom to offer.

She was startled when Norris tugged her aside. "You don't have to cling to him all night, do you?"

"I suppose not. What's the matter?"

"Phyllis says he's still adamantly opposed to her marrying."

They were in the busy entrance hall. "Norris, this is hardly the place to discuss it."

"I need to know. Do you think he'll change his mind?"

This truly wasn't the place, but he wouldn't be denied. "In all honesty, not soon. He has reasons."

"I can improve. I'll take perfect care of her."

"Not here. We can discuss it tomorrow and see if we can devise something. Did you see that Hermione Merryhew's here? Faringay now, of course."

"What do I care for that?" He almost ran a hand through his fashionably arranged hair but then collected himself. "Very well. Very well."

Ariana put a hand on his arm. "Truly I understand how strongly you must feel. But a short time of waiting won't be intolerable."

"You're the one who wanted me married by Christmas."

"I've learned a little patience."

He covered her hand with one of his. "You're the best sister a man could have."

It almost made her teary-eyed. "And you're the best brother. All will be well for you. I know it will."

He smiled briefly and hurried off. Back to Phyllis, who was standing quietly in a corner, waiting for him. She should seem like a wallflower, but it was more as if she were an island of good sense in the midst of giddiness. She'd help Norris be patient.

Ariana turned back to Kynaston—and found him not there. Not off with the brandy again!

She made her way through the crowd, keeping up a smile and exchanging light comments, until she saw him conversing normally with two gentlemen and a lady. She sagged with relief, and then realized that some time apart would help break the impression that they were devoted. They were supposed to be almost strangers portrayed in a casual moment. What was more, if he was on view, she could escape without any suspicion of an assignation.

She went in search of Hermione and found her still by the window in the drawing room, her husband devotedly at her side.

"I really don't like the heat," Hermione confessed.

"Perhaps we could slip away for a gossip."

"Go," said Faringay. "Anything that will get you out of this heat and crush."

Hermione smiled at him and kissed him on the cheek, then led Ariana out of the room by a back way to a set of stairs.

"Perhaps the greatest inconvenience of increasing," she said, going up, "is his fussing."

"You can't blame him."

"I can only hope the world will have regained sanity in seven months' time."

Hermione led the way to a bedroom and lit a candle

from the fire. As there was only one plain chair at the dressing table and another upholstered one by the fire, she scrambled up onto the high bed and patted the space beside her.

Ariana joined her, saying, "It must be ten years at least since we sat like this to share confidences."

"Is that what we're going to do? Lovely. I have missed your company."

"As I have missed yours, especially when you were in such straits and had to move north to live with your sister. You never rubbed along well with Polly. But now you're married, and so well! He seems an excellent specimen, and completely devoted."

Hermione rolled her eyes. "Sometimes too much so. But tell me all about Kynaston."

"That we're mere acquaintances?" Ariana tried.

"The truth."

Ariana leaned her head back, trying to sort through complex words, but simple ones would have to do. "I love him. It's a damnable inconvenience, because he's determined never to marry again."

"Again?"

Ariana looked at her friend. "So you didn't know, either. He thinks it strange that I didn't, but I've never been interested in society gossip."

"I, on the other hand, loved to read accounts of balls and assemblies, but I skipped over any births, marriages, and deaths. Except for the casualty lists." Hermione's younger brother had died in the war. "But if I'd happened to read of the death of the Countess of Kynaston, it would have meant nothing to me. Or you, I assume."

It would be so easy to agree. "I remembered him from my first season."

"The Great Disaster? I don't remember you mentioning him."

Ariana had never told anyone the embarrassing story, but she realized she couldn't now because it would show Kynaston in a poor light. "He was a young god," she said. "Gloriously handsome and charming."

"He's retained his looks, at least."

Ariana smiled wryly at the omission. "And he played the lute."

"That would make anyone memorable."

"Yes. He played a few days ago at an evening party we held. He's out of practice, but it was still special. For everyone, I mean."

"It matches well with your taste for the harpsichord. You do still play?"

"Yes."

"And you love him. Why won't he marry again? Grief?"

"In a way." It felt like talking of a personal secret, and yet the whole world knew. "His wife died in childbirth. He's determined never to put another woman at risk."

"Oh. I can imagine how terrible that must be, but . . . it's not practical, is it? The human race would come to an end."

"I don't think he's arguing it for everyone, though in the current mood others might join him."

"I very much doubt the whole nation has taken to celibacy," Hermione said drily. "There is rather an imperative about it."

Ariana knew what she meant, and for her it was only a half-sensed hunger. "Kynaston may have enough willpower to hold his course. The death of Princess Charlotte must have reinforced his intent. The wound is still very raw. Is there an unused bedroom here?"

"I believe so. At the back. Why? Are you planning to drag him there for a tryst? That might overcome his scruples. The imperative," she added as explanation. "I sensed a strong interest in him."

"You did?"

Ariana would have pursued that, but Hermione asked, "The unused bedroom?"

Best not to talk more about Kynaston's interests, and Hermione needed to understand the problems. Ariana wriggled off the bed. "I need to show you something."

They left the room, bearing the candle, and went to another door. Hermione opened it cautiously, but the room was empty and unused. The lack of fire made Ariana wish she were wearing a thick shawl. As soon as they stepped in, the candlelight illuminated Cleo.

"Oh, my," Hermione said, moving closer.

Ariana went as well. She hadn't anticipated the mummy's effect in a simple unused room with nothing to prevent anyone from approaching and even touching.

"Be careful with the candle. The portrait uses a wax base, I understand, and it might be damaged."

"She's lovely," Hermione whispered.

"And very like Kynaston's dead wife."

"She was Egyptian?"

"I don't think these portraits were of Egyptians, or not entirely. The ones we know of come from the time of Roman rule in Egypt. Seraphina was Italian."

"Seraphina?"

"Kynaston's wife. I'm told they were a magical couple, seeming to be blessed by the gods." Ariana took a step closer and put her hand on the mummy's shoulder. She found only a cool, dry, rough surface. Cleo's expression seemed to ask, *What did you expect?*

"I think I'm going mad," she said.

Instead of protesting, Hermione said, "Love will do that. He can't mourn forever."

"People do, but even if grief passes, his resolve will not. I thought of a celibate marriage, but I doubt it could work."

"So do I."

"And as he said, what point in him marrying other than to get an heir?"

"Companionship," Hermione said. "I would be very unhappy never to couple with my husband again, but I'd be even unhappier to be without his company and precious friendship."

Cleo seemed to be listening with rapt attention. Had she loved? Had she married, borne children? Perhaps even died in the attempt.

"We've hardly spent enough time together to discover companionship," Ariana said. "And nearly every encounter has been fraught and difficult. I should return to the company." She made herself turn and leave the room.

Hermione came with her, but at the door said, "Faringay and I spent time once—stolen, illicit time in a nighttime room—talking. In the end we kissed, and other things—though not what you're thinking! But that time of talking was a precious jewel. We do it often now, of course, but courting couples should do it."

"I should sneak into his bedroom?" Ariana asked, amused. "We don't even live under the same roof anymore."

"Neither did we," Hermione said, joining her in the corridor and closing the door. "I think I'll remain up here, if you'll let Faringay know. Do you want the candle to go down?"

"I can manage. Thank you for this. Perhaps tomorrow you can come to our house for a while."

"Certainly, and don't give up hope. Faringay changed for me, and I for him. That, too, is the way of love."

Ariana went downstairs with the aid of light at the bottom, and reentered the drawing room to the sound of a discordant twanging instrument. Kynaston was playing again, but on something ancient and odd. He was grimacing, in an amused way. "I have no idea how it's supposed to sound."

Peake said, "Much like that, my lord."

"Then heaven help us."

The company chuckled. The lighthearted atmosphere was like entering a faery glade.

The day had been so dire, and Ariana had come here fearfully. Upstairs, Cleo had reminded her of Kynaston's grief and her tragic love for him. It was almost an affront to find him here, lightheartedly playing with music.

Then others joined in. A display of unusual instruments lay on a table and another man picked up a wooden instrument that resembled a recorder. He tried a tune on it and then settled into a version of "Bobby Shafto." A lady hurried to choose a small drum and beat the time.

Entering a faery glade was said to be dangerous, but Ariana went to the front of the room and picked up some small bells to tinkle them in time with the others. Kynaston glanced up at her, eyes bright with amusement as if welcoming her to magical insanity.

The world tilted.

She'd said she loved him, but this was of a different order. Instinctively she grinned back in a way that she hoped implied fun in the moment and nothing more.

She even shared a smiling glance with the gentleman playing the wind instrument. But her mind, heart, and soul were with Kynaston.

Forever.

She'd loved him fiercely, but out of pity, with a desire to mend and remake. Here was a man she could love as he was—the man she'd idolized in her callow youth, alive here, now, today.

All magic must fade. In time he ceased playing, and laughingly turned away demands that he continue. He replaced the instrument on the table, saying something about it needing a lifetime of practice. The woodwind man began a new tune and others picked up instruments to join in. Ariana gave one lady her bells and went to Kynaston.

"All seems well," he said, still softened by the ghost of merriment. "Most of the guests have left, convinced of your innocence. Our job is done."

And that's the end of us, she heard. She could sense even now that he did care for her, and she could imagine how hard that would make continued meetings. She'd endure them if she was allowed, but she'd spare him the pain.

As if to hammer home the point, he added, "I'm told repeatedly that my estates need my care. I'll be returning there tomorrow and taking Phyllis with me."

Ariana tried to match him, step for step. "I suspect we'll return to Boxstall."

"You'll cease your husband hunt?"

"For now."

"You'll find a suitable partner in time," he said, and it fell like a blow.

She managed a smile. "I'm sure I will. But then, Norris may wed."

They both knew it could only be to Phyllis, and Kynaston couldn't like that.

"We should thank Peake," Ariana said.

They crossed the room to the old gentleman, who beamed at them. "Not at all, not at all! I regret your distress, Lady Ariana, but it's given me the opportunity to make quite a splash, especially with pieces in the papers tomorrow listing all the grandees who passed through. It was never my desire to be an *obscure* eccentric."

She chuckled. "You'll certainly not be that now, sir." She needed to speak with him about Cleo, for something must be arranged, but not now.

Not with Kynaston at her side, perhaps for the last time. What if she somehow tempted him up to that unused bedroom and faced him with the mummy? That could only lead to sorrow and discord. But it was a bedroom. . . .

"I must find my brother and mother," she said, and set off in search.

It was the end.

Chapter 13

Neither her brother nor her mother was in the drawing room, so they went downstairs. Because she couldn't ignore the subject forever, she added, "My brother is probably with your sister."

"I hope they haven't been in one another's pockets all evening."

"And if they have?"

"It's as well she's returning home with me tomorrow."

Ariana paused at the bottom of the stairs. The people around were taking farewells, finding coats and cloaks with the help of servants, and waiting for carriages. All the same, some came over to assure her of their disbelief and best wishes, and she had to respond appropriately. When she had the chance, she led the way into the small library.

"There's no one here," Kynaston said, turning to leave.

"Wait."

He did so, warily.

"My brother and your sister are truly in love," she said.

Jo Beverley

"They hardly know one another."

"How long did it take for you to know you loved Seraphina?"

He flinched. "We won't speak of her."

She wouldn't give way. "Not long, I suspect. The daughter of an Italian musician? Not the most suitable match for an earl."

"Don't, Ariana."

"I merely ask that you remember the truth of love. Would your devotion have melted away if she'd returned to Italy?"

"I can't possibly know. I won't forbid Phyllis to marry. I might want to do so, but I'm not so unbalanced as that. But not yet. She's *seventeen*! It won't hurt either of them to wait. It's your obsession with the inheritance that drives you. You want her in childbed within nine months, and I won't permit that."

That truth sent heat into Ariana's cheeks, but she said, "For the most part, I want them happy. Are you prepared for years of unhappiness as they wait?" *Will you be unhappy away from me, as I will be unhappy to be apart?* She dare not ask, for the true answer might be that he'd find separation a blessed relief.

"Let's find them," he said, and left the room.

Ariana sighed and followed, to see him being given a note by a maid. She hurried to his side. "Who is that from?"

"Phyllis," he said. "She developed a headache and Langton offered to escort her back to the Weathersteds'."

"How odd."

"Isn't it? She says she couldn't ask me, as it was important that I be here."

"But to go off with Norris . . ."

"They took a chaperone," he said.

"Mrs. Manners?"

"She's not here. Your companion, Miss Burgis."

"Ethel! Even odder, but she'll make sure your sister is safe."

"Safe from your brother?"

"Safe from folly of any sort. So, where *is* my mother?"

There was only one public room uninvestigated, so Ariana crossed to the small reception room. Her mother was there, with the Hatchards and two gentlemen Ariana didn't know, all in good spirits. Ariana hadn't seen her mother so relaxed and happy since before her father had died, and she backed away. "I dislike asking her to leave."

"Then why don't we follow precedent?" Kynaston said. "You can write her a note to explain, and I can escort you home." Ariana very much liked the sound of that, until he added, "With one of Peake's maids for propriety."

"Very well. It may lead to my mother being escorted home by one of the gentlemen. And perhaps, being of advanced years, they won't feel the need of a chaperone."

It came out tartly and she didn't mind. She was feeling positively sour. She returned to the library and found paper and pen in the desk there. She wrote the note and then gave it to a footman to be handed to Lady Langton when she emerged from the room.

Soon she was on her way in a hackney with Kynaston beside her, but a middle-aged maid opposite. The woman seemed to be enjoying time away from her duties and she obligingly looked outside all the way. Ariana and Kynaston could have held hands, shared meaningful looks, and even kissed. But they sat straight, looking forward, and kept silent.

What was there to say other than piteous arguments from her that they surrender to love? Ariana was grateful to be saved from that indignity.

Chapter 14

At the house he climbed out first and handed her down; then he went with her to the door. She didn't have a key, so she used the knocker.

"I'll be perfectly safe now," she said, wanting this painful time over.

He simply waited, and then the footman was opening the door. But he looked behind her. "The countess isn't with you, milady?"

"No. Is there some problem?"

"A note came from Lord Langton, milady, to be given to Lady Langton on her return."

Norris wasn't home? He could have gone on to a club or various other amusements, but an unease crept through Ariana. She went into the house and said, "Give it to me."

The door closed behind her, but Kynaston was at her side. "I'm sure it's nothing," she said to him, and turned to take the note. She broke the seal and opened the paper.

After a moment she said to Kynaston, "Come into the library."

He gave her that distressingly wary look, but then he told the footman to tell the hackney driver and the maid to wait a few moments, and went with her.

She gave him the note and the shocking news. "My brother and your sister have eloped."

"*What?*" A rapid read told him all that she knew. "With your companion as gooseberry? Did you have any part in this?"

"No!"

"You are in urgency to have your brother married."

"Not like this. And with your sister so young, it's outrageous!"

"I'm glad you agree on that at least. They can't be more than two hours on the way. I'll overtake them." He'd crushed the paper in his fist.

Ariana ran to be between him and the door. "If that letter tells the truth, this is your fault, not his! Dragging your sister off to a ramshackle house and forbidding her all communication!"

"Delacorte is *not* ramshackle. It's Phyllis's home and she's too young for London, as has become clear. As for communication, I merely banned it for three months. That wouldn't have killed them."

"Clearly you don't remember love."

"I remember the insanity of it. There's a purpose to chaperones, though I doubt your Miss Burgis will serve the purpose." He stalked toward her. "Move."

Ariana was instantly reminded of that time in his bedroom, when she'd commanded him out of her way, but she didn't budge. "No. I won't let you kill my brother."

"I won't kill him, but you won't delay me to help his devilish plans."

"I must come with you."

"Don't be ridiculous."

"You say you won't kill my brother, but what if he resists? Why shouldn't he?"

"Phyllis will do as she's told."

"Will she?" Ariana met his eyes. "I don't think you know her at all, Kynaston. But then, you've neglected her for so many years."

"You harridan."

"Truth stings, doesn't it? I'll come with you."

"And be compromised? Oh, no."

Heat flared in Ariana's cheeks. "I never thought of such a thing. I assume you'll use an open carriage for speed."

"Yes, and thus you'll be frozen."

"Tender blossoms don't have big feet."

He was distracted by puzzlement, but only for a moment. "You're not coming. And that is absolute."

"Then I'll follow on my own. I can drive."

"You wouldn't."

She let silence speak. She didn't at all relish driving at speed in icy weather, but she tried not to let that show. "Well?" she asked, sensing victory.

He seemed to become aware of the crushed note and turned to hurl it into the fire. "I know where I can borrow a curricle and a fast team."

"A curricle!" That was a flimsy sporting vehicle and dangerous, but it was built for speed.

"Changed your mind?" he asked.

"Never!"

"I'll return here. I suggest you dress warmly."

"If you're not back in a half hour, I set off on my own."

His jaw was working, and when he strode by her and out of the house, she could only hope he believed her. Damn Norris for this stupidity! But then, Kynaston had given the lovers little choice.

Why had Ethel not come to warn her instead of abetting him in his folly?

She summoned her mother's maid and ran up to her room to shed finery and put on a sturdy woolen gown over an extra flannel petticoat. She exchanged silk stockings for worsted and slippers for leather half boots. A simple hat, her hooded fur-lined cloak, gloves and a muff, and she was ready in twenty minutes.

She hurried downstairs and wrote an explanation for her mother, who would think both her children had run mad. She sealed it thoroughly and left it with the curious footman. As there was no good explanation to provide, she didn't attempt it.

She watched the ticking longcase clock and Kynaston didn't come.

Had he not believed her? Norris had a curricle and team stabled near there. She was going to have to pursue alone, but she deeply didn't want to. She'd only ever tooled the sporting vehicle around the estate at Boxstall. She could do it if she must, and she must prevent bloodshed. Norris wouldn't meekly turn back, and he'd be armed. Someone could get killed—her brother or the man she loved. She couldn't stand by and do nothing!

But then the knocker was used—with some violence. When the door opened, Kynaston was there, glowering. There was no other way to describe it.

Chapter 15

Ariana managed to suppress a victorious smile as she hurried out to the curricle, drawn by a pair of matched blacks. A groom was at the horses' heads, but once Ariana and Kynaston were in place and Kynaston had the horses under his command, the man stepped back. Some curricles had a seat for a groom at the back, but this did not, and in any case, Kynaston wouldn't want the extra weight.

The horses were given leave to go, and Ariana was reassured by the horses' even pace and Kynaston's sure hands on the reins, but as yet they couldn't travel at speed. They were weaving their way through Mayfair, and despite mourning, the ton was traveling from one entertainment to another. Hackneys and fine carriages, and even a few sedan chairs, went hither and thither. Yet even at a modest pace the wind of their travel combined with the cold night air to be sharply unpleasant.

Ariana raised her fur-lined hood. "Do we know which route they've taken?"

"They'll be heading north."

She suppressed irritation. North was the direction of Gretna. "There are various routes that lead to the Great North Road."

He steered neatly around a coach. "I assume they've taken the fastest one, but they can only have about two hours on us. We'll catch them."

Ariana no longer knew what to wish for. No one could want the scandal of a clandestine marriage, but it could be the only choice for Norris and Phyllis short of waiting for years. If her brother had been enamored of a girl like Cessy Weathersted, she'd believe it a passing thing. But Phyllis Delacorte? It had to be true love.

Lady Phyllis herself was no flibbertigibbet. If she'd consented to this, it would be only after careful thought. It had probably been she who'd insisted on a chaperone, and Kynaston had driven her to the scandalous course. He was unbalanced on the subjects of marriage and birth.

He had his emotions under control now and was keeping the spirited horses to a steady pace. But then they escaped the boundaries of London, and even though they'd also escaped the traces of street lighting, he gave the team their heads. Ariana clutched the side of the flimsy seat. Her purpose here was to prevent bloodshed, and that included her own!

She couldn't protest the speed through the dark. She'd insisted on coming.

There was little traffic on the toll road this late at night, but a half-moon showed the way and the carriage lamps added a little detail. She hoped it was true that horses could see better in the dark than humans. When they paused at the next tollbooth, having to wait as the keeper hurried out half-dressed, she said, "We could ask if he's seen them pass."

Without waiting for Kynaston's opinion, she called to the gatekeeper. "We're following my aunt and cousins—a young gentleman and an even younger lady. Have they passed by?"

"There was a carriage a while back, ma'am. Four horses and postilions. Gentleman looked a lot like you." He began to slowly open the gate.

"How long ago?" Kynaston demanded.

"At least an hour, sir. Likely more. I could check my record book."

"No matter," Kynaston said, and gave the order to the horses to hurtle through.

So they were on their trail.

"Postilions," Ariana noted.

"Frequent changes," he agreed.

"We'll have to change horses eventually, and we're unlikely to get such fine ones."

"I know."

He was irritated by her stating the obvious, and she was annoyed at herself for doing so.

Over the next hour or so, they encountered a variety of coaches heading into London, but at their speed, nothing overtook them in a northerly direction.

Would Norris be planning to travel through the night? Probably, and there he had the advantage over the curricle. Even if Ariana took the ribbons for a while, they couldn't drive through the night and the horses certainly couldn't go that long. If they didn't catch up within a couple of hours, all would be lost.

Or won.

Ariana had nothing to do but endure the journey, which gave too much time to think. This was hardly a romantic situation, but she couldn't help but be aware of Kynaston's presence at her side. His skillful handling of the team only added to her admiration. Which was good fuel for love.

Why couldn't they also be en route for Gretna Green and marriage?

His dread of another dead wife approached insanity.

Yet, apart from his drunkenness on those few occasions, it seemed he lived a normal life. She'd encountered him out riding, and the excellent way he drove meant he must do so now and then. And, she realized, must have done so when abroad.

Where had he traveled, and what had he done then? Caroused, she'd assumed. Wine and wenches. But if he was resolved never again to get a woman with child, didn't that mean celibacy?

Swaying and bouncing, nose icy from the wind, she reassessed what she knew of the Earl of Kynaston. It was only ten days since she'd reencountered him in the Albemarle Street library, and that had been only a week after the funeral of Princess Charlotte.

The funeral had taken place two weeks after her death, so Kynaston would have been suffering from three weeks of grief and gloom over the death of a lovely young wife in childbirth. Even in the countryside no one had spoken of much else. It must have been more intense in London. Perhaps he'd begun to pull himself together, when he'd been confronted by Cleo. Later that night she'd been afraid that he might kill himself.

He was better now. His focus now was the need to protect his sister, but he seemed steady, more solid than when she'd first met him. His merry musical play earlier had been evidence of that. And had made her love him more.

Had she once wished for a tragic love? She could

marry none but him, and he would marry none. Perhaps she should enter a nunnery!

She turned her mind from the hopeless to the possible. "When we catch them," she called, "wouldn't the wisest thing be to allow them to court in the usual manner?"

"You'd be content with that?" he asked, not taking any attention off his driving. "A courtship of a year or more?"

"Perhaps, but would they be? Love burns fiercely."

"And sometimes burns out. Whatever the truth of that, I won't have Phyllis sacrificed to your family's needs."

"There's no reason to believe that she'll die from it!"

The horses broke step, perhaps from a rough hand on the ribbons. He instantly calmed them and perhaps himself, but he said, "Enough of this."

It was steely enough to silence Ariana. Therefore she turned her mind to other matters.

Clearly the elopement must succeed. Love must have its way.

Chapter 16

They hurtled by fine coaching inns, but eventually he had to pull into one to change horses. The swinging sign announced it to be the Old Boar, and it seemed a large and prosperous place.

"It'll take a while to choose a pair that can work together," he said. "Go into the inn for some warmth."

"You won't try to go on without me?"

"I'd not abandon you here, Ariana. Order some mulled wine or punch."

She supposed he couldn't strand her there, so she hurried into the warmth of the inn and gave the order. It wasn't worth hiring a private parlor for a short while, so she sat by the fireside in the public room, ignoring the few people around. It was gone ten o'clock and the place was quiet. No one ate at the long common table, and the few people sitting close to the casks of ale were probably local.

Staring into the large log fire, she considered how to delay their pursuit.

Already there was hope. He'd said it would take time to find a good replacement pair of horses, but it could be impossible. A curricle used a single pole and two horses harnessed abreast. The vehicle itself wasn't notably expensive. It was the difficulty of finding a perfectly matched pair to pull it that made it a toy for the rich. Quite likely this inn couldn't provide two horses of similar size with an identical pace. To try to go on without would mean at best slow travel, and at worst a rapid tangle and overturn.

The bowl of hot punch came, along with two medium-sized glass tankards. Ariana filled one and cradled it in her hands as she sipped, contentedly waiting for Kynaston to join her and admit defeat.

He arrived and poured himself punch. "Your brother changed horses here not that long ago. We're gaining on them, so we can't dally." The implication was obvious.

"You found a suitable pair?"

"They'll do. A chestnut and a gray, so hardly for Hyde Park display, but they're of a size and pace. Drink up. We should be on our way."

"Let's warm up a little first," Ariana said, and sipped more of the hot drink.

"I warned you this journey would be cold. I could arrange for you to stay here."

"No. I'll be fine."

They sipped in silence, but Ariana was thinking desperately. The elopement must succeed, but if the new horses were as good as he implied, they would catch the fugitives in the next couple of hours. She wished he were getting drunk, but he seemed likely to drink only one tankard-full, and it wasn't very potent.

The conclusion was as obvious as it was unpleasant. She must do something to damage the curricle. It would

infuriate Kynaston, but it would be for the good of all
in the end. Someone must be able to enjoy love! She
asked the innkeeper for the use of a private room,
which was interpreted as the need to relieve herself
without a trip to an outhouse. Kynaston could hardly
object to that delay.

A maid took her upstairs to an unused bedroom,
which had a closestool. The room was perfect. It had
an extra door to the gallery around the innyard, and
down in the innyard Ariana saw the curricle, pole down.
As soon as she was left alone, Ariana pulled up the hood
of her gray cloak and slipped out through the door onto
the gallery, and down the stairs.

Fortunately, no vehicle was coming or going at that
moment, so the yard was deserted. From voices, she
guessed that the ostlers had sensibly taken themselves
indoors for warmth. The door to their room stood ajar
so they'd be aware of any arrival, and she glimpsed a
large fire in there. With that brightness, it must have
seemed pitch-dark out there. Shrouded in dark gray,
she must have been close to invisible.

She moved toward the back of the yard, where the
curricle waited, which took her close to the stables. A
lamp in there showed her two horses—a chestnut and
a gray—standing ready, harnessed but wearing blan-
kets. Only one ostler minded the two. She could try
to injure one of the horses, but she couldn't see how
and she wasn't sure she could bear to do such a thing.
That meant the curricle, and time was passing. Delicacy
would mean she'd be uninterrupted for a while, but not
forever.

The obvious course was to cut the reins, and she had
her small sewing kit in her pocket. The needlework
scissors would do the job, though slowly. However, it

was likely that the inn had replacements, so it would only mean a delay. The spokes of the two large wheels were thin, for everything about a curricle was designed to reduce weight. Even so, how could she break one, especially undetected?

Perhaps it wouldn't matter if she was detected. Kynaston would be furious, but if he turned against her forever, she'd be in no worse state. He wouldn't be able to summon a new wheel in an instant. Even if a wheelwright was willing to work this late, it could take hours.

Yes, she must do that.

She worked her way around to the back of the curricle, where she'd be even less likely to be observed, looking around for some means of breaking a spoke. A hammer would do, or even a large stone. She found neither, but she did see a long metal rod propped in a corner. She grasped it, and only then realized what it was.

It was the curricle bar. Once the horses were in their harnesses, it would be slid into place through rings on the top of each horse's harness and fixed in place in order to keep the horses the correct distance apart. Without it, the horses could bump into the pole or each other, risking injury and chaos.

It would be insane to try to travel without the bar.

It was quite heavy and as tall as her shoulder, but she could hold it against her body, inside her cloak. With her prize, she worked her way toward the arch into the street. She'd discard it out there and it wouldn't be found until morning.

Then, with a blast of a horn, a laden stagecoach began to turn into the innyard.

Ariana backed out of the way, encumbered by the

pole. As the ostlers poured out of their room and servants hurried out of the inn, she awkwardly edged toward the stairs and climbed back up to her room-of-ease.

At the door, she looked down over the gallery railing and saw that the coach had come to rest directly beneath her. The horses were being unharnessed and new ones made ready. The passengers were pouring into the inn in search of food and warmth, but they wouldn't be given long. The poor passengers who'd been traveling on top had probably been the first in, for there was no one up there now. A great many bags and boxes were tied at the back of the huge vehicle. No one seemed to be watching. She extricated the bar and moved it over the railing, and then she dropped it vertically into a space between two wooden chests. It fell with a clunk, but no one raised an alarm.

Content with her work, she hurried back into the room, used the chamber pot, and left to return to the public room and Kynaston. He would be fuming at the time she'd taken, but he could hardly berate her for such an intimate matter.

It turned out to be exactly so. As soon as he saw her, he rose, ready to pay their bill, but he couldn't grab the attention of any of the inn servants, who were all busy with the new arrivals. "Just a moment, sir, if you please!"

They were all attending to the urgent needs of the coach passengers, who now filled both sides of the long table. Some servants carried huge trays of bowls of steaming soup, while others put cut loaves down along the table, accompanied by dishes of butter and cheeses and ham slices. Hungry hands grabbed, and some slurped their soup too quickly, then cursed the burn. The soup smelled delicious and Ariana was thinking that if they had to wait, they could eat, but then a slurred voice said, "Well, well, well. What have we here?"

She turned to find her uncle Paul Boxstall leaning in the doorway, as if further progress was beyond him. He was clearly deep in drink.

She had to say something, especially as a few of the coach passengers were paying attention. "On a journey, Uncle?"

"Repairing lease to Derbyshire. Damned cold."

"It is, yes." She'd rather have him flat drunk than saying something to embarrass them, so she added, "The punch in that bowl is still warm. Have some."

He collapsed into the seat she'd vacated and scooped some into her tankard. After a long drink, he snorted. "Ant's piss. Needs more brandy. More brandy!" he yelled to the innkeeper.

Kynaston put an arm around Ariana to urge her out of the room. "Leave him be. We need to be off."

"Oh-oh!" Paul cried. "What have we here? An elopement?" Now he had the attention of the whole room.

"Of course not," Ariana said. Hastily, she invented, "We're on our way to a deathbed."

"Whose?"

"Great-aunt Maud."

"The old bag's finally shuffling off? Wonder if there's any money in it."

"Very unlikely. I must be on my way."

"With Kynaston? Almost as wretched as me, and merely over a woman."

Kynaston's arm went rigid. "Let him be," he muttered. "We need to leave."

"Aye, go, go! I'll not stand in the way of a wicked bedding!" Someone sniggered, and he took encouragement. "Note, my friends, that noble birth doesn't lead to noble behavior. The most noble Earl of Kynaston and my niece. Perhaps all those salty rumors were true after all!"

Ariana would have launched into a defense, but Kynaston forced her out of the room. "Anything you say will only fix the matter in their minds."

Once out of sight, she protested, "But some will remember and spread the word. It'll all start up again, and now with more cause. This is my fault. I insisted on coming."

"I can't dispute that."

"You could try."

"I can dispute the first part. Some may remember me, but he didn't name you. They'll not know who he is or who his niece is."

"He could be telling them all now."

"They're too busy eating, but . . . ah, innkeeper!"

The sinewy man was hurrying out of the public room, perhaps fearing they'd leave without paying. "My deepest apologies, my lord! Here's your accounting."

Kynaston glanced at the paper and paid, adding extra. "The man now drinking the last of our punch— give him as much brandy as he wants."

The innkeeper hesitated. "Beggin' your pardon, my lord, but he has the look of one who shouldn't drink any more."

"All the same."

"As you say, my lord."

He hurried back into the public room, leaving them again alone in the hall. Ariana said, "I suspect Uncle Paul can drink a great deal and still spew vileness."

"We do what we can. Let's be on our way. At the least we can prove later that we haven't spent the night here."

Except that they weren't going to be able to be on

their way. Again she'd created a problem. Would they end up compromised into marriage after all?

But then Norris and Phyllis entered the hall from the back. They stopped to stare, and Ariana became newly aware of Kynaston's arm around her. She pulled free.

"What the devil . . . ?" Kynaston demanded.

"Private parlor," Norris said tersely with a gesture to Kynaston to lower his voice. He was right. Kynaston's loud exclamation could have been heard by the interested crowd in the public room.

The innkeeper dashed out again, clearly worried about new trouble. Norris repeated his words, this time as a command. The innkeeper flung open a door to a large room across the hall, which already had a fire in the hearth, ready for anyone wealthy enough to want a private parlor. Or even a bedroom. A large oak bed took up half the room, but it left space for a dining table against a window, with four chairs attending. Two oaken settles bracketed the large fireplace.

"Refreshments, ladies and gentlemen?" the innkeeper asked.

"No," Kynaston said. "Leave us."

Reluctantly, the man obeyed, closing the door as he went. Kynaston and Norris were already facing off like two fighting dogs.

"I'll have your guts," Kynaston growled.

"It's you who deserves to be gutted."

". . . never see her again."

". . . see reason!"

Phyllis sat on one settle, close to the fire, and observed them as at a play.

Ariana sat opposite her. "What are you doing here?"

"Trying to be sensible." The girl rolled her eyes at the men.

Ariana focused on them. *"Stop!"*

They both looked at her in shock.

She didn't feel quite able to command Kynaston, so she pointed at the opposite settle and said, "Sit down, Norris, and let's all talk."

Her brother flung himself down at Phyllis's side, taking her hand.

Kynaston remained standing. "So you've seen the error of your ways?" he said to his sister.

"About Gretna only," she replied, meeting his eyes without a flinch. "I don't want a clandestine marriage."

"You'll have none other. I'll never give my consent."

"Then we might as well set off again."

"You won't leave this room."

"You won't stop her!" Norris exploded.

"Oh, won't I?"

Ariana spoke into a growling silence. "Where's Ethel?"

"What the devil does that matter?" Kynaston snapped at her.

"Don't swear at my sister!" Norris yelled, on his feet now.

"This sister is *losing her damned patience*!" Ariana shouted, shooting to her feet to go nose to nose with her brother. *"Where's Ethel?"*

"She abandoned us!"

"She didn't want to come back with us," Phyllis said quietly.

Ariana sat again and focused on the girl. "Phyllis, please tell me the tale. You seem to still have your wits."

"Wits enough not to try to outshout the men," the girl observed.

"Are you attacking me now?" Ariana asked.

"No, I'm sorry."

"Why did you turn back?"

Phyllis looked up at her brother with a concerned frown. "I came to see that Titus would be hurt by my elopement. And that he needed to see sense."

Titus. Ariana hadn't known his given name. A Roman emperor, rather than a god.

"I see sense perfectly," her brother said, trying to match her calm tone. "You're too young to know your mind."

Phyllis met his eyes. "We'll wait a year, then. No longer."

"You don't get to set the terms."

"Why not? If you don't promise your consent within a year, we elope again."

"I should beat you."

"Blaggard!" Norris protested, moving to stand between them.

"He won't," Ariana said.

"I won't," Kynaston agreed. "You remind me of your mother, Phyllis. Beneath her light spirits, she was all quiet steel. Yet she was unwise. She abandoned you."

"Not unwise," Phyllis said. "Norris, move out of the way, if you please." When he'd done so and sat back down beside her, she continued. "You know how young my mother was when she was widowed. She had her life ahead of her and a man she loved. She's still happily married to Thorpe. And," she added, with quiet emphasis, "the healthy mother of six other children."

Kynaston ignored that. "You've been in touch with her?" He seemed dumbfounded.

"She is my mother."

"She abandoned you in your cradle," he protested, "and was forbidden to ever make contact with you."

"*I* found *her*," Phyllis said. "Note what I said about her six children."

"My mother died trying to give birth the second time," Kynaston retorted.

Phyllis seemed completely undisturbed. "I'm more likely to take after my mother, don't you think? She was only eighteen when she bore me. Titus, I understand your distress. Seraphina was a lovely person and very kind to me, but I won't let her death make a nun of me."

Norris was looking at Phyllis with mute adoration, but Kynaston probably wanted to throttle her. All the same, her quiet reason was irrefutable.

"A year, then," he said, as if every word hurt. "If you're still of the same mind by this date next year, you may marry."

Phyllis rose, smiling. Her smile wasn't triumphant or gleeful, but gently loving. "Thank you. In the church at Delacorte, in all good order. May I hope you will already be married, brother?"

"No."

Her expression promised that she intended to change his mind.

"Do you want to stay here?" Norris asked Phyllis.

"I'd rather return to Town, but perhaps I can stay in your house? Your mother is there, after all. I truly can't endure much more of Cessy and her parents."

"Of course," Norris said. He'd have given her the moon and stars if she'd asked for them.

All was as it should be, but Ariana asked, "So, what's happened to Ethel?"

"Oh." For once, Phyllis seemed wordless, and Norris grimaced.

"Never say you abandoned her," Ariana protested. "I know she can be annoying at times, but . . ."

"Of course not!" Norris protested. "When we halted

and decided to turn back, she declared that she'd carry on north."

"Why? She knows no one in the north."

Phyllis answered, "To marry a Lord Inching."

"Inching!" Ariana's exclamation matched Kynaston's.

"Apparently he proposed to her, but she said she couldn't leave you. But when I asked her to accompany us north, she decided to seize the moment."

"'God helps those who help themselves,'" Norris said, clearly quoting. "'Adversity makes strange bedfellows.' You know what she's like."

"But that sounds as if she doesn't want to do it," Ariana said.

"The 'strange bedfellows' was us and the elopement, I think," her brother said, "though 'Better to light a candle than curse the darkness' had me foxed."

"She wants to be married," Ariana said. "She's said as much recently, but we've made her a creature of two worlds. She couldn't marry in a Burgis way, but what gentleman would take her, with her background and her height and build?"

"Except Inching," Kynaston said, even with a bit of a laugh. "They might do well enough. She's a strong, resolute woman, and he'll adore her. He'll probably be happy to stay in Cumberland now he has an Amazon of his own."

"I don't get to thrash him?" Norris asked. "For what he did to Ariana?"

"Let sleeping dogs lie, love," Phyllis said, which made him groan, in a totally besotted way. When she added, "We should leave," he agreed.

He looked at Ariana. "Do you want to travel back with us, Sis?"

The carriage would be more comfortable, but they clearly needed to be alone together, as lovers do.

As lovers do.

Her love was hopeless, and once they returned to Town, she might never see Kynaston again. She could have this little time.

"I'll return with Kynaston," Ariana said. "We'll not be far behind."

She'd truly forgotten until that moment that she'd stolen the curricle bar.

Chapter 17

Outside, the horn was blowing and in the inn hall someone was yelling that the Derby coach was about to leave. "All aboard!"

There was still time. Time to confess her crime and for the bar to be retrieved. She said nothing. She wanted to be with Kynaston as much as Norris wanted to be with Phyllis, and this could be her last opportunity.

When the door closed, he looked at her. "You should have gone with them."

"And played gooseberry?"

"I'm very much in favor of gooseberries."

"I think your sister has proven you can trust her to be sensible." She returned to her seat on the settle, which put her closer to him. "In any case, thank you."

"For allowing your brother to put my sister at risk? What of your urgency? He could kill himself in the hunting season."

She shrugged. "Perhaps he'll be more careful. He's

found his one true love. I can't try to force him to marry another."

"You could have urged them to continue their elopement."

"No. A horrid way to marry. You could let them marry in church next week."

"No. I'll see proof of constancy, especially from your brother."

"He's changing. It's astonished me, but it's so. I quite expect to soon find him with his nose in a book."

That twitched a smile on his stern lips.

"Can you bear this?" she asked him. "In good humor, for Phyllis's sake? I think she wants family around her, and you are the only family she has."

"Leaving aside her mother."

"That bothers you? It seems natural to me."

"Anabelle abandoned Phyllis when she was only a few months old!"

"For love. It seems you in turn abandoned her."

"When she was fourteen, and I left her with her reliable governess, who turns out to have been a regular bluestocking!"

"Mrs. Manners?" Ariana asked.

"I only hired her a few weeks ago. As soon as I returned, Miss Armstrong left to find more demanding pupils. Manners was to help Phyllis prepare for society. A sensible woman, or so I thought."

"What's she done?" Ariana asked, slightly amused by his air of grievance.

"Says she's going to marry Tom North! What about mourning?"

"Perhaps she's mourned long enough and, like your stepmother, deserves more life." She meant it about him as much as anyone.

He didn't have to respond, because after a knock, the innkeeper peered in. "All well, sir? Here's another bowl of punch, some soup, and some slices of pie." A maid carried in the refreshments and laid them out on the table, and then the servants bowed out.

Ariana chuckled. "They seem relieved not to have found dead bodies."

"Indeed. Would you like anything? We should leave soon."

Or not, Ariana thought, agreeing to soup and pie and moving to the table. The stolen curricle bar was now on its way to Derby, and with luck she'd never be found out. But at this moment she and Kynaston were in harmony, and she was learning about him. That was a feast on its own.

Chapter 18

He came to join her at the table and poured himself a tankard of punch. "Rather stronger than before," he commented after a sip. "Perhaps the innkeeper misunderstood my instructions."

"The soup is delicious. He thought Uncle Paul shouldn't fall further under the hatches."

"He thought your uncle was dying of drink," Kynaston said. "Didn't you notice his yellow skin, and even yellowish eyes? There were other signs."

"He might die soon?" Ariana asked.

"You sound so hopeful."

"Can I deny it? He's a hovering disaster. Without him, everything would be much simpler. Ethel suggested we murder him."

"Your Ethel seems an extraordinary person."

"She is. All in all, I'll be glad if Inching marries her. She'll keep him in line, and she'll like to be 'my lady.'"

"How did she come to be your maid?"

Ariana told him the tale as she finished her soup, and then took two slices of pie. "Her calm nature has often kept me in balance."

"You're inclined to fly into alt?"

"It has been known."

"And yet you prefer the harpsichord to the piano."

"I learned it first. But yes." She risked a direct question. "Why the lute?"

"Blondel," he said with a wry quirk of the lips. "As a boy I fell in love with the tale of Richard the First, and how, when he was secretly imprisoned, his faithful minstrel, Blondel, found him."

"By going from castle to castle singing a song only they knew."

"So that Richard could sing the next verse and be rescued. In the story, he played a lute. All nonsense, of course," he added.

"But an enchanting story."

"Perhaps all enchantments are deceit. But that led me to insist on learning the lute, and as a young man I found being different appealing."

"You play very well."

"So do you."

She considered him. "How do you know that?"

"You played once in Albemarle Street."

"I hoped no one would be disturbed."

"And at your mother's entertainment."

"I thought you'd already left."

"Or you wouldn't have played?"

That wasn't exactly what she'd meant. "I heard later that you left earlier. You sing well. I don't."

"I've never heard you sing."

"That's why." She'd eaten and drunk all that she

could, so there was no reason for further delay, even though she was relishing this conversation.

She understood now what Hermione had said. Conversation with a beloved was precious. All the same, she said, "We should leave."

"If you're ready," he said, courteously.

She rose and he opened the door to call that the curricle be made ready. Then he turned back to pick up her cloak and help her on with it. As he did so, his hands brushed the nape of her neck, sending a secret shiver through her. At least, she hoped it was secret.

How could she let him go?

How could she lose what they had?

How could he?

As she drew on her gloves, he put on his outerwear and soon they were walking out to the innyard. There, they found the two horses arranged on the vehicle, but four ostlers hunting around. An older man hurried over. "Beg pardon, milord, but they seem to have mislaid the curricle bar."

"Mislaid? How is that possible?"

"Well, milord, it had to be taken off, milord, as a new pair would need an adjustment, you see? It was set to leaning against the wall over there. But it's gone."

Everyone stared at the wall as if the metal bar might suddenly reappear.

Kynaston turned to Ariana. "Would your brother have done this?"

"No. Why?"

"To prevent my following."

"Back to London," she reminded him as carelessly as she could. She'd much rather he never discover the culprit. "There must be another bar around."

Kynaston looked at the head ostler, but he shook his head. "We don't get many curricles here, milord, a curricle not really being a traveling vehicle, you see. The smith can likely make something in the morning."

"Wood would do for a while."

"Perhaps, milord, but I'd not fancy it. Under strain it might snap and injure the horses."

Kynaston muttered a curse. "Keep looking. We'll return to the inn."

Once back in their room, he said, "You should have returned with your brother. I'm likely to be stuck here until the morning. There'll probably be a stagecoach for London passing at some time."

Ariana had no intention of returning to London on a public stage, for any number of reasons. "Maybe," she said, "but though they often leave London in the dark, most arrive in daylight. Can we hire some other conveyance?"

When he left to find out, she prayed he would fail. Her prayers were answered. He returned to say, "There's a gig, but it's a sorry specimen. He keeps one chaise for hire, but it's out."

"I'd say we could ride," Ariana said, "but I'm not dressed for it."

A hint of a smile twitched his lips. "Pity you don't have your brother's clothes."

She smiled back. "Dreadfully ill-fitting! Ethel was better suited and rather liked wearing breeches. I found it embarrassing, even though no one could see." Memories of a shirt made her blush.

"A bashful Hippolyta?" he teased.

"Don't. I mean, the Amazon bit. I'm not a warrior."

"You fought to preserve Boxstall."

"Foolishly. I discounted love."

She wanted to ask about Seraphina, but that was forbidden territory. In any case, she might not want to know.

A one true love.

Was there only one for each person? If he was her one true love, and his heart had been buried with Seraphina—ah, there was tragedy.

She refilled her tankard with the cooling punch, and sipped. Could he really be without any image of his beloved?

"Do you have a picture of your first wife?" she asked.

After a moment, he took out his pocket watch and flipped open the back cover. Inside was a miniature of that face Ariana had seen before in the portraits Lady Cawle had preserved.

She affected surprise. "Heavens, she's very like that picture on the mummy case! No wonder you were shocked."

"Yes." He considered the miniature again and then snapped the case shut and returned the watch to his waistcoat pocket.

"But that picture was of a woman thousands of years dead," Ariana reminded him gently.

"I know that. You probably know all about such pictures, but I consulted an expert. Those mummy paintings date from the time when Egypt was ruled by Italians. Seraphina was Italian, from a town near Naples, and she's buried in a lead casket."

"It's painful for you to speak of it. Don't."

"It's painful whether I speak of it or not. I should have buried her peacefully at Delacorte, her and the child, but I took the need to return her to her home and family as an excuse to escape. So she was bound in linen soaked with resin, sealed in lead, and transported a thousand miles. Have you ever heard of Mad Queen Joan of Castile?"

"No," Ariana said, not wanting to hear these grim details, but awed by his sudden willingness to speak them.

"She was born a princess of Castile, but was married to Philip the Fair, ruler of the Low Countries. She fell insanely in love with him, and when he died ten years later, she refused to have him prepared for burial, insisting that he was merely ill and would revive. When he was finally embalmed and sealed in a coffin, she opened it daily to be sure he was still there and still dead. She would caress his corpse."

"How tragic, but perhaps that is part of the power of love."

"If so, it's a vicious one. I didn't go so far, but I should have let my wife rest peacefully in England."

"Perhaps her family was pleased to have her to bury in Italy?"

He shrugged. "I told myself that, but she had only grandparents there, and some cousins. Her parents had moved to England before she was born."

"You were driven by a noble desire."

"I was driven by a desire to delay her burial, for that would be final. And perhaps I was trying to flee the pain of her death."

"Which didn't work."

"Instead, the journey etched it deep. We buried her in a rocky place beneath olive trees, close to an ancient Catholic church. It had a kind of beauty, but it wasn't her soil. She'd been born and raised in Middlesex, and was a Protestant. She should rest in a green place beneath oaks and elms where thrushes and nightingales would sing to her." After a moment, he added, "She was a singer."

"You sang together."

"Often. Even as she labored. She said it helped. She asked me to play the lute in the next room. She hardly made a sound. I had no idea. . . . Don't say anything."

Ariana wasn't sure she could have forced words out of her tight throat.

"Did my playing help?" he asked, staring down at his glass. "Or did my being there make her hold back her screams? Would shouting and screaming have helped? They said there'd never been any hope. That the baby was stuck in such a way that he could never have been born. Why is nature so cruel?"

She reached out and covered his hand with her own.

After a moment, he turned his hand and took hers. "I shouldn't have burdened you with all that."

"If it's a burden shared, I don't mind. You said that childbirth killed your mother?"

He looked up then. "Determined to turn the screw? Yes, and I was seven then. I remember the noises. Not screams so much as howls. Then silence. It's a wretched business."

"At worst. Not at best."

"I know. I witnessed some births in Italy."

"All went well?"

"In some cases with ridiculous ease. Peasants," he dismissed.

"Not only peasants. I don't know how the queen's births went, but she survived a great many of them."

"But Princess Charlotte died. I visited Prince Leopold, to offer him the sympathy of one who knew. He seemed to appreciate it. He, too, does not intend to marry again."

He produced that like a weapon, so he wasn't unaware of the trend of her thoughts.

"He may change his mind in a year or two."

He kept silent, not making the obvious comment.

Ariana thought of something to say that shouldn't be painful. "I've been wondering what to do about Cleo. I mean, the mummy case."

"Where is it? It wasn't in the cellars."

"I asked Mr. Peake to move it. It's in one of his spare bedrooms. She is. I can't stop thinking of her as she, and alive."

"She's not."

"I know that. It doesn't affect how I feel! I don't want her on display, in Peake's house or in a museum. I certainly don't want her ground up to make love potions and such."

"What?"

"You weren't there when Peake told me that. Apparently that's what happens to many of them. That's why he bought it. Her."

"Good man. I could purchase the mummy and store it somewhere at Delacorte."

"Another cellar? It doesn't seem right."

"What do you want to do?"

"I don't know."

They were still standing, outer clothes on, caught between the need to leave and the impossibility, but Ariana was feasting on every moment and thinking of more. . . .

A knock at the door broke the spell. She'd not realized they were holding hands until he stepped apart. "Come!"

It was the innkeeper again, looking anxious. "Beg pardon, my lord, ma'am, but did you say the gentleman was your uncle?"

"Why?" Ariana asked. "Has he left his bill unpaid?" That would be typical.

"In a manner of speaking, ma'am. The fact of the matter is . . . he's dead."

"What?"

"I do apologize for giving you such a shock, ma'am, but he refused to return to the coach, and when one of my maids tried to rouse him, she found him . . . already gone. He wasn't a well man."

"True enough," Ariana said, sitting. "But to be dead. Here."

"Arrangements will have to be made," Kynaston said. "That's what our host is implying."

"Arrangements?"

"By a member of the family. Perhaps you will allow me to take care of it for you?"

Ariana felt she should be able to cope, but she was relieved to agree.

Kynaston looked at the innkeeper. "Can he be moved to a bedroom?"

"Yes, my lord."

"Then afterward, a magistrate should be summoned. Or a coroner, if they be different people. Then an undertaker."

"Right, my lord. And Reverend Darraclough? He's the clergyman here."

"An excellent suggestion."

"He'll need to be moved to his home for burial, I suppose, my lord."

Kynaston looked to Ariana. "Where is your uncle's home?"

It seemed a surprisingly difficult question. "I'm not sure. Rooms in London, probably."

"Do you have any objection to his being buried here?"

"None at all. It seems simpler."

"I assume he has no wife or children."

"I don't think so. Should he be buried at Boxstall?"

"Here will suffice," he said firmly, and she was grateful for his decisiveness.

She wasn't grief-stricken over Uncle Paul's death, and in many ways she was glad he was gone, but she was unnerved by the surprise of it, and disturbed by guilt. She'd encouraged him to drink punch to shut him up, and she hadn't protested when Kynaston had told the innkeeper to give him as much brandy as he wanted.

The innkeeper left and Kynaston sat beside her. "If he'd had any say, it's probably how he'd have chosen to die. By a fire, drinking brandy."

"How do you know what I was thinking?"

"Easy enough. I'm feeling some guilt myself."

"He tried to make mischief, even then."

"True to the end."

"I think I have to stay here until the burial," she said. "As family."

"You don't have to. I can stand in for you there as well."

Ariana was aware of a weak desire to lean against him and be embraced, be taken care of. Instead, she sat straighter. "I've been weak enough. I can at least represent the family here, but I should write to Mama and my brother."

"Undoubtedly."

"I'll need a room here. We both will. Two rooms," she amended hastily.

"Of course. You might as well have this one, as it's warm and ready." He went to the door and called for the innkeeper, then ordered a room prepared for himself.

"You can have the one next door, my lord. It's not quite as spacious as this one, but it's well enough and a fire's been burning there all evening. I keep these rooms ready for any who stop and want a private one, even for a little while."

Kynaston nodded. "Very well."

He went into the corridor to inspect the next room, but returned through an adjoining door. "It'll do. This door locks." He put the key on Ariana's side.

"I'm sure I can trust you," she said, unable to resist some dryness.

"Use the key," he said, and returned to his room.

Ariana didn't.

Did he feel any pull of lust? Was it only willpower that kept them apart? If so, shouldn't she respect that?

Their earlier discussion had deepened a bond, but the bond had only increased her desire. Could she bear to let this opportunity slip by? If they bedded here tonight, how could he not marry her?

Such thinking was wicked, but it seemed wickedness could be intensely appealing, and they had all night before them.

Chapter 19

There was no immediate opportunity to sin.

The parson came to report that he'd given the last rites to Paul Boxstall, even though he was already dead.

Kynaston came through to stand by her side. Reverend Darraclough offered brusque sympathy and assured them both that Ariana's uncle could be buried in the churchyard.

A sinewy Sir George Quill turned up as both magistrate and coroner, accompanied by his plump wife, who hurried to Ariana. "Such a shocking tragedy, my dear Lady Ariana." Clearly the lady was thrilled by the small drama, and by the chance to rub shoulders with the aristocracy.

"You're very kind, ma'am," Ariana said. "It is a shock indeed, but my uncle and I were not close." She lowered her voice. "As is clear, he'd been slave to alcoholic beverages from his youth."

Lady Quill sighed. "So sad. A lesson to all so inclined. Would you like to remove to our house, Lady Ariana? We have a cozy manor house only two miles distant."

"How very kind," Ariana said, "but I feel I should stay here. Even though Lord Kynaston is handling the official matters for me."

"Another relation?" Lady Quill asked, glancing to where Kynaston was discussing details with Sir George.

Ariana remembered then the scene Uncle Paul had created and the awkwardness of her situation. She could only hope Lady Quill hadn't heard any of the London scandal, but someday she would.

"A cousin," she said as calmly as possible. "We are connected through Kynaston's aunt, the Dowager Countess of Cawle. He accompanied me here to deal with a minor matter—most fortunately as it turns out."

"Indeed. The gentlemen always know what to do in these situations, don't they?"

Sir George went away with Kynaston to view the corpse. They both soon returned.

"There'll have to be an inquest, of course," Sir George said, "but the doctor's here and says it's a clear case of liver disease. No sign of anything amiss. We can hold the inquest here tomorrow. Does he have family, my lady? Has he made a will?"

"No, to both, I think. But I'm about to write to my brother, the Earl of Langton, who can make all necessary checks."

Sir George nodded, clearly satisfied that another man would soon be taking care of everything, and left, taking his somewhat reluctant wife with him.

Ariana was suddenly deeply weary. "What a day," she said.

"Astonishing."

"I woke this morning thinking the worst was over and my life had returned to normal."

He gave her a wry smile. "What is normal?" But he came over then, and sat beside her on the settle, taking her hand. "I would have spared you this if I could."

"It's rather that I've dragged you into my family's mess. I hope Uncle Paul's words earlier won't create new mayhem."

"The coach travelers seemed a humdrum lot."

"But the inn servants heard, and Uncle Paul's death is the sort of incident they'll talk about for months."

He sighed. "True enough. Perhaps you should return to London."

"How? And in this?" Wind was rattling the windows now and rain was lashing them. "In any case, any damage is done." When he looked a question at her, she added, "You came in here through the adjoining door. Lady Quill noted it. I saw her."

"Damnation. You should have locked it."

"You should have thought!" She calmed down. "It doesn't matter whose fault it is. Lady Quill will gossip about this event all year, and sooner or later it will connect with the London scandal. Our only explanation will be to tell the world that my brother and your sister eloped."

"No."

"No," she agreed. "Though Phyllis will tell all as soon as she understands the implications."

"Wretched girl."

"I think she's admirable. Honest and courageous. But it would be better if she begins life as the Countess of Langton without scandal hanging over her. So," she added, gathering her nerve, "it would be best if we were the eloping couple."

"What?"

"Think about it. I didn't want a society wedding, which would look like an admission of guilt, but we are in love, even if we haven't sinned. So I persuaded you to an elopement."

"And I, like an idiot, agreed, even though we're both of age and could marry anywhere, anytime?"

"Oh." She grimaced. "It was such a pretty tale, with our elopement interrupted by Uncle Paul's death."

"It was an idiotic tale." But he smiled. "It's endearing to see that you can sometimes be idiotic."

"You like foolish women?"

"I like you."

"I love you." He looked down. "Titus. I want to be able to call you Titus. I give you your sister's words: Your vow will make a nun of me. I don't fancy the idea at all."

He looked at her with exasperation. "There are other men. Plenty of them. Once you put your mind to it, you'll find happiness."

"You don't believe in a one-and-only?"

"No."

"What of Seraphina?"

"You won't let her rest in peace, will you? I thought she was my one-and-only. Until you."

Ariana smiled and leaned closer. "Thank you. Is your vow entirely about childbirth, or is part of it a vow to her? I don't think she'd mind."

"You can't know."

That was true. Ariana realized she was thinking of Cleo.

"I don't believe that anyone who truly loves would

want their beloved to be unhappy after their death. I think my mother will marry again."

"That's different. Ariana, I couldn't bear to kill you."

She went into his arms to hold him. "Oh, love, you won't. Even if the worst happens, it will be cruel nature, not you. And it *won't*. There's no reason to expect it. I want you, I want our children, and I want our comfortable old age as grandparents. So many people have that. Why not us?"

"Perhaps I'm cursed."

"Why think that? *Why?* What have you done to deserve that?"

She waited, praying he didn't have some dreadful secret on his soul.

"Perhaps nothing," he said at last. "But perhaps I persuaded Seraphina into marriage before she was ready. I was an arrogant young fool, sure that every dangling fruit was my just possession."

"Did she not love you?"

"Yes, but we could have waited. Her mother wished us to. I was impatient, however, and she was dazzled by my rank."

"And your looks and charm, I'm sure."

"Feeding me compliments?"

"Truth. Don't try to deny your gifts. I suspect Seraphina wanted you equally as much as you wanted her, and her mother had no say at all."

He chuckled. "You could be right. She was willful."

"And age would have made no difference. You said the baby couldn't be born. It wasn't a fault in her, or anything to do with her youth. She could have been forty and suffered the same fate."

"You're not advancing your cause," he pointed out.

"I'm pointing out a truth. There's always a risk when a woman bears a child, but there's greater risk when a man goes off to war. That hasn't put an end to the army or navy."

"Perhaps it should."

"Perhaps it should, but it hasn't and it won't. More women die of smallpox than in childbirth, even now we have vaccination. I looked that up."

"Then we should vaccinate everyone."

"Probably. Of the women who died last year in their childbearing years, fewer than five percent died in childbirth."

"My darling bluestocking, that's five percent too many."

"But think of the ninety-five percent who lived to enjoy their children! Twenty times as many females died of consumption last year. Twenty times! Some may have been older or younger than childbearing years, but that's a huge number."

"And a risk that can't be avoided. It strikes where it will."

"Very well, consider this, sir. I intend to take my chances and bear children. It will be with you, the man I love, or with some other. Choose."

"You wretched woman."

Ariana simply waited.

"You'd do it, wouldn't you?"

"I'm determined on it. I know I'm asking a lot of you, but my life, my entire happiness, hangs in this moment. I wouldn't do it if I wasn't sure your happiness depends on it as well."

He cradled her face and kissed her. "I surrender, but I'm not eloping. We'll do it with dignity at Boxstall no sooner than the spring."

"So that if I bear a child nine months later, there'll be no raised brows? Challenging, but clever. Merely a few months to wait."

"Or not. If we're careful."

"Careful?"

"I made a vow, but I haven't been a monk. Or at least . . ."

"A monk?" she asked in surprise.

"In Italy, briefly, it seemed a solution. I found I didn't suit."

She chuckled and it turned into a giggle, a giggle of delight because it was sinking in that she'd won. She'd made a bold move, and she'd won!

"We really will marry? In the spring?"

But he moved back and rose again. "No. This is a momentary madness. You'll be sane again in days."

"No, I won't. I've loved you for years!"

"How could you have?"

She was already regretting her admission. "We did meet all those years ago. You were handsome, charming, and kind."

"I was a swollen-headed young idiot. Ariana, I hardly noticed you."

"I know. But I never forgot you, and you are now a man to admire."

"For what? I married rashly, and when fate was cruel, I ran away, neglecting my family, my estates, and my other responsibilities. I could at the least have joined Wellington's army and wasted my life more usefully."

"No!" she protested, rising to her feet. "You did what you had to do, and since returning—"

"I've resorted to drink. I'm not worthy of you."

"That's for me to decide. You've shown strength and resolution, and I love you. I need you." She managed not to say, *Don't run away again*, but perhaps he heard it, for he turned and plunged into the other room. Ariana regarded the slammed door ruefully. She was unskilled at managing men. Another woman would have done better.

She couldn't give up now, however. She sensed the same physical needs in him as raged in her, and the deeper desires and emotions as well.

She thought of Ethel, who'd clearly seen what she wanted and set about it, grasping the means of going north that Norris and Phyllis had presented. Perhaps she was even now with Lord Inching, persuading him that marriage would be a perfect conclusion. Which it probably would be. Ethel would manage Inching, and they'd live happily together in Cumberland, undisturbed by the world's opinion.

Seen in that light, her own obstacles seemed insignificant. The world would regard her marriage to Kynaston as highly satisfactory, and she felt sure that in time she could make him happy. He wanted her as much as she wanted him.

What she was contemplating was wicked, but it might win her the ultimate prize. He was too honorable to abandon her once they'd anticipated their marriage.

She summoned an inn maidservant to help her undress. "I didn't expect to stay," she explained to the plump lass, "so I have neither maid nor nightclothes."

"I could maybe find you a nightdress, milady."

"My shift will suffice, but perhaps you could sponge off my gown so it will be fit to be seen tomorrow."

"Of course, milady. And your cloak?"

"I might need that."

When the maid had taken off her corset, Ariana sent her away and considered herself in the mirror. She wasn't sure what clothing would be seductive, but her sturdy linen shift, hanging shapeless down to her calves, didn't seem likely. Nor did her thick gray worsted stockings and leather half boots.

She had to wear something on her feet, however, or she'd freeze. There were no carpets on the floor here and it was cold. The air was cold, too, despite the fire, so she picked up her fur-lined cloak and put it on, pulling up the hood.

Ah, better. More covered, but more pleasing.

The cloak reminded her of the night she'd wandered Lady Cawle's house and seen Kynaston return, dreadfully drunk. That had been the culmination of the day on which he'd encountered Cleo. "Your ghost needs to be exorcised, Seraphina," she said aloud. "Are you restless because of where he had you buried? I promise to have you brought back to rest in English soil, if you will only leave him in peace. Leave us in peace." She considered herself in the small inadequate mirror. "Not that this sight will break any man's will. Help me, Seraphina. Help me, Cleo."

The adjoining door opened and she turned to face it, to face him.

"Are you all right?" he asked. "I heard voices."

"One voice," she said hoarsely, for he was undressed down to his pantaloons and shirt, which was open at the neck. "I was talking to myself."

"You're cold. I'll order warming pans, and then you'd best be in bed."

"Two in a bed would be warmer."

"But most unwise." He left, but she shed her cloak and pursued. "Titus!"

He turned to face her, but behind him sat a larger mirror, which showed her in ugly shift, woolen stockings, and well-worn half boots. She covered her face with her hands. "I'm sorry. I'm such a sight."

Warm hands lowered hers. "You're beautiful, Ariana, as you always are."

She met his eyes. "I wish I were in filmy silk, like a woman in a harem."

"You'd be no more alluring."

"Surely I'd have to be."

"Why are you always so clearheaded?"

"It's a flaw?"

"It means you must see me for what I am."

"I see a man, no better or worse than other men, but perfect in my eyes."

"That's a heavy burden to bear."

"Then you must strive to. I'm sure you were a good husband to Seraphina, and will be a good husband to me."

"We've talked about this—"

"Clearly not enough. We are going to marry, Titus, and be happy, with a brood of happy, healthy children."

And that meant . . .

Chapter 20

His room was much smaller than hers, and dominated by the tester bed. She pushed him and the backs of his legs hit it. Another push, and he sprawled backward onto it. He wasn't resisting, as best as she could tell. In fact, he grabbed her shift and pulled her down on top of him.

She sprawled over his warmth, with only two thin layers of cloth between her breasts and his chest. The surge of hunger startled a gasp from her, but killed any qualms, so she kissed him. She had to, as a parched person must drink.

He kissed her back in the same way, but was struggling to get away. "We mustn't . . ."

"*I* must," she stated, holding tight to his shirt, "and I won't suffer for your qualms."

He ripped free. "Qualms!"

She knelt on the bed, glaring at him. "Seraphina wouldn't have wanted such a sacrifice. This is all about you. In fact, she wants to be brought back from Italy."

He sat up, glaring in return. "Oh, does she? She's written you a letter?"

"I just know. She can't rest there, and perhaps that's why you can't be at peace." She leaned into him and kissed him more gently. "Let me bring you peace, Kynaston."

"Peace," he groaned. "I haven't known a moment's peace since we met."

"Again."

"Again?"

"We met eight years ago."

"I hardly remember that."

"I remember it. I've always remembered it." She pulled off her boots and threw them on the floor, where they landed with two loud thumps. Then she untied the garter above her right knee and rolled down her ugly stocking. Her only purpose was to expose her feet. If he couldn't bear them, this must go no further. But then she saw the way he was watching her and looking at her leg.

It reminded her of Ethel's words about Inching. *Showing a bit of leg.*

Like a cat in catmint.

She pushed the stocking off her foot, watching him. No repulsion. Instead he grabbed her foot in both hands, and rubbed it. "Not too cold."

"Boots and worsted stockings," she reminded him, then added, "I have large feet."

"You said something about large feet before. It would be odd for someone so tall to have tiny ones."

"I *am* very tall."

"For a woman. You're no taller than I am."

"Which makes us a good match." The way he was massaging her foot made her want to purr and roll.

"I'm not the only tall, eligible man around."

She gently eased her foot out of his hands, and tucked it under herself. "You're the one I want. I tried to like the others, but from the start, it was you I wanted."

"From the start? I wasn't on my aunt's list."

"How do you know that?"

"Your mother showed it to me, asking my advice."

"And what did you advise?"

"The same as I advised you."

Ariana remembered what Hermione had said about talking and could sense what she'd meant. Desire still hummed, but they were both calmer now and in some way more open, there in a small bedroom lit only by the fire and one candle.

On the bed.

She crawled up to sit on the pillows, resting back against the headboard, and patted the space beside her in invitation.

"I think I'll keep my distance," he said.

"As you will. Tell me about the monastery. All about taking Seraphina to Italy."

He leaned back against one of the bottom bedposts, frowning in thought. "We sailed for Naples. Some friends came with me. We sighted some Barbary pirates once, but they didn't bother us. We were on a well-armed navy ship. My friends preferred to stay in Naples, so I went on alone, with the coffin. I'd had the notion that her family would welcome her, but they were all distant relatives who'd long ago lost touch with her father, though I could see a family resemblance."

"What of her parents, here in England?"

"I didn't even consult them. So arrogant. They, too, want her to be returned here. They want her buried in London, where they live. But she wouldn't want that."

Apparently without thought, he'd taken her other foot and was massaging it . . . no, fondling it. "Why not?" she asked on a breath.

"She loved Delacorte. Especially the wilderness area. I think she'd like it there. You don't mind me talking about her?"

"Not at all."

"I'd assumed any woman would resent me talking about my first wife. A wife I loved very much."

Ariana noted "first" with satisfaction. "Some might. But not if you have room in your heart for another."

He closed his eyes, dark lashes lying on his cheekbones. "Do I? What of the one-and-only? If we'd fallen out of harmony, it might be different."

There seemed no benefit to pursuing that, so she asked, "The monastery?"

"Once I'd realized I couldn't bear to get another woman with child, especially one I cared for, a vow of chastity seemed logical. Alas, the poverty and obedience were a challenge."

"I can imagine."

He opened his eyes and smiled at her. "As they would be for you."

"I said I'd never make a nun. How long did you stay there?"

"Nearly a year. Father Prior had to evict me, for though I knew I wasn't suited to the life, it was so calm and lovely . . . the singing, the routine, even the work in the gardens. I'd never done such work and I found it very soothing."

"I enjoy it, too. The cycle of the seasons gives a rhythm to life, and to be surrounded by living greenery . . . Perhaps there's a reason paradise was described as a garden. What then?"

"Once thrown out of paradise, I wandered, trying to avoid anyone I knew. Trying to find peace. Until my aunt summoned me."

"You must have kept in touch with her."

"Or she kept watch over me. I didn't hide my identity, so my presence was noted. She had ambassadors all over Europe on alert to report to her. She wrote frequently to remind me of my duties and responsibilities, but I ignored her."

"You returned in the end," Ariana reminded him.

"I'd come to long for home. She provided the excuse. . . ."

"But then the princess died."

"Almost exactly as Seraphina did. Healthy and happy, then cold and dead a few days later. I was glad the child died with her."

He wasn't talking about Charlotte. "You think you'd blame him or her?"

"Him. A son. I didn't care about his death. I wanted my beloved!"

The depth of his anguish hurt, but Ariana crawled across the bed to hold him, merely to offer comfort. To kiss seemed natural and inevitable, as did all that followed. She had no care for her clothing or his, or her feet, but only the ever-closer embrace, the beat of their hearts, their heat, and her own greedy desire.

When he entered her, it seemed perfect, especially his stillness. Until she realized it might come from regret. Could he still retreat?

She wanted the commitment this must mean and held him closer. Moved her hips to bring him deeper. Refused to let him go.

"It's done," she murmured against his neck. "Complete. I love you."

"As, God forgive me, I love you!" With that groan, he moved in her, harder and faster until, with a great shudder, all was done.

Ariana couldn't say she'd achieved poetic ecstasy, but she'd won her prize. He was hers now. Later, as she dozed in contentment, he kissed her and touched her. And in the end she said, "So it wasn't poetic invention," and snuggled against his hot, hard, naked body, smiling.

Morning light woke her, so she knew it must have been late.

"I shouldn't be found here," she said.

"I doubt we can hide the facts, love."

She became aware of smells and a sticky bed. "Are you just saying that—'love'? Because you feel you must?"

"No. I desired you that day in the library, which shocked me. I'd denied all desire for years, and it hadn't been hard, but then there was you. Every day you were in my aunt's house was torment. Every moment together." He kissed her. "You were assessing other men as husbands and I must help you. Torment."

She chuckled. "For me, too. No other man could ever be good enough."

"I'm not good enough. For you."

"You're the one I want. The one I need."

"My good fortune. Not my just deserts."

"So?" she asked. "We elope?"

"No. We'll do it with dignity at Boxstall no sooner than the spring."

"What if a child comes from this?"

"I did my best by separating from you when I did, so that I did not spill my seed in you."

She placed a hand on his chest and could feel his deep breathing. "Can you do that every time until we wed?"

"Wretched woman. There'll be no more times like this."

"No?"

"I've had practice at self-restraint."

She chuckled and it turned into a giggle, a giggle of delight at realizing that she was with him and he was hers. "We really will marry? In the spring?"

"On my honor." He pulled the covers off her. "I want to see you naked, my glorious beauty, and kiss you head to toes."

And he did, and didn't seem to mind her feet at all.

Easter, 22 March 1818

Ariana was pleased to find that Easter came early in 1818.

On 22 March she married Titus Frederick Delacorte in the ancient medieval Boxstall church. Norris and Phyllis married on the same day, but in a later, separate ceremony.

Lord and Lady Kynaston honeymooned in Italy, even visiting a monastery, where the elderly prior blessed them, saying that he'd always known Brother Titus's calling was in the world.

Ariana declined an offer to visit Greece and Egypt, saying she preferred to cherish the image of them in their prime. They returned to England to the port of Liverpool, bringing a coffin to be reinterred at Delacorte.

Kynaston had some business interests to pay attention to in Liverpool, but Ariana traveled up into Cumberland to visit Ethel.

Lady Inching was in fine fettle, and much loved in the area for her down-to-earth nature and true concern for the lives of the ordinary people. Inching had mumbled an apology to Ariana but then kept out of the way. It was clear he adored Ethel in every way.

"Some of the local grandees are standoffish," Ethel said over tea in an elegant drawing room, "but that's mostly an old pattern because of Inching, and he's improving. The worst ones don't spend much time up here anyway, thinking London and the area so much more important."

"But you're happy to stay up here?" Ariana asked.

"Of course. You don't mind?"

"Not at all. I have a new lady's maid, but that's all she is, and a new friend in Kynaston."

"I hope he's treating you right."

"Of course he is. We disinterred his first wife from her olive grove in Italy."

"Why?"

"It didn't suit her. She'll rest more easily at Delacorte."

"I wouldn't want a first wife's grave on the doorstep."

"She'll always be part of our lives. Do you remember Cleo, the mummy?"

"You found out who she was, then?"

"No. That's the name I gave her. I hope to bury the mummy with Seraphina, but keep the portrait."

"You do have some funny ideas. I'm expecting."

Ariana had guessed. "When?"

"In the late summer. Inching's pleased."

"No qualms?"

"Why should there be?"

"Exactly. But all good news will be welcome. Hermione Faringay will have her child soon, and if you are also safely delivered, then by Christmas we can be at ease."

"You are expecting, too, then?"

Ariana instinctively put her hand on her belly. "I have hopes. I haven't told Kynaston yet."

Ethel chuckled. "Let sleeping worries lie?"

"Exactly."

"Which brings to mind . . ."

"What?" Ariana asked.

"What's your husband planning to do about mine?"

"Nothing."

"Nothing?"

"Nothing. I pointed out that he's suffered from being short as much as I have from being tall."

"What of Churston, then?"

"We can't do much about him without involving Inching, but he is aware that his part is known, and he never expected things to go so far."

"'He who blows on an ember . . . ,'" Ethel muttered.

"'Let sleeping dogs lie,'" Ariana countered, and indeed, with so many happy outcomes, why stir coals?

Ariana and Kynaston traveled south to Delacorte, stopping off at various estates and business ventures that Titus had neglected. She thought he was being excessively conscientious, but she didn't mind the wandering, for once at Delacorte, she was going to have to accept that it, not Boxstall, was her new home.

It wasn't as difficult as she'd feared. The house was mellow Elizabethan, nothing at all like Boxstall, and there were no ruins lurking in the park. Norris had already sent her favorite books, including the *Égypte*, and some family paintings.

Ariana was sure that Phyllis had played a large part in that, perhaps nudged by the Dowager Lady Langton, though Ariana's mother was mostly absorbed by her own upcoming marriage to Reverend Corby.

On midsummer, with Seraphina's parents present, they laid the previous Countess of Kynaston to rest in the wilderness at Delacorte with Cleo's mummy alongside. Cleo's portrait already hung in the house alongside portraits of Seraphina, but a stone carver had reproduced the look on the stone that would stand over the grave, inscribed to Seraphina, Countess of Kynaston, and an unknown Italian lady who had been originally buried in Egypt.

Ariana had written a full account, which was now in the Delacorte library.

She and Kynaston were already preparing an Egyptian Hall there, done in as accurate a way as possible, and having the reproduced mural on one wall. Edgar Peake had come to see it installed, and brought as gifts the various Egyptian statues and artifacts he had. "For it never seemed right to have items that have no connection to me or my adventures."

"They have no connection to me," Ariana protested.

"Do they not?"

She smiled at him. "Perhaps they do. Perhaps they do."

They celebrated Christmas 1818 at Delacorte.

Ariana's mother also attended, as Ariana's time was due, along with her amiable and doting husband. She was positively glowing with new energy and joy.

"Though why you and Phyllis must expect your babies at the same time . . . I know, I know. Comes of marrying on the same day, but it doesn't always work just so. Her mother wanted to be with her, which only seems right, so here I am, though my experience is limited and Anabelle has borne seven!"

As it was, no experience was necessary. Ariana began her labor on December 30, but the midwife told her to carry on as normal as long as she could. That calmed Kynaston a little, though when she took to her bed in the evening, he insisted on being with her at every moment. "My love, it's far worse to be somewhere else, waiting and wondering!"

Ariana tried to stay quiet, but the midwife said, "Just let it out, my lady. Don't you worry about him. The babe's in a fine position, so there's no need to worry. But it's work, see, and it's only normal to make noise as we work hard."

So Ariana worked, and soon the baby slithered out and squawked.

"A fine boy!" the midwife declared, wrapping him up and showing him to his father. "All's well, my lord, but you can't have him yet. He's to go to the breast to help his mother."

Ariana was unprepared, but as soon as the tiny baby was put near a nipple, he took it and sucked. The sensation startled, but the midwife grunted in satisfaction.

"That's it. Good for him and grand for you, my lady. Stops any bleeding, that does, and bleeding's the danger at this point. Ah, there it is."

Ariana looked down to see she'd delivered a lump of liver.

The midwife massaged her lower belly, grinning. "All's well now! Congratulations!"

Kynaston staggered to the bedside. "It's over? They're both well?"

"Perfect, my lord. Lady Kynaston could get up now and be about her duties, but we'll keep her in bed and look after her. Ah, the little one's asleep. Here, my lord, you take him. But no wandering around to show him off. I'll have no drafts on him."

A nursery governess, Mrs. Within, had been hired and she now bustled over to claim the baby, wash him, and clothe him in silk ready for his fine cradle by the fire. Ariana watched, with a contented smile, as Kynaston hovered, trying not to claim his right to his son and heir.

When Mrs. Within moved to put the baby into the cradle, Ariana said, "My lord, bring the baby to me, please."

He obeyed, and she took the swaddled child. "Perhaps you could climb on the bed beside me?"

He did and took them both in his arms. "Thank you. For the child and for dragging me this far, my love."

She smiled at him. "It's been my delight, my lord, every step of the way."

Author's Note

If you read my 2016 book, *The Viscount Needs a Wife*, you'll already understand how deeply the tragic death of Princess Charlotte affected everyone, each in his own way. Ariana sees the chanciness of life, even for the young; Kynaston's trauma over his wife's death is exacerbated.

Fans of the Company of Rogues will have noticed that neither Ariana nor Kynaston is a Rogue, but will have spotted the Rogues' World connections.

Ariana is a friend of Hermione Faringay, who was Hermione Merryhew, sister of a Rogue. Her story is *Too Dangerous for a Lady*, and there we meet Edgar Peake. The Dowager Countess of Cawle is a recurring character brought in to use her social influence, being connected to Rogue Hal Beaumont.

More elusively, the Duke and Duchess of Belcraven and the Duke and Duchess of Yeovil are both parents of Rogues, so we know why they turned up to support

Ariana. (Lucien, Marquess of Arden—*An Unwilling Bride*—is the heir to Belcraven; Lord Darius Debenham—*To Rescue a Rogue*—is a younger son of the Yeovils.)

You can find out more about the Rogues on my Web site at jobev.com.

Read on for a sneak peek at
Beau Braydon's story in

The Viscount Needs a Wife

Available from Signet Select.

Chapter 1

7 November 1817
Cateril Manor, Gloucestershire

"Kathryn, your dog is looking at me again."

Kitty Cateril looked up from her needlework to see that indeed her King Charles spaniel was sitting in front of her mother-in-law, eyes fixed on her face. She bit the inside of her cheek to hold back a smile as she patted her leg. "Sillikin, come."

The small black-and-tan dog cocked its head, then trotted over, as if expecting a reward for a job well done. Kitty wasn't sure why Sillikin sometimes stared at people, but it seemed to be in disapproval, and her mother-in-law sensed that.

What secret sins could lurk in the soul of straight-backed, gray-haired Lady Cateril? She was the sort of woman often described as beyond reproach. These days, dressed permanently in mourning black, she had been canonized by the heroism and death of her younger son—Kitty's husband, Marcus.

Had Sillikin caught Lady Cateril wishing that the heroism and death had come together? That Marcus hadn't lived, wounded and broken, for seven more years and married someone like Kitty? That devotion to Marcus's memory hadn't required her to offer Kitty a home? Kitty and her irritating dog.

"I will say again, Kathryn, that you should rename that creature."

And I will say again, Kitty supplied silently before saying, "She's too used to the name by now."

"She's a dumb creature. She cannot care."

"Then why do dogs respond to their names as people do, Mama?"

Names. So powerful and so often poorly considered. Six years ago, she'd named a wriggling ball of fluff Sillikin. Three years before that, when Kitty had married Marcus, she'd called his mother Mama, in the hope of pleasing the disapproving woman. It had never seemed possible to change to something more formal.

Her bid for approval had been a hopeless cause. Lady Cateril's favorite son, the wounded hero of Roleia, bound to a seventeen-year-old chit? Had she hoped that by using the name Kathryn, the chit would become a sober matron? "Kitty," she'd said at first meeting, "is a romping sort of name." There'd been a clear implication that Kitty was a romping sort of person.

Better that than being starchy as a frosted petticoat on a winter washing line!

The weather today wouldn't freeze cotton as stiff as a board, but it was raining. That trapped Kitty in the house, and effectively in this small parlor, which smelled of wood smoke and the mustiness that came from long-closed windows. The larger, airier drawing room was rarely used in the colder months, so the fire there was unlit.

She would have liked to retreat to her bedroom even though that, too, lacked a fire, but in Lady Cateril's domain, bedrooms were not sitting rooms. They weren't dining rooms, either. The only time anyone was served food in her bedroom was if she was ill.

Kitty knew she should be grateful to be housed there. Her only other option was to live in cheap lodgings somewhere. At least there she had everything she needed and the estate to walk in.

She had everything except freedom.

In the beginning, she'd rubbed along well enough with her mother-in-law, united in grief. However, when six months had passed, Kitty had followed custom and prepared to put off her widow's weeds. When Lady Cateril realized Kitty had ordered new gowns in gray, fawn, and violet, she'd reacted as if she'd spat on Marcus's grave. When reproaches and then tears hadn't changed Kitty's intent, Lady Cateril had taken to her bed and sent for the doctor. Kitty had been badly shaken, but the rest of the family hadn't seemed alarmed, so she'd stuck to her guns. The first gown had arrived, a very plain gray wool round gown, and she'd worn it, quaking. The next day Lady Cateril had emerged. Nothing more had been said, but a frost had settled.

Kitty had realized then that in Lady Cateril's mind she had only one reason to exist: as Marcus's inconsolable widow. She was as much a monument to his magnificence as the marble plaque in the village church.

CAPTAIN MARCUS EDWARD CATERIL
OF THE 29TH
HERO OF ROLEIA
1782–1815

The words were inscribed on a large alabaster bas-relief that included a shrouded, mourning woman drooping over a plinth. The plaque was white, but the figure was black. Kitty had assumed at first that it was a symbolic representation of grief, but she'd since realized it was supposed to be her. Fixed in drooping black for all eternity.

She'd worn half mourning since then, but when her mourning year had ended, she'd lacked the fortitude to progress to bright colors. Her pretty clothes were stored away, becoming more out of style every day. She'd tried to think of ways to escape, but there she still was, eighteen months after Marcus's death. She had hardly any money and no possibility of desirable employment. She'd gone straight from school to marriage.

She picked up Sillikin. Through the most difficult times, the spaniel had been her confidant and consolation and had heard all that Kitty's pride had kept silent from people. *We'll find a way,* she said silently to the dog. *There has to be a way—*

The door burst open and Lord Cateril entered, eyes wild. "The most dreadful news!"

Lady Cateril started upright, a hand to her chest. "John?" she gasped, meaning her surviving son. "The children!"

"The princess. Princess Charlotte is dead!"

There was a moment of stillness as Kitty and Lady Cateril took in his words. Princess Charlotte, second in line to the throne, who'd been due to deliver her first child, the hope of the future, was *dead*?

"No!"

For once, Kitty and her mother-in-law were completely in harmony.

"The child?" Lady Cateril asked desperately.

"A son. Also dead." Lord Cateril sank into a chair by his wife's side and took her hand. "All hope is gone."

It was overly portentous, but Kitty knew what he meant. The king and queen had presented the nation with seventeen children, but now, nearly sixty years after George III had come to the throne, there had been only one legitimate grandchild, the Regent's daughter, Charlotte. With her dead, what would become of the nation? The king was old and mad and expected to die at any moment. The Regent was nearing sixty and grossly fat, and he led a dissipated life. No one would have been surprised if he died soon as well.

His sisters were all middle-aged, and those who had married hadn't produced offspring. Few of his brothers had married, and none of those unions had produced a living child. With the perversity of fate, some had bastards, which were of no use at all.

Kitty's heart ached for the people involved. "Poor woman," she said. "And her poor family. Royal, but not beyond the hand of fate."

"Amen," Lord Cateril said. "The shops and theaters have closed in respect. The court has gone into mourning, of course. But I'm told people of all degrees are putting on black, or at least dark bands."

"We must do the same," Lady Cateril said. "The family must wear full black." In spite of her genuine shock and sorrow, she shot Kitty a triumphant look.

Kitty almost protested, but Lord Cateril agreed. "You're right, my dear. And black bands, aprons, and gloves for the servants. Please gather the household together in the hall. I must read out the news."

Kitty helped to pass the word, and soon the family and servants stood together in the oak-paneled hall as Lord Cateril read out the letter he'd received. All were affected and many wept. Afterward Kitty went to her room to put on one of her black gowns. If only she'd given them away . . . but it was provident to keep mourning by. No one knew when death would strike, as had just been proved.

As a red-eyed housemaid fastened the back, Kitty resolved two things. She'd return to half mourning after the funeral, along with everyone else except the court. And she would not live this half life any longer.

Somehow she'd find a way to escape. Here was evidence that life was fleeting. She wouldn't waste what time she had left in the everlasting shadows of Lady Cateril's grief.

The princess's coffin, along with that of her stillborn child, was lowered into the royal vault at Windsor on November 15. Lord Cateril read a letter giving an account of the funeral to the assembled household, and they all prayed again for the princess and the bereaved family.

Kitty went upstairs to take off her black, tempted to move into brightly colored gowns now, but she truly was sorrowful over Princess Charlotte's fate, so half mourning felt correct. She chose gray and wore silver ornaments instead of jet. When she entered the parlor, Lady Cateril's look was flat, which seemed even worse than anger. Strenuous thinking over the past week had brought Kitty no closer to escape. The only prospect was to find employment. She'd discussed the situation with her sister-in-law and raised the possibility that Sarah give her a reference.

"Employment?" Sarah had asked, eyes wide. "Mama would never permit that."

"She can't stop me."

"But she can make my life miserable if I assist you." Sarah was plump, practical, and kind, but not courageous. She never tried to cross Lady Cateril over anything.

Kitty tried another approach. "Don't you think we should try to ease her out of her mourning? She has two fine children still, and six grandchildren—yours and Anabel's."

Anabel was Lady Cateril's youngest child, who'd married a man who lived three counties away, probably by design. Anabel had as much spine as her mother, so they easily clashed.

"She won't," Sarah said. "In some ways she likes the effect of it, but it reflects true grief. She always loved Marcus best."

"Doesn't John mind?"

"He's his father's favorite and he is the heir. Surely you're comfortable here overall, Káthryn. Why would you want to become someone's servant?"

On the surface it was idiotic. She was treated as one of the family, with everything provided for her. She hardly ever had to touch the small sum left her by Marcus, for any bills were paid by Lord Cateril without complaint.

Kitty had told Sarah the truth. "I want to wear rainbow colors and be joyful."

"I don't think governesses or companions are encouraged to dress gaudily, or romp around laughing."

Kitty had had to admit the truth of that, but it didn't change her mind. She was only twenty-seven years old and felt entombed.

Chapter 2

The next day, Kitty entered the parlor and found it empty. John and Sarah had driven out to visit friends who were celebrating the healthy birth of a child. Kitty could imagine how fearful the parents must have been with such a prominent example of the dangers. Lady Cateril must have been going over the household accounts with the housekeeper, for mourning had not led her to loose the reins of management. Lord Cateril would be in his office, where he spent most of his time when at home.

Kitty settled by the fire, Sillikin at her feet, to seek escape of another sort—in the delightful adventures of *Love in a Harem*. She'd enjoyed novels when young, but they'd become a precious escape during her marriage. The unlikely adventures had transported her far from the Moor Street rooms in London that she and Marcus had called home. Marcus hadn't liked her to leave him alone, but as long as she was in the room with him, he hadn't minded her reading. In good times she'd read to him, and they'd chuckled together over the most implausible parts.

He would have enjoyed *Love in a Harem*. The heroine had been plain Jane Brown when she'd set sail from Plymouth, but her ship had been captured by Barbary pirates and she'd been sold into the harem of the Sultan of Turkey and renamed Pearl of the North. She'd narrowly escaped being ravished by a number of men, including the captain of the ship, but now, trembling and dressed in the skimpiest silks, she awaited her lord and master. The harem door opened. . . .

"Silent reading, Kathryn?" Lady Cateril asked, coming in. "You know I don't approve."

Suppressing some salty words she'd learned from Marcus, Kitty did her best to be pleasant. "Would you like me to read to you, Mama? You might enjoy *Love in a Harem*."

She heard her own words only as she spoke them and had to fight the giggles. "Fulminating" was exactly the word for the look she received. Kitty was saved from another unwise remark by Becky, the housemaid, coming in with a letter.

"His lordship's sent this for Mrs. Marcus, milady."

She looked as if she might give it to Lady Cateril, so Kitty held out her hand. "Thank you, Becky. It will be from my friend Ruth Lulworth," she told her mother-in-law, for Ruth was her only correspondent.

"Ah." Lady Cateril's expression lightened a little. Ruth was a clergyman's wife and thus approved of. She sat. "You may read *that* to me."

It was revenge for that mischievous offer to read from the novel, and probably for Kitty's putting off mourning, but not worth fighting over. Kitty and Ruth were long past their school days, when they'd shared all the anxieties, dreams, and longings of their silly hearts. The letter would contain news about Ruth's home and family, and of her work in the parish around the Gloucestershire village of Beecham Dabittot. Kitty broke the seal and unfolded the letter, but was startled to see that Ruth had written a great deal. To save the cost for the recipient, she'd kept to one sheet of paper, turning it sideways and continuing the letter crossways. There were even a few lines on the diagonal. A sense of dramatic doings rose from the jumble, especially as one crosswise phrase stood out, because Ruth had underlined the "Yes!"

Yes! I'm sure your astonishment equals mine.

At least that didn't sound like tragedy.

Kitty needed to read the astonishing news in private, but Lady Cateril was waiting. The beginning of the letter seemed to be normal news and she didn't think Lady Cateril could see the crossways writing, so she'd make do.

My dear Kitty,

It's been a long time since I wrote, but we've been very busy here in Beecham Dab. Such terrible news about Princess Charlotte. All around put on some mark of mourning, and we tolled the bells at the time of her interment. The tragedy is a reminder to us all to be mindful of our brief lives and the judgment to come.

Sadly, we have been visited by death more frequently than usual here this year. In August a sickness carried off ten souls and weakened many others, even at harvesttime, so Andrew went out when he could to help in the fields.

"Andrew is Reverend Lulworth, Mama."

"So I remember. A charitable act, but not, perhaps, suitable for a man of the cloth."

Kitty was tempted to debate how any charity could be unsuitable for a clergyman, but she returned to the letter.

> *By God's grace, we are all well. Little Arthur is babbling very cleverly for three. Maria is still quiet, but that makes her an easy babe.*

Kitty remembered that Ruth's second birth had been difficult, but she and the child had survived, unlike poor Princess Charlotte.

She continued to read more descriptions of the children, the work of the parish, and about a pair of clever cats they'd acquired who were keeping the vicarage completely clear of mice.

At that point she invented a farewell and folded the letter. She longed to leave the room immediately to read the rest, but that could stir suspicion, so she used Ruth's comment about the cats to introduce a subject she needed to discuss with her mother-in-law. The housekeeper had asked her to try to persuade Lady Cateril to allow some cats in the house.

"Mice are causing problems in the kitchen area, Mama. A cat or two would control them."

"I could tolerate cats *there*, Kathryn, but cats do not stay in their allotted space." Kitty had no answer to that. "I'm pleased you see for once that I am right. It's a pity that your dog doesn't kill mice. Dogs do generally obey orders."

Sillikin half opened her eyes, as if commenting on that.

"I've never known her to kill, Mama."

"If she weren't fed, perhaps she would."

Preferably kill you!

Seething, Kitty called Sillikin and left the room without explanation. She retreated so she wouldn't say something unforgivable, but she needed to read Ruth's astonishing news.

Perhaps Andrew Lulworth had been offered a grander parish, or even a place in a bishop's establishment. Kitty had no idea how advancement in the church was achieved, but she was sure Ruth's husband deserved it, if only because Ruth had chosen him. Perhaps they'd received an unexpected inheritance, or found buried treasure in the garden. Perhaps the Regent had dropped by for tea!

Her flights of fancy were interrupted by the sight of the portrait of her husband hanging over the stairs in such a way that it always confronted her as she went up. It had been painted after Marcus's death, but based on a miniature done in 1807, before his heroic maiming. It showed a young dark-haired officer in his gold-braided regimentals, bright with vigor and life. It showed the Marcus Cateril she'd never known, for she'd met him after he'd lost a leg and an eye, been scarred in the face, and broken in other ways that caused him pain till his dying day.

She fought tears, as she still often did, not of grief over his death, but of sadness for all he'd lived with. He'd often said he wished he'd died alongside others during that magnificent assault at Roleia, and she knew he'd meant it. The overdose of laudanum that had killed him had not been accidental, no matter what the inquest had said.

She hurried on into the refuge of her room and wrapped

herself in two extra shawls. Fires in bedrooms were left to die down in the morning and not lit again until close to bedtime. Then she unfolded the letter, hoping for truly diverting news.

Now for the main impetus for writing, Kitty. The sickness carried off our local lion, Viscount Daun-try, and his only son, a lad of eleven. That was sad, to be sure, but it also produced an interregnum. There's a daughter, but of course she can't inherit, so no one knew who the heir was or, indeed, if there was one at all.

Now the new Lord Dauntry has arrived. He's a very distant relation of the fifth viscount, who had no notion of being in line and has never been here before. By blessed good fortune, he and Andrew both attended Westminster School only a few years apart, though he was plain Braydon then.

Ah. A friendship with the new viscount might advance Reverend Lulworth's career.

Dauntry has joined us to dine quite frequently in the weeks he's been here, and thus we have become familiar with his situation.

At this point Ruth had run out of paper and begun the crosswise writing, so Kitty turned the page.

He did not rejoice to find himself a lord. He didn't need the wealth or want the running of estates. To make matters worse, the late Lord Dauntry's will makes his successor guardian of his daughter and imposes a duty to care for his mother, who lives on in the house. In short, Dauntry has decided he needs a sensible woman to assist him with these responsibilities. I immediately thought of you.

A laugh escaped. What was Ruth thinking of? Then she read the next line.

It would mean you living close, Kitty. Only think of that!

Oh. Yes. Only think of that.

She and Ruth had met when they were both parlor boarders at school in Leamington. They'd become inseparable, but when they'd left school their paths had gone in different directions. Ruth had found employment as a governess. Kitty had returned home and soon been wooed into marriage by Marcus. They'd rarely met since, and not at all since Ruth's marriage four years ago.

To be close again.

Wondrous, but surely impossible.

I know it would mean exchanging life as part of a noble family for one as a servant, but I have the feeling that you're not entirely comfortably situated.

It was so like Ruth to read between the lines. Kitty had tried to put a bright face on her situation there, just as she had during her marriage, for she didn't believe that a trouble shared is a trouble halved. It seemed to her that complaining of trials that couldn't be changed was merely sharing the misery.

Was this a possible escape? What would this position be? Surely the girl had a governess. Was she to be companion to the elderly lady? That might be no better than being trapped with Lady Cateril—except that she'd be free of mourning and have Ruth nearby. There could even be weekly visits.

Kitty focused eagerly on the page again.

> *I put forward your name and explained why you might be suitable, which I confess involved a little exaggeration of your sober nature, but then Lord Dauntry shocked me by saying he'd resolved that the lady he needs must be his wife. My hopes were exploded.*

Kitty's were, too.

How could Ruth lead her on like that?

She crumpled the letter and threw it across the room. But Sillikin ran to retrieve it and bring it back to her, stub tail wagging.

"This isn't a game, you foolish creature."

But she took it, picking up the dog to hug. "I don't suppose I'd have liked the position anyway. I'd have been a servant, no matter how it was dressed up, and with no other company than my lady, who could be even worse than Lady Cateril." The dog licked her chin. "Yes, I know I have you. But would I be allowed to keep you?"

Sillikin turned to settle on Kitty's lap, but pushed the letter sideways with her paws so it slid toward the floor. Kitty caught it and realized she'd not yet reached Ruth's astonishing news. Perhaps that would raise her spirits. She smoothed the paper and found her place.

> *I was bold enough to ask why, and Dauntry pointed out that his ward is hard to handle and the dowager*

Lady Dauntry difficult in her grief. Then he asked if you would fulfill his requirements as wife.

Yes! I'm sure your astonishment equals mine.

It did indeed. Marriage? To a viscount? Was it a full moon?

I was cast into a tizzy. He, however, continued as if discussing whether to plant turnips or cabbages to say that he needs his household under sensible management without delay, and asked again if my friend might be suitable and willing.

I didn't know the truth about either, but the thought of you within miles, not to mention the opportunity for you to become my lady, was too much to resist, dear Kitty. I said you might be. Of course, that commits you to nothing, and I know you've said you will not marry again, but do please give it thought, for Lord Dauntry means what he said.

"He must be mad," Kitty muttered. "Would I marry a madman to escape?" She answered herself. "Perhaps. If he was safely mad."

Ruth was correct in saying that Kitty didn't want a second husband, but that was largely because she couldn't imagine finding a comfortable one. After the storms with Marcus, she needed calm waters, but she was not in a position to pick and choose. She had no great beauty or elegance, and a pittance of money.

This offer tempted, but it was too good to be true. There must have been something markedly wrong with a man who sought a wife in such a way. A difficult marriage would be far worse than life at Cateril Manor, and there would be no escape.

I respect your devotion to Marcus, but can you continue as you are for the rest of your life? Upon hearing of the death of Princess Charlotte, I found myself contemplating the uncertainties of life and our duty to use our time on earth well. I fear your current situation leaves you idle. However, my desires might cause me to overpersuade you, so let me tell you of the problems.

The writing was becoming even smaller. There must have been a great many problems, and that was a relief. Kitty could feel the pull of this ridiculous plan, and she needed reasons to resist.

Lord Dauntry stated plainly that he sought a wife who would not seek to change his ways. Kitty, I fear those <u>ways</u> include <u>carousing</u> and wicked women. He behaves with complete propriety here, but he is a very <u>fashionable</u> gentleman. I understand he is commonly called Beau Braydon, in the style of Beau Nash and Beau Brummell! His life since leaving the army has been mostly in London. You are more familiar than I as to what that might involve.

Kitty was, but she was fixed on the words "since leaving the army."

Kitty had lived in London all her married life, often surrounded by Marcus's army friends. He'd not been able to get out much, so his military friends and acquaintances had come to him when in Town on furlough or official business, sometimes in numbers that threatened to burst the walls. Some were good company, but she'd learned that soldiering often left scars, visible and invisible.

Major Quincy had been silent, with such a dark look in his eyes. Captain Farrow had mostly been quiet, but occasionally he'd fall into a kind of fit in which he thought he was fighting the French; it had taken two or three others to restrain him. Lieutenant Wynne had a strong voice and had often led jolly songs, but she'd sensed something wrong. According to Marcus, his wounds had affected his manhood. Marcus had thanked heaven that his had not, but they'd affected so much else.

She wasn't attracted to the idea of any second marriage, and certainly not to another ex-soldier. She'd done her share in that regard.

> *He asked if I would put the proposal to you. I made no promise, but later Andrew and I discussed the matter. He is uncomfortable with the situation for many reasons, but he sees how advantageous it could be to you, and he confirmed my assessment that Lord Dauntry would be a tolerable husband, as long as you kept to his conditions.*

And if not? Rages and bruises, then weeping contrition and threats to kill himself?

If she'd been a meeker woman, perhaps Marcus's life would have been more tolerable, but his unpredictable anger had developed an echo in herself. To begin with, she'd agreed and soothed, and even apologized for imagined faults, but her patience had worn down until she'd answered sharp words with sharper, and rage with rage. She'd rebutted accusations with ones of her own. That had worked better, but she'd hated his dismal repentance for days afterward.

Men wanted meek wives, and she didn't think she

could ever be one again. Ruth's plan was a fairy tale. But the next line leapt out at her.

> *Remember, Andrew and I would be close by to offer loving support.*

To be close to Ruth and have her loving support . . .

What was more, if she became Lady Dauntry—astonishing thought!—she'd be able to visit the parsonage whenever she wished. She could invite Ruth and her family to her own grand home. What was the name? Beauchamp Abbey. Was it pronounced in the French way—*BOW-shamp*—or did it match the village name, Beecham? That was irrelevant, but relevant thoughts, weakening thoughts, were trickling in.

Here, at last, was escape from Cateril Manor.

Might it be bearable?

The married life of Lady Dauntry would be vastly different from hers with Marcus, no matter how odd her husband was. She wouldn't be trapped in four rooms, and it seemed unlikely Lord Dauntry would demand her presence most of the time or insist on her sharing his restless bed.

She and he could have separate bedrooms, separate suites of rooms. Separate wings, perhaps! Given what Ruth had said, he might rarely be at the Abbey at all. In a normal marriage, she might object to his amusements elsewhere, but not in this one.

"Am I seriously considering this?"

Sillikin's cocked head seemed to send the question back at her.

"I am."

To escape Cateril Manor. To live close to Ruth. To

have a home of her own again, with a frequently absent
husband . . .

She read on, now fearful of something to make it impossible.

> *If you are willing to consider the matter, it must be*
> *soon. Dauntry is a man of brisk action. If you don't*
> *give him hope, he will proceed to other ways of obtain-*
> *ing the wife he wants. I can't imagine it will be diffi-*
> *cult. He's a handsome man, though in a cool way.*

Ruth had run out of space and turned the page to
write diagonally.

> *If you agree to consider the match, he will arrange*
> *your journey here at his expense, and your journey*
> *home if you decide he will not suit. You need only*
> *reply to me for all to be put in hand, but remember,*
> *it must be soon.*
>
> *I don't know this man well, Kitty, and I fear my*
> *ardent desire to have you nearby influences me, but*
> *Andrew believes you should at least consider this,*
> *and his judgment is sound.*

That was it.
Ardent desire.
Yes.
Kitty rose and paced her room, Sillikin in her arms.
Escape!
But through marriage.
She hadn't rushed into her first marriage, but she'd
been swept along on a torrent of ecstatic romance, with
no one attempting to slow her down. Her parents had
been dazzled by her being wooed by a member of the

nobility. If they'd suffered any doubts, Marcus's wounds and true adoration had silenced them. Marcus had wooed her so desperately, with gifts, flowers, and passionate entreaties, that she would have had to have been made of stone to refuse him.

Here was a very different situation. The offer was cool, the promises minimal, and there were no tempting gifts. The man was a stranger, but she must decide in a moment, and this time she had no one no advise her.

"I must go to Ruth."

With that, everything became clear. She must go to Ruth, for advice and for the joy of it. Once in Beecham Dab, once she met Lord Dauntry, she'd know whether to make this marriage or not. Mere travel there wouldn't commit her.

"How to escape?" she muttered. One thing was sure: Lady Cateril would never tolerate Marcus's widow marrying again.

She thought she had enough money to cover the cost of a coach ticket to Gloucestershire, but how to escape the house? She was devising complicated ways, some inspired by novels, when she came to her senses. No one here knew about the offer of marriage. She could simply ask to visit her old friend.

She hugged Sillikin. "I don't know why I haven't done that before. I've allowed us to be glued here by Lady Cateril's grief, but even she can't object to a short visit to an old friend, can she?"